ATMOSPHERE OF
VIOLENCE

By

Michael & William Henry

Michael & William Henry

Atmosphere of Violence

Other books available by these authors:
Three Bad Years – *A Willie Mitchell Banks Novel*
(Michael Henry)
At Random – *A Willie Mitchell Banks Novel*
(Michael Henry)
The Ride Along – *A Jake Banks Novel*
(Michael & William Henry)
D.O.G.s (Michael & William Henry)
Veterano (William Henry)

Acknowledgments

Much thanks to readers David Fite, Chick and Lil Graning, Bill Byrne, Wendy Jenkins and Pat Austin Becker; to Chuck Thomas for military tactics; to Dr. Pat Wojtkiewicz for criminalistics expertise; to the indomitable Regina Charboneau for her support; to Christine Maynard for her creative enthusiasm and literary skills; to Gayle for her tolerance and kindness.

To view more of Michael & William Henry's work, visit: http://henryandhenrybooks.com

Michael & William Henry

Dedication

To Tom Murchison, who died January 7, 2012. Tom was a scholar, historian, reader, raconteur, and friend; an honest lawyer and man of integrity—he will not be replaced.

Chapter One

When he saw the well-dressed mark pull his credit card from the gas pump and stick the aluminum nozzle in the shiny new Taurus, Lester "Mule" Gardner lurched from his spot against the faded green Waste Management dumpster. He needed a drink.

Even though Mule's head was pounding and his stomach queasy, he had to move while the mark was trapped holding the nozzle. For reasons unknown to Mule, a year ago Gas & Go Fast convenience store management had removed the metal clips from the nozzle triggers. If customers wanted gasoline to flow, they had to keep squeezing the trigger, creating a captive target for Mule.

Mule straightened his crumpled straw cowboy hat with red and black feathers and walked, sort of, toward the pump. With his right leg three inches shorter than the left, Mule's walk was something to behold. He moved up and down and side to side as much as he did forward.

Mule was delivered with difficulty in the fifties by a mid-wife who lived near his parents' shotgun tenant house on a cotton farm in rural Yaloquena County. He was the fifth of six children and was deprived of oxygen in the birth canal long enough to cause developmental defects in his limbs, especially the right leg. It never grew to its proper length.

No one in Sunshine was sure of Mule's age. He appeared to be in his fifties. Even standing on his long leg, Mule was no more than 5'5" and skinny, weighing about one-thirty. His skin was very black and he rarely shaved. He wore a pre-Super Bowl New Orleans Saints jersey, now looking more brown than gold, and always pushed a Jitney Mart shopping cart when working.

Mule was one of Sunshine's premier drunks. He bragged that he had never done blow, crack, horse, or crank, though he owned up to smoking a little weed in his younger days. An inveterate accomplished panhandler, he used his dramatic limp to great advantage. He alternated his venue among the C-Stores on the main highway, averaging twenty-five dollars a day in alms. Given the quality of wine and gin he drank, it was more than enough to keep his blood alcohol level acceptably high. Most of his marks were sympathetic out-of-towners stopping for gas or a snack. Locals shooed him away; they knew what he did with the money.

Mule closed in on the stranger, who glanced Mule's way, trying to avoid eye contact. Mule recognized the ploy. It was the most common first defense—pretend Mule wasn't there. Undeterred, Mule moved piston-like toward the clean-cut black stranger in a navy blue sport coat, gray slacks, white shirt and dark red tie. The mark concentrated on the pump dial's spinning numbers as if he had never seen anything so fascinating.

"Excuse me, sir. Could you help a brother out?"

When the stranger turned, no longer able to ignore the panhandler, Mule gave him a big grin. The stranger looked directly into Mule's eyes and continued pumping gas.

"Come on, please sir, I just need a couple of bucks for some food. You look like you've done well for yourself."

The stranger shook his head.

"Come on, man. How 'bout a measly dollar for a brother down on his luck?"

The mark left the nozzle in the Taurus but released the trigger. He reached into his back pocket and pulled out his wallet. Before he opened it, he studied Mule.

"That's a nice pin you got there," Mule said, pointing a crooked finger at the green crescent moon pin on the man's lapel. "Really fine."

"It's the symbol of my faith."

"I'm cool with that. I'm a Baptist. My church is out in the country. Meets every third Sunday."

The stranger removed a five dollar bill.

"Now you talking," Mule said. "All right. All right. Thank you, my brother. I knew I could count on you. I just got laid off and having the hardest time gettin' back on my feet. Bless you, man. Bless you."

The mark put the five on the trunk of the car. Mule went for it, but the stranger snatched it back.

"Aw, man."

Mule had seen this trick before. It made his head hurt worse and his stomach churn.

The man fixin' to say some shit about savin' my black ass or buying me some healthy food or shit like that.

"Okay, sir. What do I got to do?"

"Pray with me."

"What?"

"A simple prayer with me and this is yours."

Mule closed his eyes and bowed his head slightly. He pictured a chilled half-pint of London's Best gin.

"Most Merciful Allah, receive the prayers of this troubled soul...."

Mule was desperate for a drink, but this was bull shit.

"Nah, nah. I ain't prayin' to no Allah with you Uncle Tom-looking Muslim mother-fucker. Don't gimme that Allah shit. I ain't no troubled soul. I just want a couple of bucks for a drink. It ain't no major transaction, you lettin' me hold a dollar or two."

Mule started moving in a circle, pivoting on his longer leg, up and down like a carousel horse on speed. The faster Mule revolved, the more agitated and louder he became.

"Goddamned camel jockey lovin' bastard. Keep your Goddamned five dollar bill."

"You make me sad, my brother."

Mule stopped. He stuck his right index finger in the man's face.

"Sad? Sad? You feelin' sorry for me now? You think you so much better than me 'cause of your nice suit and tie, and that dip shit pin you wearin'? You think your shiny black ass is special?"

The stranger gave Mule a stern look.

"Oh, now you think you bad. Mad-doggin' me. You ain't bad, Muslim boy. This here's my town. Everybody know me. You in my town, nigger. I'm Mule. I'll tear your head off you mess with me."

The stranger turned his back on Mule and resumed filling his tank. Lester amped up the volume, getting angrier.

"Don't be turnin' your black ass to me. I own that pump you holdin'. I own this station. My gas. American gas for Americans. Not some sand nigger lovin' piece of shit like you."

"That's enough."

"Ain't near enough. I'm fixin' to hurt you bad."

Mule planted his long leg, raised his short one, and jerked the ancient Converse All-Star tennis shoe off his right foot.

Chapter Two

Trevor crumpled the empty cigarette pack and threw it on the floor of his smooth-running 1990 Ford F-150 pickup truck.

"Shit," he said, and stroked the scraggly triangular goatee that hung a full two inches below his chin. Trevor's beard was almost transparent on his cheeks, wispy blond on his upper lip, but acceptably dense and amber around his chin and below. He was a wiry six-footer weighing in at one-fifty-five. Like most Brewers, he was tough and raw-boned, the kind of guy who, despite his slim build, knew how to hurt a man. Trevor had engaged in more than his fair share of fights in his twenty-eight years.

He was closing in on Sunshine, having driven from Brewer Hill, his family's ancestral land on a hardwood ridge in Dundee County, just east of Yaloquena and west of I-55. Trevor turned up the volume on the CD he and his band burned the day before. Trevor did some engine work for the owner of the primitive recording studio in the woods just outside the city limits of Kilbride, the only incorporated town in Dundee County. The owner bartered some studio time for Trevor's mechanical skills. The Brewer Hill Skins weren't great, but they were heavy and loud. As he listened in his pickup, Trevor thought his voice, rasping and guttural, sounded better than any of the instruments on the BHS CD. What he liked most was his lack of hesitation, the forcefulness of his words.

It had been busy for a Thursday at Tom's Automotive, his father's auto repair shop. Trevor had been working since seven a.m. replacing an engine in the 1973 Pontiac GTO his dad was trying to keep running for a regular customer. Trevor was feeling the need for a break when his father Tom told him to jump in his truck and hightail it to the Green Light Auto Parts store in Sunshine to pick up an alternator for the 1998 Lincoln Town Car they were trying to get ready for Mr. Jerry Hedges by six o'clock.

Trevor was glad to do it. He didn't care for Sunshine much, but the Green Light was the closest auto parts store to the shop. Trevor glanced at his watch. He had plenty of time to pick up the alternator and get it back to the shop for his dad to install. Tom worked fast. It was about 4:15 when Trevor pulled into the Gas & Go Fast on the east end of the Sunshine main drag, a four-lane highway running east and west.

Trevor sped by the Gas & Go Fast pumps and made a wide turn to bring the truck into the diagonal parking space closest to the front door. He noticed the new Taurus at the island because he liked the Ford's new styling, but paid little attention to the two black men next to it. He jumped out of his F-150 and hustled into the store.

"Doral Reds," Trevor said to the young black woman in the red and yellow uniform behind the counter. When she turned to retrieve the cigarettes, Trevor glanced outside. He saw the two black men arguing. The bigger man in the coat and tie was calm, but the little scruffy guy was really mad, hopping around in a circle, shaking his fist and yelling. When the clerk placed the pack of Dorals on the counter, Trevor pointed to the men outside at the gas pump.

"Trouble."

"That's just Mule. He got a big mouth and he bother everybody with it. Ain't nothing to it. He too little to hurt anybody."

Trevor paid and walked out. He saw the small man with the crumpled cowboy hat take off his tennis shoe. Trevor stopped on the concrete outside the front door to watch.

"Uh-oh," Trevor mumbled. He chuckled when Mule threw his tennis shoe, hitting the big man in the head. Mule wasn't through. He flew into the bigger man. The man easily brushed Mule away and pulled the gas nozzle out of the Taurus tank. He pointed the pale green stream of gas at Mule, soaking him from the chest down.

"Shit, shit," Trevor whispered. He watched Mule reach into his grocery cart and pull out a small chrome-plated semi-automatic pistol. Mule fired twice at the man in the suit. Behind him, Trevor heard the heavy deadbolt on the steel door. He turned to re-enter the store but saw the yellow and red uniformed store clerk hiding behind a stack of beer cases near the front door. Trevor tested the door. *Locked.* He ran in a crouch the short distance to his truck, glancing at the shooter. Mule fired twice more.

Son of a bitch looks like he's shooting at me.

One bullet whizzed past Trevor's head. Trevor knew from the report it was a .22 or .25 caliber.

Enough firepower to kill me.

Trevor put his truck between himself and the shooter, ripped open the passenger door and grabbed his nine-millimeter Smith & Wesson M&P semi-automatic pistol from under the front seat. He chambered a bullet and eased around the truck to get a better vantage. He saw the bigger man grab the shooter's gun hand. Trevor watched the two men struggle again, and was surprised the big man couldn't manhandle the weak-looking shooter like he had earlier.

Trevor understood why when the two men turned toward him. The big man's face was covered in blood. He had been shot. The big man faltered, let go of the shooter and fell back against the gas pump. Mule aimed his pistol at the bloody man leaning against the pump.

"Hey. Hey," Trevor yelled.

Mule was startled. He turned the gun toward Trevor. Trevor fired twice at Mule just as the bigger man pushed away from the gas pump and lunged into Mule. Both men fell onto the concrete, twenty feet from Trevor. Mule's semi-automatic skittered across the concrete toward Trevor. He picked it up and banged on the front door. Inside, the clerk peered around the tall stack of Bud Light at the front door.

"9-1-1," he yelled through the glass.

While the clerk made the call, she stared for thirty seconds through the store window at the two men on the concrete before unlocking the steel and glass door. Trevor walked in. He felt light-headed. The clerk stared at him.

"You shot."

"Yeah, yeah," Trevor said, holding up his gun.

"No," she said and pointed at Trevor's left chest.

Trevor looked down. The left side of his shirt was soaked in blood. He knew Mule fired twice in his direction. Now that he thought about it, he remembered hearing only one bullet whiz past his head.

So that's where the other one went.

The clerk helped Trevor sit on a short stack of Coors Light cases. He placed his nine millimeter and Mule's .22 caliber on the Old Milwaukee cases next to him. Trevor tried his best to take a deep breath, but couldn't.

Two black men wearing paint-spattered white coveralls and painter's caps walked in tentatively, checking out the store while holding open the front door. They spoke to the clerk.

"The man wearing the tie is dead," one of them said. "Mule bleeding like he hurt pretty bad."

"But he's breathing," the other painter told the clerk.

"9-1-1 said the cops and ambulances are on their way," she said.

Trevor felt himself growing weaker. His mouth was parched. He gestured to the clerk. She brought him a bottled water, twisting the cap open. He looked down at the bottle and did his best to raise it to his lips. No luck.

Trevor noticed blinking bright blue light filling the store.

"Cops are here," the clerk said.

Trevor concentrated but could not understand a word the clerk said. Everything grew dark around him. The last thing he remembered before waking up in the hospital was dropping the water bottle.

Chapter Three

All the deputies working the Gas & Go Fast homicide scene turned to watch Kitty Douglas step out of her 1996 E36 BMW convertible with the top down. Kitty was by far the best-looking law enforcement woman any of them had ever seen. She was 5'8" with long dark hair and olive skin. Her form-fitting dark blue Yaloquena Deputy Sheriff's uniform emphasized her perfect figure. Susan Banks and Ina helped tailor the uniform so that there was no surplus cotton fabric for a bad guy to grab. Kitty told them she didn't want anything to interfere with her drawing and using her weapon.

Though she wore the uniform, she was not an employee of the Sheriff's office. She was a Special Agent of the Federal Bureau of Investigation, on loan to Yaloquena County Sheriff Lee Jones through an intergovernmental program that the FBI and Justice Department ran to assist rural, cash-strapped law enforcement agencies. In her first week, Kitty balked at wearing the deputy uniform, but Lee insisted.

"I want people to know you're law enforcement," Lee told her. "In your FBI outfit you could be anyone. They see you in one of my uniforms they know you work with the Sheriff's office. Trust me on this."

Such FBI Special Agent assignments were rare. Politics had a lot to do with which counties benefited from the intergovernmental appointments. Kitty was the only FBI agent currently working in the program in Mississippi. Though the Mississippi Delta would have been at the top of any list of regions in the country to qualify for a Special Agent because of the grinding and insoluble poverty and lack of an educated populace, Kitty knew she was working with Sheriff Lee Jones because of the political connections of District Attorney Willie Mitchell Banks, banker Jimmy Gray, and U.S. Senator Skeeter Sumrall. Jake Banks helped, too.

Every person who knew Kitty and was in a position to help her get the appointment pushed hard for it. After what happened to her in New Orleans, no one wanted Kitty to take on a new FBI posting in another city. She still needed time to heal, physically and emotionally. The relatively mundane criminal activity in Sunshine was the right tonic for her. And, there was Jake.

Jake and Kitty were on again. He was a Justice Department attorney in D.C. under the direct supervision of Deputy Attorney General Patrick Dunwoody IV, the number two man at DOJ after Attorney General Danny Okole. Even so, it seemed to Kitty that Jake spent much of his time in Sunshine or at training camps in remote areas around the United States.

Regardless of how or why she received the appointment, Kitty was by far the best trained, most professional, and smartest officer currently under the command of Sheriff Jones. Training the other deputies in state-of-the-art criminal investigation techniques was a big part of her job, but so was helping investigate high-profile crimes in Yaloquena County. A three-victim, daylight shooting on Sunshine's main drag, with one dead and two seriously wounded certainly qualified.

As she walked, Kitty adjusted the .40 caliber semi-automatic matte finish Glock 23 in the leather holster on her right hip. It was one of the things she liked about wearing the uniform—she could carry her weapon in a leather holster on her hip, fully exposed, instead of concealing it under her jacket in accordance with FBI protocol. Having grown up in Tacoma, she was still unaccustomed to the heat in the South. Her first assignments as a Special Agent were in Jackson, Mississippi and New Orleans, where the jacket or top she was required to wear to conceal her gun made her uncomfortably warm most of the time. The Yaloquena deputy's uniform was short-sleeved, much more practical on this hot mid-September afternoon in Sunshine.

It was 5:30, about seventy minutes after the shooting.

"Thought you might like to get in on this," Sheriff Lee Jones said to Kitty standing over the corpse. "Sorry to call you on your day off."

"No problem, Sheriff. I'm glad you did. I was driving back from Jackson when I got the call. Had to swing by the camp to get in uniform. What have we got here?"

"A mess is what we got," the Sheriff said. "The two shooters have already been taken to the hospital. This one didn't need any medical care. Doc Clement says he died almost immediately."

Kitty made a note on the form on her clip board. She lifted the white cotton sheet back to look at the victim on the concrete.

"At least he's already dressed for his funeral," Kitty said quietly while she looked at the victim. "Who is he?"

"Name's Abdul Azeem, according to the Virginia driver's license in his wallet. There's also an old picture i.d. in the name of Joseph Randall. I guess he did a name change at some point. Clerk said he's stopped here before on his way through."

Kitty looked around at the officers spread out on the concrete.

"All the casings accounted for?" she asked.

"We think so," Lee said. "Double checking now. We've got both weapons, marked the locations of the spent rounds and bagged them. Every inch of this property was photographed before we moved anything. EMTs got the other two victims out right away, but we took photographs of how they were situated."

"You don't need me working your investigations, Lee."

"Let me be the judge of that, Kitty. I'm not going to be Johnny-on-the-spot every time we have a major crime, and until you and I can get my investigators up to speed on the basics, I need your help. With this new position with the state organization, I'm going to be at meetings in Jackson at the Capitol on a regular basis. If you're here I won't have anything to worry about."

Lee Jones was a Yaloquena native, four months from turning forty-nine. He was a professional—ex-military, ex-state trooper, and smart. Sheriff Jones was physically intimidating. Six feet tall and 195 pounds, with a thick chest and muscular arms, he looked like he did when he was the fastest and hardest-hitting middle linebacker in the Southwestern Athletic conference in his college days.

D.A. Willie Mitchell Banks told Kitty that Lee was the best Sheriff ever elected to serve in Yaloquena County. His peers across the state recognized his abilities. Four months earlier, just before Kitty began working with Sheriff Jones, he was elected president of the Mississippi Sheriff's Association, the first black man to serve in such capacity.

"Has the Coroner been here yet?" she asked.

"No. Dr. Clement has. Examined the body, confirmed he was dead. Coroner Cecil B. DeMille called and is supposed to be here any minute. He gave orders not to move the body until he showed up with his crew."

Lee Jones shook his head. Kitty had seen the elected Coroner in action. Mississippi did not require a medical degree or any medical training for a citizen to qualify and run for the office. Yaloquena County voters had seen fit to elect Alphonse "Al" Revels in a landslide. Sheriff Jones said the closest Al had come to any medical training was when he got his flu shot at the County Health Unit.

"What exactly happened?" Kitty asked. "Do we know?"

"You know who Mule is? Little trash-mouthed panhandler with a bad limp and an attitude to match. Usually pushes a grocery cart."

"I see him all the time."

"We've interviewed the clerk. Mule was hassling our victim here for a donation. They had words, the man sprayed Mule with gasoline. Mule pulled a little .22 caliber pea shooter out of his cart and started firing. The clerk hid in the store as soon as the shooting broke out. The white guy, Trevor Brewer, is going to be our best witness. The clerk said he was outside and saw it all. Trevor did some shooting, too. But it doesn't really matter what the witnesses say."

"Why is that?"

Sheriff Jones pointed to the two security cameras on the front of the store, mounted high on the brick wall.

"They have sixteen of these cameras inside and out. This one covers the pumps with a wide angle. That one," he said, pointing to the other, "is a tighter shot on the area between the pumps and the front door."

"Were they both working?"

"We're lucky," Lee Jones said, nodding. "The system is digital. The computer inside and all the cameras were just serviced a few days ago. They caught the whole thing. We called the Gas & Go Fast office and they sent out their tech man right away. He downloaded everything to a disk for me. Willie Mitchell called his pal Robbie Cedars at the state crime lab. I've got a deputy driving the disk down to Jackson right now for analysis. They'll take custody of the original and burn some copies for us. Everything that took place is on the disk except for audio."

"Can the technician preserve the original data in the system?"

"I asked him to. He said it was no problem."

"Why did the Trevor guy start shooting?"

"Don't really know yet."

"Is he going to make it?"

"Doc Clement says he will. Bullet went into his left chest and is still in there somewhere, but Doc said he should be all right."

"Trevor ought to be able to tell us what was said."

"I don't know," Sheriff Jones said. "He's a Brewer."

Kitty was about to ask Lee what he meant when the Coroner's extended length white Econoline van roared into the Gas & Go Fast's parking lot followed by an older model white panel truck. AL REVELS, YALOQUENA COUNTY CORONER was painted in big black letters on both sides of each official vehicle.

Two black men in white jump suits hopped out of the panel truck and hurried to set up portable light stands. The taller of the two men retrieved a Steady-Cam from the panel truck and adjusted the settings. He nodded to his partner who opened the Econoline door.

Like General McArthur wading ashore at Leyte Beach, every step of the Coroner's dramatic arrival at the scene of the homicide, and his studied examination of the corpse while kneeling next to it on the concrete, was captured for posterity and for Al Revels' re-election campaign.

Chapter Four

As usual, Willie Mitchell finished his early morning jog at Jimmy Gray's driveway. The temperature had been in the high seventies when he started forty minutes earlier. It was still hot and humid, and Willie Mitchell was soaking wet. As usual, his left leg ached. The four mile run seemed exceptionally difficult today. It might have been because of his gimpy left leg, or the fact that he was closing in on fifty-eight. Maybe it was just the oppressive humidity this morning. Whatever the reason, it had been a long, hot summer in the heart of the Mississippi Delta and Willie Mitchell was ready for it to end.

Jimmy Gray burst from his side door onto the carport and jogged, more or less, the fifty feet to Willie Mitchell. He wore royal blue nylon trunks that ballooned and sagged below his knees, a matching blue cotton and elastic headband, and a tight white wife-beater that had seen better days.

"Frisky," Willie Mitchell said.

"You bet," Jimmy Gray said, simulating Ali's rope-a-dope posture, moving daintily from one foot to the next, his head back, fists at waist level. "Good weigh in."

"How much?"

"Three-eleven, butt naked."

"It's buck naked."

"You're wrong."

"Google it. Buck naked. We've been through this before. Anyway, you got any pictures?"

"Martha took some. She says I'm beautiful when I'm naked. This is how I call her when I step out of the shower."

Jimmy Gray spun around and spread his arms, baying like a coyote, then yelling at the top of his voice.

"I'm nekkid. Butt nekkid."

Willie Mitchell stared at the spectacle.

"Call her for what?"

"Whatever she wants. Ladies' choice."

"Your breakfast menu these days, I want to know exactly what pharmaceuticals you're taking."

"Just one joyful dude these days, pods. I'm all about dropping the weight now," Jimmy Gray said with a straight face. "I attribute it to this strenuous exercise program you've got me on."

"Right. But you need to be careful. Going from three-twelve two days ago to three-eleven this morning may be too fast to be healthy."

"You got a point. Maybe we ought to skip walking today."

"No. However, let me say I am very proud of you."

"Thanks."

"But don't overdo it. Lose any more and you're skin and bones."

"I'll be vigilant."

"What do I have to do to get you to stop wearing these gross undershirts on our walks? How about a regular tee shirt?"

"These are cooler. It's what body builders wear."

Willie Mitchell raised his eyebrows for a moment, then he and Jimmy burst into laughter. Willie Mitchell squeezed Jimmy's fat bicep and clapped him on the shoulder.

"Let's get going, Charles Atlas."

They were an odd-looking couple. Willie Mitchell had been in shape his entire life. He was 6'1" and weighed the same as he had when he finished undergraduate and law school at Ole Miss. He walked on and made the Ole Miss freshman basketball squad, but a bad ankle injury sidelined him for six weeks his first year in school and convinced him that focusing on academics and limiting his basketball to Panhellenic intramural play was the right career move. He was handsome, with dark hair starting to gray and blue eyes like his oldest son Jake, who was better-looking, an inch taller, ten pounds of muscle heavier, and thirty years younger.

Willie Mitchell started his watch and they walked onto the street. The banker was already sweating from his antics in the driveway.

"Let's make it an easier pace today," Jimmy said.

"I'll try, but I don't think I can walk any slower."

"Well, let's cut the distance."

"We'll see. Just do your best."

It had been four years since Willie Mitchell finally succeeded in shaming Jimmy Gray into walking for fifteen minutes, three days a week. Willie Mitchell was still running four miles five days a week, and he tacked on the fifteen minute walks at the end of his runs. He was trying to get Jimmy to exercise and eat healthier because he needed him.

Jimmy Gray and Willie Mitchell were closer than brothers. They were born a month apart in 1955 to parents who were best friends and business partners. Their fathers founded Sunshine Bank and worked together all their lives. Jimmy and Willie Mitchell started first grade at the Catholic school run by nuns. Jimmy Gray said the cranky sisters belonged to an order called "Little Sisters of the Homely and Disgusting Poor." When the nuns left Sunshine the school closed. Their parents enrolled Jimmy and Willie Mitchell in junior high in the newly-formed Sunshine Academy. They finished high school at the Academy and graduated Ole

Miss together. Willie Mitchell went on to law school and Jimmy Gray returned to Sunshine to work in the bank, eventually becoming Chairman of the Board, CEO, and largest stockholder. When Willie Mitchell finished his law degree, he hung out a shingle in Sunshine and ten years later was elected District Attorney for Yaloquena County. He was the second largest bank shareholder. Together they owned a majority of the stock.

Jimmy Gray had one older brother, Rod, an unmarried architect in New Orleans. Willie Mitchell was an only child. The two men lived a couple of blocks from each other close to downtown Sunshine and had been through a lot together.

Five-and-a-half years earlier, Willie Mitchell and Susan separated for three years, for reasons they never shared with anyone. Two years into the marital sabbatical, Willie Mitchell had become involved with a younger woman whom he ended up prosecuting for the death of her husband and an innocent six-year-old black girl. Jimmy Gray helped the D.A. through the dark days of Willie Mitchell's personal and professional crisis—talking things through, mainly just being there.

Jimmy Gray owed him, because a couple of years earlier Willie Mitchell helped Jimmy overcome the worst tragedy a parent could suffer—the death of his youngest son in a hunting accident. Beau was nineteen when his rifle slid off the fence he was climbing and discharged accidentally into his stomach. Jimmy tried to drink the tragedy away, sinking so low into depression no one thought he would pull out of it.

Willie Mitchell never gave up on Jimmy. He spent as much time with Jimmy every day as the banker needed. There were many afternoons when Willie Mitchell would not let Jimmy Gray go home. He would call Jimmy's wife Martha and insist that Jimmy stay in one of the Banks' guest rooms so Willie Mitchell could keep an eye on him. He never told Martha it was so he could make sure the banker did not have access his well-stocked gun cabinet. She probably knew.

"So Mule's going to make it?" Jimmy asked, huffing.

"That's what Nathan told me this morning. He talked to the doctors in Jackson late last night after they had stabilized him. Probably going to be paralyzed from the waist down."

"And the Brewer boy?"

"Nathan said he's fine. They removed a twenty-two slug in the back of his lung close to his shoulder blade. He's a strong kid."

"He the one used to be on Jake's team? When you were the coach?"

"That's him. The eleven and twelve-year-old league. Trevor lived here for two summers. A good little athlete, and seemed like a nice kid. He and Jake were buddies for a while until he moved back to Dundee."

"Brewer genes usually kick in during the teen years."

"He hasn't been in any serious trouble, far as I know."

"You talk to Jake?"

"Not since last week. He's training somewhere. Incommunicado."

"I drove past the Gas & Go Fast after work yesterday. Kitty was busy writing on a clipboard, working with Lee." Jimmy Gray paused a moment. "Two pistols, three people shot, two black and one white, one dead. The white one a Brewer. You're going to have a great time with this one."

"I won't be the one trying it."

"Famous last words."

"I'm serious. I'm letting Walton handle this. He's fully capable, and I'm ready to slide into senior status."

"So you're like the hunting dog old man Fite brings up from time to time, the one having sex with a skunk," Jimmy Gray said. "You've had just about all of that fun you can stand."

"Kind of."

"I say bull shit. I got money says you'll be right there, slap-dab in the middle of it."

"I'm serious this time."

"Just because you've got a bad leg, a left eye that only half-works, and a brain that seizes up at inopportune times is no reason to be a pussy, Willie Mitchell."

"That's not why I'm letting Walton try it," Willie Mitchell said as they stopped at Jimmy Gray's driveway, their fifteen minutes over.

"Then how come?"

"To see if I can stand it," Willie Mitchell said.

"Stand what?"

"Giving up some control," Willie Mitchell said. "I'm not sure I can. I've never been much of a delegator."

He cleared his watch and took off jogging for home.

Chapter Five

Sheriff Lee Jones leaned against the wall in Willie Mitchell's office in the Yaloquena County Courthouse. Willie Mitchell sat behind his desk. Across from him were his First Assistant District Attorney, Walton Donaldson, and Kitty Douglas. It was five-thirty and had been a busy day for each of them. There were no smiles. All four were deadly serious.

"Damn," Willie Mitchell said. "I should have known it wasn't going to be as easy as it seemed."

"What are we going to call the dead guy?" Walton asked. "Azeem or Joseph Randall?"

"He filed the name change petition in Prince William County, Virginia in 2002," Willie Mitchell said, "it's all legal. I spoke to the Clerk of Court up there who pulled the records for me, including the fingerprint cards Virginia law requires. A District Court Judge signed the name change order and it was all properly recorded. There are service returns on the Prince William County District Attorney and the Virginia Secretary of State. We have to call him by his legal name, Abdul Azeem."

"Crap," Walton said. "I'd rather refer to the victim as Joseph Randall if it goes to trial. An Abdul Azeem might not be as sympathetic a character as a Joseph Randall to a Yaloquena jury."

"The fact he's Muslim will make that much difference?" Kitty asked.

"Lots of black Baptists don't care too much for converts to Islam," Lee Jones said. "It'll be an issue to some jurors."

"You'll have to explore that in *voir dire*," Willie Mitchell said to Walton. "Let's get back to the charges."

"Crime lab is sure of the ballistics?" the Sheriff asked.

"I talked to Robbie Cedars," the D. A. said. "He did the comparison himself. He's a perfectionist. The slug Dr. Clement removed from Azeem's chest was fired from Trevor Brewer's nine-millimeter."

"And Dr. Clement says that's the bullet that killed him," Lee Jones said. "Kitty and I were there at the autopsy. Azeem had a twenty-two caliber bullet lodged in his shoulder, and a crease through his scalp from another. That's how all the blood got on his face. Dr. Clement says neither one of those would have been fatal."

"In fact," Kitty said, "Dr. Clement said the twenty-two bullet in the shoulder did minor damage and the one that creased his forehead was no more than a scratch. Just bled a lot."

"So the shots Trevor Brewer fired in self-defense," Willie Mitchell said, "ended up killing Azeem and paralyzing Mule from the waist down."

"If it *was* self-defense," Kitty said. "We've got to look at the disk from the crime lab before we draw any conclusions."

"No way," Walton said. "Brewer is minding his own business, picking up an alternator, stops to buy some smokes, gets shot and uses his gun to defend himself. The way I see it, he's a victim."

"I agree," Willie Mitchell said. "Lee?"

"I want to look at the CD," the Sheriff said. "There's going to be a lot of people watching us on this. He's a Brewer from Dundee County. People around here know what that means. And even though Mule's a pest, everybody in town knows him."

"I'll give you two some background on the Brewer family later," Willie Mitchell said to Kitty and Walton. "In the meantime, we'll charge Mule with felony murder but I don't want him arrested yet."

"We'll wait until he's released from the hospital," Sheriff Jones said. "We arrest him, we'll have to pay all his medical bills and keep him under guard. Let the state Medicaid office worry about the cost for now."

"Mule's not going anywhere," Willie Mitchell said. "Nathan told me there's nothing that can be done for him. His lower lumbar spine is severed. He'll be in a wheelchair the rest of his life. Doc said there's no other organ damage."

"How long did Dr. Clement say he'd be in the hospital?" Walton asked Willie Mitchell.

"A week at the most. Then he'll go to rehab. Before we make the arrest, we can talk to the judge about letting Mule out on a recognizance bond. There's no need to put him in the jail."

"You're right about that. No way we can take care of a paraplegic up there," Lee said. "Judge Williams will let us use an ankle bracelet if we explain the situation to her."

"What did Dr. Clement say about Brewer?" Walton asked.

"Day or two he'll be going home," Willie Mitchell said.

"No charges on him?" Lee asked.

"Not right now," Willie Mitchell said. "We'll look at the disk when we get it from the crime lab, but based on what we know now, I can't see charging Trevor Brewer with anything."

"I asked a friend of mine at the Jackson FBI office to talk to Mr. Cedars at the crime lab," Kitty said, "and get the serial numbers off both weapons and run a trace on them, just to cover all the bases."

Lee laughed. "I'm sure Mule's twenty-two was pawned locally at some time. Probably for no more than ten bucks. Mule probably bought it there. And no telling where the nine-millimeter originally came from. Brewer Hill is like an elephant's graveyard for weapons. They say they've accumulated an arsenal up there."

"These Brewer people sound dangerous," Kitty said.

"Tomorrow morning we'll go by the hospital and I'll introduce you and Walton to Trevor," Willie Mitchell said. "You can judge for yourself."

Chapter Six

Trevor Brewer sat up in bed in the Yaloquena County Hospital. It was Saturday morning. The scrambled eggs before him on his breakfast tray were such a vivid yellow, Trevor thought they might be radioactive. He pushed them around the plate a little, but did not dare eat any.

Trevor's father helped with breakfast, opening the small butter and jelly packets and spreading them on the whole wheat toast, the only thing Trevor ate. He tasted the coffee, but it was so weak one sip was enough. A blue medical sling held his left arm against his chest. The television mounted on the wall was on ESPN, the volume muted in deference to his father.

"I'm going to head on back to the shop," Tom Brewer said rolling the breakfast table away from Trevor's bed.

Trevor was surprised his father showed up at all. Tom Brewer rarely left Brewer Hill, and only then to drive the short distance on the dirt and gravel road down the steep hill to his mechanic and body shop on the paved highway to Kilbride. He was fifty-one and slightly built, the same size as Trevor, with large hands and knuckles, scarred and discolored from years of working on automobile engines. He always wore old jeans and a faded blue shirt with "Tom" embroidered over his left chest in red letters. His red cap bore the STP logo on the front. Tom's kinfolk on the hill said if Trevor shaved his scraggly goatee, Tom and he would look just alike.

"All r-right, Tom," Trevor said.

Trevor's only sibling, Leonard, was two years younger and lived in the woods between Aniston, Alabama and the Talladega Superspeedway. Leonard had spent his teen years working in the shop with Tom, and like his father, was a natural with gasoline engines and anything related to cars. He left Brewer Hill nine years earlier when he was seventeen after he and Tom had a fifteen-minute knock-down drag-out fist fight over Leonard wanting to marry a seventeen-year-old girl from Greenwood. Leonard was bleeding and angry when he swore to Tom he was leaving Brewer Hill and never coming back. Leonard married the girl and moved to work on cars at Talladega. He impressed the shop foreman of longtime NASCAR champion driver Danny Ray Johnson with his work ethic, and won a permanent job traveling with the crew to races all over the United States.

Like all Brewers, Leonard was hard-headed. He kept his vow, having never returned to Brewer Hill. He and Trevor talked on the phone occasionally, but the cell service at Brewer hill was so spotty the phone visits were rare. Trevor and his father never spoke about Leonard. Trevor saw Leonard with Johnson's pit crew on television from time to time. Trevor missed his brother and wished Leonard would come home to visit. He knew it unlikely because Tom and Leonard were at loggerheads; neither one would take the first step to reconcile.

Trevor admired Leonard's guts and independence, standing up to Tom like that. Trevor was almost as good with motors and body work as Leonard, but Trevor would never leave Brewer Hill. He didn't think he could make it on the outside because of his stutter.

It started when he was a kid. Tom got sent to the penitentiary for raping a woman in Kilbride. Trevor fought every kid in the third grade who teased him about having a jailbird for a daddy. It got so bad Trevor walked down the dirt road to the school bus stop at the paved highway but disappeared into the brush when the other kids from the hill started lining up to step into the bus. He spent his truancy days playing all over Brewer Hill, bow hunting small game. Trevor skipped school so many days the school administration held him back, making him repeat third grade. He didn't care. By then he was stuttering so badly he was embarrassed to answer the teacher. The teachers knew Trevor's situation at home, and passed him along, never calling on him in class or insisting that he do his homework. As soon as Trevor was sixteen and it was legal for him to quit school, he did. He went further in school than Tom, and stuttering did not present as big a problem on Brewer Hill as it was at school.

"Be back to work s-soon as they l-let me out of h-here," Trevor said as Tom opened the door to leave. "M-Maybe this afternoon."

Tom said nothing. Trevor watched the door close. Alone in his room again, his heart rate slowed considerably.

Chapter Seven

Willie Mitchell met Walton and Kitty at the Quick Stop across the highway from the hospital. The Subway Sandwich counter in the west half of the store didn't open for business until ten on Saturday mornings, so Quick Stop's coffee customers sat in the booths on the Subway side of the store.

Kitty wore her dark blue deputy uniform. Walton wore khakis, a knit shirt, and Top-Siders. He was thirty-one and handsome, with near black hair and blue eyes. He and his wife had healthy four-year-old twins and planned on one more child, but were afraid they would have another set of twins. The first two were just now getting to the age where they were fun. The thought of two new babies in diapers was still too scary for them to commit to another birth, but they were getting there.

Walton hailed from Clarksdale, an hour north of Sunshine, and went to work for Willie Mitchell as an Assistant D.A. right out of Ole Miss Law School. He had prosecuted a lot of cases in his seven years as an assistant, trying more jury trials than anyone of his law school classmates.

Willie Mitchell sat in the booth across from Kitty and Walton, and told them everything he knew about the history of the Brewers. Originally from Tennessee, the first Brewers moved to Dundee County in 1825 and bought Brewer Hill and the three sections of land around it. Old timers said the Brewers were highwaymen who robbed and killed people along the Natchez Trace west of Pulaski in southern Tennessee, eventually getting run out of the state by the law. They used the money they stole to buy the almost two thousand acres around Brewer Hill on the edge of the Mississippi Delta. Some said the Brewers were hill people in Tennessee and when they settled in Mississippi they wanted the hilliest land they could find.

Willie Mitchell said the Brewer Hill legend was enhanced in 1855, when one of the Brewers was arrested for attempted murder of a shopkeeper in a small Delta town not far from Brewer Hill. All of the Brewer men folk descended from the hill into the town to free their kinsman, killing the Sheriff and burning down most of the buildings. According to the story, two more lawmen went up on Brewer Hill to make arrests for murdering the Sheriff, and were never seen or heard from again. No one from the state attempted to draft the Brewers to fight on the side of the Confederacy, so the Brewers ignored the Civil War. There was good water on the hill and the clan grew corn and tobacco in the flats and raised cattle, sheep, and hogs on the hill. They didn't like the outside world much, and rarely saw the need to leave Brewer Hill.

Around 1890, a federal census worker heard stories about Brewer Hill from people he interviewed in Dundee County. Some said Brewer Hill was haunted, others said the Brewers would raid communities in the county and kidnap women and children and take them to the hill. According to the stories, the victims were never heard from again. The census worker rode a horse loaded with whiskey, sugar, and bolts of brightly-colored cloth up Brewer Hill. The Brewers accepted his gifts and let him set up camp for one night on the hill, then asked him to leave and never come back.

The census worker later documented what he saw, estimating that approximately eighty men, women, and children occupied the hill in five or six groups or "families." He said it appeared that some of the women were of native Indian descent, speculating that the Brewers married Cherokee or Choctaw women who remained in the remote parts of Dundee County after most of the Indian population was relocated west of the Mississippi in the federal government's Indian Removal Act, the "Trail of Tears" in the 1830's.

Willie Mitchell said the Brewers became less isolated during the twentieth century, trading and interacting with the small Delta communities near Brewer Hill. Brewer children attended Dundee County public schools. Some, like Trevor's brother Leonard, moved away when they were able, but most stayed.

"The Brewers never really assimilated," Willie Mitchell told Walton and Kitty. "They've always been suspicious of outsiders and the government, and constantly in trouble with the law over here. Some of the Brewer men have done hard time. Trevor's father Tom did six or seven years in Parchman on a rape conviction. I've never seen Tom's half-brother Freddy, but they say he's done federal and state time and is the worst of the Brewers."

"Sounds like they're just a bunch of redneck outlaws," Kitty said.

"I've heard stories about the Brewer clan ever since I moved to Yaloquena," Walton said, "but I've never prosecuted one."

"I've convicted a few of them on minor charges," Willie Mitchell said. "Most of the serious cases against Brewers have been in Dundee County. They don't like to stray far from the hill."

"So," Walton said, "our man Trevor Brewer is from a clan of criminals whom everyone in Yaloquena and the other jurisdictions around Dundee County knows about."

"That's right," Willie Mitchell said. "According to what I've heard from people who claim to know, the Brewers don't like blacks or anyone of mixed race. Then again, supposedly they don't like anyone who doesn't live on Brewer Hill. They don't like flatlanders, Yankees, Asians, and anyone affiliated with the federal, state, and local government regardless of ethnicity. They don't know any Jews, but if they did, they'd hate them, too. They're equal opportunity bigots."

"Great," Walton said.

"Let's go on across the street. I know you and Kitty are dying to meet your star witness."

Chapter Eight

Trevor clicked back and forth between the baseball highlights on ESPN and a show about alligator hunters on the History Channel. He was getting restless, ready for the doctor to check him out so he could get in his truck and go home. Tom had left the room ten minutes earlier and Trevor was glad he was gone. His father was a hard man to talk to. He didn't say much in the repair shop, and even less when he was outside his comfort zone. Tom was most at ease on Brewer Hill, then the shop. Anywhere else, Tom was tense and paranoid. Even in Trevor's hospital room, Tom jumped when a nurse opened the door.

Trevor hated to admit it, but he wasn't much different. He didn't like leaving the hill or the shop, where everyone knew about his stutter. Here in Sunshine, Trevor was uncomfortable around everyone. He tried to keep his communication to a bare minimum.

Better they think I'm a slow-witted retard than opening my mouth and proving it.

NASCAR highlights popped up on ESPN and Trevor strained to pick out Leonard on the thirteen-inch screen mounted high on the wall. He turned up the volume when the announcer mentioned Danny Ray Johnson, but the pit crew on the screen was so small, there was no way to recognize his brother.

One of the good-looking blonde ESPN announcers filled the screen. Trevor studied her, paying little attention to what she said. Maybe getting shot was just what he needed to get himself up off his ass and get himself a full-time woman. He had his eye on a sixteen-year old on the hill. She had flirted with Trevor a few times when he was cane pole fishing in one of the Brewer Hill ponds that was full of bream. He had stuttered at her at first, but calmed down enough to put some whole words together and not sound so stupid. She seemed to like him in spite of the way he talked, or tried to talk. Trevor noticed she was fully-developed. He had been thinking about her a lot.

There was a light knock on the door.

"O-k-kay," he said.

Willie Mitchell, Kitty, and Walton walked in.

"Trevor?" Willie Mitchell said.

Trevor stared at Willie Mitchell and the two strangers. He looked at Kitty longer than the others. She was good-looking. He shook hands with the District Attorney.

"You remember me?" Willie Mitchell said.

Trevor nodded.

"C-Coach Banks."

"Right. You know I'm still District Attorney for Yaloquena County, just like I was when you were on Jake's little league team."

Trevor nodded.

"This is my first assistant, Walton Donaldson." Walton shook Trevor's hand. "And this is Kitty Douglas. She works with the Sheriff's office." Kitty shook Trevor's hand, too.

Trevor smiled at Kitty. Her hand was warm and soft. Trevor knew Coach Banks was going to start asking him questions about the shooting at the Gas & Go Fast. He felt his chest begin to tighten and his throat constrict. His heart started to pound; his ears roared.

"You feel well enough to talk to us this morning about what happened day before yesterday at the store?" Willie Mitchell asked.

Shit. Shit. Shit.

"Q-Questions?"

Trevor noticed Walton cutting his eyes at the D.A.

Didn't take that guy long to figure out what a loser I am.

"We've got a lot more to do in the investigation," Willie Mitchell said, "but right now it looks like Mule started shooting at the man at the gas pump while you were standing at the front door."

Thoughts raced through Trevor's mind. Tom preached to him over and over at the shop: never talk to lawyers and cops. Tom said "no matter what happens or what they say, they ain't your friends." One time Tom made Trevor repeat "they ain't your friends," which Trevor said over and over to Tom that day until he could say it without the usual hesitations and stammers. Trevor knew he was in the right, defending himself at the Gas & Go Fast, but Tom said lawyers have a way of twisting your words. He said the six years he spent in the pen was because of the way the lawyers twisted his words, even his own lawyer. Trevor remembered Tom swearing to Trevor's mother that he didn't do it, that the lawyers put words in his mouth and lied to the jury.

Even if I could get some words out, I better not.

Trevor said nothing. After thirty seconds of awkward silence, Willie Mitchell tried again.

"We don't have any current plans to place you under arrest. We're thinking you were defending yourself. Is that how you feel?"

More silence. Trevor turned his head away from his visitors.

"All right, Trevor," Willie Mitchell said. "I can understand your being reluctant to talk to us. We'll just be on our way."

Trevor turned back to Willie Mitchell and extended his hand. Willie Mitchell shook it and smiled at Trevor.

"C-coach. How's J-Jake?"

"He's good. All grown up like you. I'll tell him you asked about him. We'll talk later if you want."

Willie Mitchell led Kitty and Walton out.

"Why didn't you tell us he stuttered?" Walton asked in the hall.

"I thought he might have outgrown it."

"He didn't," Kitty said.

~ * ~

Six hours later, around four that afternoon, Kitty and Sheriff Lee Jones walked into Willie Mitchell's office. Walton was proofreading a barebones press release that Willie Mitchell had written to placate the local media. It was a joint statement by the D.A.'s office and the Sheriff's office, updating the information they provided the night of the homicide.

"What's up?" Willie Mitchell asked.

"Bad news for Trevor," Lee said.

"The trace on his nine-millimeter Smith and Wesson came back," Kitty said. "It was reported stolen in Oklahoma City three years ago."

"Uh-oh," Willie Mitchell said.

"That's not all," Lee said. "Your friend Robbie Cedars at the crime lab ran the digital images of the nine millimeter cartridge casings from the Gas & Go Fast through the National Integrated Ballistics Information Network identification system. The casings ejected from Trevor's nine matched casings found at the scene of a double homicide in Oklahoma City two years ago."

"They're sure?" Willie Mitchell asked.

"Pretty much," Lee said. "Robbie's going to test fire a few rounds and send them some actual reference casings so they can do a physical comparison, but Robbie said the NIBIN comparison was an easy match. He eyeballed the images himself and is sure the computer is correct."

"Trevor's looking at possession of a stolen weapon at a minimum," Kitty said. "I'll check into the Oklahoma murder investigation and let them know we've got the weapon used in their unsolved double homicide. Maybe they've got a description of the killer."

"Call the hospital," Willie Mitchell said to Walton. "See if Trevor is still there."

Chapter Nine

That night, Jake Banks held his cell phone to his ear as he lay across the tattered sofa in the upstairs common room of the two story Georgian in the edge of Rock Creek Park they called "the barracks." DOGs administrator Billy Gillmon purchased the property in an LLC in late 2008 from the federal government at a GSA surplus property auction. It was formerly the embassy of a small eastern European country that ceased to exist after the restructuring of the Soviet Socialist Republics in the nineties. In typical fashion, the federal bureaucracy took eight years to declare it surplus after title reverted to the U.S., and another six to dispose of it. No one took care of the place in the meantime, but vandals and the homeless failed to discover the building because of its remote location on the edge of the heavily wooded park fifteen minutes from Massachusetts Avenue. David Dunne lived in the barracks; he had no other home. Bull lived in Chicago and Hound in Miami with their families when they were off duty. Doberman lived in San Diego near his newly-discovered maternal grandmother.

Jake stayed in a small efficiency apartment in downtown D.C. not far from D.O.J. when he wasn't in Sunshine or on a training mission. Jake was early for tonight's meeting and used the time to talk to Kitty.

"Sure. I remember Trevor," Jake said. "He was on our baseball team for two summers when Daddy was coaching. He and I were buddies."

Jake listened for several minutes. David Dunne and Doberman walked in. Jake held up one finger to them. He interrupted Kitty.

"We're starting a meeting," he said. "I'll call you back soon as we're through." He listened for a few seconds. "Me, too," he said. "Call you in a little while."

"You can tell Kitty you love her in front of us," Dunne said smiling. "We've both been in that situation before." He turned to Doberman. "Haven't we?"

"Hundreds of times."

Jake shrugged. Hound and Bull walked in laughing.

"Big Dog's right behind us," Hound said. He was Salvadoran, with short black hair and *café au lait* skin. At 5'10" and about 170, Hound was the softest-looking of all the DOGs, but looks were deceiving. He was Dunne's best stealth killer and the second-best long-range marksman on the squad after Doberman. His long-distance swimming ability had been critical on several missions.

Hound and Bull pushed Jake over and joined him on the ratty brown couch. David Dunne and Doberman sat in the matching brown chairs with wispy white stuffing escaping from the overstuffed arms. Hound put a headlock on Bull and rubbed his knuckles into Bull's short blond crew cut. Still in the headlock, Bull grabbed Hound around the waist and stood up from the couch, Hound and all.

Hound looked down at the floor, four feet below him.

"You give?" Hound asked.

Everyone laughed. Bull gently placed Hound on the couch and sat on top of him just as Big Dog walked in the room holding his back. Big Dog was sixty-eight, with broad shoulders, thick white hair and a bushy white walrus mustache. A ten-year-old scar from a 2001 DOGs mission ran diagonally from his forehead, through his left eyebrow and eyelid on to his left cheek. The razor blade creating the scar had also passed through his left pupil, rendering it useless, cloudy and gray.

Lieutenant General John Evanston, code named Big Dog, was there at the beginning. He was called out of retirement two days after September 11, 2001 by a covert consortium of representatives of DOD, DOJ, FBI, CIA, and the White House. The group met in secret at a Holiday Inn in Chevy Chase on Sunday, five days after the twin towers fell. The mission Big Dog undertook that day was to head up the Domestic Operations Group, DOGs. DOGs' first directive was to eliminate any person in the United States who aided the 9/11 terrorists. No arrests, no trials, no due process, no publicity—just quiet eradication. Big Dog's first recruit was his former son-in-law, a special forces Captain he code-named David Dunne.

Big Dog grew the DOGs organization in staff and operatives in the early years, fulfilling the prime directive then broadening its scope to include any domestic action the federal government could not officially undertake. After the 2008 election, the new administration grudgingly agreed to forego prosecuting Big Dog, Dunne, and the other DOGs in a standoff negotiated by Deputy Attorney General Patrick Dunwoody IV. No one in the new executive branch knew Dunwoody had represented DOJ in the September 16, 2001 meeting in Chevy Chase. Big Dog agreed to the 2008 shutdown, but immediately recruited his best men, David Dunne, Doberman, Hound, and Bull, along with two administrators, Billy Gillmon and Helen Holmes. DOGs went underground. Aided by Billy Gillmon's computer expertise and knowledge of agency budgets, Big Dog procured his own funding. From early 2009, DOGs continued to operate in secrecy without government authority, carrying out missions critical to the protection of the United States.

Two and a half years before tonight's meeting in the Barracks, events in Mississippi and New Orleans tangential to DOGs missions led David Dunne and Big Dog to recruit Assistant U.S. Attorney Jake Banks.

Ostensibly an AUSA working out of the DOJ office in D.C. under the supervision of Patrick Dunwoody, Willie Mitchell's oldest boy was now a full-fledged DOG, waiting with the others for the start of the meeting.

Soon as he entered the room, Big Dog did a double-take, glaring at Bull sitting on Hound's lap.

"Playin' grab ass, huh?" Big Dog said smiling. "Looks like you two boys been away from your women a little too long."

"How's your back?" Bull asked.

"The same as always," Big Dog said in his usual pose, leaning slightly forward at the waist. He put both hands behind his back at waist level and arched his waist forward.

"Before we get into this new business," Big Dog said to David Dunne, "is there anything you want to update the men on?"

"Just some interesting intel from one of our associates in N.O.P.D.," Dunne said. "Remember when I left you guys in New Brunswick to help Jake out of a jam in New Orleans?"

"Yeah," Hound said. "The gun smuggling gang led by that Cuban Santeria freak Brujo."

"Right," Dunne said. "It turned out to be a nice little piece of work. We took Brujo out and put the kibosh on their weapons going to the Mexican drug cartels."

"Then ATF picked up the slack for the cartel gun supply in Operation Fast and Furious," Hound said looking around. "Can anyone here believe that shit? Our own government supplying those killers?"

Jake kept his head down.

"Let's stay on message here," Dunne said. "You men remember N.O.P.D. and the FBI never found the two guys that almost killed FBI Special Agent Kitty Douglas, Jake's friend," Dunne said. "If you recall they attacked…,"

Raped her, cut her, left her for dead is what they did, Big Dog.

"Four hundred stitches," Jake interrupted quietly, supplying all the detail he thought was necessary for the men to know.

"Yeah, well," Dunne said, "the two men in Brujo's outfit, Hispanic gangsters that attacked Kitty, one was named Panik and the other Smokey. They went underground after Brujo passed away suddenly last year on Chartres Street in the French Quarter."

Dunne paused for a moment to look directly at Jake, who seemed distracted, distant.

"Anyway, our friend, a captain at N.O.P.D., called me this afternoon. They found Panik and Smokey in a dumpster a week ago. Took a while to identify the bodies, get a positive i.d. Somebody dispatched them professionally, permanent-like."

Everyone in the room turned and looked at Jake.

"Did you hear me, Jake?" Dunne asked. "You paying attention?"

"Yes, sir. I heard you," Jake said, looking straight at Dunne. "Sounds like they got what they deserved."

"Before we went on the mountain training mission," Dunne said to Jake, "you were gone for a week or so. Where'd you go?"

"Nowhere much," Jake said.

"Good," Big Dog said. "Jake, I know you're aware of our rule against solo activity, no matter how justified."

"Yes, sir," Jake said, looking first at Big Dog, then Dunne.

"I'm glad we cleared this up, then," Big Dog said. "Let's get on with the new business."

Doberman, Hound, and Bull stared at Jake.

"All right," Dunne said. "Listen up, girls. We've been asked to do something we've never done before. We're not going to do it unless every one of you is on board. Big Dog will give you the basics, then we'll talk about it. We want your input."

Chapter Ten

Wide awake at 4:45 a.m. for no reason, Willie Mitchell put on his running gear and drank two cups of coffee while reading Monday morning's Wall Street Journal on his HP laptop. He strapped his square iPod Nano on his arm, opted for the "purchased" song list and took off out the front door, jogging toward the eastern sky. It was getting light later these days, but no cooler. Weather Channel Local On The 8's said it was seventy-eight degrees when he started his run, looking for a high today of 96. Only four days to the autumnal equinox, but cool weather seemed light years into the future.

He sang along with Adele for a few minutes until his brain compartmentalized the music. Willie Mitchell would not be walking with Jimmy Gray this morning. They walked yesterday because Willie Mitchell wanted to get an early start at the office today with Walton. They had a lot of details to go over. Willie Mitchell wanted to keep the investigation moving forward as fast as possible.

Yesterday's big Sunday lunch with Jimmy and Martha Gray and Kitty was fun, except for Kitty bringing up the Mule Gardner case at the table. Willie Mitchell did not want to discourage her enthusiasm and answered her first question. He politely deferred the rest until after they finished Susan's fried chicken and the last of the Hudson brothers' sweet corn on the cob Susan had kept in the freezer since July.

Kitty had lunch every Sunday with the Banks family, whether Jake was in town or not. She lived in Willie Mitchell's duck camp, several miles outside Sunshine. Kitty liked the peace and quiet of the remote cabin on the forty-acre black water cypress-studded pond. When Jake was in town, he spent a lot of time at the duck camp with Kitty, but always returned to his bedroom in the Banks home in the wee hours. Kitty agreed with Jake's need to maintain a veneer of propriety in Sunshine. His mother Susan deserved no less.

The Hudson brothers' sweet corn was delicious this year, with big ears and kernels full of juice. Willie Mitchell leased the 990 acres inherited from his father to the Hudsons, who planted half in cotton and half in sweet corn. Cotton prices were through the roof for the first time in decades, and Midwest ethanol production had driven the price of corn higher as well. The Hudsons were going to have a banner year. Willie Mitchell took one-fourth of the crop as his rental income, so this year was going to make up somewhat for the previous four years of lean returns on the land. Willie Mitchell would never sell the land and unlike most lessors, refused to move to a cash rent. He liked participating in the crop.

It was almost like being a farmer. He watched the prices and the weather, and bellyached like a real farmer when things went bad. He didn't need the money. Susan's DeSoto Parish natural gas income was down because of the glut of product coming on line from the shale discoveries all over North America, but her monthly checks were still massive. Willie Mitchell's large block of Sunshine Bank stock continued to pay dividends like clockwork, the annual total now exceeding his D.A. salary. Under Jimmy's management, the dividend increased each year.

He thought for a moment about what Jimmy told him yesterday after Sunday lunch. The big regional bank out of Nashville was making a run at Sunshine Bank again. They were offering much more than the two-and-a-half to three times book value multiple that was the going rate for bank acquisitions. Jimmy said under the terms of the offer, he was to keep running the bank for five years then walk away, "free as a bird," to use the Nashville bankers' expression. Jimmy said the terms of the five-year non-competition agreement they wanted him to sign as a condition of the sale were too severe.

"Well, hell," Jimmy Gray told Willie Mitchell, "if I'm going to run the bank we might as well keep on owning it. I ain't too good at taking orders."

"Whatever you say, partner," Willie Mitchell said.

He told Jimmy the decision was his to make. They would both make a lot of money if they sold, but Willie Mitchell knew the stock would continue to grow in value with Jimmy managing the bank. When Jimmy had grown Sunshine Bank to $400 million in assets, he converted the corporate structure to a Sub-Chapter S. The bank was over-capitalized at fifty-two million, more than the FDIC and state auditors required. Jimmy was a banking wizard, inside and out. He knew bank accounting and financial standards regulations, but also had the best personality of any small town banker in the South. His loan customers loved him; so did his correspondent bankers.

A sharp pain in his left hip brought Willie Mitchell's focus back to his running. Within minutes his home was in sight. In spite of the ache shooting down his left leg, he turned into the pea gravel circular drive in front of his two-story house and took the front steps two at a time.

~ * ~

Walton and Willie Mitchell were talking on the speaker phone to Robbie Cedars, Willie Mitchell's buddy at the State crime lab, when Louise Kelly, his forty-eight-year-old receptionist with dark brown skin and neatly trimmed Afro stepped into the D.A.'s private office.

She knew they were talking to the crime lab and waited for a signal from Willie Mitchell before saying anything. He held up one finger, and Louise nodded. In less than a minute, Willie Mitchell and Walton had wrapped up with Robbie.

"What's up, Louise?"

Only then did Willie Mitchell recognize the look he rarely saw. Louise had worked for him for fifteen years in the front line of the D.A.'s office. Hundreds of odd people with bizarre stories to relate had appeared at Louise's front desk over time. Very little surprised her. This morning, Willie Mitchell knew Louise was about to describe something out of the ordinary.

"There's a man out front..., well, three men."

Willie Mitchell waited.

"The man doing the talking is wearing a bow tie and a brown suit. He says his name is Mohammed X."

"Muhammad?" Walton asked.

"No. He was very precise. Mohammed."

"And the other two men?" Willie Mitchell asked.

"One is little with a shaved head and glasses that are too big for his face. The other is the biggest black man I've ever seen in my life. Those two are wearing bow ties and black suits."

"What do they want?"

"They won't tell me exactly. Mr. Mohammed says he wants to talk to you and no one else."

"Bring them in," Willie Mitchell said.

"You want me to wait outside?" Walton asked.

"Nope. Pull up a chair next to my desk."

"You know who this Mohammed is?"

"Mohammed X heads up the Freedmen's Creek commune. Lee's told me about him. Glad I'm finally getting to meet him."

Louise stopped at the door and gestured the men in. Willie Mitchell sized them up. Louise's description was accurate.

"I'm Willie Mitchell Banks," he said, extending his hand.

Willie Mitchell took the man to be mid-fifties. He wore a broad smile, was well-groomed and clean-shaven. He parted his hair on the left side and wore it straightened and slicked down. He wore rimless glasses and a dark green bow tie against his bright white shirt. His light brown suit looked expensive and was not as dark as the man's milk chocolate skin. The other two men were as different in appearance as two adult black men could be.

"My name is Mohammed X, and I am here to seek justice."

"All right," Willie Mitchell said. "We'll see what we can do about that. This is my first assistant, Walton Donaldson."

Mohammed nodded to Walton, who almost extended his hand but stopped when Mohammed did not extend his.

"Very well," Mohammed said. "These are my associates. Samson al Kadeesh." The big man bowed slightly. "And Abud Rahman."

Louise had not exaggerated. Willie Mitchell guessed Samson al Kadeesh was at least 6'6" tall and 300 pounds of muscle. The man was not soft. His skin was jet black, his head shaved. Abud Rahman, on the other hand, was a small man. No more than five-six, he could not have weighed more than 140 pounds. His head was shaved and his skin was dark, but not as black as Samson's. Louise was right about the oversized glasses. Willie Mitchell thought Abud looked like Tweety-Bird.

"Mr. al Kadeesh is well-named," Willie Mitchell said.

"Yes," Mohammed said. "May we speak frankly?"

"By all means," Willie Mitchell said and sat down, as did Walton.

Mohammed sat in the heavy barrel-backed oak chair across from Willie Mitchell. Samson and Abud stood behind him, their arms hanging down in front, crossed at the wrists.

"Abdul Azeem was a friend and associate."

Willie Mitchell waited.

"He was cut down in his prime, murdered for no reason."

"It's unfortunate," Willie Mitchell said. "Sorry for your loss. We have arrested a local man, Lester Gardner and intend to charge him with felony murder. Our investigation so far indicates that Gardner started the whole thing, that Azeem was minding his own business."

"I am sure Azeem did not bring this on himself," Mohammed X said. "He was a serious man, a business man. I am aware that although this Gardner did shoot Azeem, his weapon did not actually kill Azeem. Is that correct?"

"Yes," Willie Mitchell said. "It appears that the bullet that killed Azeem was fired by the young man at the store who was also shot by Mr. Gardner."

"Who told you about that?" Walton asked.

Mohammed ignored him.

"We would like to know how you learned these details?" Willie Mitchell asked. "That information has not been released to the public."

"I spoke to the County Coroner, Mr. Alphonse Revels."

"He's not supposed to give out any information about the investigation until we've examined all the evidence," the D.A. said.

"I am a resident of this county," Mohammed said. "He is the elected coroner and I should be able to confer with him, or so it seems to me. He doesn't work for you, does he?"

"Certainly not," Willie Mitchell said. "But there are protocols to follow in releasing information after a homicide."

"In any event, we expect you to bring murder charges against the person who actually killed Azeem, this Trevor Brewer."

"We're looking into it," Willie Mitchell said. "Azeem was killed only four days ago and we have a lot of investigating left to do."

"Yet you have decided to charge this Gardner with murder."

"Yes. We are presenting the case to the Grand Jury Monday."

"And this Trevor Brewer has not been charged with anything."

"So far."

"Could that be because you and this Trevor Brewer share some of the same sentiments regarding white transgressors and black victims?"

Willie Mitchell felt heat moving from under his collar along his neck to his ears. He knew from experience they were getting red.

"And what would those sentiments be?"

"I've lived in Yaloquena County only a short time," Mohammed said, "but long enough to know that this Trevor Brewer is part of a racist white supremacist family that has terrorized, murdered, and lynched African-Americans in a number of counties in this area."

"I'm aware of the Brewer family reputation," Willie Mitchell said. "I can tell you that since I've been District Attorney in Yaloquena County, no Brewer has been involved in any serious criminal activity in this county."

"You mean until this Trevor Brewer murdered Azeem in cold-blood for no reason."

"We're still investigating," Willie Mitchell said.

"Given the history of this Brewer clan, have you considered charging the killer with a hate crime?"

Willie Mitchell took a deep breath.

"There's no evidence so far to indicate a racial motive. The evidence seems to indicate Brewer was shot before he armed himself and acted in self-defense."

"That's your opinion."

"In Yaloquena County," Willie Mitchell said. "It's my opinion that counts." He paused for a moment. "If you'll give me your phone number and address I'll make sure we keep you informed of the progress of the investigation."

"I do not talk on the telephone. Abud will leave his number with the woman at the front desk."

"And your address is Freedmen's Creek?"

Mohammed did not answer.

"We expect you to charge Trevor Brewer with the murder of Azeem," Mohammed said, "and we want him sent to prison."

"No death penalty?" Willie Mitchell asked.

"I have no problem with him being put to death for this," Mohammed said and walked out, followed closely by his two men.

Walton exhaled loudly.

"You notice how he smiled the whole time," Willie Mitchell said, "no matter how derogatory and abrasive his comments?"

"Kind of a weird affect, if you ask me."

Willie Mitchell simulated taking a final drag on a cigarette, tossing the butt into the center of the office and covering his ears awaiting the imaginary explosion.

"I give," Walton said.

"Lloyd Bridges, the first Airplane! movie."

"Who?"

"Father of Jeff and Beau. He played the same ditzy character, an admiral in Hot Shots! I used to watch him on Sea Hunt on our black and white television when I was a kid."

"Whatever," Walton said, not in the mood. "This trial is not going to be what I expected."

"Yep," Willie Mitchell said. "You picked a bad month to stop sniffing glue."

Chapter Eleven

By noon Willie Mitchell, Walton, Kitty, and Sheriff Lee Jones were on their way to Dundee County in Lee's black Tahoe with the official Yaloquena County Sheriff emblem on each of the front doors. Willie Mitchell rode shotgun. After Mohammed X, Samson, and Abud left the D.A.'s office, Willie Mitchell asked Lee to call the Dundee Sheriff, Bob Cheatwood, to set up a meeting in Kilbride today if possible. By asking Lee to make the first contact with his counterpart in Dundee County, Willie Mitchell was following rural county political protocol.

"Not much to this place," Lee said turning off the two-lane state highway onto the street that led downtown to the courthouse and the post office.

"Never has been," Willie Mitchell said. "Courthouse was built with WPA help during the thirties. The post office was built by the government in the fifties when art deco was all the rage for public buildings."

"I bet there's no one in Dundee County that would disagree with your take on the architectural style," Walton said.

"Or agree with you for that matter," Kitty said.

Lee chuckled. "I'm just glad I'm not coming over here by myself."

"Aw, Lee," Willie Mitchell said. "Times have changed."

"I'm not so sure about that," Lee said.

Neither was Willie Mitchell. He started coming to Dundee County in the eighth grade to play basketball for Sunshine Academy against Kilbride School. Sunshine played the Kilbride Demons a home-and-home in basketball every year, so by his senior year Willie Mitchell knew a few of the Kilbride players. One of them, Clyde Guthrie, played against Willie Mitchell for five straight years, but in Willie Mitchell's senior year, Clyde said he was a sophomore. Willie Mitchell told Jimmy Gray that Clyde was apparently doing graduate studies at Kilbride High.

A hundred-twenty-two pounds ago, Jimmy Gray was on the Sunshine Academy team with Willie Mitchell. He wasn't a scorer. His job was to rebound and set picks to get Willie Mitchell open for jump shots. At 6'0" and one-ninety, Jimmy Gray was a wide body in those days, good at blocking out and clearing the boards. Willie Mitchell laughed when he thought about Jimmy saying if any player on the Kilbride Demons bit him, he was going to get a tetanus shot.

The drive through Dundee County reminded Willie Mitchell how different Dundee was from Yaloquena. Yaloquena was 100% Mississippi Delta, not a natural hill to be found. The soil was incredibly fertile and agriculture still accounted for almost seventy per cent of the economic activity. Yaloquena citizens were more genteel than people in Dundee County. Most of the old Yaloquena farming families had dispersed and much of the land was now owned or managed by corporate farm operations. Yaloquena County was almost seventy-five per cent black. Many of the black citizens were the progeny of the men and women who worked in the cotton fields for the plantation owners.

Dundee County was more rural. Only the western third of Dundee was suitable for row crops. The rest was hilly and covered in some pine, but mostly hardwood. The people were poorer and rougher, the population whiter. Almost all of Dundee's black population was in the Delta, the western third of the county, and made up around ten per cent of the county census. No African-American Dundee County citizens lived in the hills, especially around Brewer Hill. Willie Mitchell remembered the Dundee County D.A. telling him he had "the black vote" in the hills locked up, then chuckling as he explained that there was only *one* black voter in the hills, and he wasn't sure she was still registered.

Willie Mitchell and his basketball teammates referred to the Kilbride players as hillbillies, but never in their presence. Thinking back on it, it was an apt description. They were raw-boned with dark hair and bad skin. Many of them had heavy beards, even as teenagers. Dental care was substandard, and the Demons' lack of personal hygiene, especially in the fourth quarter of close games, became a real issue for Willie Mitchell and his teammates.

Lee parked the Tahoe at the courthouse and the four of them walked into the Sheriff's office. Bob Cheatwood had been Sheriff when Willie Mitchell was first elected and still held the position. Willie Mitchell had only a half-dozen contacts with Sheriff Cheatwood over the years. The Sheriff was always cordial and helpful. Willie Mitchell remembered Cheatwood as the typical good old boy Sheriff who tried to mediate disputes between his voters, making arrests only if no alternative resolution by the Sheriff was possible.

The four of them stood in the Sheriff's waiting room less than a minute. He walked out of his office with a big smile. He grabbed the closest hand to shake as Lee started the introductions.

"How's the presidency treating you?" the Sheriff asked Lee.

"Not bad, Sheriff. You coming to the annual meeting this year?"

"Not unless someone carjacks me. I don't leave Dundee County much these days. Getting up in years."

Except for his hair being totally white now, Cheatwood looked about the same to Willie Mitchell. His uniform was tight around his middle, and the frayed and yellow edge of a tee shirt peeked out from his uniform's open collar. Lee told Willie Mitchell that the other Sheriffs in the area didn't think much of Bob Cheatwood because he was lazy and had retired on the job. Said he spent all his time hunting and fishing and laid up drinking with his hairdresser girlfriend in his cabin on a fishing pond on some acreage he owned out in the county.

Lee told Willie Mitchell Sheriff Cheatwood's personal faults didn't bother him. Lee said he didn't think Cheatwood liked him, though there was no bad blood between the two. Lee told Willie Mitchell the dislike was deeper, as if Cheatwood didn't like what Lee represented.

"I wouldn't spend a lot of time thinking about that," Willie Mitchell told Lee when they talked about it. "He's not worth it."

"I don't," Lee said. "It can't be anything personal because we hardly know each other. The other stuff is his problem, not mine."

They gathered in Sheriff Cheatwood's tiny private office. Cheatwood closed the door and sat down hard in his old wooden swivel chair and leaned back. The chair made an awful noise, creaking and groaning, badly in need of Three-In-One Oil. Willie Mitchell glanced around the filthy office. The dust and dirt on every surface had been there a while. The cramped office was in need of a good cleaning. He studied the faded photographs and yellowed framed certificates on the walls from three decades earlier. Lee and Willie Mitchell sat in the only two chairs in front of the Sheriff's desk. Kitty and Walton stood behind them leaning against three beige filing cabinets. Two mounted deer heads with large racks of antlers hung on the tan paneling behind the Sheriff. Between them was a large painting of a yellow Labrador Retriever with a duck in it's mouth.

"Thanks for seeing us on such short notice," Lee said.

"No problem, Sheriff. I read in the Jackson paper about that shooting in Sunshine involving the Brewer boy. Damned shame."

"Yeah, it is," Lee said.

The Sheriff rocked back and forth in his chair, apparently oblivious to the grating noise it made. The dust and dirt made Willie Mitchell's nose stop up, and the chair's noise made his teeth hurt. Time to get down to business and get out.

"We need to see Trevor Brewer," Willie Mitchell said. "We were hoping you'd help us locate him so we could talk to him about the shooting."

Sheriff Cheatwood opened his middle drawer and pulled out a gnarled twist of Cotton Boll chewing tobacco. He leaned back and bit off an inch of the hard dried tobacco and moved it around in his mouth to get some moisture in it. Willie Mitchell had chewed tobacco a few times in his teen years, and had tried Cotton Boll once. Within minutes of putting a piece of the bitter black twist in his mouth, Willie Mitchell had thrown up. It was worse than the Castor Oil his mother made him take when he was a five-year-old, which also made him gag.

Sheriff Cheatwood picked up the metal trash can from under his desk and spit a stream of dark Cotton Boll juice into it. He rested his elbows on the desk and leaned forward. It was obvious to Willie Mitchell the Sheriff was not keen on helping them with Trevor.

"Sheriff Jones, Mr. Mitchell," Cheatwood said, "I don't think that's a good idea. Not a good idea at all."

Kitty cleared her throat. Willie Mitchell remembered now that Sheriff Cheatwood had referred to him as "Mr. Mitchell" in all of their past dealings. Willie Mitchell didn't mind.

"Mr. Mitchell, I know you gotta talk to that Brewer boy but I don't really think going up on that hill's a good idea."

"Why not, Sheriff?" Kitty asked from behind Willie Mitchell.

"Brewer Hill's like a whole 'nother country, Miss. They don't like deputies or troopers or any law enforcement, or any kind of government agents. We go up there, we're gonna have a problem. Believe me when I say you go up there unannounced and try to pry the boy from that hill you're gonna need an army."

"What do you suggest?" Lee Jones asked.

"Probably the best thing to do is go over and see Tom at the shop. That's what you should do."

"If you think we need to go that route," Willie Mitchell said, "we'll take your advice, Sheriff. That's why we came to you."

"I do, Mr. Mitchell. I think it's the only way without stirring up a hornet's nest. Maybe getting somebody hurt, or worse."

Sheriff Cheatwood swiveled his seat to the side and stood.

"Tell you what. You fellows go on over there to Tom's Automotive. I got some things I gotta do around here. You need me for anything just give me a holler."

Back in the Tahoe, Lee Jones left the parking area next to the courthouse and drove toward Tom Brewer's repair shop.

"I guess we're on our own over here," Lee said. "The Sheriff didn't seem interested in joining our investigation."

"No kidding," Walton said. "Looked like he was scared to me."

"I think it's primarily not wanting to get up off his lazy butt," Willie Mitchell said, "coupled with the will to live out what life he's got left in peace. He's dealt with Brewers his entire career and at his age he knows he can't go up against them."

"What was that foul stuff he put in his mouth?" Kitty asked. "It looked like dried buffalo chips."

"Cotton Boll, Kitty," Willie Mitchell said. "Chewing tobacco. I've never tasted buffalo chips, but I bet they taste better than Cotton Boll."

"You've actually tried that stuff?" Lee asked.

"I've always admired your courage, boss man," Walton said.

Willie Mitchell studied the people in Kilbride he saw out his window on the way out of town, confirming his belief that Dundee County was a different place, filled with strange people. Even as a seventh grader, he had the sense Dundee County was inhospitable, an ominous, forboding place. The people were suspicious and rarely smiled, even the junior high kids. Fear seemed to permeate the place.

Willie Mitchell recalled the fights they had on the basketball court his junior and senior years. The year he graduated, Sunshine Academy dropped the Kilbride Demons from the schedule. He thought it was the right thing to do. His fondest memory of playing in Kilbride was getting on the team bus in one piece after the game and leaving the creepy place.

Tom Brewer's body and repair shop was on the paved two-lane state highway that ran between Sunshine and Kilbride, no more than a hundred yards from where the dirt and gravel private drive the Brewers controlled teed into the paved state road. There was only one way into Brewer Hill and one way out: the dirt and gravel road they passed just before turning into Tom's shop. Sheriff Cheatwood did mention that Tom's repair shop was the best in the county for older vehicles. He said quite a few Kilbride residents made the drive to Tom's Automotive because their work was good and they stood behind it.

"So that's Brewer Hill?" Kitty said while she stretched outside the Tahoe in Tom's parking area. Willie Mitchell, Lee Jones, and Walton joined her. She stood staring at the heavily wooded hill into which the dirt and gravel road disappeared.

"It's a pretty good hill, all right," Walton said.

The sky had grown overcast since they left Sunshine, and it seemed cooler to Willie Mitchell. He watched the dirt road rise at a steep angle and disappear under the dark green blanket of hardwood leaves. It was about two p.m., but the remnants of thin clouds still clung to the tops of the broadleaved oaks on top of the hill, a remarkable sight for someone born and reared in the Delta.

"Spooky," Kitty said and turned to Willie Mitchell. "I still don't know why we can't just go up there and talk to Trevor. Surely the Brewers wouldn't ambush us."

"We wouldn't know where to look," he said, "and nobody's going to help us. "We'd be up there the rest of the day getting the runaround. The garage is a smarter choice. Don't you think, Lee?"

"The shop makes more sense."

"When are you going to tell Trevor or his father about the double homicide in Oklahoma?" Kitty asked.

"I'm not sure. Let me be the one to broach that. It might make them dig in, make it even tougher to talk to them. Just have to see."

"Okay by me," Lee said. "You take the lead." He paused to look up at Brewer Hill. "When I was a kid, my grandmother told me stories about black kids being kidnapped by the Brewers and taken up the hill. Scared the hell out of me."

"You think it was true?" Kitty asked.

"Who knows? Probably not. But I've seen enough horror movies to know it's always the colored guy gets killed first by the monster."

"That is the general rule, Lee," Willie Mitchell said.

~ * ~

Up close, the shop was bigger than Willie Mitchell expected. The front was a one-story brick veneer structure attached to a much larger pre-fab metal building. He never paid much attention to the building in the past when he drove by. The four of them entered through the glass front door. Metal chairs ringed the waiting area, and a full-length counter separated it from the open office behind the counter. There was no one in the office. While waiting at the counter, Willie Mitchell walked over and looked through a large plate glass window at the interior of the repair shop. He counted at least five men dressed in dark blue overalls working on vehicles. Some of the cars were up on lifts, some rested on the concrete. The shop floor was clean and the equipment well-organized. There were no jacks or tools on the floor, and each station had its own computerized diagnostic machine. It was not what Willie Mitchell was expecting.

Behind the counter a woman with long dark hair and high cheekbones walked out of a back room through a maze of desks and computers. Wearing tight jeans and a tighter shirt, she approached the counter, drying her hands on a paper towel. He noticed a name tag on her blouse, but could not make out her name, TRACY BREWER, until she stood at the counter.

"May I help you?" she asked.

"Yes, ma'am," Willie Mitchell. "We're looking for Tom Brewer."

She walked over and pressed a button on the wall next to the plate glass. Looking out on the shop floor, she leaned close to the button.

"Tom," she said into the intercom. "Please come to the office." She waited a moment then said it again.

Willie Mitchell heard her voice echo through the garage. He watched through the glass and saw a man walking toward them rubbing his hands with a dark red rag. He wore blue jeans and a blue work shirt, a red hat with an STP logo. He was slightly built. To Willie Mitchell, he looked like an older version of Trevor, stringy but tough-looking.

~ * ~

As usual, Tom looked down at his hands as he walked toward the office. He scrubbed the oil and grease with the dark red rag he pulled from his back pocket. As he got closer, he caught a glimpse of the four people waiting for him in the office. A glimpse was all he needed.

The law.

Before he opened the door, Tom glanced behind him and saw his men gather in the middle of the repair shop and start to walk his way.

"No big deal," he said and gestured for them to get back to work.

No big deal my ass.

Tom knew his men would be more than willing to back up his play with the law men. They didn't care for them either. It wouldn't come to that. Tom didn't need any help talking to the law about Trevor.

Tom opened the door and immediately felt his "fight or flight" response begin to kick in. Some of what he felt was anger, some was fear. He was never good at talking to the law. The six years he spent in prison was proof of that. Tom raised his eyes to the three men and the woman, but immediately looked down. It was a defense mechanism he'd learned as a child. He never looked his adversaries in the eyes. It was safer for them and safer for him. If he had to do something, his eyes wouldn't give it away.

He continued to wipe his hands with the red rag. The lawyer stuck out his hand but Tom raised his, scrubbing his hands harder.

"Grease," Tom said, begging off.

Not interested in shaking a law man's hand.

"No problem," Willie Mitchell said and introduced Lee, Walton, and Kitty. All the while, Tom scrubbed his hands, looking down, holding their eyes no longer than absolutely needed, focusing on the rag.

"What's this about?" Tom said, impatient.

"Sorry for intruding in your work day," Willie Mitchell said. "We just want to talk to you for a second, then we'll be on our way."

Tom raised his head slightly to meet Willie Mitchell's eyes then dropped his head again.

"Mr. Brewer, we're here looking for Trevor," Lee said.

Tom looked up a moment to give the Sheriff a cold stare. He didn't like blacks, especially blacks in uniform.

"You got a warrant, law man?" Tom said.

"Not yet, Tom," Willie Mitchell said. "We don't have a warrant and we're not here to take Trevor away. We just want to talk to him about the shooting last week in Sunshine. I'm sure you know about it."

Willie Mitchell's calm words made Tom a little better. Trevor told Tom the D.A. over in Sunshine was a good man, always fair with him when he lived over there in Sunshine as a kid. No matter, he was still a law man. Tom knew better than to trust any of the people in the room, including the D.A. They wouldn't think twice about twisting around whatever he said so it didn't mean what he intended. Just like the lawyers did him before when he ended up in Parchman.

"Trevor ain't here. He ain't working today."

"The gun that Trevor used at the Gas & Go Fast," Willie Mitchell said, "came up stolen in Oklahoma. Possession of a stolen weapon's a crime, state and federal."

Tom stared at the floor and gritted his teeth.

Fuckin' Freddy. I should've known.

"Trevor ain't never been to Oklahoma," Tom said. "Trevor ain't never been out of Mississippi."

"I'm sure that's true, Tom. I know Trevor. He's a good boy. I coached him in baseball when you were away. He and my son Jake were friends. We believe he acted in self-defense in this shooting. He didn't go there looking for any trouble. But he can't hide out up on that hill."

Tom took a deep breath and thought about what to say next.

"I don't know."

"Just talk to him and tell him we were here. Tell him about the gun being stolen in Oklahoma. We need you to arrange it so we can talk to him. You can come in with Trevor, stay with him the whole time."

Tom looked down while Willie Mitchell spoke. He knew he could not keep Trevor from these men without asking for a lot of trouble. He'd have to bring him in or the law would come down hard on them. Tom pointed his finger at Sheriff Lee Jones.

"I'll bring my boy in. But you better let him go or there'll be problems. I ain't a threatenin' man. I just want straight talk." He turned to Willie Mitchell. "You'll let him go, you say?"

"You have my word."

"All right. I'll bring him in." Tom jammed his red rag in his back pocket. He held open the door to the garage and turned back to the D.A.

"Anything else?" Tom asked.

"No," Willie Mitchell said. "That's about it."

Tom watched the four visitors leave. Willie Mitchell tipped an imaginary hat to Tracy on the way out.

"Thank you, ma'am," he said.

Tracy looked hard at Willie Mitchell, watching him leave with the rest. She didn't smile or wave.

Tom looked at Tracy a moment, stuck his red rag in his back pocket and walked back to the garage. He didn't blame Tracy for being stern to the Yaloquena County law men or prosecutors. It wasn't the first time Tracy had law men come into the shop looking for a Brewer. Tom knew it certainly wouldn't be the last.

Chapter Twelve

While the Sheriff drove Willie Mitchell, Kitty, and Walton from Tom's Automotive back to Sunshine, Mule lay in the Yaloquena County hospital bed, a half-eaten lunch in front of him. Only bones remained of the baked chicken. Cold mounds of mashed potatoes and broccoli were left untouched on the plate. There were corn bread crumbs stuck in his mangy beard and clinging to the front of his hospital gown. Mule thought the nurse's aide must have forgotten to pick up his tray. It had been sitting in front of him a couple of hours. With his right hand still slick from the chicken, Mule grabbed the T.V. control, muttering and thrusting the remote toward the wall-mounted television each time he punched the channel up-or-down button. He was not the best of patients.

The day before, the nurses told Mule he should be more appreciative of the clean sheets and his comfortable room. Given his normal accommodations in the projects, of which the nurses were all aware, the room and amenities should have seemed like paradise. Mule told the nurses his idea of heaven involved fountains overflowing with gin, wine, and beer on every street corner, free for the taking.

To his credit, after the first day in the hospital Mule had not spent time complaining or fretting over the loss of the use of his legs. "What's done is done," he told the head nurse the day after the doctor told him the bad news. "One of my legs wasn't worth much anyway."

Mule usually talked loud and a lot, but this afternoon he was uncharacteristically quiet, watching Judge Judy, when a nurse's aide finally came in to remove his lunch tray.

"Where you been?"

She ignored him. Mule shrugged and pointed the remote at the T.V. "That's one mean white woman," Mule told her.

"You ain't got to watch her," the aide said. "Anyway, you turn it off. You got two visitors waiting outside to see you."

"Visitors? Who?"

"I don't know. That black lady lawyer Bernstein and a white man."

Mule looked down at the mess on his gown and in his bed.

"You need to clean me up," Mule said.

"I ain't your cleaning lady," the aide said. "You clean yourself up. I'll bring you a dust buster. You need to vacuum your beard, too."

"You just like Judge Judy," Mule said reaching up to brush his beard. "You get out of here and send my visitors in. It must be something important."

Mule shook the sheets and cleaned off what crumbs he could. His door opened. In walked the man and woman.

The white man took the lead, extending his hand to Mule.

"I'm Jordan Summit, Mr. Gardner. And this is Eleanor Bernstein. We are attorneys. We want to talk to you about your case."

Mule wiped his right hand on the sheet and shook hands with the man. He recognized the attractive woman in the pale lavender suit.

"I know you," he told Eleanor Bernstein. "I see you around. Up and down the highway mostly."

"We have met several times before," Eleanor said. "Sorry about your situation."

"And I think I've seen you somewhere, too," Mule told the man.

"Probably on television," Jordan Summit said.

Mule snapped his fingers. "That's it. You the man standing in front of the giant Benjamins."

"That's right," Summit said.

"Get some," Mule said. "Ain't that what you say? 'Call me and get some of these Benjamins'."

"Very good," Summit said. "That's part of the reason why Ms Bernstein and I are here."

Mule looked at the man. He was stocky, square-built with black hair and glasses. He didn't look like most of the lawyers Mule saw advertising for wrecks. They were flashy; this man looked like an undertaker, maybe a bookkeeper.

Before the shooting, Mule spent his nights watching television at his apartment in the projects on the east side of Sunshine, but only if he wasn't out honky-tonking. His place was walking distance from the main highway. Lying in the hospital bed, he had been thinking about his apartment. Now that he was going to be in a wheelchair, he figured the Yaloquena Housing Authority was going to have to build him a ramp over the steps so he'd be able to roll his chair inside.

"Can you get me one of those scooters they show on t.v.?" Mule asked. "I mean I know I got to have a wheelchair, but the scooter is different. You sit in it and you drive it with one hand. I see people riding them all over town, right down the middle of the street. They say on t.v. if they qualify you and the government won't give you a scooter, the people on t.v. say they'll give you one free."

"We'll certainly look into that for you, Mr. Gardner."

"Mule. Call me Mule, Mr. uh…."

"Summit."

"Lawyer Summit," Mule said and turned to Eleanor. "And lawyer Burnside."

"That's close enough for now," Summit said. "Let me first say, how deeply sorry I am about your injuries, Mule. You have been done a grave injustice. Ms. Bernstein called me and told me about the shooting and your incapacity. We are here to help you."

The way the man stared right into Mule's eyes made him uncomfortable, made him turn away. But he liked the way the man was talking. No nonsense, just right to the point. The bookkeeper-looking lawyer made sense to Mule.

"They say the Muslim man died, the one doused me with gasoline. What was I supposed to do?"

"I know, Mule. Believe me, I know. I'm on your side. You were doing what you had to do. I know I would have been expecting the man to pull out a lighter or matches and burn me to death, had I been in the situation in which you found yourself."

Mule's eyes grew brighter.

Hadn't thought of that. That's a good thing to say.

"That's right. Yeah. That boy was gonna light me up. Shit."

"You only shot in self-defense," Summit said. "It's obvious to me and Ms Bernstein from the way it all happened." The lawyer paused. "However, we are sure the State is going to arrest you on a charge of felony murder."

"Murder. I ain't murdered nobody. That Muslim was trying to murder me."

"Clearly. And you with your pre-existing disability," Summit said. "It is my belief this entire incident could have been avoided had the owner and operator of the Gas & Go Fast followed the law and made sure certain precautions were in place."

"What precautions?"

"Ms. Bernstein tells me this store has a substantial history of altercations at this location on the highway where you were shot, yet they failed to implement certain safety measures. Gas & Go Fast has an affirmative obligation to provide its customers with a safe environment in which to shop. We all know that. It's just common sense. You're at the store frequently I understand. How many times have you seen fights and disturbances? Ms. Bernstein tells me this store location has experienced one serious crime after another, yet they've obviously failed to protect the store invitees. All they had to do to protect you was hire a security guard to maintain order on the premises."

Mule glanced at the woman lawyer behind the white man. She was listening, nodding her head. She didn't smile much, and didn't seem very friendly. She was good-looking enough.

Maybe she mad at me for axing her for money all those times.

"We will subpoena the Sheriff's records to verify, of course, but based on what Ms. Bernstein tells me, there's more than enough to establish an atmosphere of violence at this location, enough to put the store owners on notice that they should provide security."

I see where he's going. This bookkeeper-looking white man is right on the money. Smart.

"Shit, yeah. They just care about their money. If they got a security guard or somethin' there this wouldn't happened. I've seen a bunch of fights there myself. In fact, I've broken up fights at that store."

Jordan Summit opened his briefcase and pulled out a stack of papers. He placed them on the table in front of Mule.

"Those people do owe you, Mule. You have a strong case here. If you hire Ms. Bernstein and me, we'll start on a two-step process. First, we will represent you in the criminal charges the D.A. is going to throw at you. We're sure he will claim it's murder. On a separate track, we want to sue the owners of Gas & Go Fast on your behalf for failing to take the proper safety precautions at that location in spite of ample notice. Their negligence caused your paralysis from the waist down, and it's only fair that they pay you for the pain and suffering you've experienced, past present, and future, and for your loss of economic opportunity and earnings."

"I like the way you talking," Mule said, "What do I need to do?"

"Sign these contracts," Summit said. "The first set retains us for the criminal charge. The next set authorizes Ms. Bernstein and I to sue the Gas & Go Fast people for damages. I assure you we will do all in our power to make sure you get what you deserve."

Mule took the pen, stuck his tongue out of the side of his mouth and concentrated while he signed the papers. Summit gave them to Eleanor Bernstein. She brushed corn bread crumbs off the contracts and walked out of Mule's room.

"Did I make Mrs. Burnside mad or something?"

"No, no, Mule. She's a busy young woman. She's headed to her office to set the wheels of justice in motion for you."

The lawyer stepped to the door. He peeked out to check the hallway, looking both ways. He closed it and walked back to Mule's bedside, his hand reaching inside his coat. He pulled out a small flask, picked up a paper pill cup from a stack on the table next to Mule's bed and poured it full of clear liquid.

"This is a celebration to our partnership, Mule. Now don't tell anybody I gave you this."

Mule sniffed the liquid and his face lit up. He downed the gin in one gulp. The lawyer poured the cup full again. Mule threw it back like the first one. Summit emptied the remaining gin into the cup and put the empty flask back into his inside coat pocket.

"Now I know you're tired and in pain. Ms. Bernstein and I have a lot to do. I'm leaving now, but we'll be talking soon."

Mule finished his third shot, leaned back and closed his eyes.

Mule Baby, your ship has come in.

Chapter Thirteen

Willie Mitchell walked into the reception area. Louise was reading her Kindle. She looked up at her boss.

"Sorry. Sorry," he said. "I thought I would have been back sooner. You didn't have to wait for me."

"I wasn't going to, but a federal agent stopped in to see you and I didn't feel comfortable leaving him here alone in the office or locking him outside to wait in the hallway."

"You did right. Who is he?"

"He's with ATF. Here's his card."

She picked up her purse and walked toward the door.

"He asked to use the men's room so I let him use the one in the back. You need me for anything?"

"No, thanks. Leave early tomorrow."

Willie Mitchell read the card: GARY NEEDHAM, BUREAU OF ALCOHOL, TOBACCO, FIREARMS, & EXPLOSIVES. There was an Oklahoma City office address.

I know what this is about.

"Mr. Banks?"

Gary Needham was in his mid-thirties, clean-cut in a dark suit.

"That's me," Willie Mitchell said and held up the card. "You're Gary Needham?"

"That's correct."

"Sorry you had to wait so long."

"No problem. It hasn't been that long a wait. I didn't call."

Willie Mitchell made sure the main entrance to the D.A.'s office was locked. He guided the agent into his private office.

"What can I do for you?" Willie Mitchell asked.

"It's about your recent shooting at the Gas & Go Fast on the highway last week."

"We're still investigating the murder."

"I'm here today as a courtesy call."

Federal Government Courtesy. Major oxymoron.

"The Smith and Wesson M&P used in your shooting was used in a double homicide in Oklahoma a couple of years ago."

"We knew that. State Crime Lab ran a NIBIN check for us."

"My supervisor sent me down here to let you know that we are prepared to charge this Trevor Brewer with possession of a stolen firearm under the federal statute."

"Penalty's the same under Mississippi law. We're planning on charging Trevor with possession of the weapon. I am well aware these are strict liability crimes and lack of knowledge by the defendant that the gun was stolen is not a defense. But just so you'll know, Trevor's never been out of the State of Mississippi."

"That's why the statute makes possession the offense, not the theft. Easier to prosecute that way."

"I'm just saying he didn't go to Oklahoma and steal the weapon. You a lawyer?" Willie Mitchell asked.

"I am. Went to OU."

"Did you ever practice?"

"I worked for a big firm in Oklahoma City for a while. Hated it. I've always been interested in law enforcement, so I applied for an ATF position five years ago and been there ever since."

"More and more law graduates are dissatisfied. Do you know how many new lawyers the law schools in this country graduate every year?"

Needham shook his head.

"Forty-five thousand," Willie Mitchell said. "Guess how many new doctors and engineers graduate each year?"

"Not a clue."

"Me either," Willie Mitchell said, "but I'm sure it's fewer than forty-five thousand. No wonder our country's going down the tubes." He paused. "What was involved in the double homicide?"

"I don't really know."

Cannot be true, Mr. Needham. Five years with ATF. They send you all the way to Sunshine just to let me know the feds want Trevor if we don't charge him, and you know nothing about the double homicide?

"I appreciate your coming all this way. You could have just called."

"I know. I like getting out of the office sometimes. See part of the country I've never seen."

"We've got a Grand Jury coming in next Monday," Willie Mitchell said. "They were already scheduled to come in before the Gas & Go Fast shooting happened. One of the charges I'll ask them to consider is the possession of the weapon by Trevor. They'll indict him."

"Good. If for some reason you decide not to pursue it, would you hold the Brewer fellow for us? If you end up not prosecuting, we'll charge him and take him through the federal system."

"Right," Willie Mitchell said. "You made that clear. Anything else I can do for you? We need to go over any other details?"

"This kind of goes without saying, but we'll need that Smith & Wesson as evidence in the event we charge someone with the murders."

"Sure," Willie Mitchell said. "We'll have to offer it into evidence to prosecute the stolen weapons charge. We'll preserve it in the evidence room for you and I'll prepare a motion and order to withdraw it and turn it over to you for the murder case in Oklahoma if you ever solve that case. Anything else?"

"That about covers it. You've got my card."

Willie Mitchell placed the agent's card in his middle drawer.

"I'll keep you posted."

"Thanks," Needham said. "I might call occasionally to check on the status."

"By all means."

Willie Mitchell gave Agent Needham a card and led him out the door. He locked it behind him and punched Kitty's name on his cell phone. He glanced out his window waiting for her to pick up.

~ * ~

At 8:15 the next morning Kitty walked through Willie Mitchell's reception area on the way to his private office. She said good morning to Louise, who was accustomed now to Kitty's unscheduled "pop-ins". Since Kitty was practically family, Louise never stopped her unless Willie Mitchell was with someone.

"I spoke to the FBI agent in Oklahoma City, like you asked."

"He know Needham?" Willie Mitchell asked.

"He does. ATF and FBI are in the same building. Says Needham's all right. It's Needham's supervisor who wants to send a strong message to you that if you didn't prosecute Trevor they're taking the case over."

"I got that loud and clear. I told him we were."

"Had you planned on charging Trevor on the firearm?"

"I don't know the answer to that. Tell you the truth, until Needham showed up I was kind of hoping to finesse the weapons charge. I know Trevor didn't steal the gun in Oklahoma." He paused a moment. "I don't like this. Lots of people trying to tell us what to do with our prosecution of the shooting at the Gas & Go Fast. Mohammed X insists we charge Trevor with murder. Now the feds want Trevor's head on a weapons charge. Technically he's guilty of possession of the stolen gun. But I am positive Trevor didn't know anything about it."

"You sure about Trevor?"

"I've been doing this job a long time. I'd bet money on Trevor."

"What are you going to tell Tom? You said if he brought Trevor in he could leave with him."

"I've got to tell Tom what's happened. The threat of the federal charge has changed everything." Willie Mitchell pursed his lips. "What did you find out about the homicides from your FBI contact?"

Willie Mitchell leaned back in his chair.

"The pistol was used in a murder of a man and his girlfriend. They were walking out of a bar at three in the morning in downtown OKC and they were shot and killed on the sidewalk a half a block from the bar. I had the agent scan and e-mail me a crime scene photo."

Kitty placed the grainy photograph in front of Willie Mitchell.

"Now I understand. Black man, white woman," he said, looking at the dead bodies. "DOJ is hot on this weapons charge because of the civil rights aspect. Your agent say anything about the murders being race related?"

"He volunteered they thought it was but there was no proof. No witnesses, nobody hassled the couple in the bar. No physical evidence at the scene, nothing the cops could work. He said the cops handled the crime scene investigation and the feds came in a week or so later when the girl's mother came into the FBI office. She insisted it was racial and said OKC cops weren't trying to solve it."

"DOJ is focusing on the gun to keep the case alive," he said. "After the FBI investigation on the homicide didn't go anywhere the ATF gun investigation is all they've got. Is the FBI working any kind of angle on the homicide or is it dormant?"

"The agent told me that weekend was a big biker rally in Oklahoma City. They call it The Grand Southern Plains Road Rally. Tens of thousands of bikers in town. He told me the OKC cops said there were a handful of bikers in the bar in question, but no problems. No interaction at all between the victims and the bikers. The murders were Sunday morning, last day of the rally, and by mid-afternoon, all the bikers were long gone."

"Was this rally like the ones for Harley-riding dentists and lawyers, or where there some hard core, outlaw bikers there?"

"He said the OKC cops' gang intel was non-existent. By the time the feds got involved the biker trail was cold."

Willie Mitchell thought about the investigative nightmare it would have been for the FBI. A week late, no suspects, no motive, and the nomadic bikers dispersed in every direction. It would have been a miracle had they come up with a suspect.

It's why the feds are all over Trevor's Smith and Wesson. The only lead in a two-year-old double homicide with racial animus as the motive.

"The agent said the FBI brought in their gang specialists and did some after-the-fact investigating. They concluded there were several major outlaw biker gangs at the rally. The agents have informants in a few of the gangs. They pulled them in and asked them to sniff around, but no luck."

"It would be easier to get information out of a rock," Willie Mitchell said. "Those biker gangs close ranks. Who were the gangs they questioned?"

Kitty looked at her notes.

"The Outlaws, Bandidos, some Hell's Angels offshoot, and a few smaller gangs I never heard of. They all camped outside of town."

"Anything else?" he asked.

She took a moment to check her notes again.

"That's about it."

"You talked to Jake lately?"

"Last night."

"What did you talk about?"

Kitty shook her finger and giggled. "None of your business."

Willie Mitchell laughed. "Next time you talk ask him to call me. I want to find out what he's up to."

She came to attention and saluted. "Yes, sir," she said.

Chapter Fourteen

Willie Mitchell pulled his silver Ford pickup truck onto the parking pad at Tom's Automotive. Kitty and Walton stepped out of the truck.

"Why don't you guys let me talk to Tom by himself about this. He's not going to like it, and it might go down better if it's just Tom and me alone. Less intimidating. Okay?"

They stood by the truck while Willie Mitchell walked in.

"Good morning," he said to Tracy Brewer.

She looked up from her computer and scowled. Tracy pushed her chair back from her desk and walked to the counter, flipping her head so that her long dark hair fell over her shoulders, away from her face.

"What is it now?" she said.

"I need to see Tom and Trevor."

"Trevor ain't here."

"How's his injury?"

"How do you think? He cain't work for a while."

"Is Tom here today?"

She gave the D.A. a hard look. Willie Mitchell pretended not to notice and plowed ahead.

"I need to talk to him, Ms. Brewer."

She arched an eyebrow and moved to the intercom box on the wall.

"Tom. Needed in the office. Tom. Needed in the office."

She sat back down in front of her computer without acknowledging Willie Mitchell. While she tapped on her keyboard, Willie Mitchell moved to the big plate glass window to look out onto the shop floor. After a minute, Tom Brewer slid out from under a red eighties Pontiac Firebird. Willie Mitchell watched him walk toward the office. Tom's head was down and he was trying to rub grease off his hands with a dark red rag.

"Mr. Brewer," Willie Mitchell said when Tom walked in. They didn't shake hands. Willie Mitchell knew better than to offer his. Tom glanced into Willie Mitchell's face only for a moment, then lowered his eyes and worked the red rag into his oil-stained hands.

"Something's come up. I need to talk to you and Trevor."

"Trevor ain't got nothing to say to you. Neither do I."

"After I left here Monday, I had a few other things to do in Sunshine. When I got back to my office, there was a fellow waiting to see me. This is his card."

Tom squinted at the small writing and the gold seal on the card.

"His name is Gary Needham and he's with ATF, the federal...."

"I know what ATF is. Years back they tried to start something with us up there." He pointed toward Brewer Hill. "They ain't been back."

"Until now. This ATF agent drove all the way from Oklahoma City to my office in the Yaloquena County court house to tell me the federal government was going to charge Trevor with possession of the stolen Smith & Wesson unless…."

"Unless what?"

"Unless I prosecute him in state court for the same thing."

"How can they do that?"

"They can, believe me. In fact, if they wanted, even if Trevor is convicted or pleads guilty to possession of the stolen gun in state court, the feds can still charge him with the same thing and prosecute him all over again. It's not double jeopardy."

Tom cursed under his breath.

"And under the law, both state and federal, they don't have to prove Trevor knew anything about the gun or where it came from, just that he had it on him."

"You here to take him in?"

"Nope. I'm here to talk to him, and you. What we talked about doing on Monday is off the table. Because the Department of Justice is bird dogging this case, I've got to do something with it in Yaloquena County. If I don't, the feds will swoop down on Trevor and they won't be interested in talking."

Tom looked up at the D.A. for a moment, then down again. For the first time, Willie Mitchell felt Tom's anger and mistrust subside. He sensed Tom edging into resignation. Willie Mitchell glanced at Tom's hands. They looked raw from all the rubbing.

"I've got to do something, Tom. If I don't, I'll have no say in what happens to your boy. And I know Trevor's a good boy."

"What is it you're planning on doin'?"

"I'm going to have to charge him for the weapon possession. I've got a Grand Jury meeting next Monday. I didn't call them in because of this shooting. They've been scheduled to come in on Monday for over a month now. I'm going to present the shooting and they'll indict Mule Gardner, the man that started it all, for felony murder."

Tom looked up.

"And they'll bring back an indictment against Trevor. It's a felony."

Tom nodded. "He going to jail?"

"I can get the judge to set a really low bond, maybe a few thousand dollars. I'll try for recognizance, but she might feel he needs a bond. He won't have to spend a single night in jail. It'll take a couple of hours to arrest him and go through the process, then you can take him home."

Tom stuffed his rag in his back pocket.

"I'm going up on the hill," Tom told her. "I'm gon' be a while. Tell Grover to finish up Dickie's Firebird. Ain't much left to do."

"Follow me," he said to Willie Mitchell.

On his way out the door, Willie Mitchell noticed Tracy Brewer pick up the handset from her desk phone and make a call.

~ * ~

Tom Brewer took the lead in his GMC truck and threw up a lot of dust when he left the paved road. Willie Mitchell followed about fifty yards behind to avoid rocks kicked up by the GMC. No need to break a windshield. There was little conversation in Willie Mitchell's truck. Kitty coughed a couple of times because of the dust.

A steep incline on the dirt and gravel marked the end of the flatlands. So did the shade. The first quarter-mile off the paved road was flat and in full sun. Where the hill began, large Red Oaks, Water Oaks, Cherry Bark and White Oaks grew on either side of the road as far as the eye could see.

Willie Mitchell recalled the Roman *viae* Susan and he had walked in Tuscany. Like the *viae*, the Brewer Hill road was straight as an arrow. The incline was severe as far as Willie Mitchell could see.

"Jeez," Walton said.

"No switchbacks or turnarounds," Kitty said. "I guess it's wide enough to turn and head back down if we had to."

"If we didn't turn over once we got sideways," Willie Mitchell said. "It's like driving straight up the side of a levee."

The shade ended with the incline, and Willie Mitchell's truck entered bright sunlight as the road carried them onto a treeless, flat plain the size of two football fields. Willie Mitchell slowed to a crawl and stopped. The dust was so thick in front of him he could not see.

After a moment, the dust and dirt settled.

"It's like a mesa," Kitty said before she coughed.

"Or the parade grounds at college," Walton said.

There were log structures that looked abandoned on the edge of the open area. He put his truck in gear and began driving toward Tom's GMC, seventy-five yards away across the flat expanse. Halfway to Tom's truck, Willie Mitchell stopped. Pickup trucks came at them out of the trees and from behind the dilapidated wooden buildings. Willie Mitchell counted seven vehicles, some with a driver and two passengers, others with passengers in the beds of the trucks holding shotguns and rifles.

"Holy crap," Walton said. "Road Warrior."

"We made a mistake not bringing Lee with us," Kitty said, reaching for the Glock on her side.

"Relax," Willie Mitchell said. "They're not going to hurt us. Bringing Lee Jones up here with us would have made matters worse with these people. Just sit in the truck and stay calm. Your pistol wouldn't do us much good anyway against all this firepower."

"You sure it's safe?" Walton said.

"Tom's a little backward, but he's not stupid. He's probably as surprised as we are at this reception. You two keep your seats."

Willie Mitchell stepped out of the truck and started walking toward Tom's GMC. The pickups moved around the mesa in a circle, kicking up dust, Brewers whooping and yelling every few seconds. Tom left the GMC and walked toward Willie Mitchell. When he reached the D.A., Tom held up his left hand, stuck his thumb and second finger of his right hand into his mouth and whistled.

The sound was so piercing Willie Mitchell winced, but it did the trick. The pickups came to a halt around them, all eyes focused on Tom and the intruder.

"Sorry about this," Tom said. "This ain't my doing."

"I know. I saw Tracy calling when we left your shop. Is she your wife?"

"Naw. She's a lake Brewer, lives up here on the other side of the hill around Kettle Lake, just this side of Broken Hill."

Willie Mitchell gestured to the flat field around them. "What is this place out here in the open?"

"It's the *cummins*. Been called that forever. We gather here when something's up. Whoever Tracy called blew an air horn. That's one of the signals to gather."

Cummins? Commons. He meant to say the commons.

"Trevor around?"

"He's at his place ov'air next to mine. Trevor's still stove up with the gunshot and all. It ain't far. Just keep following me."

Tom stuck his hand in the air and twirled his hand around. The trucks revved up and retreated into the woods. Willie Mitchell cranked his pickup.

"This is really strange," Kitty said. "I wouldn't have believed it if I hadn't seen it."

"They do seem fairly insular up here," Willie Mitchell said.

"Insular?" Walton said. He began humming "Dueling Banjos."

Willie Mitchell laughed. "Don't he have a purty mouth?" he said.

"What are you two talking about?" Kitty asked.

~ * ~

Tom drove between two abandoned log buildings and into the trees on a trail no bigger than a logging road. He glanced in his rear view mirror to make sure Willie Mitchell was following. The road wound through the old growth oaks, twisting and turning, until Tom stopped in front of the smallest of three cabins in a clearing surrounded by towering hardwoods. He hopped onto the porch and opened the door. Trevor was on his cell.

"Who you talking to?" Tom asked.

Trevor spoke into the phone. "I'll c-call you b-back." He switched it off. "N-nobody."

"Who I said?"

"L-Leonard."

"What'd he want?"

"N-N-nothing."

"He ain't part of us no more, and there's no need you talking to him. Leonard made his choice and I got nothing for him. Neither do you. I already told you don't talk to him no more and I mean it."

Trevor nodded.

"Come on outside. That D.A. from over at Sunshine wants to talk to you about the shooting."

~ * ~

Willie Mitchell stood with Walton and Kitty outside the truck in the clearing in front of the cabin. He could hear everything Tom was saying to Trevor, and he felt bad for the boy. Willie Mitchell moved some dirt with his foot and studied the cabins. All three were built entirely out of logs and rough-finished wood, with the same design: a pitched roof of hand hewn wooden shingles, wide front porch with tree trunk columns, and a substantial stone and mortar chimney on one side.

"Looks like they were built entirely out of materials from this hill," Walton said, "which makes good sense, because you couldn't get anything of any size up that grade."

"Fairly efficient," Willie Mitchell said.

"Medieval," Kitty added quietly.

Tom walked out on the porch. Trevor followed and walked down the wooden steps to shake hands. He went back on the porch and stood next to his father. Tom kept his eyes on the dirt much of the time.

"I want you to know, Trevor," Willie Mitchell said, "that nothing you say to us up here, if you do want to say anything, will be used against you in any way."

Trevor nodded. He smiled when he made eye contact with Kitty.

"I told Tom that something's come up since we saw you in the hospital on Saturday. We're not going to be able to handle this in the way I discussed with Tom on Monday."

Willie Mitchell told Trevor about ATF agent Gary Needham and the federal government's plan to charge Trevor if Willie Mitchell didn't. Willie Mitchell explained that Monday's Grand Jury would indict Trevor for possession of the stolen gun, but Trevor didn't have to appear before them to testify. He said Trevor would have to come in Monday afternoon and be arrested and processed and could go home that night.

"I t-trust you, C-Coach. I'll do what you s-say."

Tom glanced up occasionally but continued to stare at the dirt. Willie Mitchell noticed Tom wringing and rubbing his hands, even though his red rag was stuffed in his back pocket.

"I'll bring him in," Tom said.

Willie Mitchell took a deep breath. "Now, I'm going to tell the both of you something I didn't mention to Tom at the shop. I kept it to myself because I thought it might make Tom so mad he would have kept us from talking to you."

"I knew it…," Tom said, his voice rising.

"Now, hold on Tom. Hear me out."

Tom pursed his lips and jammed his hands in his back pocket. He walked off the porch into the clearing behind Willie Mitchell.

"There's two additional things you need to know about this mess that you don't know now. Neither one of them are good news for you."

"Shit," Tom said and kicked a dirt clod away.

"The first explains why the feds are so bound and determined to prosecute the weapons charge. Your gun, the Smith and Wesson that you used last Thursday in Sunshine, was used in a double murder in Oklahoma City two years ago."

Trevor rocked back on his heels on the front porch.

"He don't know nothing about that," Tom yelled. "Neither do I."

"I know you didn't have anything to do with it," Willie Mitchell said. "But I promise you the federal government's going to stay after Trevor until someone tells them how he came to be carrying that particular gun. The reason is this: the victims were an interracial couple in Oklahoma City. A black man and a white woman."

"Aw," Tom said, kicking another dirt clod, this time harder. "Here we go. Ain't it always that way? They don't care much for our kind, but they always looking out for them others." Tom spit tobacco juice in the dirt. "I say to hell with the Goddamned federal government and to hell with those two dead people in Oklahoma," he yelled. "We don't know nothin' about them, live or dead. Keep your mouth shut, son."

Tom walked toward the center of the small clearing. He turned around to Willie Mitchell, staring at the dirt and pointing at the D.A.

"You claimed there was two things," Tom said.

"Dr. Nathan Clement is a good doctor and friend of mine. He's assistant coroner. He said the twenty-two caliber bullets Mule fired, one of them just creased the top of the man's head, and the other lodged in his shoulder without doing much damage."

"Aw, Goddammit to hell," Tom said. "It was Trevor's bullet."

"That's what killed the man."

"I w-wasn't sh-shootin' at that man."

"We know that, Trevor. We've got the disk from the front of the store coming back to us from the crime lab today or tomorrow. It's going to back you up."

"The l-little m-man already shot m-me."

Walton whispered to Willie Mitchell.

"And there's people who were friends with the victim," Willie Mitchell said, "they want me to charge you with murder."

Tom screamed something Willie Mitchell couldn't make out.

"But I'm not going to do that," Willie Mitchell said loudly. "That's not going to happen."

"I think you best be going," Tom said, his voice shaking.

"This is all bad," Willie Mitchell said, "but I wanted you to hear it from me, not from somewhere else."

Trevor walked down the wooden steps and stood toe to toe with Willie Mitchell. He shook the D.A.'s hand.

"I t-trust you, C-Coach. I'll c-come in Monday."

"Over my dead body," Tom barked.

Trevor walked to Tom and whispered something.

"I'll b-be th-there," Trevor said. "What t-time?"

"Sometime in the afternoon. I'll call you with the hour."

"B-better tell me n-now," Trevor said, pulling his cell phone from his pocket and holding it for Willie Mitchell to see. "Service h-here is no g-good."

Willie Mitchell looked over at Walton.

"Three o'clock ought to work," Walton said. "I'll be through with the Grand Jury well before then."

"Three o'clock at my office. I'll walk with you down to Sheriff Lee Jones' office and stay with you the whole time. I'll talk to the judge about your bond and get that set up before you get there."

"Thanks," Trevor said.

"We'll get through this, Trevor. I'll do everything in my power to see that it turns out right for you."

Tom turned his back on Willie Mitchell. "You better," he hissed.

Chapter Fifteen

The next morning, Willie Mitchell breezed into Jimmy Gray's carport and tapped on the door in the process of making a u-turn back out to the center of the driveway. Fifteen seconds later, Jimmy walked out in bright red nylon shorts and a gray tee shirt.

"That's more like it," Willie Mitchell said.

Jimmy Gray spun around. I BEAT ANOREXIA in bright red letters spread across the back of the shirt.

"Beat the hell out of it," Willie Mitchell said. "No contest."

"Martha got it for me in Jackson."

"She knows her man."

"Damned straight. Let's walk."

Willie Mitchell started his watch.

"You think Trevor'll show Monday?" Jimmy Gray asked.

"I'd bet money on it."

"What if he doesn't?"

"We'll prepare the warrant and try to get in touch with Tom, talk some sense into him. But I'm sure Trevor will be there."

"I want you to take me up on Brewer Hill when all this is over."

"I don't think so. You're much too big a target."

"I want to get their banking business."

Willie Mitchell laughed. "You mean away from their current financial depository, empty Chef Boyardee cans buried in the backyard?"

"I like conservative investors."

A minute later, Jimmy Gray began to sweat. It was seven a.m. and eighty degrees.

"Can you stand a little inside scoop on your big murder case?" Jimmy Gray asked. "I mean Walton's big case."

"How bad is it and how reliable?"

"Absolutely reliable, and probably not bad for you."

"Then let me have it."

Jimmy wiped sweat off his brow with a red sweat band then put it around his head.

"You know the Gas & Go Fast people bank with us?"

"I knew that. What about it?"

"I talked to their operations guy late yesterday. He wanted to see about coordinating their bad check policy with the bank, make it consistent."

"They shouldn't have taken a check from Mule."

"You're right, but that's not it. After we finished talking about the hot check thing, the guy says 'you're not going to believe the phone call I got this afternoon'."

"I'm all in. What did he say?"

"Jordan Summit's paralegal called to get their main office mailing address. She told the operations man Summit is sending a letter requesting the name of their insurance company and amount of coverage on their premises liability policy. Going to be a suit for damages."

"That's no surprise. Who's he representing, the dead guy's estate?"

Jimmy Gray rolled his eyes. "This is so good," he said. "It's Mule. Summit is representing Mule, going after those Benjamins."

"You know what that means."

"What?"

"No public defender for Mule. Jordan Summit will be representing Mule in the criminal case, too."

"Is that good or bad?"

"Bad for us. Jordan Summit's a good lawyer. Really detail oriented. Nothing will get past him. He's got the financial resources to compete with any expert we might call. He'll probably associate a criminal defense attorney. He only takes criminal cases when there's a big civil case attached."

"I don't care how good he is," Jimmy Gray said. "Mule is guilty as sin. He started the whole thing."

"You been living under a rock?"

"What do you mean?"

"This case is not going to be about Mule's guilt or innocence."

"Then what's it going to be about?"

"Everything but that."

"Man-oh-man," Jimmy said. "What a fine legal system we have."

"Yep, partner. It's a beaut."

As they approached Jimmy Gray's driveway and the end of the walk, Jimmy surged ahead of Willie Mitchell. When the big man arrived first at the carport, he raised both arms high, danced and twirled on his toes like Rocky on the top step of the Philadelphia Museum of Art, humming Rocky's theme as loud as he could. He turned toward Willie Mitchell with eyes closed and began to stumble around yelling "Adrian. Adrian."

"Played by?"

"Talia Shire," Jimmy Gray said. "Francis Ford Coppola's sister. Too easy. Who played Adrian's brother Paulie, Rocky's trainer?"

"Burt Young. Apollo Creed was…?"

Jimmy frowned. "I know this. Just having a senior moment."

"Carl Weathers."

Jimmy snapped his fingers. "I'd have gotten it in regulation time. That was too quick."

Willie Mitchell took off running for home.

"You owe me two bits," he yelled over his shoulder.

~ * ~

Two hours later, Willie Mitchell and Walton were on the speaker phone talking to Robbie Cedars at the Crime Lab, trying to get him to rush the analysis of the physical evidence collected at the Gas & Go Fast, especially the disk.

"Lee will send someone to pick it up," Willie Mitchell said.

"My computer tech has been out sick," Cedars said, "but he's here today and he'll get it done."

"All right. Call me when it's ready."

Louise appeared at the door as Willie Mitchell ended the call.

"The guy who was here Monday morning with Mr. Mohammed, the little one...."

"Tweety Bird?" Walton asked.

"That's him," Louise said. "He'd like to see you. He's got Bobby Sanders with him."

Walton shook his head. "You're not going to see Bobby, are you?"

Willie Mitchell shrugged. At thirty-four, Reverend Bobby Sanders had the fastest growing black church in Sunshine. He overcame his early years as a ladies' man and a rounder in the local bars, turning his life over to God and starting a church. Lee Jones doubted Bobby's conversion. Lee said Bobby realized he could enhance his financial and personal situation by using his con artist skills in the role of a pastor. Even so, Sanders had become the most politically influential preacher in town. Reverend Sanders led the protest march on the Sunshine Courthouse that turned into a riot several years before, resulting in the death of wheelchair-bound Little Al Anderson. Sanders had publicly accused Willie Mitchell of protecting Little Al by refusing to prosecute him for the vehicular homicide of a six-year-old black girl that Little Al struck and killed with his Mercedes. Willie Mitchell blamed Bobby Sanders for the riot and resulting fire that burned Little Al to death in his bed. There was no love lost between the D.A. and Preacher Sanders.

"Send them in," Willie Mitchell said to Louise. "And you stay in here, Walton. I like to have a witness present when I talk to the Most Reverend Bobby Sanders."

Not one of the four men offered to shake hands. Abud Rahman and Bobby Sanders sat down. Rahman pushed his big glasses up on his tiny nose. Rahman was young-looking, but Willie Mitchell guessed that he was at least ten years older than Bobby. A casual observer might think they were the same age. The D.A. knew Bobby was thirty-four; Rahman probably in his mid-forties. Bobby Sanders wore his signature outfit: a tailored dark gray suit and a stark black shirt with a stiff white collar encircling his slender neck, affecting the Roman collar. Willie Mitchell was raised Catholic and could not understand why Bobby wanted to dress like a Catholic priest. After all, Bobby labeled his church "non-denominational."

"We want to talk to you about the man that killed Abdul Azeem," Bobby Sanders said. "His name is Trevor Brewer. One of the Dundee County Brewers."

"No pleasantries first?" Willie Mitchell asked. "We haven't spoken in some time, Bobby, and I thought you'd want to chat for a while before we get down to business."

"You're a busy man, Mr. D.A.," Bobby said smiling, "and I don't want to waste your precious time."

"You know my first assistant, Walton, don't you?"

"I am acquainted with Mr. Donaldson."

You should be. He almost died the night of the riot, the night your marchers torched the Anderson mansion and killed Little Al.

"You and Mr. Rahman are both here about Mr. Azeem's death?"

"The Honorable Mohammed X contacted my office about this matter. He supplied me with the relevant details of their grievance."

"I didn't think Mohammed X spoke on the phone."

"He makes exceptions," Abud said.

"Where is Mr. Samson today?" Walton asked Abud.

"Brother Samson's calling is the protection of the prophet, Mohammed X," Abud said. "Our supreme leader is a holy man with many enemies. Brother Samson never leaves his side."

"What is it you want, Reverend Sanders?" Willie Mitchell said.

"Mohammed X has asked me to help them seek justice for their dead Muslim brother, Abdul Azeem."

"Your Full Gospel Non-Denominational House of the Lord is aligned with disciples of Islam?" Willie Mitchell said. "Isn't that a conflict of religious interests? Don't they consider you an infidel?"

"In this case our interests are perfectly compatible," Bobby said. "We're both out to see that the racist policies of this office are exposed to the public. We seek justice."

Willie Mitchell was determined to keep his cool.

"Do you have any evidence to suggest that Trevor Brewer intentionally shot Abdul Azeem?" Willie Mitchell asked.

"Or that he even knew Abdul Azeem or Mule before he stopped at the Gas & Go Fast to buy a pack of cigarettes?" Walton asked, raising his voice. "He was minding his own business, and only got his gun out of his truck after he had been shot in the chest by Mule."

"He is a Brewer," Sanders said. "That family has a long and well-documented racist hatred for black people. Untold numbers of innocent African-Americans have been raped, brutalized, and lynched at the hands of the Brewers."

"Name one," Willie Mitchell said.

"One what?" the preacher said.

"Name one black man or woman lynched by the Brewers."

"Don't play games with me," Reverend Sanders said smiling. "Our last confrontation did not work out all that well for you, Mr. D.A."

Walton stood up, his face and ears red.

"You little…." Walton growled.

Abud Rahman leaned back in his chair, his eyes wide. Bobby Sanders didn't move a muscle. He continued to smile.

"Hold it, Walton," Willie Mitchell said, reaching out to take Walton by the arm. "Let's not overreact here. Mr. Rahman has lost a friend and business associate and Reverend Sanders is just being an advocate on behalf of Mohammed X."

Walton grimaced and sat back down. Willie Mitchell didn't blame Walton for losing his temper, but he was playing right into Bobby Sanders' hands.

"Isn't that right, Reverend Sanders?" Willie Mitchell asked. "We're all after the same thing here, justice for Mr. Azeem's family and friends. Let the investigation continue and the facts develop. We're scheduled to get the disk back from the crime lab late today or tomorrow, and we'll see what it shows. My information is the entire sequence of events was caught on the two cameras on the front wall of the store. Unlike most cases we prosecute, we should be able to see exactly what happened."

"If it hasn't been doctored," Bobby Sanders said. "How can we be assured of that?"

Willie Mitchell stared at the preacher. Even for Bobby Sanders, it was an outlandish suggestion. Walton kept his head down, his eyes focused on his hands clenched in his lap. Willie Mitchell noticed Walton's knuckles turning white.

He's trying to think about baseball.

"If we have time before Walton presents the case to the Grand Jury on Monday," Willie Mitchell said, "you gentlemen are welcome to come back in and view the disk with me."

"We just might do that," Reverend Sanders said. "Though it seems to me your mind is already made up just like in the Takisha Berry case, or in the killing of little six-year-old Dee Johnson. You're going to throw the book at the disabled black man and let the racist Brewer go free."

"All right," Willie Mitchell said, "I think we've accomplished about all we can this morning." He turned to Abud Rahman. "Mr. Rahman, is there anything you'd like to add?"

"We've been at Freedmen's Creek less than two years, Mr. Banks, and we've tried to be good neighbors and live peacefully." Rahman's voice was steady, quiet. "Abdul Azeem was a peaceful man, a devout Muslim believer who never hurt anyone. All we want is justice, and it does appear that the deck is stacked against us in this case. It seems these Brewers will continue to enjoy immunity in this county for the crimes they commit against black Muslims or black Christians. I will report to leader Mohammed X what I've witnessed here this morning and pray that we can maintain good relations with the small number of white citizens in your county. I must say I have my doubts if this is the kind of justice system we must live under."

Willie Mitchell stood and extended his hand to Rahman who hesitated, then shook it. Bobby Sanders walked toward the door followed by Rahman.

"Let me know if you'd like to see the video," Willie Mitchell said.

The preacher stopped and turned back to the D.A.

"I want to be up front with you, Mr. Banks. I don't want you to hear this on the street. Regardless of the outcome of this matter, I am supporting a candidate against you next year. Twenty-four years of your plantation-owner attitude is enough. It's time the black citizens of Yaloquena County have fair representation in this office, and I intend to do everything in my power to replace you. I already have a commitment from a well-qualified black attorney to run for District Attorney next year."

Willie Mitchell took a deep breath. He didn't quite understand it, but at that moment, his long-standing animosity toward Bobby Sanders began to dissipate. Willie Mitchell felt no anger, only resignation. Bobby's pointed threats seemed to take on an abstract quality, as if Willie Mitchell were a bystander instead of the target of the preacher's wrath. His destiny appeared to unfold before his very eyes, playing out at a distance. Willie Mitchell knew at that moment nothing he could do would change the coming events. The die was cast. He felt very odd.

This is not me. I hope I'm not about to have a seizure.

"Our constitution certainly gives you that right," Willie Mitchell said as they turned to leave. "That's why we have elections. It's been a pleasure as usual, Bobby. I'll be in touch when we get the disk."

Walton closed the door behind them.

"What an asshole," Walton said. "I do not see how you kept your cool talking to that bastard."

"I don't either," Willie Mitchell said. "A couple of years ago I'd have thrown him out of my office."

Willie Mitchell walked to his window and looked across the street at the firemen playing basketball behind the fire station two stories below.

"Maybe he's doing me a favor," Willie Mitchell said.

Chapter Sixteen

That same night in the DOGs barracks in D.C.'s Rock Creek Park Jake sat with Hound and Bull on the raggedy furniture in the big room upstairs waiting for a follow-up meeting on the proposed mission. The previous Saturday Big Dog laid out the general parameters of Operation Camelot, a DOGs operation in London. An international mission would be a significant departure from the unwritten charter of the *Domestic Operations Group*. Big Dog asked the men to give the idea a few days to sink in. He scheduled tonight's meeting to provide more details.

"I probably shouldn't get a vote," Jake said. "I'm pretty new."

"I don't think it matters," Hound said. "Everyone's going to go along with whatever Big Dog and Dunne recommend."

"I'm not a big picture man myself," Bull said. "I like the action."

"Seems to me a foreign venue ramps up the danger and potential for discovery," Jake said. "Not to mention the likelihood of failure."

"You don't think Bull can pull off a British accent?" Hound said.

"Aw," Bull said, "listen to Fidel's bull shit. Like he's a man of the world. He ain't ever lived more than a few hundred miles from the equator."

Jake laughed. Hound and Bull enjoyed jacking each other around. They were at ease in each other's company, like childhood pals. Though their friendship dated only to 2001, Jake knew it was forged in battle and unbreakable.

Doberman and Dunne walked in. Doberman sat on the couch with Hound and Bull. Dunne leaned against the wall.

"So, what's the verdict?" Hound asked Dunne.

"I don't know. Big Dog and I met with Dunwoody and the Brit on Sunday and Monday at Bellingham. The Brit wants us in London bad. We covered a lot of details, but I'm still not sold. Foreign soil operations require support in country, and we don't have anything like that set up. We might be too small to gear up for it, no matter how significant the opportunity. I think it's high risk. Big Dog believes the risk is manageable. He says the Brit can provide the infrastructure."

"What's the guy like, the Brit?" Jake asked.

"Very impressive, very rich, very personable. He's a real patriot and makes a good case for our involvement."

"Why don't our agencies get involved with MI6 or MI5?" Hound asked. "The Brits have all kinds of anti-terrorist capacity."

"Leaks," Doberman said.

"This would be MI5," Dunne said, "and Doberman is right. The Brit thinks all their domestic intel operations are compromised."

"Are they?" Bull asked.

"I don't know," Dunne said. "Big Dog says our own government can't keep a secret. Look at the Wikileaks crap. How could they give the Manning guy such a broad security clearance? A private, for God's sake. What were they thinking?"

"And you have to wonder," Hound said, "how many other Mannings there are out there?"

"And it's worse in Great Britain," Jake said. "England's got a long history of moles in top management in their spy agencies. Kim Philby and the other Cambridge Five, George Blake...."

"But we're no better," Dunne said. "Look at Robert Hanssen and Aldrich Ames."

"That's the good thing about us DOGs," Bull said. "After all these years, and all the time we've spent together, Anita and I still don't know that Hound's real name is Carlos Tomas and his fiancé is Teresa and his parents moved to Miami from El Salvador."

Hound leaned back from Bull. "How did you know that?"

Dunne looked over at Jake and winked, then laughed along with everyone. Big Dog stressed to Jake when he came on board that DOGs knew each other only by their code names, that personal information was off limits. Jake figured out early on that it made sense to use only code names in all forms of communications, but it was not reasonable to expect that Dunne, Doberman, Hound and Bull could spend so much time together in remote locations planning and waiting to implement operations and not know every intimate detail of each other's lives.

"Don't spill the beans with Big Dog," Dunne told Bull.

"I won't if you tell me whether Big Dog and Helen Holmes are still an item," Bull said.

"Since you're feeling your oats, Bull, why don't you ask Big Dog about Helen when he gets here? See what happens."

"Wouldn't do that," Doberman said.

"Why?"

"Big Dog doesn't want his uh..., friendship with Helen discussed," Dunne said. "He's our C.O., Bull, and he does not like to be teased."

"As we speak, the devil," Doberman said when Big Dog walked through the door bent over at the waist, holding his back.

"I hate those stairs," Big Dog said. "So I was the topic of discussion?"

"The men were just saying how much they enjoyed being under your command," Dunne said. "They took turns telling stories about the great times we've all spent together."

Big Dog smiled. "Yeah, right. Let's get down to business. We've got a lot to cover before my back gives out totally. I have more details about the proposed Operation Camelot that will help each of you make your decision. Before we get to that, I've got some scuttlebutt I'm hearing from The Earl about our legal status."

Big Dog had everyone's attention. In the short time Jake had spent in the organization, this was something they didn't talk about, though Jake knew it was foremost in each DOG's mind. From 2001 through the end of 2008, DOGs operated covertly, but with the imprimatur of legality from the agencies that set up DOGs in the week following 9/11. The agencies' official positions were to deny DOGs' existence if ever asked. They assured Big Dog and Dunne privately that the U.S. Government had their backs and would protect them as needed.

After the agreement Dunwoody hammered out with the new administration in early 2009 exchanging a DOGs shutdown for immunity from prosecution, every DOGs operation undertaken by Big Dog's downsized force had been illegal. If prosecuted, each DOG faced life imprisonment, or in some states, the death penalty.

Each DOG believed in the righteousness of every mission. However, the slightest hint of the possibility of becoming legitimate again was priceless; sweet music to each ear in the room.

"Dunwoody says there are some adults in the founding agencies who support returning us to legal status. The possibility of the current administration serving one term seems to be growing and if that happens, The Earl says he thinks it's very doable for us to come under the umbrella of legitimacy the agencies provided us for the seven years through December of 2008."

"Thank you, Jesus," Bull yelled, pumping his fist.

The others clapped and whistled. Jake laughed along, feeling for the first time the DOGs' intense desire to come in from the cold.

"Hold on, now," Big Dog said. "This is still just a possibility. Even if the voters turn the current set of politicians out, there's still many a hurdle for us to overcome to regain our pre-2009 status." Big Dog was very stern. "So, don't count on it, but I wanted to keep you informed. I'm not promising anything."

They all clapped and laughed again. David Dunne gestured for his men to be quiet.

"All right," Big Dog said. "On to Operation Camelot."

~ * ~

That night in his small apartment downtown near DOJ's main office and not far from his brother Scott's condo, Jake listened while Kitty brought him up to date on the Gas & Go Fast shooting. Jake delighted in hearing the excitement in her voice. She was clearly enjoying the investigation, working in the trenches. Her description of the visit to the mesa on top of Brewer Hill was hilarious.

"I guess they don't have folks like that in Tacoma," he said.

"They probably do, but I've never been around them. Did Dunne say when you're going to be able to come home?"

"They still haven't made a decision about this thing they're considering." Jake had been careful not to share any details of Camelot. "The meeting tonight was just more information."

"When will they decide?"

"Don't know. They're not sure themselves, but they said we have to stick around. I'm lowest on the totem pole, so I'll be the last to know"

"Your Daddy wants you to call him."

"I will tomorrow." He paused a moment. "I'm getting sleepy."

"What are you doing?"

"In bed, watching some crummy college game. I miss you."

"I think about you all the time."

"Except when you're working the homicide investigation."

"Even then. I love you, Jakey."

"I love you, baby. Where are you?"

"At the duck camp, thinking about the last time we were here together. How wonderful it was."

"Wish I were there instead of this apartment."

"Want to know what I'm doing?" she asked.

Not waiting for an answer, Kitty told him, taking her time.

"You're alone I hope."

She laughed. "You know I am."

Kitty continued talking, her voice lower, suggesting this, and that.

Jake answered, quietly and in great detail.

Fifteen minutes later, the phone call ended. They both fell asleep quickly, as satisfied as they could be with their long-distance intimacy, each eager for the touch of the other.

Chapter Seventeen

The next morning, Willie Mitchell, Walton, Sheriff Jones and Kitty sat in Willie Mitchell's darkened office, watching the Gas & Go Fast video disk for the fifth time. No matter how many times they replayed the critical part, the actions of Mule and Trevor were subject to interpretation.

"It looks to me there's no question Mule turned the gun on Trevor," Walton said flipping on the light switch.

"I can't believe we don't have a better angle on the disk," Lee Jones said. "I can't say beyond a reasonable doubt that the disk shows Mule's gun pointed right at Trevor."

"I'm with the Sheriff," Kitty said. "There's movement on Mule's part toward Trevor, and Mule's face certainly turns to look at Trevor. I just don't think the gun makes it around before Trevor takes his shots."

"So Trevor should have waited until he was certain Mule had him dead to rights before Trevor fired?" Walton said. "That's asking a lot for someone in Trevor's position. Mule had already shot Trevor once."

"Right," Kitty said, "but the clerk said Trevor didn't know he had been shot until he came in the store after he fired his gun twice."

Willie Mitchell's lips rested on the tips of his fingers, his hands together as if praying. He sat up straight.

"I agree with Walton's point," he said, "but Lee and Kitty are correct that from the camera angles we have to work with, it's hard to say exactly where Mule's gun is aiming when Trevor shoots."

"The critical facts are these," Walton said, "and they're backed up by the video. Azeem turned the gas nozzle on Mule. Mule pulled his twenty-two from the grocery cart and shot Azeem, grazing his head with one bullet and plugging him in the shoulder with the other. Everyone agree with me on that?"

Each person nodded.

"The disk also shows Mule shooting twice in Trevor's direction as he moved toward his truck," Walton said. "Now we know one of those bullets hit Trevor in the left chest."

"Though he didn't know it at the time," Lee said.

"Then we see Mule point the pistol at Azeem again, this time when Azeem is leaning against the gas pump" Walton said. "But before Mule can shoot, he turns suddenly toward Trevor, moving the pistol toward Trevor. Can we at least agree on that?"

Lee Jones and Kitty said yes. Willie Mitchell nodded.

"Even though there's no audio and we can't see Trevor's face," Walton said, "Mule's reaction corroborates what the clerk told us about Trevor yelling at Mule. Isn't that the most reasonable interpretation?"

"It is," Willie Mitchell said. "No question. Trevor acted in self-defense."

"But if Trevor hadn't shot at Mule," Kitty said, "Azeem would be alive and Mule wouldn't be paralyzed."

"Trevor's yelling at Mule saved Azeem," Walton said. "Mule was about to shoot Azeem leaning against the gas pump."

"But then Trevor squeezed off the kill shot," Willie Mitchell said. "And we can't hear or see Trevor yell at Mule. But the clerk's statement is clear on that point."

Lee Jones shook his head. "What a mess."

"Walton's going to show this video disk to the Grand Jury Monday," Willie Mitchell said, "and ask them to indict Mule for felony murder. We're going to ask the Grand Jury to indict Trevor for possession of the stolen firearm." He looked at Kitty and Sheriff Jones. "Do either of you disagree with my decision? If either of you think we ought to ask the Grand Jury to consider any grade of homicide for Trevor, tell me now."

"I don't," Lee said.

"Neither do I," Kitty said. "My only point is the video is not as clear cut as I thought it would be."

"Same here," Lee said. "Have you called Bobby Sanders yet?"

"I wanted to wait until we all had plenty of time to review the tape," Willie Mitchell said. "I'm going to call him as soon as y'all clear out."

"See you early Monday morning," Lee said. "You or Walton need me for anything this weekend, call my cell."

Kitty and Sheriff Jones left.

"You want me to hang around until you call the preacher?" Walton asked. "I will if you need me."

"No. I'll issue the invitation and let you know what time. I'd like you to be here when and if Bobby comes to watch it."

"After all the crap he dished in here yesterday," Walton said, "he's going to want to watch it for sure, probably with Tweety Bird."

"Don't count on it," Willie Mitchell said.

~ * ~

Willie Mitchell closed his door and called Bobby Sanders' church. A young, professional-sounding black woman answered.

"Full Gospel Non-Denominational House of the Lord," she said. "How may I help you?"

"This is Willie Mitchell Banks," he said. "I met with Reverend Sanders yesterday in my office in the courthouse and told him I would call him when a disk of the shooting was ready for him to view."

"He's not here," the woman said.

"Do you know when he will be back?"

"I don't know that, Mr. Banks."

"I can call him on his cell. Can you give me that number?"

"I'm sorry. We're not allowed to give out that information."

"Then would you call him yourself and tell him?"

"Reverend Sanders doesn't like to be disturbed when he's ministering outside the office. He sometimes calls in for his messages. I'll let him know then."

"Miss, this is pretty important. He might want to see this today. Please make sure he gets the word. I'll be in my office until five this afternoon."

"I'll tell Reverend Sanders you called, Mr. Banks."

"Let me give you my office number," he said.

The young woman paused for several seconds.

"All right."

Willie Mitchell gave her the number and hung up.

"That went well," he said quietly and looked up. Louise was standing in the door.

"Problem?" she asked.

"Nah. I left word with Bobby Sanders' secretary for him to call. If he calls today and I'm on the phone or out, tell him we've got the disk and he's welcome to come watch it this afternoon."

"Was she rude to you?"

"She wasn't very helpful. Like pulling teeth to get anything."

"I'm not surprised. We don't have many fans over there."

"You need me?"

"Eleanor Bernstein and Jordan Summit, the t.v. lawyer with ads featuring the big Benjamins, are here to see you."

"Did he give you a few?"

Louise laughed.

"Send them in, please ma'am."

Eleanor Bernstein led her co-counsel into Willie Mitchell's office. Willie Mitchell was surprised at how short he was. The television ads made him seem much bigger. His hair was dense and dyed jet black, so dark it reflected no light. Eleanor was well-dressed as usual, in a gray business suit, white blouse with a ruffled front, and a black scarf.

"Welcome to Sunshine, Mr. Summit," Willie Mitchell said.

"Please call me Jordan. Thank you Willie Mitchell. This is my first criminal case in your jurisdiction, first time in your office."

"Well, you've associated an excellent lawyer to guide you over the rough spots. Eleanor has spent a lot of time in that chair right there, and in the courtroom down the hall. How long is it you've been public defender, Eleanor?"

"Six years now," Eleanor said.

"Eleanor's been on the defense side in most of our jury trials during that time, and we've probably plead out how many others?"

"Thousands," Eleanor said.

"So, you're here about Mule?"

"Right," Jordan said, placing a document on the desk in front of Willie Mitchell. "Here is a copy of our Motion to Enroll as Counsel of Record in State versus Lester Gardner. Eleanor is co-counsel and retained, so she's not acting in her capacity of public defender."

"She's getting some Benjamins," Willie Mitchell said.

Jordan laughed and Eleanor chuckled. Eleanor was so much prettier when she smiled, Willie Mitchell thought. She always appeared so stern and unsmiling in court and his office. He didn't blame her. With her case load and the type of defendants she represented, Eleanor had very little to smile about.

"It's nice to be retained for a change," she said, "instead of appointed."

"I'm looking forward to working with both of you," Willie Mitchell said. "I know Eleanor's capabilities, and your reputation precedes you."

"As does yours, Willie Mitchell. Eleanor says you never lose."

"That's nice of you to say, Eleanor, but I've lost plenty of cases. In my experience, the only lawyers who have never lost a case are lawyers who haven't tried many."

"Amen to that," Jordan said.

"My first assistant Walton Donaldson is presenting the case to the Grand Jury Monday, as I'm sure you're aware."

"Right," Jordan said. "Eleanor may be in and out up here Monday, and she will definitely be in court when the Grand Jury returns its findings, but I'll be in Jackson. We don't have any witnesses we want to present. I assume you're not going to call our client."

"Certainly not. We'll put on the Sheriff, who led the investigation, and the Coroner, if he's not on location filming a re-make of Citizen Kane Comes to Yaloquena."

Eleanor actually laughed out loud and slapped her knee. Willie Mitchell was proud of himself. He'd never see her guffaw.

"That must be an inside joke," Jordan said.

"Eleanor will explain it to you. We're also going to play a copy of the video disk from the store's security cameras. It pretty much shows the whole thing, from Mule's first encounter with Azeem to the shooting."

"We'd like to see that this afternoon if we could," Jordan said.

"No problem," Willie Mitchell said. "There's a computer you can watch it on in our conference room. The original digital format has been preserved if you want to have an expert look at them. You can watch my copy as many times as you want. I'll make myself a note to call Robbie Cedars Monday at the crime lab to make you a copy."

"That would be great," Jordan said. "I can pick it up next week in Jackson. I doubt we'll have an expert examine it. It is what it is."

"Anything else?" Willie Mitchell asked.

"Just something for you to consider," Jordan said. "We don't plan on doing a lot of discovery or filing any pre-trial motions of any significance. Eleanor tells me you don't like to drag things out, that you like to move cases to trial quickly."

"That's always been the way I've prosecuted," Willie Mitchell said. "In my experience, the testimony of witnesses and the presentation of evidence has never been helped by the passage of time."

"I agree," Jordan said. "Delay always helps the defense, except in this particular case."

Willie Mitchell declined to bite. He figured Jordan was anxious to conclude the criminal case so he could get on with his civil suit against Gas & Go Fast and the company's insurer. No reason to bring that up.

"Before I forget," Willie Mitchell said, "you're welcome to spend all the time you want watching the disk today. Only caveat is that I got word to Reverend Bobby Sanders he could watch it today if he wanted."

Jordan and Eleanor nodded. They didn't seem surprised.

"He's been up here twice to talk to me about it. He's somehow involved with the Freedmen's Creek Muslim community that Mr. Azeem was apparently affiliated with. I don't know the exact relationship."

Eleanor cast her eyes down. Willie Mitchell knew Bobby and Eleanor were tight; they had worked together on things in the past, including the defense of McKinley Owens whom Willie Mitchell prosecuted for the arson murder of Little Al Anderson.

Willie Mitchell had a feeling. He decided to push further.

"Reverend Sanders doesn't think too much of me, Jordan. He and I have had our differences. Eleanor can tell you. You two should know when he was in here yesterday with a representative of the Freedmen's Creek encampment he railed against me for not prosecuting Trevor Brewer for murder."

"Trevor Brewer's involvement is certainly something we believe your office should pursue, Willie Mitchell," Jordan said in a pleasant way. "We believe without his intervention no one would have been seriously hurt as a result of the confrontation at the store."

"I understand your position," Willie Mitchell said. "I don't agree with it, but I fully expect you to argue that at the trial. That's why we have juries, to sort these things out." He paused. *Might as well get this out there.* "Bobby's taking his animosity toward me and the way I run this office to another level. He told me yesterday he's already recruited a well-qualified black attorney to qualify against me next year."

Eleanor looked at her hands folded in her lap, then toward the door. She was ready to leave.

At that moment, Willie Mitchell knew it was Eleanor.

Chapter Eighteen

Friday afternoon Eleanor Bernstein and Jordan Summit watched the shootout at the Gas & Go Fast on the disk in Willie Mitchell's conference room. At the same time twenty miles away, in the woods in the northeast corner of Yaloquena County, Abud Rahman *nee* Andre Nelson pushed his oversized prescription glasses above the bridge of his nose. He walked with Reverend Bobby Sanders from the Freedmen's Creek community center to the outdoor amphitheater he had been describing to Bobby in glowing terms. When they arrived at the edge of the grassy bluff and Bobby was finally able to look down on the facility at the edge of the creek, he was sorely disappointed.

There were six levels descending to the small wooden riser resting on the high bank overlooking Freedmen's Creek. Bobby estimated the total drop from where he stood down to the riser to be about twenty-five feet. After a dry September with no rain anywhere in its watershed, the creek was a trickle of clear water no more than four feet across, moving slowly over a bed of sand and gravel.

The six tiers had been excavated and flattened somewhat, with a drop of four feet between levels. The seating was rudimentary, consisting only of two-by-eight pine boards resting on the dirt. There were uneven wooden stairs from the top level down to the riser next to the creek. Bobby noticed erosion under some of the boards and wondered how anyone could sit comfortably on them for any length of time. So far, Freedmen's Creek was strictly rinky-dink to Reverend Sanders, not nearly as impressive as his own Full Gospel sanctuary.

"Very nice," Bobby said to Abud. "What sort of worship do you have here?"

"Prophet Mohammed teaches and lectures here. Worship takes place only in our mosque." He pointed to the metal building east of them with a makeshift wooden minaret attached. The mosque building looked second-hand to Bobby. "All of these facilities are temporary. When our funding reaches the appropriate level we will build a beautiful stone mosque with a lofty minaret for a real *muezzin* to call us to prayer. Right now, we have recordings playing over small speakers throughout the compound."

"It's the prayer that's important," Bobby said.

"That is what our leader says. We must crawl before we walk."

They had been touring the facility for an hour. So far the front entrance and the fence surrounding the encampment were the most impressive things Bobby had seen. When he first arrived, Reverend Sanders was stopped in his black Escalade at the metal and brick front gate by a tough-looking guard in camouflage gear, a black beret and black boots. He held a military-type rifle at an angle across his chest.

Bobby estimated the mechanical steel gate to be at least ten feet tall. Inside the gate, he noticed a large flag raised on a stainless steel flagpole. A slight breeze gently moved the flag. It was green, black, and red with a black crescent moon in the center. The metal fence extending out on each side the gate was the same height, topped with concertina wire.

Bobby tried to appear nonchalant waiting as the guard said something into a cheap-looking Walkie-Talkie. The guard closed his phone and directed Reverend Sanders to the asphalt parking area near the gate, where two large silver buses with extremely dark tinted glass were parked. Abud arrived at Bobby's Escalade in less than a minute to escort Bobby on a walking tour in advance of his meeting with Mohammed X.

Bobby Sanders knew the history of the original Freedmen's Creek settlement in the remote northeast part of Yaloquena County. It was founded by slaves freed by Lincoln during the Civil War and thrived until the end of the nineteenth century when its founding father, William Almonds, died without a succession plan in place. Blood was spilled in the course of rival factions fighting for control. The lack of cohesion and leadership coupled with financial need of the residents caused a steady exodus to cities up north. By 1905, the village lay abandoned and empty. When they stood on the grass above the amphitheater, Abud pointed out to Bobby the remains of the original village buildings on the other side of the creek.

Abud said the encampment covered twenty acres, but Bobby estimated it closer to thirty. There were at least ten acres devoted to crops and cattle near the parking area inside the entrance. Abud led Bobby through the community center building with its adjacent kitchen and cafeteria, the largest metal structures on the campus. On the walk-through they passed at least fifteen young girls at one end of the community center building being taught by three black women in traditional Muslim attire.

Abud pointed out to Bobby the dozen or so small residential trailers inside the concertina enclosure not far from the gated entrance.

"Those are FEMA trailers," Abud said. "The government let us buy them for $1250 each. FEMA paid nine or ten thousand per trailer right after Katrina. They're not all that pretty, but they're solid, and cheap."

Bobby Sanders envied their deal on the FEMA trailers. He was irritated with himself for neglecting to get some for his people. He knew Yaloquena County was in the GO Zone after Katrina and residents were eligible for all sorts of grants, even though the hurricane produced only a small amount of rain and no more than twenty-mile-an-hour winds. It did no damage in Yaloquena, but many in his congregation lined up for the

$1500 grants Red Cross gave out and the larger grants FEMA funded a month later. Bobby spread the word about the free money and encouraged his flock to show up for the checks.

He knew Full Gospel's status as a not-for-profit inside the GO Zone would have qualified the Church for a grant to purchase FEMA trailers. Bobby estimated he could have picked up at least twenty or thirty at no cost to his people. He thought about applying when they were available, but failed to follow through. Abud interrupted Bobby's internal lament over the lost opportunity.

"Let's look at the gym," Abud said, "then we'll walk through the mosque to the prophet's residence, where he receives visitors."

Bobby followed Abud into the gym, a small, metal building with rusted gutters and downspouts. The concrete floor inside was covered with faded green artificial turf. The only athletic equipment consisted of free weights and benches, and an area covered with mats. Two of the half-dozen young men lifting weights were flanked by a huge black man bench pressing what Bobby thought had to be well over three hundred pounds. The giant did not need the spotters' help. He grunted and cleared the press easily, then stood up and directed one of the young men to take the bench. Bobby estimated the young men to range from seventeen to the early twenties, and noticed how serious they appeared, concentrating on building strength.

Two of the young men left the weights area, faced off on the mats and began circling each other. When they began fighting, Bobby could see they weren't wrestling or boxing. It looked to him more like the mixed martial arts he saw occasionally on cable. When Abud led him outside the gym, Bobby took a deep breath of the country air.

"Who is that giant in there?"

"Samson al Kadeesh. He is the prophet's principal protector and instructs our young men on strength conditioning and weight training...."

Bobby hit the dirt when he heard loud, rapid gunfire. From his days running the roads, he knew a gunshot when he heard one, and recognized these to be from three, maybe four semi-automatic rifles.

Abud started laughing and helped Bobby to his feet.

"You're in no danger," Abud said. "That's the firing range through those woods," Abud said pointing. "We have several weapons instructors with military experience. The instructors supervise the young men who are practicing, making sure all guns are fired in a direction away from the encampment. As you can see, the prophet wants all our young men to be proficient with weapons, and with self-defense techniques."

"Why is that?"

"We hunt deer and wild hogs to help feed the community," Abud said. "We also provide our own defense. There are many enemies of Allah in this state, and we doubt that your Sheriff can provide us the security we believe we need in this remote location."

"I believe you are right about that," Bobby said. "What kind of rifle did the guard have at the gate?"

"The AK-47, the best gun ever invented, or so I am told. All of our weapons here, including the ones you just heard, are AK-47s."

"How do you pay for all this?" Bobby asked.

"You should direct all such questions to the leader."

"Well, let's make our way to the prophet's residence."

"This way. We'll walk through our place of worship."

They walked through the mosque, another large metal building. It was the only building in the encampment that looked new to Bobby. The mosque was bare inside except for the fifty-or-so prayer rugs Bobby noticed rolled up and scattered around the room on the bare concrete floor.

"The women worship back there," Abud said, pointing to one corner of the building enclosed by blue lattice work.

Abud and Bobby exited the mosque and walked into the building Abud said was Mohammed X's office and residence. Bobby glanced at the satellite dish securely anchored in a concrete slab near the front door as they walked inside.

~ * ~

"*Assalamu alaikum,*" Mohammed X said to Bobby.

"And the same to you, Mohammed X," Bobby said.

The prophet sat on a large pillow behind a wooden table no more than three inches off the floor. He extended his arm to Bobby, gesturing for him to join Abud on the pillows on the other side of the table.

"Tea?" he asked Bobby.

"No, thank you."

Mohammed X wore a full-length black robe and a black turban covering his slicked-down hair. His eyes sparkled behind rimless glasses; a constant smile creased his milk-chocolate skin.

"You must excuse my ignorance of your customs and religious ways," Bobby said. "Yours is the first Muslim congregation I've ever visited."

"Others may not be like us," Mohammed X said laughing. "We have some special requirements because of our peculiar situation."

"You mean like being in hostile territory," Bobby said. "I feel like that myself sometimes and I been living in this county all my life."

Mohammed laughed. So did Bobby. Even Abud chuckled. Mohammed was pleased to see Reverend Sanders loosen up. He seemed ill at ease when he entered. Mohammed needed Bobby's assistance in avenging Azeem's death, and wanted Bobby to leave today feeling like he made a friend.

"I am very impressed with your grounds and buildings," Bobby said. "One day when it's convenient I'd like to bring out some of my flock to see what you've created here, or maybe just the elders and deacons."

"I would love to accommodate your parishioners," Mohammed said, "but I am afraid it's not possible. We strive to stay under the radar out here. Most people in the area already consider us a very strange phenomenon, and we cannot turn this holy ground dedicated to Allah into a tourist attraction."

"Oh, I certainly understand. No problem. Seeing all this has caused me to aspire to building an encampment like this for my followers at Full Gospel. Do you mind if I ask how you raised the money?"

"Not at all," Mohammed said with a big smile, "but I am afraid that also falls under the umbrella of confidentiality. Let me just say that followers of Allah all over the world contribute to our cause. Our detractors spread lies about sinister financial sources behind us, but I can assure you it's principally Muslims from all walks of life who want to help us spread the word."

"Like missionaries," Bobby said.

"Exactly," Mohammed said. Abud nodded in satisfaction. "Abud tells me your second meeting with the District Attorney about Azeem's murder met with the same obstructionist attitude we saw this past Monday in the court house. Mr. Banks seems determined to protect the actual killer."

"He's a difficult man," Bobby said. "With his own agenda."

"This Brewer family everyone seems to know," Mohammed said, "are they members of the Ku Klux Klan?"

"I don't know," Bobby said. "I'm sure they were in the past. Don't get me wrong. The Klan is still around, I'm certain of that. It's just that these days the Klan is totally underground."

"Is it possible the District Attorney has links to the Klan?"

"I don't think so," Bobby said, "I think he's racist on his own. He doesn't need anyone's help to abuse the delivery of justice to our people."

Mohammed continued to smile broadly.

"What is your plan to help us achieve justice, Reverend Sanders?"

"I've got a short-term plan, and a long-term plan."

"Let's hear them."

Bobby began a monologue about his past exploits mobilizing public opinion against the District Attorney, describing marches, pickets, and spreading the word among the black preachers in town. Mohammed closed his eyes, lowered his head and listened, smiling all the while.

"And your long-term plan?"

"I've gotten a commitment from a black attorney to run against Willie Mitchell next year. I'm certain we can turn him out of office using the power of the vote. Our people make up 78% of the registered voters in this county."

"Is this the woman attorney we've heard about this week?"

"Yes. Is that a problem?"

"In our faith and teachings, we don't believe it's a woman's place to do a man's work in the justice system." He paused and grinned. "But as they say, when in Rome...."

Bobby cackled, and Mohammed was pleased to see the preacher so easily amused.

"I believe we can help you financially with this electoral matter," Mohammed said, "but you must keep our participation absolutely secret."

"That's easy to do. I've worked openly or behind the scenes in many political campaigns. Your contributions will have to be cash."

"Of course. Reverend Sanders, I'd like to speak frankly. Do you feel in this case it might be necessary to use more than pickets and peaceful marches and protests to bring about the goals you describe as short-term?"

"I'm not sure what you mean," Bobby said.

"My experience is that sometimes when faced with an intractable, racist authority, protesting is not enough. Sometimes there's a need for confrontation. Sometimes the use of force. Significant force."

Mohammed saw confusion in Bobby, then fear. He decided to tone it down, let the preacher think about that a while.

"I'm not sure what you mean," Bobby said.

"You're much too young to remember the water cannons and dogs used against our people not far from here."

"I've seen it on television," Bobby said.

"No matter. I just bring this up for discussion. I certainly have no plans to resort to violence, but I believe in being prepared. Abud has shown you this morning a sample of our training regimen and our ability to defend ourselves from attacks by outsiders."

"Yes, sir."

"You must keep all this secret as well. I wanted you to see our facility so that you understand we are more than capable of avenging the death of brother Azeem if the authorities fail us, and of course, obtaining justice for Mr. Gardner."

"I see that. Yes, sir," Bobby said. "I see that."

"Good," Mohammed X said, gesturing for Abud and Bobby to leave. "Let's hope it doesn't become necessary."

Chapter Nineteen

It was nine-thirty and warm Sunday morning. The biker rode east on U.S. 82 in the Arkansas Delta between Montrose and Lake Chicot, one of the scores of oxbow lakes in Arkansas and Mississippi created eons ago when the river changed course. He veered right on 82 when the highway divided, heading toward the newly-opened Mississippi River Bridge at Greenville. Like the deltas in Mississippi, Louisiana, and Tennessee, the Arkansas countryside he passed was flat and desolate after the corn and soybeans were cut and cotton picked.

It was too early to row up the fields for the winter. The farmland was ragged, with volunteer corn stalks here and there, or stiff brown cotton plants, denuded except for tiny pieces of stringy white fiber clinging to empty and broken bolls. On both sides of the highway, the land seemed devoid of prosperity or promise. It was exactly the way the biker remembered it.

The Arkansas state highway hugged the oxbow on an arc to the bridge. The fifteen mile stretch from the fork to the river was dotted with churches, some brick with asphalt parking lots, some white frame buildings built out into cotton fields with parking areas of grass, the churches badly in need of paint. Though he was in no hurry now that he was close to the end of his trip, he was fed up with all the church people poking along on 82.

He slowed to twenty-five behind an old white couple in a fifteen-year-old Buick. Other churchgoers filled the oncoming lane, one after another, so the biker decided to take the Buick on the right. He gunned the motor on his 1994 Harley Blockhead and zipped along the passenger side. The old lady's window was down. He decided to have some fun.

When he was even with her door, he slowed to keep pace with the Buick. The woman's eyes popped wide open when she saw how close the biker was. He winked and flicked his tongue at the lady. Still staring at the biker, she reached over to paw at her husband. When the old man turned to look, the biker flicked his tongue at him, too.

Their mouths gaped at the same time. The biker threw his head back and laughed, gunned his Harley and took off. In thirty seconds he was around the curve and out of sight, the wind slapping his long gray ponytail against his sleeveless black leather vest.

He slowed down to the speed limit, chuckling at raising the old couple's blood pressure. As he drew near the Cow Pen on the right before the bridge, he recalled from the old days two memorable fights in the parking lot. The biker pulled off the highway into the Cow Pen lot and stopped. He reached behind him and released one side of the bungee cord tie down, removing his Nazi-style helmet. It met every state standard of safety, he made sure of that. Arkansas was a rider's choice state over the age of twenty. In Mississippi helmets were mandatory for motorcyclists of any age. The helmet was one of the first things a state trooper checked in a compliance state, and the biker did not want to give the law an excuse to hassle him. They made up plenty on their own.

He watched a muddy pickup enter the parking lot and drive to the restaurant entrance. The truck driver leaned over and kissed his passenger. She opened the door and stepped out. As he drove out of the parking lot, the driver eyed the biker.

Perched on his idling bike, he watched the woman stand at the door and light a cigarette. She had long red hair and a pretty face. Slightly plump, her tight-fitting uniform emphasized her significant curves. The biker put-putted the Harley toward her and stopped, resting the helmet under his forearm on top of his left thigh.

"Morning," he said to the woman.

She sucked on her cigarette and blew smoke into the air.

"You work here?"

She nodded.

"What time do they open?"

"Should be open now. Start serving at eleven."

"You're mighty conscientious, getting here before everyone else. You must be trying to please the boss."

She took a long drag.

"My husband had to drop me off early 'cause he had some bush-hogging to do."

"I like bush hogging," the biker said with a big grin. "What about you, pretty lady? I could show you thing or two about bush hogging, have you back before your boss gets here I bet."

She blew a stream of smoke his way and shook the cigarette between her index and middle finger at the biker.

"I think you better head on out of here, mister. The boss's brother is Chief Deputy Sheriff in this county. So far, I ain't got a reason to tell him about you. But you're getting' close to giving me one."

The biker laughed and strapped on his Nazi helmet.

"No cause for that," he said, putting his Harley in gear. "See you around, sweet thing."

He roared out of the parking lot onto the road leading to the bridge. He gunned the Harley and in seconds, he was over the speed limit. The biker throttled back and took his time, admiring the Mississippi River below him.

He passed the sign in the middle of the bridge that read "Entering Mississippi, The Hospitality State," and took a deep breath. It had been over two years, but Freddy Brewer was back home. He had serious business to tend to.

~ * ~

Freddy was fifty-three, a couple of years older than his half-brother Tom. They shared the same father, but that was about it. At 6'2" and 220 pounds, Freddy was much bigger. While Tom kept his hair in a burr like Trevor, Freddy's gray hair hung down to the middle of his back, usually in a ponytail, plaited if he had a woman around. Freddy looked every man or woman he encountered straight in the eye, invading their space when he talked to them. Tom was reticent, retiring; angry. Freddy was loud and charismatic, ever-grinning, a born leader. Tom spent his entire life on Brewer Hill, in Parchman Penitentiary, and in his repair shop. Freddy was a nomad, having ridden his Harley through every state in the union, most of Canada and parts of northern Mexico.

Every day Tom wore the same pants, blue cotton work shirt with his name, and a hat with the red STP logo. Freddy's outfit from day-to-day was also the same, but there was a lot more to see. DREGS was stitched in an arc along the top of the vest. Under the arc in the center of his back was the face of a demonic, horned woman with burning eyes. Her red tongue was forked, reptilian, and snaked almost to his waist. "One Per Center" diamond-shaped patches were stitched into the leather around the front and back of the vest. His jeans were well-worn and tattered, his boots heavy and square-toed, good for kicking.

Freddy sported a lot of tattoos: SS lightning bolts on his neck, a large Nazi War Eagle atop a swastika on his chest, and on each forearm, woodpeckers with sinister grins. 1% in a diamond frame was tattooed on the back of each upper arm for passing motorists to admire. The eagle on his chest was a piece of art, done with precision by a talented man in Daytona Beach. Freddy had the woodpeckers done in Austin, at a parlor recommended by a Bandido friend of his. All the other tats were crude and ragged, acquired in prison.

Freddy spent some of his life behind bars, in locales he thought superior to Parchman. Having run away from Brewer Hill at sixteen, he lived on the streets of Little Rock until hooking up with a thirty-year-old stripper who got him a job as bouncer in her club. After he turned eighteen, he and his girl friend broke up in the middle of her act, inciting a club-wide brawl that required six cops to break up. Freddy left in the middle of the fight and escaped arrest, showing up the next day at an Army recruiting office. After four years driving a transport truck in Fort Carson, Colorado, he left the army and hung out in communes in the mountains for a couple of years. Freddy enjoyed the dope and the sex, but the Colorado hippies were too peace-loving for him.

While scoring some coke in the mid-eighties in Greeley he met Jacko McManus, who introduced Freddy to the Sons of Silence Motorcycle Club. Jacko sponsored Freddy as a "probate" and in 1987, Freddy was patched in as an SOS member. He was an active member of SOS MC for almost nine years. He was a good earner, his specialty being crystal methamphetamine, which he produced, marketed, and smoked, especially on long runs, when the bikers had to stay awake for days at a time. Freddy killed a biker from a rival gang in a Colorado motel room in 1990 in a fight over meth distribution franchises. He and Jacko cut up the body and spread the parts in the high desert. Neither the authorities nor the rival gang ever figured out how the victim disappeared.

With the blessing of his SOS brothers, in 1990 Freddy opened a strip club in Colorado Springs, fulfilling a lifelong dream. For three years the club was a money-maker. The strip business up front broke even, but the meth sales and prostitution divisions run out of the back offices were SOS profit centers. Freddy enjoyed a surfeit of dope and stripper girlfriends, but was arrested in 1993 for distribution of methamphetamines, earning him three years in a Colorado pen, where he absorbed the collective wisdom of the white supremacist prison gangs. His upbringing on Brewer Hill had been a thorough introduction to the concepts.

When his mentor Jacko was stabbed to death in a dispute with a civilian over a woman, Freddy was allowed to leave SOS MC on the condition that he continue to make quarterly payments to them. From 1997 to 2004, Freddy roamed the Southwest, staying clear of Colorado, selling crystal meth to bikers on an *ad hoc* basis.

Missing his true calling, Freddy opened a strip club in Killeen, Texas. It did so well he opened another in Abilene in 2006. The clubs prospered until the Spring of 2008, when the city of Killeen shut down the club after Freddy and his friends severely beat three black men who had the nerve to enter the club and order a drink. Abilene's police department had also started hassling Freddy and his customers. Freddy decided his business career had run its course. He closed the clubs.

The liquidation of his strip club business wasn't a total loss for Freddy. He made a little money and met the love of his life, a tough little Oklahoma stripper named Brandi Trichel who worked for him in the Killeen Club. After he departed the strip club industry, Freddy married Brandi in a ceremony on the outskirts of Oklahoma City presided over by a justice of the peace in the large recreational vehicle the j.p. used as his official place of business and courtroom. They lived together for six months in Oklahoma City, until Brandi told Freddy she had about all his lying she could put up with. She hired a lawyer, served Freddy with divorce papers, and kicked him out of their matrimonial domicile, a double-wide her parents co-signed for and put in Brandi's name only. All the Trichels were glad to see Freddy depart, and were thankful Brandi wasn't pregnant.

Freddy and what little he could carry on his Blockhead Harley left Oklahoma City and returned to Texas. While operating the clubs in Texas, Freddy had become friends with several Bandidos who were good customers. He obtained permission in early 2009 from The Bandidos to start his own biker gang, The Dregs, in a northern suburb of San Antonio with three of his friends. Though it was Bandido territory, Freddy got their approval by committing to them he would not engage in any business, especially the drug trade, in competition with theirs. Freddy's second in command was James "Wizler" Kohler, who had developed formidable computer skills in Austin working for several computer and electronic companies before he became bored with the straight life. Using Wizler's skills, The Dregs concentrated on identity theft, ATM theft, and selling high quality fake i.d.s, passports, green cards and other documents, markets in which the Bandidos had no aptitude or interest. Freddy also sold a few guns here and there, but not enough to step on Bandido toes.

An hour and a half after Freddy crossed the bridge into Mississippi, he cruised into Kilbride, his Harley puttering barely above idle. He parked in the street next to the courthouse and cut the engine. Freddy took off his helmet, sat on the bike and rolled a thin brown cigarillo. He knew it would be only a matter of moments before word spread through the court house. When it circled round to Freddy's old nemesis, Freddy was certain the man would walk out and say hello.

Sure enough, Freddy spotted Sheriff Cheatwood walking carefully down the court house steps, holding on to the iron handrail. Freddy exhaled and peered through the blue tobacco cloud to take note of how old and fat Cheatwood had grown. The Sheriff stopped on the sidewalk, ten feet from the Harley.

"Well, look what the cat done drug up," Cheatwood said. "Boy, what the hell are you doing back in these parts?"

"I just got to missin' you so bad, Sheriff."

Freddy laughed. So did the Sheriff. The two of them had gone round and round for five years in Dundee County before Freddy left for Little Rock when he turned sixteen. Freddy recalled the Sheriff beating him but good on two of the occasions he caught him. When Freddy's old man asked Cheatwood how the boy got his nose broken in the Kilbride jail, the Sheriff said "Freddy must have slipped and fell in the cell. He was pretty drunk when we brought him in." That didn't fool anybody.

Freddy hadn't killed anyone in Kilbride before he left for Arkansas, but it wasn't for lack of trying. He was the ring leader of a half-dozen Brewer Hill boys that used to come to Kilbride on Saturday nights just to get in fights. They liked to drink and cut up, but mostly they liked to fight. When he was fifteen, Freddy almost killed two Kilbride teenagers. The Sheriff didn't charge him with anything because he figured it was a fair fight. Freddy took on both boys and single-handedly beat the hell out of them using just his fists.

"I know it ain't likely you just showed up here for old times sake," Sheriff Cheatwood said. "You here to support Trevor?"

"What's Trevor gone and done, Sheriff?"

Cheatwood waved off the question. Freddy grinned. Freddy knew the Sheriff was on to him. Cheatwood had tangled with Freddy often enough to know Freddy never did anything to support anyone, except himself.

"If you come here looking for information," Cheatwood said, "I ain't got none. The shooting happened over in Sunshine and I ain't got nothing to do with it. Don't even know what happened. The D.A. and that nigger Sheriff they got over there come to see me about talking to Tom and Trevor and I told'em where to find Tom at the shop. That's all I did. It ain't none of my business what happened over there."

"Trevor is one of your constituents," Freddy said. "I'm surprised you don't take more of an interest."

"You wore me out chasing you around on top of that hill, and I ain't been back since. Don't plan on going up there in the future, neither."

"Trevor's out, right?"

"I heard he's back up on that hill, and I heard that D.A.'s been up there on the hill talking to Tom and Trevor, but that's all hearsay. I don't know it for a fact. You talk to Tom?"

"Nah," Freddy said. "I thought I'd surprise him."

"I 'spect you will if he don't know you're comin'. It's Sunday so Tom's up there. Every other day he's in his shop. Your brother's got him a good business going there on the highway."

"Half-brother," Freddy said. "He wants everyone to know we ain't full blood kin."

"Cain't imagine why?" the Sheriff said.

Freddy took a final drag on the cigarillo and tossed the brown unfiltered butt in the street. He grinned and winked at Cheatwood, started the Harley and shook his Nazi helmet at the Sheriff.

"You gonna make me wear this thing in your county?"

"I don't care what you put on your fool head, but you run up on a trooper and he'll bust you in a heartbeat if you ain't wearing it."

Freddy put on his helmet and slightly revved his engine. Over the noise of the Harley, Freddy yelled "great seeing you, Sheriff" and rode off. Ten minutes later, he turned off the paved highway onto the dirt and gravel road to Brewer Hill. He stopped to tie down the helmet with two bungee cords, glanced in his mirror to make sure his long gray hair was just right, and roared up the steep hill.

Chapter Twenty

Jake kicked back with an ice cold Corona on the expansive brick work surrounding the sparkling blue water of Bellingham's infinity pool. He admired the view of the Blue Ridge beyond the pool as he squeezed the lime wedge and stuffed it into the clear bottle. He placed his thumb on the mouth and turned the bottle upside down for a second.

"Ah," Jake said after he took his first taste. "There's nothing like the first beer of the day."

Bull turned his Corona up and drank half of it.

"Yeah," Bull said. "The twenty-fourth one ain't bad, either."

Hound and Jake laughed and raised their Coronas to toast Bull just as Big Dog, David Dunne, Doberman, and Patrick Dunwoody IV walked out of the house to join them.

"Here come the grownups," Hound said. "Bull, you behave."

"Gentlemen," their host Patrick Dunwoody IV said, "I'm sorry we took so long. I do hope you haven't been bored."

Bull pointed to the aluminum wash tub full of ice and Coronas.

"No, sir. We've been through much worse."

Dunwoody was the number two man at the Justice Department behind the president's appointee Danny Okole, the first Attorney General of the United States of Hawaiian descent. Deputy A.G. Dunwoody had made a career at DOJ, and kept the department running in spite of Okole and his political predecessors. He was the last of the Dunwoodys, sole heir to the family fortune and Bellingham, the two thousand acre estate near Charlottesville that the Dunwoodys had owned since before Thomas Jefferson built Monticello. Parts of the Georgian mansion at Bellingham were constructed in the mid-1700s. Dunwoody and his longtime companion and executive assistant at DOJ Donald Monroe added the pool and brickwork in 2006, using old brick manufactured on Bellingham grounds and harvested from *pigeonnaires* and other outbuildings that had deconstructed before Patrick IV took over the estate. It worked out fine, because Patrick never liked the French towers behind the big house. His ancestors added them in the mid-1800s, and Patrick considered them in derogation of his family's British roots.

Dunwoody was in his early sixties, thin and elegant. He was present at the creation of DOGs at the Holiday Inn in Chevy Chase in 2001 five days after 9-11, recruiting David Dunne as the first hire. He negotiated with the incoming administration in December of 2008, dissuading them from prosecuting DOGs in exchange for the termination of the official program. Dunwoody counseled Big Dog when he took DOGs private in early 2009. He maintained enough distance and deniability to survive if Big Dog's unofficial operations came under legal scrutiny, and was currently leading the quiet campaign to bring DOGs back into official status when the current hostile administration was no longer in power. DOGs had no better friend than Patrick Dunwoody IV. At Big Dog's office in the basement of Homeland Security and in the barracks in Rock Creek, Dunwoody was referred to as "The Earl."

"We've made a decision," Big Dog said to his men. "We've decided to green light Operation Camelot. Patrick will notify our British sponsor and we'll begin the planning stage."

No one clapped or whistled, but none of the DOGs were disappointed, either. They knew the mission was important to the security of the country. Big Dog and David Dunne would have never agreed if the need weren't critical. The Earl would never have asked them to consider it.

"Something else, men," Big Dog said. "Dunne, Doberman, and I are leaving at the end of this week for London for planning and recon. We may be there quite a while. We're going to spend as much time as necessary to educate ourselves on the viability of the operation."

"And guys," Dunne said, rubbing the two-inch scar on his left jaw line he acquired from an I.E.D. in Iraq, "rest assured that if we are not one hundred per cent certain that we can safely pull this thing off, we will not undertake it. If any of us has doubts after this scouting trip, we'll call it off. You have my word on it."

Hound, Bull, and Jake were silent. Each of them knew Dunne and Big Dog had not made the decision lightly. It was a serious moment.

"Doberman," Big Dog said, "do you have anything to add?"

"Nope," Doberman said.

"Doberman's going with us," Dunne said, "because his particular skills are going to be critical in several phases of the operation."

Hound raised his hand.

"Hound and Bull, you two are off duty until Gillmon or I get word to you," Dunne said. Hound lowered his hand. "I know it's bad news for your ladies," Dunne said with a smile, "but that's just the way it is."

"Jake," Patrick Dunwoody said. "You go on home, too, at least for the time being. I don't want to get you a new assignment inside DOJ until we know how long this planning stage will take. If it looks like they're going to be over there months rather than weeks, I'll bring you back to D.C."

"All right men," Big Dog said to the three of them. "You all get on out of here. And stay out of trouble."

~ * ~

Jake, Hound, and Bull drew straws to see who would be the designated driver and abstain from the Coronas on the drive back to D.C. The Earl had packed a Styrofoam chest with a case of long-necked Coronas in ice, lime wedges, and a silver bottle opener with Bellingham engraved on the handle. Jake was glad that Hound lost because if Bull had drawn the short straw, he would have demanded a re-draw, or two out of three, or three out of five.

Hound was sober and remained so on the drive up 29 North. Part of the deal was the right of the driver to keep whatever Coronas were left after the two hour drive. Bull took it as a personal challenge to drink all the Coronas so Hound's reward for sobriety would be meager. Bull enlisted Jake's help, but after six beers, Jake reached his limit. His bladder was about to explode because Hound would not pull over.

Jake lost count of how many Coronas Bull drank, but there were only two left in the ice chest when Hound stopped in the circular gravel drive in front of the barracks. After six beers he couldn't be positive, but Jake thought The Earl had given them a full case. Jake did a quick calculation.

Bull must have drunk sixteen, an average of one every seven and a half minutes.

The last ten minutes of the drive, during which Hound appeared to be in no hurry, Bull was transformed. He had been jovial and funny up until then. Nearing the barracks, Bull began to twitch and jump in his seat, crossing one big thigh over the other, sitting on his hands and humming, sweat pouring from his brow.

Hound stopped but didn't unlock Bull's door. Bull frantically tried to get out. Hound pretended to search for something in the console between them. Bull began to whimper, then screamed.

"I'm going to...."

Hound tapped the unlock button on his door. Bull burst out of the passenger seat straight into the center of a large oleander bush next to the vehicle. The bush closed in around him. After Bull had been deep inside the bush for several minutes, Hound yelled.

"Whatever you're doing in there, don't eat the oleander leaves. They're poison."

Jake and Hound walked into the barracks laughing. Jake put on a pot of coffee to sober up before driving to his apartment.

~ * ~

That night, Jake called Kitty. She told him Walton was presenting the Gas & Go Fast shooting to the Yaloquena Grand Jury the next morning. Kitty said Willie Mitchell wanted Mule indicted for felony murder and explained why Walton would be asking the Grand Jury to indict Trevor for possession of the stolen Smith & Wesson that caused the death of Azeem and Mule's paralysis. She also told him about the double homicide in Oklahoma City with possible racial overtones.

"Damn," Jake told her, "Having that pistol in his truck turned out to be bad luck for Trevor."

"No kidding," she said and filled him in on Willie Mitchell's two meetings with the Freedmen's Creek contingent. She told him what the Muslim commune leaders were demanding. She said Bobby Sanders attended the office conference on Thursday.

"That ass? Unbelievable," Jake said. "Tell Daddy I'll be home Wednesday. Maybe I can do something to help Walton and him."

"You're kidding. You can't fly out tomorrow or Tuesday?"

"I've got a few things I have to take care of at DOJ tomorrow, things I have to do in person. I've booked a flight out early Tuesday and I'll be landing in Memphis before noon."

"So you'll be home Tuesday afternoon."

"I'll be in Yaloquena County on Tuesday," he said, "but I thought I might go right to the duck camp from the airport. Didn't you tell me there's something that needs tending to out there when I had time?"

"Oh." She paused. "Yes. As soon as possible. Sweet of you to remember."

Chapter Twenty-One

Tom Brewer was worn out from working on Bubber Forman's 1965 Mustang, and mad at himself for letting Bubber talk him into promising he'd have the job completed before the weekend was done. Here it was, Sunday afternoon, almost six, Tom's only day off shot to hell.

He drove the Mustang out of the shop and left it locked up on the parking pad next to the highway. Tom called Bubber and told him it was ready and he could get his old lady to bring him over to the shop and pick it up. He reminded Bubber to bring his extra set of keys, because the others were locked inside the car. Bubber asked Tom if he could pay him at the end of next week when he got his paycheck. Tom was too tired to remind Bubber about his promise to give Tom payment in full when he picked up the Mustang.

Tom cranked up his GMC truck and headed home. He was looking forward to sitting in front of the T.V. with a cold beer, hoping Trevor hadn't come over from his own cabin to eat everything in Tom's refrigerator. For such a skinny kid, Trevor sure ate a lot. Tom figured he did the same thing when he was that age.

As the GMC crested the hill onto the flat, treeless field, Tom saw Freddy sitting on his Harley holding court with a dozen Brewer men and boys. There was a pile of logs and brush not far from the Harley and four pickup trucks, set up in the commons where the Brewers gathered for a bonfire.

Shit. They throwin' the sum'bitch a party.

As Tom drove the GMC closer he noticed someone running away from the others and heading for the lane between two of the old wooden buildings. He recognized the man from his gait.

Trevor. I ought to tan his hide.

Tom stopped his truck and walked up to the Harley. Freddy dismounted and grinned.

"Tom," Freddy said. "You're a sight for sore eyes."

Tom sensed the others waiting for his reaction. They all knew there was bad blood between them, half-brothers or not. Tom wasn't going to give Freddy or the others the satisfaction.

"Freddy," Tom said, glancing briefly at his half-brother before looking down at the dirt.

"Trevor was just here," Freddy said, looking around, all smiles.

"I saw him. What you doing back on the hill?"

"Ain't been here for a couple of years. I been kind of missing the old place. You know what I mean?"

Tom nodded as if he did.

Lyin' sack of shit.

"Everybody's gatherin' up in a little while," Freddy said. "The women went off to get some supper together so we can eat out here by the fire."

"I see."

"Why don't you sit with us a spell? You and me can catch up."

"Been working on Bubber Forman's Mustang all day," Tom said. "I'm pretty much tuckered out. Filthy, too."

"Come on, Tom. It's been a long time."

"Let me get on to my place and clean up and we'll see."

"Bring some beer," Freddy said as Tom cranked the GMC. Before he drove off, Freddy hollered at him, loud enough for everyone in the *cummins* to hear.

"I heard about what Trevor did in Sunshine," Freddy said. "I wish'd he'd killed them both. You should be proud of what your boy did. I surely am."

~ * ~

Tom walked into his house and slammed the door, causing Trevor to jump in his chair in front of the T.V.

"What's he doing here?" Tom barked at Trevor.

"Who?"

"You know who. I seen you running from the *cummins* when I come over the hill. Did you call him?"

"N-no s-sir."

"Then who did?"

"H-he s-said L-leonard did."

"Goddammit. One deserter calls another. I guess you called your brother and told him about the mess you're in?"

"Somebody else c-called and t-told Leonard and h-he called m-me."

"You ask'em to call Leonard?"

"N-no, sir. I s-swear."

Tom opened the refrigerator and popped open an Old Milwaukee sixteen ounce. He moved to the pantry and pulled a fat can of Chunky soup off the shelf and put it on the counter, then plopped down in his tattered La-Z-Boy recliner and jerked the handle to rare back with his feet up on the footrest.

"He's no good," Tom said.

Tom hated the way everyone always made such a fuss over Freddy, with his big grin and braggin' about all the places he'd seen and all the things he'd done. Here he was, working his ass off at the shop supporting half the shiftless Brewers on the Goddamned hill and nobody'd ever lit him a bonfire. Freddy's nothing but a criminal. He'd climb a tree to tell a lie. The truth just wasn't in him. Tom looked over at Trevor and felt bad about jumpin' on him. He was just a boy.

"I don't want you hanging around Freddy," he told Trevor. "I know he's fun and everybody's glad to see him, but he ain't nothin' but trouble. Never has been. I don't want to know the details about the Goddamned Smith & Wesson he give you, either. The less you and me know the better. But I done figured out he give the damned gun to you, didn't he."

"Y-yes, s-sir. Better'n t-two y-years ago when h-he was h-here last."

"And he didn't tell you the gun was stolen and somebody'd used it to kill two people in Oklahoma City, did he?"

"N-no, s-sir."

"I know he didn't. He's a bad seed. He don't give a shit about nobody but himself."

"H-he s-said he w-was here t-to help m-me."

"That's a lie. He ain't never done anything his entire life to help nobody but himself. That's a fact. I want you to stay away from Freddy. You hear me?"

"Wh-what about the f-fire and s-supper?"

"I ain't going." Tom took a sip of beer and looked at Trevor. "You do what you want. Just get back plenty early to your cabin. You and me got to go into Sunshine tomorrow and meet with that D.A."

Trevor nodded and walked slowly out the door.

Tom turned off the television and finished his beer. Tom was fourteen when Freddy left for good. Didn't say kiss my ass, goodbye, or nothin'. Just woke up one morning and the old man said Freddy was gone. Even back then, everyone loved Freddy and the boys all did whatever Freddy said. Tom never joined in the fighting in Kilbride. Didn't make much sense to him. Before the old man died he asked Tom to find out where Freddy was and ask him to come see him before he passed on. Tom made the call and Freddy said to tell the old man he was coming but he never showed up.

Tom walked outside and tossed the beer can into the burn pit between his place and Trevor's. He started the GMC and drove slowly through the trees on the narrow dirt lane to the edge of the *cummins*. He kept his headlights off and stayed between the abandoned buildings so no one could see him.

Tom admired the bonfire. He'd had many a fine time out on the *cummins* around a fire such as that. Over a dozen Brewer pickups surrounded the bonfire and Freddy's Harley. Tom was close enough to see the women had set up tables. He knew from experience there'd be plates of sandwiches, biscuits, and meat. There were steaming cast iron pots, probably full of beans and corn.

Tom watched several of his cousins pat Freddy on the back and raise a beer can to him. Freddy put his arm around Trevor's shoulders and whispered something. Trevor drew back and looked his Uncle Freddy in the eyes and started laughing. Tom knew he didn't stutter when he laughed. In fact, people on the hill told Tom that Trevor didn't stutter near as bad when Tom wasn't around.

Tom put the GMC in reverse and backed up between the buildings, turned around and started home in the dark to heat up the Chunky soup on the stove.

Tom knew it was no need in blaming the boy for liking Freddy. Everyone else did. It had been that way all Tom's life.

First time he had Freddy off by himself, with no one else around, Tom figured he'd ask Freddy the real reason he was back on the hill. Both of them knew he wasn't there to help Trevor. Tom would tell him he wasn't buying that bull shit. Tom swore he was going to ask Freddy if he hadn't already done enough to Trevor, giving him a stolen gun used in some badass murder, getting the Feds and the Sunshine D.A. after the boy. Knowing Freddy, he'd deny he knew about the gun. Tom wasn't going to call Freddy a liar to his face, but he was going to make sure Freddy knew Tom was laying it all at Freddy's feet.

Chapter Twenty-Two

Walton Donaldson first saw the two dogs when he got close enough to the court house steps to see around the big magnolia tree with limbs that grew all the way to the ground. As he came nearer he recognized them as Catahoula Curs and was grateful they were leashed. On the other end of the leashes were two smokers, medium-sized white guys in their early to mid-twenties. Walton stopped to admire the dogs. They were black and white with brown splotches. One had bright blue eyes; the other cur had one brown eye and one gray-blue.

"Good-looking curs." Walton asked.

The man with faded jeans and a gold tee shirt with GEAUX TIGERS across the front grunted. The other said nothing. Walton would have bet a dollar against a dime the one in the LSU shirt had never set foot on LSU campus.

"You hunt them?" Walton asked.

"Some," the other man said. His jeans had holes in the knees and his gray tee shirt said U.S. ARMY in white letters. "Mostly hogs."

"I've seen a cur tear into a big old boar before," Walton said. "That dog had some fierce energy. The guy I was hunting with had a dog team of pit bulls and curs. We got two boars and a sow that day. Those boars stunk to high heaven."

"Hmm," the LSU man said blowing a stream of smoke away from Walton. "Curs and pit bulls don't usually git along all that well."

"Catahoula Curs are supposed to be really good working dogs and swimmers," Walton said, "and the guy that I hunted with said he had one could climb a tree."

"I heard dat," the Army man said. "We got a cousin up on the hill got a cur can climb a pine tree, or so he says."

"We ain't never seen it," LSU said. "He tells it for a fact."

"What hill? You guys Brewers?"

They both took drags off their cigarettes and nodded.

"Curs is smarter than pit bulls," LSU said. "You can train'em to do all kinds of thangs."

"Trevor doesn't have to show up until this afternoon."

"That's what they said," Army said.

Walton glanced at his watch. It was eight-thirty.

"Y'all going to leave and come back?"

They shook their heads no.

"You're going to stay around until this afternoon?"

"Suppose so," LSU said. "We're here for Trevor."

Walton started to pet the big square head of the closest cur, the one with blue and brown eyes. The dog emitted a low growl.

"I wouldn't do that if I's you," Army said.

"No kidding," Walton said. "See you later."

Walton walked up the steps and into the front door. Sheriff Jones was on the other side of the security check, saw Walton and waved him through the metal detector. The two large deputies working the security table told Walton good morning.

"Good idea, Lee," Walton told Sheriff Jones.

"You ought to see upstairs. They started showing up at six, when the courthouse doors were still locked. I got a call at home and told my men to restrict access to the front door and set up the security station."

"I'm going on up."

"You and Willie Mitchell get this Grand Jury in and out as soon as possible," Lee Jones said. "We don't need this going on all day."

"I'll be through by noon," Walton said and walked toward the stairs to the second floor.

"Hey, Walton," the Sheriff said, "it's not just Brewers up there."

"Who else?"

"You'll see."

Walton bounded up the stairwell and walked out the heavy wooden door to the second floor. There were people everywhere. Sturdy oak benches designed like church pews were spaced along the walls. Every seat was taken. Those who didn't have a place to sit leaned against the cream colored walls.

Walton knew they had to be Brewers. He walked toward the D.A.'s office. There were men, women, and children of all ages on either side of him, most wearing jeans. Only a handful of the women Walton passed wore dresses. Several of the men wore faded denim bib overalls. Walton smiled and nodded like always on jury day. Some of the men nodded, but not one of the men or women smiled at the Assistant D.A.

There were three men seated on the bench by the entrance to the Grand Jury, and Walton was sure they weren't Brewers. Reverend Bobby Sanders, Tweety-Bird Abud Rahman, and the giant, Samson al Kadeesh took up almost the entire bench. Abud and Samson wore dark suits, white shirts, bow ties, and sour expressions. Bobby sported his *faux* Roman collar. There was room for one more person to sit on their oak bench. Walton knew it highly unlikely one of the Brewers would fill the spot. Walton waved to acknowledge the three black men before ducking into the District Attorney's office.

~ * ~

Willie Mitchell had been at his desk since seven. He woke up at five, did a quick four miles after only one cup of coffee, showered and hurried to the office to review the file in the Gas & Go Fast shooting one more time. He and Walton had gone over everything relating to the Grand Jury presentation in detail on Saturday. He knew Walton was ready and the morning's presentation, like any case before a Grand Jury, would be a piece of cake. Nevertheless, here he was grinding each detail again before the Grand Jury started at nine. He shook his head as he read the coroner's report for the tenth time. Segueing into senior status was not going to be easy.

Old dog. Old tricks.

Walton walked in and stopped. Willie Mitchell grinned.

"How about all those people?"

"I couldn't believe it when I stepped into the hall," Walton said.

"Looks like Hee-Haw out there."

Walton chuckled. "My father used to watch Hee-Haw on Saturday nights and would laugh until he cried. I was little."

"Junior Sample was always my favorite."

"Which one was he?"

"The fat guy in the overalls that could hardly read the cue card."

"Oh, yeah. What are you working on?"

"Just going through the file."

"No matter how much you go through it the video's not going to change and neither is the cause of death," Walton said. "And just in case you're thinking about coming into the Grand Jury room with me, don't."

"I know. I know."

"I'm calling Lee Jones to give the Grand Jury an overview of the investigation. I'll get into the Crime Lab report and the video disk through him. I made Al Revels swear he'd just answer my questions and not go down some pig trail. You know how he does."

"Thank God he's not a doctor. Be sure to keep his film crew out."

Walton laughed.

"The best thing you got going for you is the fact that this is the end of the Grand Jury's term."

"No kidding," Walton said. "They're ready to be dismissed. All they'll want to do is find out what indictments we want, hear as little testimony as possible, and go home or back to work."

"I want you to pay attention to them while they watch the video. Encourage them to ask questions about it. Use this Grand Jury to help us gauge how the trial jury might react to it."

"Like we talked about Saturday, I'm going to show them the video first thing, right at the beginning of the Sheriff's testimony. Neither Lee nor I will have commented on what it shows. Let's get their honest take on what they think about Trevor's involvement. This is my sixth session with this Grand Jury. Believe me, they won't bite their tongue. We got some real talkers on this one."

"I'm sure they'll have heard a bunch of crap about it on the street."

"As usual. I should be through in a couple of hours. Noon at the very latest."

"Did you stop for a visit with Bobby Sanders in the hall?"

Walton laughed. "He didn't seem very happy in the middle of all those Brewers. I don't think there will be any dust ups as long as Samson is there. That is one big man."

"Yeah. Even the Brewers can figure that out."

Louise appeared in the doorway. She patted her neat Afro.

"We've checked in ten Grand Jurors so far," she said. "The bailiff took them into the Grand Jury room. I made sure the custodians fixed a big pot of coffee in there."

"Thanks, Louise," Willie Mitchell said.

She lingered in the doorway.

"Something else?"

"I don't think I've ever seen a rougher looking bunch of white people in one place," she said.

"You ought to go fishing with me in South Louisiana sometime," Walton said smiling.

"No, thanks," she said.

Kitty squeezed past Louise into Willie Mitchell's office.

"What are all those kids doing in the hallway?" Kitty asked. "Doesn't anyone go to school around this place?"

Chapter Twenty-Three

Willie Mitchell sat at the antique pine kitchen table working on the second half of his chicken salad sandwich. He studied the burn scars and worm holes in the wood next to his plate, and rubbed the rough surface of the table with his fingertips. The table had been in the house since the sixth grade, when he moved in with his parents. His late parents ate almost every meal on it. They rarely entertained or ate in the exquisite dining room, though they collected and furnished it and the rest of the house with fine English antiques.

Susan and Willie Mitchell had turned down substantial offers from several antique dealers for the Regency Period English mahogany table with ten of the twelve original chairs and matching sideboard. Willie Mitchell remembered the experts estimated 1815 as the year the pieces were made but could not recall the name of the English district the experts claimed was the origin. He knew the date because the dining room furniture was almost a hundred years older than his house, a two story Neo-Classical Revival wooden house he was pretty sure was built in 1905.

Susan walked in the kitchen door from outside in tennis whites and a pink Hilton Head visor. She set her tennis bag stuffed with towels, water bottle, extra racket, and cans of new and used balls by the door.

"How'd you do?" he asked.

"We had fun. We rotated doubles teams and whoever had Julia as a partner won."

He swallowed. "There's nothing better in this world than your chicken salad."

"You save any for me?"

"There's enough left in the refrigerator for your-sized sandwich. If you go upstairs and take a shower before you eat I can't guarantee it'll be there when you come back."

"Then I guess I better eat just like I am."

"You look mighty fine to me."

Susan laughed. "All sweaty and smelly."

"Not hardly. You look fresh as a peach. You never smell bad."

She walked around the table and mussed his hair on her way to the refrigerator. After she set the bread and Hellman's on the table she kissed him on the cheek and stood while she made her sandwich.

"How'd it go this morning?"

"Just like we expected."

"What did they think of the video?"

"Walton said they pretty much agreed that Mule was to blame for the whole thing. He said a few Grand Jurors asked if we were going to charge Trevor with any kind of homicide. Walton said we thought the video showed he acted in self-defense and explained that we wanted them to indict him for the stolen weapon. They were fine with it. He said they all clapped when he told them it was their last session."

"I don't blame them. I'd hate to be on a jury."

"Trevor's coming in at three to be booked."

"I feel sorry for him," Susan said. "He was such a cute little boy. His stutter any better?"

"No. He's had a rough go all his life. Now he's in the middle of this fiasco. You should have seen all the Brewers in the courthouse. They're still there, waiting."

"For what?"

"I guess to make sure I follow through on what I promised would happen this afternoon."

"And if you don't?"

"Aren't we glad we don't have to find out. Zelda agreed to set a $2500 bond. Trevor shouldn't be at the courthouse more than an hour."

"Then what?"

"Jordan Summit told me last week he's ready to get it on."

"You're not backing up on letting Walton try it, are you?"

"No, ma'am."

Susan finished making her sandwich and sat down. Willie Mitchell stared out the window.

"What are you thinking about?"

"Nothing."

"I know that look," she said. "Your Restless Brain Syndrome kicking in?"

He chuckled and focused on Susan. He was so glad they survived the rough spot several years ago. She was as pretty to him as she was the day they married.

"These days it doesn't kick in," he said. "It's there all the time."

~ * ~

Willie Mitchell sat in the courtroom at the prosecution table that afternoon. As promised, he met Tom and Trevor at three o'clock in the Sheriff's Office to baby sit Trevor during the arrest and booking procedure. Walton and Trevor stood in front of the bench listening to Judge Zelda Williams.

"There are no special conditions of your release, Mr. Brewer," she said. "When you post the bond downstairs you're free to go, your only obligation undertaken under the terms of the bond are to appear in court whenever summoned, and to notify this court prior to your venturing outside of the State of Mississippi. Do you understand all that?"

Willie Mitchell winced watching Trevor trying to form the words to answer Judge Williams. He opened his mouth wide and strained, contorting his face, but nothing came out. Walton glanced at Willie Mitchell, who looked back at Tom sitting on the front row in a courtroom full of Brewers.

Deputy Clerk of Court Eddie Bordelon, a small, bald Cajun transplanted from Acadia Parish, Louisiana looked over his rimless glasses at Willie Mitchell. Eddie was Judge William's minute clerk for the bail hearing. He was a hyper Type A who had run the Circuit Clerk's office for over thirty years for a succession of elected Circuit Clerk's who knew how to get votes but nothing about the internal operations of the office. Circuit Clerk Winston Moore was the current politician for whom Eddie was running things. Willie Mitchell acknowledged Eddie's silent plea and stood up. Zelda appeared relieved.

"Your Honor, Mr. Brewer understands the terms of the bond. His father is seated in the courtroom and he and Trevor Brewer have already committed to me earlier that they will honor the commitments Your Honor mentioned."

Judge Williams looked at Trevor. Willie Mitchell saw compassion in Zelda's eyes, exactly what he expected. She had just turned fifty, and Willie Mitchell had begun to notice a few gray hairs above her dark brown forehead. She was born and reared in the county and was in her second term as Circuit Court Judge for Yaloquena County. She was not the first black jurist Willie Mitchell had practiced before in Sunshine, but she was by far the best. Willie Mitchell and Judge Williams had been through a lot of difficult cases together, including the Al Anderson and McKinley Owens cases, the Takisha Berry prosecution, and the jurisdictional battle with the U.S. Attorney's office in the case of State vs. Adolfo Galvan Zagarra, a.k.a. "El Moro."

Willie Mitchell considered Judge Williams fair and impartial, highly intelligent and motivated. During her second term, he felt they had become friends, sharing as much of a friendship as the constraints of the Code of Ethics and the Sunshine ethos would permit. Zelda did not always rule in his favor. He didn't expect her to. All Willie Mitchell wanted from Zelda for the D.A.'s office was a fair shake in the courtroom. He felt that was what Zelda gave him, and that was all he asked.

"Is that correct, Mr. Brewer?" Judge Williams asked.

Trevor nodded his agreement.

"Very well," she said. "After you post your bond you're free to go."

Trevor nodded and turned to walk past the prosecution table to join Tom in the first row. Willie Mitchell studied Trevor as he passed. His downcast face was beet red, his eyes burrowing into the carpet.

His father's son.

"This court is adjourned," Zelda said tapping the gavel.

Willie Mitchell turned to watch all the Brewers stand when commanded by the bailiff. He wondered what was running through the Brewer minds as they saw Judge Williams walk out the courtroom. Dundee County had never elected a black judge, and Willie Mitchell knew the Dundee voters never would.

Willie Mitchell and Walton walked out with Trevor and Tom through the center aisle, all the Brewer eyes on them. They walked down the stairs to the first floor and into the Sheriff's office where a local bondsman waited. Tom told Willie Mitchell he had already put the bail money up with the bondsman, who had the paperwork ready for Tom and Trevor to sign.

Willie Mitchell and Walton shook hands with Tom and Trevor. They turned to leave the Sheriff's office but were stopped by one of Lee Jones' deputies in charge of serving civil suits. Eleanor Bernstein stood behind the deputy.

"Trevor Brewer?" the deputy asked.

Trevor nodded. The deputy placed a legal document in Trevor's hands. He and Tom studied the paper a moment then looked up at Willie Mitchell. He walked over to them and quickly read the first page. It was a petition for damages styled "Lester Gardner versus Trevor Brewer and Gas & Go Fast, Inc." Willie Mitchell looked up to see Eleanor's back as she walked out of the Sheriff's office, her task completed.

Jordan Summit and Eleanor Bernstein were wasting no time.

Chapter Twenty-Four

Jake walked from his arrival gate into the flow of passengers headed for the center of the main terminal at Memphis International. He felt sorry for the people he passed at the baggage claims carousels praying fervently that their luggage followed them to Memphis. Jake was making his way to the ground transportation exit to pick up his rental car when he saw her.

Kitty was holding a sign over her head. MR. BANKS was all it said. He started laughing as he hurried to her. Jake took her into his arms and kissed her—an exciting, delicious kiss.

"What are you doing here?"

"What do you think?"

"I like the sign."

"I've had several men stop and tell me their name was Mr. Banks."

"I don't blame them," he said. "As beautiful as you are."

"I bet you say that to all airport chauffeurs."

"Actually, you're my first. I've never had a sign before."

"Now you have."

"Like I'm a celebrity."

"You're my celebrity."

Jake kissed Kitty again. He felt his heart speed with anticipation and his chest flutter. Good to have those feelings.

"We need to get out of here," Jake said. "We're creating a spectacle."

"Who cares? We'll never see these people again."

"You drove your car up here," Jake said. "I've got a rental."

"Not any more. I canceled it. You're riding with me."

"How'd you do that?"

"I flashed my FBI i.d. I told the lady at the counter I was taking you into custody."

Jake laughed. "How much was the cancellation fee?"

"I talked her out of it. Told her what a sweet boy friend you were and that your safety was a matter of national security."

Jake put his arm around Kitty. They followed the short-term parking signs and after a ten minute stroll, Jake threw his soft carry-on into the back seat of Kitty's 1996 BMW E36 convertible. It was uncomfortably warm in the parking garage.

"Lot hotter than D.C. You want me to drive?" he asked.

"No," she said. "I'm in a hurry."

"All I've been thinking about is making love to you," he said buckling his seat belt.

She leaned across the console. They kissed. A long, slow kiss.

"Whew," Kitty said and turned the key.

She guided the BMW out of the garage, put the air conditioning on high, and took the south exit out of the airport onto I-55. Within fifteen minutes they were in Mississippi, passing the huge billboards for the giant gambling casinos along the Mississippi River in Tunica County.

"How'd everything go yesterday?" he asked.

Kitty told him about the crowd in the hallway, the Grand Jury indictments of Mule for felony murder and Trevor on the weapons charge. She described Trevor's inability to respond to Judge Williams.

"He had that stutter when he lived in Sunshine and played on our eleven and twelve-year-old team, when his father was in Parchman."

"I felt so sorry for him," Kitty said.

"He was small for his age, but tough, and a good baseball player. His aunt let him spend the night with me a couple of times. I always liked him. We rode bikes all over town. Scott got a new bike and Daddy had Scott's old bike repaired and gave it to Trevor."

Jake glanced at the speedometer. Kitty was driving eighty-seven.

"I guess you are in a hurry."

"Things to do," she said, pressing on the accelerator.

"May I make a suggestion?" He opened the glove box and pulled out a Mississippi map. "Let me show you a shortcut to the camp."

~ * ~

Jake woke up for the second time at eight-thirty Wednesday morning. The first time was at five-thirty, when Kitty aroused him from a deep sleep by tracing the scars on his chest with her index finger. Jake intended to look up on the web why his scar tissue was more sensitive than his regular skin, but he kept forgetting. He fell back asleep at seven, intending to nap another thirty minutes. It was unusual for him to sleep an hour past his wake up time, but he was all right with it, considering the situation.

He slipped out of the bed and tiptoed naked into the bathroom. Five minutes later he walked quietly out the front door onto the porch in his running shorts and a thin singlet. Jake sat on the top step and tied his shoes. He strapped his iPod Nano to his arm and took off on the dirt farm road in front of the duck camp. The air was warmer, more humid, but cleaner than D.C. Jake was glad the cotton around the duck camp had been defoliated and picked in the first two weeks of September. Inhaling defoliant always gave him a sinus infection.

The three farmers who used the duck camp road to get equipment to their farmland were through for the year, so there was no activity on the road this morning. No one in the fields, either. Jake's legs were rubbery, weak from yesterday's travel and the long night and early morning with

Kitty. He was thankful they were back together. In the three years they had known each other, it seemed they had already been through a lifetime of trouble.

Thirty-five minutes later, Jake bounded onto the porch and sat in the wooden swing. He checked his watch. The seven minute pace was slow, no doubt due to pre-run activity with Kitty. One of the things he wanted to focus on while in Sunshine was stretching his aerobic limits through faster runs and longer swims. The swimming he would do in local lakes to simulate real life situations. It wasn't likely that any of his future DOGs missions would involve swimming in chlorinated pools.

Jake planned on doing some strength training and yoga or pilates for flexibility, as well as work on his marksmanship and hand-to-hand fighting, if he could find someone to spar with. He heard the front porch screen door creak.

"You're supposed to be on vacation," Kitty said, her voice sleepy. "You want a cup of coffee?"

"If you're making some I will. Otherwise I'll get some in town."

"You can't go into Sunshine until later this morning," she said. "Remember. You didn't fly into Memphis until this morning. What time is it anyway?"

"Nine-thirty," he said.

"Mule's arraignment isn't until two this afternoon."

"I want to stop by the house first."

Kitty wrapped her thin cotton robe around her and walked onto the porch. She threw Jake a towel, sat down on the swing and yawned. Jake pushed off the cypress floor planks with his Saucony running shoes, moving the swing slowly, back and forth, wiping down.

"Hot," he said, still sweating.

He removed his singlet and dried himself.

"You're not supposed to play with my scars when I'm sleeping."

"I couldn't help it," she said. "I didn't think it would wake you up."

"Bull. You knew it would."

She yawned and nodded. "You're right. I'm lying."

"You wanted to wake me up."

"I did."

They kissed on the swing, gently at first, then with passion. She rubbed his chest, outlining the scar in the shape of an eye above his sternum. Jake drew back from her. Kitty moved and her robe fell open. He picked her up, opened the screen door and walked through the camp to her bedroom. On the bed, he kissed the scars Smokey and Panik carved on her stomach in her Marigny apartment in New Orleans, then her breasts, then her lips.

Sunshine can wait.

~ * ~

On her way to check in at the Sheriff's office, Kitty dropped Jake off at the Banks home a little before noon. He checked the kitchen and Willie Mitchell and Susan's room. No one home. Jake guessed that Willie Mitchell was at the court house helping Walton get ready for Mule's arraignment. No telling where Susan was. He walked up the stairs, inhaling the familiar smell of the spray starch Ina used. He stood in the doorway of the upstairs room where Susan worked on her computer and Ina ironed. Ina was singing as she pressed one of Willie Mitchell's blue oxford cloth shirts. When Ina took a break from her Gospel tune he clapped.

"Bravo," he said.

Ina whirled with her iron held high.

"I come in peace," Jake said, his hands up.

"You trying to give me a heart attack, ain't you?"

Jake walked in and hugged Ina. She smiled, only for a moment.

"I thought you would be here for lunch," she said.

"I wasn't sure myself when I would arrive," he said.

"I was going to make some corn bread and fry some pork chops late this morning to surprise you. Your Mama and them don't tell me nuthin' anymore."

"You know where they are now?"

"Nope," Ina said.

"You can still cook the corn bread and chops if you want. We can keep them in the oven until dinner. Kitty's eating dinner with us. She loves your home cooking."

"Nope. I'm leaving in a few minutes. Let me get to the kitchen and make sure we have everything. Your Mama will have to cook supper."

She patted Jake, then squeezed his arm.

"You sure do have muscles now," she said. "Not soft like Scott."

Jake tapped his temple with his index finger.

"Scott's muscles are more powerful than mine. He uses his brain."

"I don't recall you being no dummy."

Ina walked slowly down the stairs holding the rail. Jake remembered when she could walk up or down the steps with an armload of clothes or bedding without holding on to anything. In his mind when he was away, Ina never changed. She was always busy or on the move from one room to the other, ornery but on top of everything. Today he realized Ina was growing old.

He closed the door to his room and laid his carry-on bag on the carpeted floor next to his bed. The room had changed little since Jake was in junior high. His high school trophies filled the shelf over his desk along with novels and non-fiction he read in junior high. Jake reached up and pulled down his outdated copy of *Guinness' Book of World Records*. He thumbed through it and put it back on the shelf. He looked over some of his other books: *Lord of the Flies*, *Chariots of the Gods, Animal Farm, Cosmos.*

Jake glanced at the time. He needed to check his weapons before Susan or Willie Mitchell came home. Jake pulled out a small Glock 36 from his bottom dresser drawer. He checked to make sure it was loaded and placed it back in its leather holster under his Ole Miss sweatshirts.

Jake looked under his bed and grabbed a sawed-off Ithaca 37 shotgun with a pistol grip. It rested on two metal hooks on a side rail under the slat supports. He installed the hooks when he was home recovering from the injuries he received from Brujo in New Orleans.

Jake ejected three twelve gauge shells, reloaded and replaced the shotgun on the hooks. He crawled under his desk to make sure his KA-BAR knife was in the sleeve he screwed to the underside of the drawer.

Jake heard Ina say loudly from downstairs that she was leaving. Jake opened the door to his room and told her he'd see her tomorrow. She told Jake to make sure he put "all them damned guns" up so Susan wouldn't find them, and warned him in a loud voice not to shoot himself fooling with them.

"Okay, Ina," he yelled back.

Jake pulled out the folding step stool from his closet and stood on its top step to open the large cabinet above the closet. He pulled down three long plastic cases and a large black tote bag.

The first case contained his Colt M4 Carbine, the next an H&K 416 assault rifle Hound gave him after a weapons training session in Florida. The third case held a Mossberg 590 shotgun, a present from Dunne after Jake was officially added to the DOGs team.

Jake smiled at Dunne's mantra inscribed on the barrel.

You Never Know.

The black tote bag held the weapons Dunne left with him in his New Orleans apartment before the raid on Brujo's headquarters: a Glock 30 and a Glock 21, both .45 caliber, a couple of frag grenades, three flashbang grenades, a machete, two SOG knives, night vision goggles, and a good supply of ammunition for every weapon he owned. Also in the black tote was Jake's Stainless Steel Colt XSE .45 caliber 1911. It was not part of the arsenal Dunne left Jake in New Orleans.

Jake checked the weapons quickly and put them back into the tote. He returned the three gun cases and the tote to the cabinet above the closet. The only gun he kept out was the Colt XSE. Jake ejected the Colt's magazine. He inspected the rounds and the chamber before inserting the magazine back into the gun.

Six months earlier, Jake decided on the Colt XSE 1911 as his primary handgun, replacing the Sig Sauer P229 he had carried for three years. He liked the stopping power of the .45 caliber, and the Colt felt more natural in his hand. More importantly, he shot more accurately with the Colt. He owned two. He kept one in Sunshine, one he carried in D.C. He did the same thing with the two Glock 36's he owned—one for D.C., one at home.

Jake went downstairs to the kitchen to find something to eat before heading to the court house to watch the arraignment. He made a mental note to go to the Sheriff's practice range with Kitty in a few days. Shooting was a perishable skill. Now that he was a DOG, he wanted to stay sharp.

Chapter Twenty-Five

Jake drove to the courthouse in the 1995 red Ford F150 the Banks family referred to as "the farm truck." In a compromise with Susan, Willie Mitchell kept it behind the garage under a big Water Oak where it could not be seen from the street or the back porch. Susan said Willie Mitchell only drove it when he wanted to play farmer, driving on the dusty or muddy turn rows through the 990 acres he leased to the Hudson brothers. Jake thought it was running a little rough, but it was clean and it fit the bill for him to use while he was in Sunshine except for one thing: the air conditioner blew hot air. He was grateful he could wear jeans and a light blue Polo knit shirt to watch Mule's arraignment.

Jake walked into court and sat on the second row behind the prosecutor's table. Walton Donaldson stood behind the table addressing Judge Williams. Willie Mitchell sat next to Walton.

"Your honor this is just an arraignment we set for this afternoon at the request of Mr. Summit to accommodate his schedule. We're not prepared to go into...."

"Hold on, Mr. Donaldson," Judge Williams said. "Let's hear Mr. Summit out."

"Thank you, Your Honor," Summit said, continuing.

Jake had seen Jordan Summit standing in front of the giant $100 bills on his television spots, but this was the first time he had seen him in person. He was much shorter and stockier than Jake expected, and his jet black hair was off-putting, as were his ads. Jake could tell from his presentation he was an intelligent lawyer at the top of his game. He didn't understand why Summit had to run the sleazy ads and chase no-win civil cases like Mule Gardner's.

Mule sat enveloped in a wheelchair behind the defense table with Eleanor Bernstein. Jake had known Eleanor for some time, and was impressed with her capabilities and her attention to detail, in spite of the hopeless nature of her indigent clientele. Eleanor wore a dark suit this morning, well-fitted to her slender physique. There wasn't much of Mule showing above the backrest of the wheelchair, which seemed to Jake to be much too big for Mule. Mule was clean-shaven and his hair cut short. He wore a long-sleeved white shirt that also swallowed him, but he looked much more presentable than the last time Jake saw him in his feathered straw hat and Saints jersey, pushing his grocery cart on the shoulder of the four-lane highway that was now Sunshine's *de facto* business district. Mule appeared almost child-like in his oversized shirt and wheelchair. Jake thought Jordan Summit might have orchestrated the look to generate sympathy for Mule as a small, powerless victim facing not only the full force of the State's prosecutorial machinery, but also a little guy battling Gas & Go Fast corporation and their insurance company in the civil suit for damages.

"Let's back up a second," Judge Williams said, interrupting Summit. "Before we get into all these other issues let's have Mr. Gardner enter his plea to the Grand Jury indictment, then I'll hear what you and Mr. Donaldson have to say on these other issues."

"Very well, Your Honor," he said.

"Mr. Bordelon, will you hand me the bill of indictment, please?"

The small, bald deputy clerk gave her a document and whispered something to the Judge.

"Most definitely, Mr. Bordelon. I'll wait." She watched the clerk put on his slender earphone set and fiddle with the recording apparatus on his desk. "We're having a slight technical problem," she said to the parties. "Mr. Bordelon wants to make sure the recording equipment is picking up everything."

Jake and everyone else in the courtroom focused on Eddie Bordelon making adjustments on the machine. The clerk listened intently for a moment, and nodded to Judge Williams.

"Let's proceed with the reading of the bill of indictment," she said.

Jordan Summit began to move Mule's wheelchair.

"That's not necessary, Mr. Summit," Judge Williams said. "Mr. Gardner may enter his plea from where he is."

"In the matter of State of Mississippi versus Lester Gardner," Judge Williams read from the document, "bill of indictment number 11-3424 charges that on or about September 15 of this year in the City of Sunshine, County of Yaloquena, Lester Gardner did commit murder by killing Abdul Azeem while in the commission of a non-enumerated felony as set forth in Section 1, paragraph C of Section 97-3-19 of the Mississippi Criminal Code of 1972 as amended, namely aggravated battery with a dangerous weapon." Judge Williams looked down at Mule and Summit. "To which charge how does the defendant plead?"

Mule looked up at his lawyer. Summit whispered in Mule's ear. Mule answered the Judge in a loud voice.

"Not guilty, Judge."

"Very well. Let the record so reflect. Mr. Summit, Mr. Donaldson, do we have any motions? You first Mr. Donaldson."

"Not at this time, Your Honor," Walton said.

"Now, Mr. Summit," she said.

"Thank you, Your Honor."

Summit gestured to Eleanor, who delivered a stack of motions to Walton and Willie Mitchell. Jake watched his Daddy and Walton scan the first page of each filing and turn it over. Jake counted ten.

"The first motions are for discovery purposes, Your Honor," Summit said. "Bill of Particulars, Witness Statements, Results of Scientific Analysis, Motion to Suppress the Defendant's Statements, if any such statements exist and the State intends to use them at trial, and another routine motion or two. Additionally, Your Honor, there are other non-discovery motions that Ms. Bernstein and I are filing this morning, on which I would like to be heard briefly."

"Let's first hear from the State on the discovery motions," Judge Williams said. "Mr. Donaldson?"

"We will answer these discovery motions right away, Your Honor," Walton said. "We've already made arrangements for Mr. Summit to pick up a copy of a video disk from the crime lab that we intend to offer."

"That's correct, Your Honor," Summit said, popping up from his seat. "I picked it up yesterday. And let me add that the District Attorney's Office has been very forthcoming with the defense in already producing evidentiary matters that we have included in the motions."

"We will have our answers to these discovery motions finished by the end of this week, Your Honor," Walton said. "We don't anticipate any dispute over the production of the matters requested by the defense."

"Your Honor," Summit said, remaining on his feet. "In light of the State's cooperation in discovery, I'd like to file this Motion for a Speedy Trial and would ask the Court to consider using this opportunity to set an early trial date. Ms Bernstein and I have brought our calendars to coordinate with Mr. Donaldson and Mr. Banks."

"We don't object to the speedy trial request," Walton said, looking down at Willie Mitchell. "Judge Williams, we have a criminal jury term before Thanksgiving, starting on the 7th. I know what cases are already docketed for that term and I don't anticipate any of them going to trial. Most will plead or continue. We have no objection to setting the case for trial November 7, if that's suitable for the defense."

"A moment to consult, Your Honor," Summit said and sat down quickly to huddle with Eleanor. He stood up. "The 7th is acceptable to us Your Honor, and we do not anticipate the need for any continuances."

"All right," the Judge said, "I cannot remember when this Court has set this serious a criminal case for trial on such an ambitious schedule, but since both parties agree, I will reserve the date. Mr. Donaldson, Mr. Summit, State versus Gardner is first on the docket on November 7 at 9:00 a.m. Anything else?"

"One moment please, Your Honor," Summit said.

Summit sat down to confer with Eleanor. Jake used the time to scan the courtroom. He was the only person on the prosecution side except for an older woman on the back row Jake recognized as a perennial courtroom observer from the Tax Assessor's office. On the defense side of the center aisle, there were four black men in suits in the first row. The only one he recognized was Bobby Sanders, who wore his dark gray suit and the white collar that made him look like a Catholic priest. Based on what Kitty and Willie Mitchell had told him, the others had to be from Freedmen's Creek.

One was a small man with oversized spectacles, no doubt the one Walton referred to as Tweety Bird. The next man was a giant, the bodyguard Kitty described. The third man was much older than the other two. He wore his hair parted on one side, straightened and slicked down. Jake could not see his face clearly except to note he wore rimless glasses and a bow tie. Jake couldn't remember the name of Tweety Bird, but he did recall Kitty saying the bodyguard was named Samson. Jake knew the older man was the leader, Mohammed X.

On the fourth row behind the Freedmen's Creek crew, there was a white man Jake guessed was in his early fifties. He was big, over six feet and two hundred plus pounds. He turned and smiled broadly at Jake when Jake first walked in. The man's hair was mostly gray. When Jake was in the center aisle on the way to his seat he noticed the back of the man's hair was braided and stuffed inside the brown corduroy sport coat he wore. Jake deduced two things: the man wanted to conceal his pony tail inside his jacket to be less conspicuous; and the man had to be hot as blazes in that coat. The man also wore a high-collared white shirt buttoned all the way to the top.

"Your Honor," Jordan Summit said, "we are filing at this time a Motion To Compel the District Attorney to present the Gas & Go Fast shooting case to a new Grand Jury so the charges against Trevor Brewer can be reconsidered."

Walton jumped up but Judge Williams gestured for him to hold on.

"You may file such a motion, Mr. Summit, but you and Ms. Bernstein know it is not in my power to grant such relief. The District Attorney has the sole constitutional authority in this county to decide whom to charge with what. I can no more order Mr. Banks to do what you request than I can order you to file or not file certain pleadings."

"I would ask for a hearing on this motion," Summit said.

"Denied. I don't need to hear any testimony or read any briefs. Here is my ruling. This motion is denied based on the Mississippi State Constitution. Anything else?"

"Please note an assignment of error to the Court's ruling."

Judge Williams nodded to Eddie Bordelon. "Duly noted," she said.

"Anything else, Mr. Summit?" Judge Williams asked.

"Ms. Bernstein is handing to the Court at this time a Motion to Produce the nine millimeter Smith & Wesson in the custody of the State so that defense experts may examine it."

"Objection," Walton said. "That weapon is at the crime lab your honor and we object to it leaving the custody of the lab. If Mr. Summit wishes to have his ballistics experts test fire and examine the weapon, they are welcome to do so at the crime lab."

"Mr. Summit?"

"We want to have the weapon examined and tested by the lab of our choosing, Your Honor, without the crime lab personnel looking over their shoulder."

"May we approach, Your Honor?" Walton asked.

Judge Williams nodded. Jake watched as Walton, Summit, and Eleanor stood directly before the bench discussing the motion. Judge Williams, probably out of habit since there was no jury, cupped her palm over the small microphone on her bench. Jake thought the examination of the weapon that fired the fatal shot was something that could easily be worked out to the satisfaction of each party, until he heard Summit name the lab he had chosen to examine the S & W.

"We would like the FBI Criminalistics Lab in the J.Edgar Hoover building in Washington, D.C. to examine the weapon, Your Honor," Summit said, back at the defense table.

Jake watched Willie Mitchell whisper to Walton. Walton stood.

"Your Honor, the State would like time to consider the defense request and file an appropriate response."

Judge Williams appeared puzzled.

"Mr. Donaldson, is there any reason the State would object to the FBI examining the weapon? If it is a question of possibly delaying the trial, I could certainly understand your position because my experience is that sending a piece of evidence to the FBI does not produce a quick turnaround. They ignore our time constraints and take their own sweet time doing their work and reporting."

Summit jumped up. "Your Honor, the District Attorney's office does not want the United States Government to have possession of the gun."

"That's out of line," Walton said. "The defense has blindsided us with this motion and we've barely had time...,"

"Hold on, Mr. Donaldson," she said and turned to Summit. "Do you know how long it will take the FBI to examine and test it?"

"I am told no more than two weeks," Summit said.

"Who told you that?" Judge Williams asked.

"A high ranking official at DOJ," Summit said. "He's head of the Office of Inspector General and former U.S. Attorney in Jackson."

Son of a bitch. Summit's been talking to Leopold Whitman.

"I know Leopold Whitman," the Judge said. "In fact, I've spent too much time in this courtroom with Leopold Whitman. Why would Leopold Whitman and DOJ take such an interest in this gun?"

"It is my understanding, Your Honor," Summit said, "that the Department of Justice is looking at the Gas & Go Fast shooting as possibly a civil rights deprivation case they might be willing to prosecute. They may have other reasons to which I am not privy."

Jake watched Willie Mitchell lean back in his chair and look at the ceiling. Jake knew exactly what he was thinking. This was a bunch of bull shit. Willie Mitchell had told Jake about the ATF Agent's visit to the Sunshine courtroom. Judge Williams turned her executive style leather chair to face the wall behind her, then spun back to face Jordan Summit.

"Whose civil rights were allegedly deprived, Mr. Summit?" she asked. "I guess Mr. Azeem's?"

"I believe that would be correct, Your Honor."

"We object and request time to respond, Your Honor," Walton said.

"You two agree on a time for a hearing," she said, "and I would suggest sooner rather than later. Unless there's something else, I believe I've heard enough for one day."

Summit barely had time to say the defense had no more motions before Judge Williams banged her gavel and left the bench.

Jake watched Bobby Sanders and the Freedmen's Creek trio rise in response to the bailiff's call to stand for the Judge's exit. They walked into the center aisle to leave. For the first time, Jake saw Mohammed X's face full on. Jake felt a rush.

I've seen him before. I know I have.

Jake knew better than to ignore his intuition. The facial recognition software hardwired into his brain was uncannily accurate, unlike the software DOGs administrator Billy Gillmon said the FBI and Homeland Security had been working on unsuccessfully for years. Everyone at the meeting laughed when Gillmon said the only place facial recognition software worked was on CSI and Mission Impossible.

Jake didn't need help from a computer. Once he saw a face or even a photograph of a person, the image seemed indelibly etched in his mind. Jake didn't think it logical that he had seen the man before, but the feeling was strong. Sometime in the past, Jake and Mohammed X crossed paths.

~ * ~

Freddy Brewer left the courtroom before anyone else. Outside in the hallway, he waited against the wall next to the Coke machine near the public bathroom. He could see everyone leave the courtroom, but they couldn't see him. Freddy watched the four black men walk out into the hallway and head toward the Coke machine. They stopped outside the bathroom when the older man asked the others to wait while he stopped in the men's room.

Leaning against the wall partially obscured from their vision by the Coke machine, Freddy removed his phone from his coat pocket and pretended to send a text, keeping his eyes down and focused on the message. He was no more than ten feet from the three men waiting on the older one in the bathroom. He listened closely as he typed in nonsensical strings of letters.

"Do you think Mohammed X was pleased with the proceedings?" the black man with the white collar said to the one with the big glasses.

"I believe so, Reverend Sanders," big glasses said. "It appears the defense attorney has taken the first step in holding the true guilty party responsible."

"That's the first time I've seen Jordan Summit in court," Sanders said. "He's very good. If anyone can get the Judge to focus on the Brewer boy, I think Mr. Summit can."

Freddy listened intently as he continued hitting random letters.

"I know Mohammed X," big glasses said, "if this woman judge refuses to see this as the racist killing it is, our leader will insist we seek justice ourselves."

"I listened carefully to what he said last Friday out at Freedmen's Creek," Bobby said. "I believe he means business."

Freddy heard the bathroom door open. He did not look up, continuing to send the imaginary text. The four men walked past him and out the door, down the stairs to the first floor.

Freddy closed his phone and walked outside. On the sidewalk in front of the court house he made three calls. He spoke to two men, left a message for the third.

"Get your ass down here right now," is what he told each of them.

Chapter Twenty-Six

Willie Mitchell was dragging.

He stayed up too late visiting with Jake and Kitty after dinner the night before. Susan cooked the pork chops and corn bread Ina had prepared, and the four of them caught up on everything, except what Jake was up to. Jake kept his explanations vague, never shooting straight with what was going on with Dunne's outfit and what Patrick Dunwoody had him doing at DOJ.

They all knew Jake was sworn to secrecy, but the covert nature of his life was getting to Susan. Kitty seemed all right with knowing the bare minimum. She was Quantico-trained and accustomed to being on a "need to know" basis in her FBI duties. Willie Mitchell was so grateful to Dunne for rescuing Jake in New Orleans, and saving Jake and him in the Jackson Reservoir, he was willing to suspend his curiosity about his oldest son's new organization. Deputy A.G. Patrick Dunwoody's buttonholing Willie Mitchell at the Jefferson Hotel and having him to breakfast at Dunwoody's D.C. *pied a terre* had gone a long way to calm Willie Mitchell's nerves about David Dunne's organization, the need for Jake's involvement, and the importance to the security of the country.

It wasn't Susan's fault that she was distraught about Jake. She was his mother, and Willie Mitchell knew there was no stronger human bond on the planet. Willie Mitchell was close to both Jake and Scott, loved them dearly, but because of the nature of men, he knew he could never be as close as Susan was to her sons. She gave birth to them, gave them life. To be sure, Willie Mitchell made his genetic contribution, but Susan carried each boy in her body for forty weeks, fed them with milk from her breasts for another six months, then spent almost every waking hour with them until they entered first grade. No wonder she cried more than they did on the steps of the elementary school. Like Jimmy Gray said about the chicken and the pig and their relationship to a ham and egg breakfast. The chicken was involved, but the pig was committed.

Putting one foot in front of the other, Willie Mitchell struggled through the run. Even the shuffle function on his Nano seemed to be conspiring against him, suppressing the upbeat songs. Jake said he was going to get up early and do five or six miles at a six minute pace before Willie Mitchell started. Jake planned to run Willie Mitchell's four mile route with him, regardless of the slow pace. Willie Mitchell said there was no way Jake could run as slow as he did these days.

Jake joined his father at the one mile mark.

"How far'd you go?" Willie Mitchell asked.

"Six, I think."

"I heard you stirring around upstairs. It was early."

"I woke up at four-thirty and did an hour of plyometrics in the garage."

"Don't feel like you have to stick with me."

"This is fine. Let's me cool down. How's your leg holding up?"

"It does all right most days. Tell you the truth it usually hurts more in bed or at the office than when I'm walking or running. I guess it likes to keep moving."

Willie Mitchell struggled to pick up his pace. After pushing it for another mile, he was ready to coast in.

"Jake, you go on ahead. I need to slow down. Missing my music."

"You sure?"

"Yes. I'm embarrassed making you run at this speed. Tell you what, meet me at Jimmy Gray's driveway for his fifteen minute walk. He'll get a charge out of your joining us."

Jake took off like a shot. Willie Mitchell slowed down and tried to think about anything other than what he was doing. Two miles later, he jogged into Jimmy Gray's driveway, thanking God it was over.

"About time," Jimmy Gray said. "Jake and I were about to take off without your slowpoke skinny butt."

Willie Mitchell chuckled. Jimmy wore bright red nylon trunks that hung loosely below his knees and a tee shirt with ASK ME ABOUT MY HEMORRHOIDS printed across the front.

"Nice shirt," Willie Mitchell said.

"Keeps the civilians at a distance when I'm training."

Jake laughed.

"Let's get going," Willie Mitchell said.

"You sure you can hang with us, boy?" Jimmy Gray asked Jake.

"Do my best," Jake said.

"When you get in as good a shape as I am," Jimmy said, "you won't have to do all that speed work. You can cut down on your distance, too."

Willie Mitchell re-set his watch and they started walking.

"I cannot believe Eleanor is going to run next year," Jake said. "You said you haven't asked her point blank yet."

"I haven't," Willie Mitchell said, "but I know she's the one."

"I did some nosing around," Jimmy said. "I've got some good customers go to Bobby's church. Bobby's got her running all right."

"Damn," Jake said.

"She's got nothing to lose," Willie Mitchell said. "And who knows, she might not have an opponent."

~ * ~

- 128 -

They dropped Jimmy Gray off at his house and walked home.

"Jimmy's shirt was soaking wet," Jake said.

"I know it. I'm trying my best to help, but he cannot lose weight."

"He's going to have a heart attack."

"You'd think so, but Jimmy's father was a big man, too. He smoked and drank and lived into his eighties." Willie Mitchell tapped Jake on the arm as they reached their house. "Walk another block or two with me. I want to talk to you."

They passed by the pea gravel circular drive and the hedges that gave the Banks privacy from passing motorists on their corner lot.

"I need you to do a couple of things for me while you're home."

"Sure," Jake said.

"I don't know if this creates some kind of conflict or violates some kind of oath or code you took."

"Why don't you tell me what it is and I'll do it if I can."

"Okay. I want you to go see Trevor Brewer."

"Any particular reason?"

"He's our star witness in the Azeem shooting and he was so nervous at the bail hearing last Monday he couldn't get a word out."

"Anything you want me to ask him?"

"No," Willie Mitchell said. "This is strictly personal. I remember when he played ball on our team. He used to follow you around. Other day he asked about you. Makes me think he looks up to you. We sure could use his cooperation. Maybe you can help."

"You want me to talk to him about testifying?"

"I guess, if it comes up naturally. Tell him the video disk pretty much lays everything out. There's not going to be too much we're going to ask him. Maybe warn him about cross-examination, tell him just answer the questions asked, don't volunteer anything. Most of all, see if you can put him at ease about the whole thing."

"I'll do it," Jake said. "I'll try to get over to Dundee County today. What's the other thing?"

"Be sure to stop by Tom's Automotive shop and talk to his dad before you go up the hill. The second thing I need is substantive."

"Freedmen's Creek," Jake said.

Willie Mitchell stopped walking for a second and stared at Jake.

"How did you know that?"

"Common sense," Jake said. "You said last night you don't know anything about the victim, this Abdul Azeem and his connection with Freedmen's Creek."

"Exactly. He was born Joseph Randall according to the Prince William County name change petition."

"I can check him out. No problem."

"And I need you to find out what you can about Freedmen's Creek. That commune popped up in the woods out there within the last two years and no one knows anything about what they do or how they support themselves. I get the feeling Mohammed X and Abud are stalking us. Abud's been in my office twice, and his boss once. They both showed up for arraignment yesterday with man mountain...."

"And Bobby Sanders. What's his angle?"

"Anything to stir the crap and make himself feel important. He's the one responsible for Eleanor getting into the race."

"I don't imagine he came out and said that."

"He told me he's gotten a commitment from a qualified black lawyer to run. Eleanor's body language told me the rest."

"I'm still not sure that's going to happen."

"Right now I don't really care. I'm supposed to be easing into senior status and here I am in the middle of all this."

"At least Walton's first chair."

"Right. I don't have to worry about seizing up in the middle of a question."

"You had any lately?"

"Couple of weeks ago. I was watching the last few minutes of Alabama and Florida play in The Swamp. Next thing I know, they're walking off the field. It's weird the way it happens."

"Lee's office know anything about Freedmen's Creek?"

"No. They've never had a call out there. It takes money to run a place like that, and I want you to find out the source if you can. What goes on in the commune, too. Lee checked with the school board and Freedmen's Creek has an approved home school curriculum for all the kids. Maybe something you turn up will help us figure out why they're so dead set on us charging Trevor?"

"You know anything about Mohammed X? His real name?"

"Not a thing."

"Fairly certain I've seen him or his photograph before."

"Where?" Willie Mitchell asked as they walked up the front steps of the Banks home to the porch.

"No idea. I'll get started on this today," Jake said. "By the way, did you see the guy yesterday in the brown corduroy sport coat three rows behind Bobby Sanders and the others? Gray hair, big guy?"

"I saw him. I don't have a clue who he is."

Chapter Twenty-Seven

At two that afternoon, Jake stepped out of the farm truck and walked into Tom's Automotive. He thought it was better to show up unannounced. Susan always said it was easier to get forgiveness than permission.

The woman in the office was nice looking. Long dark hair and high cheekbones, Jake thought she might be early thirties or so, with American Indian blood in her lineage. She walked to the counter, all business. Jake glanced at her tight jeans and the cotton shirt stretched tight across her chest.

"I know you," she said.

Jake read her name on her shirt. She did look familiar. He didn't know how it was possible, but he had seen her face before.

"You're Tracy."

"No shit, Sherlock. Easy to figure out when it's plastered across my chest."

Jake laughed. Finally Tracy smiled.

"You used to play high school basketball in Kilbride. You were on the Sunshine Academy team."

It clicked. She flirted with him in the Kilbride gym after one of their games. She was older, and Jake was flattered.

"The trophy case at the entrance to the gym. We talked."

"You were shy," she said. "You married now?"

"No. But I've got a steady girl friend."

"Lucky girl. What are you doing over this way?"

He extended his hand. "I'm Jake Banks. I'm an old friend of Trevor's. Wanted to see him if I could."

A shadow passed over Tracy's face. She withdrew her hand without shaking his. Jake knew that was the end of the banter.

"You're the District Attorney's son. You look like him."

"Yep. Trevor played two seasons of Little League with me in Sunshine. Willie Mitchell was the coach."

"Now he's trying to send Trevor down the river. Some coach."

"That's not exactly so. And I'm not here on business."

Tracy walked to intercom and called for Tom.

In a little over a minute, Trevor's father walked from the garage into the office, wiping his oily hands on a dark red rag.

"This is that Sunshine D.A.'s son," Tracy said.

Tom glanced at Jake for a moment then looked down.

"They favor," Tom said.

"I wanted to see Trevor," Jake said. "We used to be friends."

"I know. Better'n fifteen years since you Banks people been around Trevor. Now, you and your Daddy cain't seem to get enough of us Brewers."

Jake heard Tracy mumble "damned right." He turned to catch her smirking as if Jake were getting what was coming to him. Jake decided to wait Tom out. After an awkward minute, Tom spoke.

"What for?"

"This isn't about the case. I figure Trevor could use a friend right now. Could you call him?"

Tom thought a minute.

"Call up there, Tracy and tell'em this boy's comin' up."

"How will I find him?" Jake asked.

"Don't worry," Tom said. "He'll find you." He turned to go back into the garage. Tracy hadn't moved. "Call'em, I said."

Tracy moved quickly to the phone.

~ * ~

Jake gunned the farm truck up the dirt and gravel hill. Willie Mitchell hadn't mentioned how steep the grade was. Jake could see how it made the Brewers inaccessible to casual passers-by, aiding their isolation. To get on Brewer Hill, you really had to want to be there.

When the farm truck came over the crest of the hill, Jake was surprised at how the terrain flattened. He slowed down and the dust he stirred up on the climb caught up with him. Jake rolled his window up to keep out what dirt he could.

He stopped in the middle of the field and waited. A GMC pickup truck appeared out of the trees, picking up speed on a trail between two dilapidated buildings, heading toward Jake. The driver's left arm was in a blue sling against his chest.

Trevor. Except for the goatee he looks the same.

Jake stepped out of the farm truck. Trevor grabbed Jake's extended hand and pumped it, a giant smile across his face.

"Jake Banks. When they s-said you was comin' up I thought they w-was lying. Now I see you here and I still c-cain't hardly believe it."

Jake nodded and laughed. He was truly happy to see Trevor. He always liked him. At the same time, he always felt sorry for him.

"That's some hill," Jake said.

"K-keeps out the r-riff-raff." Trevor laughed loud. "C-come on. Let's ride to my place in your truck. They won't b-bother m-mine here in the *cummins*. Might yours."

Jake was glad Willie Mitchell mentioned the commons. He thought about his decision to leave his Colt XSE at home. If what everyone said about the Brewer sharpshooters were true, the handgun would have been of little use anyway. Supposedly the Brewer marksmen could pick him off with their rifles at quite a distance. That was part of the lore. Jake didn't know if they could or not. Maybe he'd ask Trevor.

"You drive," Jake said. He climbed into the passenger seat and rolled down the window. "Air conditioning is out."

Trevor nodded and cranked the engine. He revved it, turning his head to listen to the engine, then revved it again. Trevor put it in gear and drove between the old log buildings, which Jake now saw were abandoned and falling down. There were gaping jagged holes where windows used to be. Trevor followed the one-lane trail winding through the trees.

"Nice timber," Jake said. "And those oaks on either side of the road coming up the hill must be a hundred years old."

Trevor smiled. "You bet."

He parked in front of the smallest of three wooden cabins, reached across his body with his right arm and opened the door. Jake met him in front of the truck. Trevor tapped the hood.

"N-needs a tune up. Be glad to d-do it for you."

Trevor gestured for Jake to follow him inside. Jake was pleasantly surprised. It was rustic and small, but very clean.

"Nice bachelor pad," Jake said, "assuming you're single."

Trevor nodded. "You?"

"Got a girl friend. FBI agent. She's was up on this hill last week with Willie Mitchell."

"I met her. She's real pretty."

"Smart, too. Not much of a cook."

"She can l-learn to cook. Cain't l-learn to be pretty," Trevor said and led Jake into the next room. It took a minute for Jake to realize he was staring around the room with his mouth open. There were posters of metal and rock bands covering the walls, along with framed records and autographed photos of rock stars.

"Damn," Jake said. "Impressive."

"I've got every one of Slayer's albums. S-sabbath. Maiden, too."

Jake noticed Trevor's stutter almost disappeared when he talked about his music.

"You started me on it. You gave me those tapes and that t-tape player. Remember?"

Jake did remember.

"I've got a b-band. Brewer Hill Skins. We've been playing f-five years now. Listen."

Trevor slipped an unlabeled CD out of a plain white sleeve and fed it into the CD player on a homemade, rough-hewn table. They stood in silence for a moment. Jake jumped when the music blared from the speakers on the wall. Trevor chuckled and turned down the volume. They listened for a few minutes. Trevor moved from track to track, commenting on the song as he went.

"Who's the singer?" Jake asked. "He's good."

Trevor pointed his thumb at his chest.

"I don't st-stutter when I sing."

Trevor turned the music lower and led Jake out of the music room. He grabbed two Budweisers from his small refrigerator. They sat on the front porch and sipped the Buds. Trevor's screaming on the CD was more tolerable with the front door closed.

"Nice view," Jake said, pointing to hills in the distance. "Those are mountains by Mississippi standards."

Trevor took a long drink from the Bud.

"I d-didn't mean to k-kill him, Jake."

"I know you didn't. So does Daddy. If it weren't for your gun being stolen out of Oklahoma you wouldn't have been charged with anything."

Jake could tell Trevor didn't want to talk about it. Jake took a sip and saw two men appear in the center of the clearing in front of the three cabins. They carried rifles. Jake could not imagine how they got there from the trees without his seeing or hearing them. They wore jeans and green and brown camouflage shirts and caps. One was barefoot.

"Stay h-here," Trevor said and walked off the porch to the men. Trevor looked down at the dirt and listened to the two men. Jake tried but couldn't make out a thing any of them said. Nobody smiled. Trevor stepped back and emphatically flipped the back of his hand at the men. Jake figured Trevor was telling them to get out of his clearing.

The two men lingered for a moment, then walked off without making a sound. Trevor rejoined Jake on the porch.

"Y-you best be going."

Whatever the two men said, Jake could tell Trevor took them seriously. It was time to leave.

"I'll r-ride to the *c-cummins* with you."

The stutter was back. Jake gave his empty beer can to Trevor, who threw his and Jake's into the burn pit next to the house. Jake cranked the farm truck and followed the trail through the trees. Trevor gestured for Jake to drive past the GMC truck parked in the center of the field. Jake stopped at the crest of the hill. Trevor got out and leaned into the farm truck through the open passenger window. Jake wrote his cell number on a small note pad from the glove compartment.

"This is my cell number. Call me if you want to talk about anything. We don't have to talk about the case. If you do want some tips on how to answer questions or anything in court, I can help. You're not going to have any trouble with Daddy's questions or his assistant. The defense lawyer might try to trip you up."

Trevor said his cell number and Jake entered it into his phone.

"I may n-not need your h-help," Trevor said.

Jake could sense the anguish Trevor felt at the idea of testifying.

"May not do it," Trevor said.

Jake didn't like the way Trevor said it. He wasn't kidding.

"Come on, man," Jake said. "Don't talk like that. You can do this. You don't have a choice. You have to appear. I'll help you."

"B-better go."

Jake said "call me anytime, Trevor. For anything."

Jake paused the farm truck on the edge of the hill for a moment. All he could see beyond the red hood were oak leaves and blue sky. It was exactly how he felt when he was a kid in Colorado mustering the courage to push himself over the edge to ski down a black slope. Jake put the truck in low gear and removed his foot from the brake a little at a time. The F150 moved in fits and finally tipped over the edge. He rode the brake to slow the truck to a comfortable speed. If the old Ford's brakes failed, Jake was toast.

A third of the way down the hill, Jake relaxed enough to take his eyes off the dirt and gravel. He glanced out the passenger window and caught a hint of flesh and a blue steel rifle barrel against a massive oak trunk. He thought he might have imagined it until he saw a shotgun barrel sticking out from behind a tree on his side of the truck less than a hundred yards downhill from the rifle.

Jesus. What's it like to grow up in a place like this? It's a wonder Trevor doesn't have more problems.

Jake breathed a sigh of relief when he stopped where the Brewer Hill dirt and gravel road teed into the paved highway. To his right, he saw Tracy Brewer in the parking lot of Tom's Automotive, fists on her hips, elbows out, staring at Jake. He waved but she didn't.

Jake turned left onto the pavement to head back to Sunshine. In his rear view mirror, he saw Tracy watching him drive away. She hadn't moved.

Chapter Twenty-Eight

Billy Gillmon was glad it was Friday. He didn't have a big weekend planned, but was pleased to have a day to catch up on work in his basement office in the Homeland Security Building at 7th Street S.W., not far from the metro station at L'Enfant Plaza. For the last month, Big Dog kept Helen Holmes and Gillmon going full speed on the logistics of the planning mission for Operation Camelot. Gillmon was proud of what he and Helen accomplished, including arranging travel for Big Dog, Dunne, and Doberman without generating a single phone call from any agency of the government. The three DOGs hitched a ride out of Andrews AFB bound for Ramstein Air Base near Kaiserslautern, Germany on a KC-135R Stratotanker assigned to the 459th Air Refueling Wing. The gigantic refueling tanker was participating in U.S. Air Force Europe's 86th Airlift Wing joint maneuvers with what was left of NATO Air Operations. With NATO Air deferring to the USAF whenever any problem arose in Europe and the Middle East, joint maneuvers with NATO were window dressing for the moribund alliance and a monumental waste of money for U.S. taxpayers. The only good coming out of the maneuvers was, in Gillmon's opinion, the transportation of his three "packages" to Ramstein, where it was easy for Gillmon to stow them without raising an eyebrow on one of the many daily USAFE flights between Ramstein Air Base and Royal Air Force station Lackenheath in Suffolk, about a hundred kilometers northwest of London.

Gillmon was sixty-six and Helen sixty-one. They were two-thirds of the entire DOGs management team. The third member was their boss, Big Dog. Gillmon had thirty-plus years with GAO and CBO internal audit teams and knew every operating system in almost every government agency, including their budgets. More importantly, he knew how to access the systems through wormholes he built after he discovered the covert entity retired General John Evanston, "Big Dog," was putting together and running out of the basement of Homeland Security. Gillmon approached Big Dog, told him about the wormholes, and offered his services. Big Dog immediately engineered Gillmon's transfer to his team.

Helen's husband Jules was a civilian employee burned to death in the Pentagon on 9/11. She had two grown children and six grand-children, plus an encyclopedic knowledge of people in each agency in the government. She was pretty, kept her silver hair short and wore black rimmed glasses. Gillmon was skinny, balding. With his rimless glasses he looked like a CPA from Central Casting. Gillmon was a self-taught computer genius who used his skills and his access to government systems to generate funding, investigate missions, and assist in planning operations. Helen did everything else, including getting information or favors from friends in federal agencies. Though her friends were unaware of DOGs, they knew and trusted Helen, and were willing to accommodate any reasonable request she made.

Helen was at her monthly lunch with girlfriends from USDA and Gillmon was by himself in the DOGs basement office when the phone rang. He had caught up on some of the work he let slide while arranging Camelot reconnaissance and was now on his computer tracking Big Dog's movements through London. The call came in on the line reserved exclusively for use by DOGs operatives.

"Hello, Mr. Gillmon," Jake said.

"How many times do I have to ask you to call me Billy?"

"Sorry, Billy. I need to ask you something."

Gillmon recognized the tone in Jake's voice as the same Gillmon's daughter used on occasion when she was a teenager.

"What do you need?"

"I've been online and I think I've narrowed it down. How quickly could you get me some Steiner binoculars and a spotting scope down here to Sunshine? Bushnell makes the spotting scope I think I need."

Gillon began a search on his computer contemporaneous with Jake's mentioning the equipment.

"I can get those to you...," Gillmon paused while his computer searched. "Monday's the earliest. I'll have it at your folks' address by special courier."

"Perfect. You want to know why?"

"Only if I need to know."

Jake was silent on the other end for a moment.

"I also need some satellite surveillance photographs, and maybe some real-time access to what's going on now at this particular site."

"Do you have the coordinates?"

"Not yet. I plan on taking my GPS out there this weekend. I can give you the parameters of the search Monday."

"You going out Saturday or Sunday?"

"Saturday."

"Send me the coordinates Saturday. I'll get to work on it soon as I have your info."

"I hate to ask you to do it on a weekend."

Gillmon laughed. "I assume this is important, Jake. Otherwise you wouldn't be calling me."

"I'm going to check out a few things and get back to you."

"Tell you what," Gillmon said, "you get me the GPS info Saturday and in the meantime I'll see what satellites we can access. The location is in Mississippi?"

"Not far from Sunshine."

"Soon as I stowaway on a geosynchronous bird and plug in your data I'll start snooping on the location on Saturday, checking things out. You call me Monday."

"Yes, sir, Mr. Gillmon."

There was silence on the phone.

"Billy," Jake said.

"How's Kitty?"

"Just fine. Just fine."

"The courier will be there Monday with the binoculars and scope"

"Thanks, Billy."

"No problem, Jake. I was looking for something to do."

~ * ~

Mule had enough of sitting in his wheelchair. The walls of his government housing apartment were starting to close in on him. He had to hand it to Jordan Summit. That little man was something else. In court Wednesday Lawyer Summit had that young District Attorney lawyer tongue-tied and red in the face when he said he was getting the federal government involved to check out that big gun the white boy used to kill the Muslim at the Gas & Go Fast. Stingy son of a bitch would still be alive if he had just come across with a dollar or two from the get-go. Serves him right.

Lawyer Summit did impress Mule in the courtroom, but Mule considered what the lawyer did concerning the ankle bracelet his best accomplishment of the day. First, he talked the lady Judge into letting Mule stay in his apartment under house arrest instead of in the jail. Then Lawyer Summit talked the Judge and the High Sheriff into letting the deputies put the ankle thing around his wheelchair axle instead of his skinny little ankle.

Lawyer Summit told the Judge that Mule's ankles were so pitiful and the skin so easy to tear that it was bound to cause medical problems. He said Mule couldn't leave home without the wheelchair, so putting the ankle bracelet on the wheelchair axle would work just as well. The lawyer got the High Sheriff to say it was fine with him.

But Lawyer Summit wasn't through. He had Mule sign up the next day with a special finance company set up to give money every week to injured people until their damage claims go to court. He told Mule he'd have to pay it back out of the eventual settlement he got from the lawsuit.

Mule was fine with that and got his first bit of cash money. All he had to do was sign his name.

Mule heard a knock and rolled himself toward the door.

"Come in," Mule yelled. "It ain't locked."

Two black men walked in. Mule did his current favorite fist bump and finger routine with them. Mule called the big one Red, the average-sized man he called Albert. Mule gave Albert a twenty dollar bill. With little effort, Red picked Mule up out of his wheelchair and carried him to the car outside. Albert drove, and in five minutes, they were seated at a table next to the bar in Club Ivory, Mule's favorite juke joint in the Sunshine quarters.

Mule slammed a ten on the table and hollered out to the Club Ivory bartender. "Bring me an ice cold pint of London's Best and a Coca-Cola, Mr. Jackson. I got a thirst that needs satisfying."

In short order Mule consumed the first pint. He was starting to feel better, and began to share the news of his good fortune not only with Red and Albert and Mr. Jackson, but everyone else in Club Ivory.

"Yessirree Bob," Mule said loudly, "Mule's fixin' to be in high cotton. My lawyers say that store's going to have to pay me big money for lettin' me get shot up right there on their property."

Several patrons gathered around Mule's table and patted him on the back. Mule yelled at Mr. Jackson, gave him a twenty and told the bartender to give everyone in the club a drink on him.

Midway through his third chilled pint of London's Best, Mule began to nod. Before the shooting and his time in the hospital it took a lot more than three pints to bring him low. Mule was slurring his words now, and told Albert it was time for Red and him to take him home.

The last thing Mule said to the patrons was his lawyers told him the Gas & Go Fast people had let too much violence go on at the store, and that caused Mule to be paralyzed and they had to pay. He had such a hard time saying the words he wasn't sure anyone understood him, but they nodded and smiled at Mule like they did.

Chapter Twenty-Nine

Freddy waited a good while in the booth at Buddy's Truck Stop on the four lane running through Sunshine. At first the Saturday morning regulars cut their eyes at him every ten minutes or so, but after an hour of his sipping coffee and quietly reading the Jackson paper, they began to ignore the stranger with the long, gray ponytail and leather vest.

Before he sat in the booth he made sure he could see his Harley in the parking lot through the plate glass window. He checked on it more often than the regulars looked at him. Freddy glanced at the time.

Damned crazy meth head.

Ten minutes later he saw Wizler pull into the parking lot and park his Harley Shovelhead next to Freddy's Blockhead. Wizler removed his Nazi helmet and round desert goggles. He squinted through the glass. When Freddy waved, Wizler grinned. Even through the grimy glass, Freddy could see the quarter-inch gap between Wizler's front teeth topped with a dark Hitler moustache. Wizler rubbed his buzz cut, pointed his index finger at Freddy and walked bowlegged in leather chaps and dirty denim into Buddy's. Every patron in the place stared at Wizler, continuing well after he sat down in the booth across from the other biker. As soon as Freddy saw Wizler's eyes and goofy grin, he knew Wizler was high as a kite.

"Glad you made it," Freddy said.

"Rode all night," Wizler said, rotating his neck to work out the kinks, and pushing his chin to the side with his open hand, repeating on the other side.

"Stiff, huh?" Freddy said.

"Every place but one," Wizler said and winked. "Ain't much of a town this Sunshine ain't."

"It's the Big Apple compared to Kilbride. There's not a single stop light in all of Dundee County." Freddy paused. "You got here quick."

"You say jump, I say how high. Speaking of high, Goddamn crank, man. Needed it to stay on the road all night, but I'm still flying, bro."

"I noticed."

Freddy put up with a lot from Wizler because he was the smartest biker Freddy ever met, the highest octane, too. He was no more than five-six, wiry and wild-eyed, even when sober. He kept his head almost shaved and wore the same vest as Freddy, with DREGS arcing between his shoulder blades above the serpent-tongued demonic woman with horns and burning eyes. Matching diamond-shaped "One Per Center" patches were stitched on the front and back of the vest.

James Kohler was thirty-seven, a whiz with computers and a devotee of Adolf Hitler, hence the nickname. In addition to the Hitler moustache, Wizler had gold swastikas implanted in his two front teeth and the dictator's face tattooed in the middle of his upper back. There were Germanic phrases tattooed on his arms, legs, and chest. Freddy never asked him what they meant.

Wizler was fascinated with anything associated with the Third Reich. He was a collector and walking encyclopedia of Nazi memorabilia and uniforms. In his spare time, Wizler dubbed portions of speeches delivered by *der Fuhrer* into the heavy metal industrial music he created.

Wizler was the most virulently racist of all the Dregs. He played the music he created at skinhead rallies, bouncing around the stage, goose-stepping and giving the Nazi salute. He lip-synched the portions of Hitler's speeches in the music, mimicking the dictator's mannerisms. When Wizler encountered blacks, he made sure he leaned into their space, grinning to expose the gold swastikas. Even by Dregs standards, Wizler was a piece of work. To Freddy, he was MVD, most valuable Dreg.

Wizler was born into a blue collar Cleveland family in 1974. A late blooming tech nerd, he was harassed by his bigger classmates at public high school, especially the black kids, who called him a midget and made fun of the gap between his front teeth. The ridicule drove him into isolation. After school he hung out at an electronics store, doing odd jobs for the store manager in exchange for the old p.c.s and other electronic gear customers returned. By his senior year in high school, Wizler's room was packed with networked computers. He went to trade school and honed his programming skills. By the mid-nineties he was sick of Cleveland. He moved to Austin and went to work for Dell. He was doing fine at Dell until he set every screen saver in his department to a photograph of Buchenwald's wrought iron front gate and its notorious slogan *Jedem das Seine* or "everyone gets what he deserves." Dell fired him. Because of his prodigious computer skills, he was subsequently hired at a series of computer and electronics manufacturers, staying until his employers had enough of his antisocial personality and behavior.

In 2003, Wizler finally found his sweet spot. He ran a website for a white supremacist gang in San Antonio. In 2004, he spent a year in Bexar county jail for internet crimes and met a host of Texas Aryan Brotherhood members. When he got out, Wizler made decent money setting up internet scams for the Texas ABs on a contract basis around San Antonio. He met Freddy Brewer in San Antonio in 2009 after Brandi ran Freddy out of Oklahoma City. Freddy recognized Wizler's value as an earner and was willing to overlook his idiosyncrasies. Freddy told him about Dregs, the gang he wanted to start, and Wizler was immediately on board. Freddy was the boss, but Wizler was proud to be considered a founding member of the Dregs.

Sitting across from Freddy in the booth, Wizler grabbed a pack of Saltines from a tray on the table. He tore open the first package and stuffed the crackers in his mouth. He did the same with a second package just as the waitress arrived. She put a small glass of water in front of him and asked for his order. Wizler spewed cracker crumbs when he tried to answer the waitress.

"Sorry ma'am," Freddy said, "he's been riding all night."

Wizler shook his head in agreement and puffed, throwing off additional cracker crumbs. The waitress stared at him a moment and walked away.

"Hey," Wizler said to Freddy, "don't I get to eat?"

As more crumbs flew his way Freddy covered his coffee.

"Yeah, but first thing I need you to do is come down off that crank and act like a normal person for a change. We got important shit to do."

Wizler turned up his water glass and drained it.

"How's it going with the ATM play?" Freddy asked.

"Dude," Wizler said, wiping his mouth on the back of his hand, "we're gonna make bank. I placed the scanners last week, three locations on the eastside. I'm already getting good reads on the cards."

Wizler turned his glass up again, disappointed the water was gone. He looked around for the waitress, and jumped when he turned back and saw Freddy sitting across from him. Wizler's mood changed.

"Why the fuck am I here?" he said loudly.

Every patron in Buddy's turned and glared at Wizler. Freddy gestured for him to keep it down and mouthed "sorry" to the regulars.

"Shut up," Freddy said.

"I need to get back to do the beta testing right now," Wizler said with urgency. "You need me back in Texas, bro. Breed and Wrench can do this muscle shit."

"Hey, there's more than muscle called for right here. You can get back to do your testing when this shit storm here is cleared up." Freddy leaned toward Wizler and whispered. "We don't get done what I need done in this place, I'm fucked. If I'm fucked you are, too. Won't matter how sweet the ATM deal is."

Wizler seemed to focus long enough to understand.

"I'll fill you in on the details when the others get here," Freddy said. "And no more junk. I need you sober."

Freddy's phone buzzed. He listened for a moment, and spoke quietly. While Freddy turned to watch their bikes and concentrate on the call, Wizler crumpled Saltines in the package, opened a small hole and poured several lines of crumbs. He unwrapped the straw the waitress brought with his water and began to snort the crumbs through the straw. When Freddy closed the phone and turned back, he swatted the straw from Wizler's hand and brushed the crumbs off the table. Wizler appeared confused. Freddy glared.

"Sober, I said. Quit fucking around in front of these people."

Freddy stood and threw a couple of bills on the table.

"I'm still hungry," Wizler said. "Where the fuck we going?"

"Motel. Wrench went straight there instead of stopping here. He's in the parking lot out there with Breed, waiting for us."

They cranked their Harleys. Freddy winked and waved at the regulars in Buddy's, all of whom were watching the two bikers. Freddy led the way onto the four lane through Sunshine. They rode for twenty minutes on the highway toward Dundee. They were almost out of Yaloquena County when another two-lane road teed into the highway from the northwest. On one side of the intersecting road was a closed gas station, on the other a ranch-style motel built in the fifties. It had twenty rooms and from the looks of the parking lot and the exterior building maintenance, was on its last legs. Freddy knew the history. The place was built on the eastern edge of Yaloquena County when Dundee was dry. Men from Kilbride, Brewer Hill, and other parts of Dundee made regular visits to the motel, which sold liquor by the bottle in a small building next to the motel office. In addition to alcohol, the motel owner stocked a half-dozen ladies available on request for his patrons. Freddy heard stories that it was a jumping place in the sixties and seventies, but Dundee's voting wet in 1978 put an end to its prosperity.

Two rough-looking men wearing Dregs vests sat on their bikes in the parking lot.

Freddy and Wizler stopped next to them.

"My bad, Freddy," the biker with a thick beard said. "I thought you wanted us to come straight to this motel."

"You thought wrong, Wrench. But it don't matter. I'm just glad you made it."

Freddy and Wizler shook hands and hugged the two bikers. The one with the beard was Rodney Russo. He stood about 6'0" and weighed two hundred pounds. Freddy nicknamed him "Wrench" when he started working for Freddy in the Abilene strip club because he had a knack for fixing motors and anything mechanical. Wrench struggled with alcohol and meth addiction. He was totally devoted to Freddy, and would do anything he asked. Wrench was useful for two things: keeping the bikes running, and strong-arming. He didn't mind beating or killing with his fists. All Freddy had to do was ask.

The other Dreg was Vinton Boswell, originally from Sabine Parish, Louisiana. He was the same size as Wrench, and was also a good mechanic. He wore his black hair in a long, braided ponytail kept in place by a beaded headband. Breed didn't care for meth, but he had a difficult time staying off alcohol. Freddy named him "Breed," because he was at least half American Indian. The other half was a mystery, though Freddy had seen Breed try to kill a man in a Texas road house for calling him a redbone. Like Wrench, Breed was muscle for the Dregs. Both of them were killers.

"You stayin' here with us, Freddy?" Wizler asked.

"Yeah. You and me will share one room and Breed and Wrench in another. I'll check us in."

Freddy was polite to the terrified Pakistani hotelier. He paid for a week's stay in advance for each room. Freddy was charming, assuring the owner they would cause no trouble at the motel. Freddy distributed room keys to his men and told them to mount up. He knew they were hungry and after several days on the road eating bugs, needed to do some drinking.

"After we get a few beers and a little food in us," Freddy told them, "I'll tell you guys exactly why we're here and what we need to do."

Chapter Thirty

"You see this crap?" Walton Donaldson said walking into Willie Mitchell's office and tossing a document onto his boss's desk.

Willie Mitchell glanced at the caption and title of the motion.

"Eddie called up here a few minutes ago to tell me about it."

"They can't recuse you just for being Trevor's baseball coach fifteen or sixteen years ago."

"They probably know that," Willie Mitchell said, "but they just want to get it out there for everyone to focus on Trevor and the fact we're not going after him on a homicide charge. Wait until we get the case before the trial jury. Jordan Summit will take every opportunity to remind the jury it was Trevor's bullet that killed Azeem"

"Bastards. How the hell did they find out you coached him?"

"This is a small town, Walton. Who knows? Like I've told you, if you're going to live and practice law or prosecute in a small town, you have to get used to this fact: if you find out something critical about someone, a witness or a defendant, you can bet your last dollar there's other people in Sunshine know the very same thing."

"I know," Walton said, "but whether we go through with the prosecution of Trevor on the gun charge or not, it makes no difference to the charges against Mule."

"There you go again," Willie Mitchell said, "thinking logically."

"Judge Williams…?"

"No. To answer your question, she will not recuse me or this office from Mule's case based on these facts. She knows the law."

"We'll have to have a hearing."

"Eddie told me it's this Friday. Judge already set it."

"They just want to throw a bunch of crap at the wall and see what sticks. Pisses me off."

"Yep. The hearing is what they want."

Ethel Morris walked in and gave Willie Mitchell the morning mail. Walton smiled and hugged her lightly.

"Welcome back," Walton said.

"Thank you. It feels good to be in the office again."

"You're looking good," Walton said.

"I'm feeling well. I've gotten two good reports in a row, so I'm optimistic for now. I missed everyone here when I was home."

She walked out.

"That a wig?" Walton whispered.

"It is."

"Looks real. Same gray as her hair. Is she back for good?"

Ethel Morris was sixty-two. She had been Willie Mitchell's private secretary for thirty years. She started with him when he hung out a shingle in Sunshine and moved with him to the courthouse when he was elected D.A. She was efficient and smart. Ethel had been on medical leave the prior four months recovering from a mastectomy and chemotherapy treatments.

"I hope so."

"Louise is doing okay, huh?"

"Louise is great. She does everything I ask her to, but she needs to be the full-time receptionist and gate keeper. She's tough and can handle anything that comes in the door. Ethel doesn't like confrontation, but she prepares pleadings as well as most lawyers and knows how to run this office."

"She looks pale."

"I know. And really frail. I'm not sure she's telling me everything."

"I hope she's got it licked."

"Me, too," Willie Mitchell said. "Puts all this other crap in perspective, doesn't it?"

~ * ~

Jake sat at the rough hewn table in the big room at the duck camp studying the instructions for the spotting scope and binoculars. He walked out the front door and tested them on the porch.

Kitty walked out holding two glasses of red wine. She sat in the swing and held up his glass.

"Join me?"

"I believe I will."

"Figured out how you're going to proceed out there?"

"Not yet," he said. "It's fairly flat around the place so I'll have to climb a tree I'm sure. Probably a pine."

"You know how to do that?"

Jake recalled working his way up the Ponderosa Pines in the foothills of the Rockies with the reinforced nylon loop and spikes that fit over his boots.

"It's not hard. I use a loop and spiked heel clamps that fit over my boots. The rest is just muscle and balance. Where the big pines grow close together they don't have limbs until the very top."

"Oh," Kitty said, snuggling next to him, "I'd love to see you in a pair of spiked heels."

Jake laughed. "These are different. Like crampons."

Kitty raised her wine glass and clinked Jake's.

"To my favorite spy. Banks. Jake Banks."

"Not exactly," Jake said.

He put the wine glasses on the porch rail. He pulled Kitty firmly to him and looked into her eyes, waiting. He brushed his lips across each of Kitty's closed eyelids. She moved, her lips meeting his. He kissed her lightly at first. After a moment, she wanted more. She placed her hand on the back of his neck and pulled him closer, pressing her hungry mouth on his, probing. Jake stood and lifted her in his arms. He carried her inside to the bedroom.

They made love in the disappearing light, and fell asleep. Jake hopped out of bed when his phone began to chime on the table in the other room. He glanced at the number and walked quietly outside, standing naked in the darkness on the porch in the warm night air.

"Hello, Billy," Jake said.

"You get your stuff?" Gillmon asked.

"Got it today. Thanks. My coordinates work?"

"Oh, yes. I've been watching this place since late Saturday. It's some kind of commune or camp I take it?"

"Religious," Jake said.

"Well, I've been watching what they've been doing. It's not praying, I can tell you that."

Chapter Thirty-One

The bartender put two Budweisers, a Coors, and a Michelob, all longneck bottles, on the table. He looked at Freddy.

"What's the problem, Buster?" Freddy asked. "My credit no good?"

"That's the third round," the big bartender said. "A dozen beers."

"And you think I'm going to stiff you?"

The bartender shrugged, continuing to wait by the table. Breed made a move to stand up, but Freddy put his hand on Breed's forearm to keep him in his seat.

Freddy pulled a fold of cash from his jeans and gave the bartender two twenties.

"This ought to give us a lead on you, Buster." Freddy flashed his wide grin. "Come on back for more when you get nervous. And we may want to order something from your grill later. What kind of food do you serve here?"

"Hamburger," Buster said.

"Anything else?" Wizler asked. He sucked air through the gap in his front teeth and stroked his Hitler moustache while he waited for Buster to respond.

"Cheeseburger," Buster said.

"What kind of cheese?" Wrench asked.

"Yellow," chef Buster said.

Freddy had introduced himself the previous week to Buster Cloud, the owner, bartender, and apparently sole employee of the Lonely Road Bar & Grill. The low-profile, flat-roofed cinder block establishment was aptly named, located on the Rivercrest Road about a hundred yards from its intersection with the Sunshine to Kilbride highway. The bar was in the middle of nowhere, five miles southwest of the Dregs' motel. According to Buster, only ten families lived on Rivercrest Road from the Dundee highway to where it dead-ended at the Dundee River. Fortunately, he told Freddy, the men folk in those families were commercial fishermen who drank heavily and often.

Freddy told Buster some friends from his social and riding club would be joining him in the area for a while, and the Lonely Bar & Grill was a perfect hangout for them. When Buster said he "didn't want no trouble," Freddy regaled Buster with a couple of stories from his career as a strip club owner, emphasizing his grasp on Buster's need to make sure the place remained peaceful. Freddy said his friends were friendly and good-natured, and asked Buster about the kinds of customers who frequented his establishment.

Buster was puzzled for a moment. "No niggers, if that's what you mean," he said to Freddy, who nodded in appreciation of the house rules.

Buster was a big man with a salt and pepper moustache and white stubble. Freddy figured him to be six-three and weight about two-fifty. Probably about sixty years old—sixty hard years. Much of Buster's weight appeared to have drifted south from his chest and shoulders into his gut. His skin was yellowish-gray, his fingertips brown from nicotine. When Freddy made his acquaintance the previous week, Buster's dirty tee shirt was partially hidden by the filthy, greasy apron he wore. This night, with all Dregs in attendance, Freddy noticed that Buster had selected the same outfit.

"This place sucks," Breed said.

"You're lucky he's serving you fire water," Wizler said, grinning to show off his swastikas. "He's too stupid to know you're a redskin."

Breed smiled. "You're lucky I like you, Wizler."

"I know this place sucks," Freddy said, "and so does the motel, but we've got to lay low until we get this thing done."

"How long?" Wrench asked Freddy.

"As long as it takes me to figure out how to get that gun."

"You got a plan?" Breed asked.

"Wizler and I are working on it. They've got a hearing of some kind in court this Friday and I'm going to be there to check things out."

"So what are we supposed to do in the meantime?" Wrench asked.

"Catch up on your rest. Relax."

"I done all that already," Breed said. "I'm bored as shit."

Freddy gestured to Buster, who brought another round.

"Why don't you bring us each a hamburger," Freddy said.

"What comes on it?" Wizler asked.

"Mustard and mayonnaise." Buster pronounced it *my-nez.* "Lettuce, onion, pickles."

"No onion on mine," Wizler said.

"I make 'em all the same way. Take off what you don't want."

"Tomatoes?" Wrench asked.

"Out of season," Buster said.

He waited for a moment, looking at Freddy.

"Well," Freddy said, "four of your best burgers, Buster. Put some of your finest yellow cheese on mine."

Buster took a step toward the bar.

"Hold on, Buster," Freddy said, gesturing with his index finger for the bartender to come close. He pointed to Breed and Wrench.

"These two friends of mine, they're very social, and they like to date girls. Nice girls, you know. Now don't take this the wrong way, but they're not from around here, and I was thinking you might know a couple of girls they might date while they're in this part of Yaloquena."

"I'll think about it," Buster said after studying Breed and Wrench for a moment.

Buster opened a small, rusted refrigerator on his way behind the bar and grabbed four patties separated by wax paper. Freddy watched Buster do a half-assed job of scraping the grill with a metal spatula and toss the burgers on the grill. The air filled with blue smoke and the sizzle and smell of frying beef. Freddy looked around the room at the small windows, the panes of which were blurred by a crusty film of smoke and years-old grease.

Freddy took a long pull on his Coors.

"I've been in worst places," Freddy said.

"Me too," Wizler said, "but they had guards with guns and fences with razor wire keeping me in."

"Yeah," Breed said. "Hurry this shit up."

"I'll do my best," Freddy said.

~ * ~

Jake drove the farm truck a couple of miles over the speed limit on the highway headed toward Dundee County. He hadn't seen a single vehicle since he left Sunshine. It was Wednesday in the first full week of October and almost midnight, but the temperature was in the high seventies. Jake drove with both windows down but the outside air blowing into the truck was hot.

As he neared the turnoff to the Rivercrest Road, Jake watched four vehicles enter the highway in front of him and head northeast toward Dundee County. Their lights were confusing at first, but Jake figured it out. They were motorcycles, not automobiles. Jake maintained a steady speed. The motorcycles stayed ahead of him for five miles or so. As Jake approached the road to Freedmen's Creek, the bikers turned left off the main highway. He slowed down. Jake didn't want any company on the road to Freedmen's Creek. When he reached the intersection, he was relieved that the bikers weren't on the road to the commune. They made a left off the highway into the old motel parking lot just east of the turnoff. As Jake turned in a northwesterly direction onto the road to the encampment, he saw four Harleys in the motel parking lot. He was grateful they were there.

Jake had memorized the route from Sunshine to Freedmen's Creek. He plotted it on the satellite map he printed from the encrypted files Billy Gillmon sent him two days before. Jake knew the general area from float trips he took with high school buddies when the area creeks were high.

They would put in at Bandit Lake landing and paddle Cross Creek to Freedmen's Creek, where they would disembark their canoes and rubber rafts and load them on a truck. He had seen the remains of the original Freedmen's Creek community and knew the history, but it had been ten years since the float trips.

Jake slowed the farm truck to a crawl and turned off his headlights. He spotlighted the woods until he found the old logging road he had identified on the map. Jake left the truck running on the shoulder and used his flashlight to check the shallow ditch and undergrowth he had to cross to access the logging road. Satisfied the Ford would make it, he drove it through the brush into the narrow lane. A few small pine trees had taken root on the logging road but nothing so big the F150 couldn't run over and flatten it. After ten minutes of slow going with parking lights on the logging road, Jake stopped. He studied the coordinates marked on the map, comparing them to the reading on the GPS Velcroed to his belt. He did a quick computation and drove further into the blackness of the woods, grateful for the dim orange glow of the parking lights on the logging road.

Satisfied he had reached his destination, Jake cut the parking lights and engine. He slipped off his jeans and put on his black and green camouflage gear and boots, smeared black greasepaint on his face and neck, and checked the rest of his equipment, including the binoculars and scope Gillmon sent him. Jake locked the truck and secured the key into a zippered pocket on his arm. He put on his night vision goggles, stuck his arm through the strap of his H&K 416 assault rifle, and checked his compass. Jake walked quietly through the woods toward Freedmen's Creek.

In less than an hour, Jake reached his destination, a thick stand of pine trees on a low ridge a fourth of a mile south of the encampment. He checked his watch. Two o'clock. He figured an hour to skinny up the pine with his cleats and nylon loop and get situated.

It was after three a.m. when Jake secured himself to the pine, fifty feet off the ground. The makeshift seat was more comfortable than he expected. Jake double-checked the blood flow in his extremities to make sure the straps and seat did not impede circulation. Jake planned to spend at least a day in the tree, maybe longer, depending on what he saw. He was certain he was well-hidden by the thick pine needles and branches between him and the commune. He knew they couldn't see him.

Jake checked his watch and waited for dawn.

Chapter Thirty-Two

By six-thirty that morning there was a lot of activity at Freedmen's Creek. Jake studied the buildings on Gillmon's map the day before and made educated guesses of their uses based on size and location. He was about to find out how good his guesses were.

Jake's pine tree was almost due south of the southernmost edge of the encampment. The buildings closest to him were the smallest on the property. He had guessed they were dormitories or housing, and based on the foot traffic from the trailer-type buildings to other parts of the camp, he knew he was right. Beginning at six, there had been a steady stream of residents leaving the residential trailers. By observation, Jake concluded inhabitants of the dorms were segregated by sex. They walked past the big building in the center of the commune to enter a smaller building on the edge of the creek. Because of the minaret-type structure attached to the front, Jake figured it was their mosque. When the slight breeze shifted from time to time, he heard the faint sound of the call to morning prayer.

At about seven, everyone spilled out of the mosque. Most walked to the building next to the large one in the center. Jake guessed it was their mess hall. Most of the men headed west from the mosque to enter a metal building next to the creek. Jake focused his binoculars on the building. About half of the men or boys that entered the building came out in shorts and sneakers and began jogging inside the perimeter of the fenced compound. The rest came out of the building in camouflage clothing holding something. Jake adjusted the glasses.

Assault rifles. AKs.

Jake switched from the field glasses to his scope. He watched the males walking down a hill west of the building. They gathered to listen to one man who spoke for a few minutes. The men separated and began firing their AKs at targets on the west side of the firing range. Jake concluded that his vigil in the tree had been worth the effort, even if he saw nothing else the entire day. He had confirmed what Billy Gillmon thought he saw on the satellite images.

Why is a religious community training with AK's?

To his right Jake watched a man in a military-type uniform run a green and red flag up a metal pole and take up a position at the entrance with a rifle. The joggers ran past the guard and the two silver busses in the parking area. Jake followed them on their path inside the perimeter fence back to the building where they started. Outside the building, their leader gathered them in a circle around him. Jake watched him pull a boy into the circle and demonstrate the rudiments of knife fighting.

Jake noticed a man walking toward the fight training. The man wore a brown business suit and bow tie. His hair lay flat on his head. Jake recognized him from the courtroom.

Mohammed X.

Two more men approached the training circle and joined the leader. One dwarfed the other.

Samson and Abud.

Mohammed X left the circle with Abud and Samson. They talked for a moment and walked until they entered a building past the mosque. There was a satellite dish near the front entrance. Jake studied different parts of the compound for another thirty minutes, then took a break for water and breakfast, and a ten-minute nap.

In the pine tree before daylight, Jake wondered how long he should observe. Based on what he had seen in the first hour and a half of daylight, Jake made his decision. He was staying in the tree all day and into the night. No telling what else he would see.

Chapter Thirty-Three

By the time Jake entered the courtroom quietly on Friday, Judge Williams had already taken the bench. Walton and Jordan Summit were on their feet at their respective tables. Willie Mitchell and Eleanor Bernstein were seated. Mule occupied his oversized wheelchair between his lawyers, wearing the white shirt that swallowed him. Eddie Bordelon, the diminutive, bald Deputy Clerk sat at the clerk's table, taking the minutes on his computer and operating the recording equipment.

Jake took a seat next to Kitty in the second row behind Walton and Willie Mitchell. Judge Williams nodded to acknowledge Jake. He smiled at the Judge. Jake winked at Eddie Bordelon when the Deputy Clerk made eye contact. Jake and Kitty were the only spectators on the prosecution side of the court room.

"It is agreed by the State and defense that all discovery motions have been satisfied?"

Walton and Jordan both said yes to Judge Williams.

"Today's hearing is just on the Motion to Recuse," she said. "Are there any other outstanding motions we need to address before the jury selection begins on November 7?"

"Just two, Your Honor," Jordan said. "The Motion to Produce the weapon used by Trevor Brewer, the weapon that actually caused the death of Abdul Azeem."

"Objection to the characterization by Mr. Summit," Walton said.

"Overruled," the Judge said. "Mr. Donaldson, you're going to have to get used to Mr. Summit's description of the Smith & Wesson. I'm sure we'll hear it many more times, especially after the jury is seated. As I understand it, his statement is accurate."

"Thank you, Your Honor," Jordan said.

"Which brings me to this point, gentlemen," she said. "From my review of the State's responses to your discovery motions, it is my understanding that there is no dispute between the parties as to Mr. Brewer's gun firing the bullet that Dr. Nathan Clement said actually was the cause of death, is there?"

Walton stood. "That is correct, Your Honor."

"Right, Your Honor," Jordan said. "The evidence is clear on that."

"Then why, Mr. Summit," she said, "do you want the weapon produced to do your own ballistics examination and testing?"

Walton and Willie Mitchell turned to the defense lawyer. Jake had discussed the same issue with them.

Why not just stipulate to the fact that Trevor's gun killed Azeem?

"The defense wishes to examine and test the weapon fired by Trevor Brewer, Your Honor. We do not intend to stipulate to anything."

Judge Williams shook her head.

"You must have your reasons, Mr. Summit, but I must confess I have difficulty understanding what they might be. That hearing has been set for two weeks from today, October 21, isn't that correct?"

Both Walton and Jordan said yes. Jordan whispered something to Eleanor Bernstein.

"All right, that leaves us with what?"

"The motion we filed to submit written questionnaires to the jury venire," Jordan said.

"The State doesn't necessarily object to this, Your Honor," Walton said, "but we've just been supplied the proposed questionnaire this morning and Mr. Banks and I would like to have time to review the proposed questions. We may have some of our own to add to Mr. Summit's list."

"My experience with questionnaires is that rather than shorten jury selection, it tends to drag it out," Judge Williams said. "Some of the prospective jurors' answers require counsel to ask more questions than they ordinarily would in an attempt to clarify some of the answers."

"We've kept the questions simple as possible," Jordan said.

"That's good," she said. "The typical Yaloquena juror cannot deal with complexity, Mr. Summit. You can ask Ms. Bernstein."

Jake could see Eleanor nodding in agreement with the Judge.

"How much time do you need to review the questionnaire, Mr. Donaldson?" she asked.

Walton conferred quietly with Willie Mitchell.

"Mr. Banks advises that he's looked over the questions while we've been before the Court and we think another ten minutes would enable us to respond."

"All right," Judge Williams said. "We'll adjourn for ten minutes while the District Attorney's office completes its review. When we resume, we'll deal with any objections to the questionnaire then move on to the Motion to Recuse."

Judge Williams tapped her gavel and walked out. Walton and Willie Mitchell huddled at the prosecution table. At the defense table, Mule appeared to be dozing while his lawyers conferred.

"How'd it go?" Kitty asked Jake.

"Good. Fill you in later."

Jake put his left arm on the back of the bench and turned to the defense side of the courtroom. Abud, Mohammed X, Samson, and Bobby Sanders sat on the first row directly behind Mule and his lawyers. Jake wondered how they would react if he told them he spent the entire day yesterday fifty feet off the ground in a pine tree watching the three of them and everything that went on at Freedmen's Creek.

The only other spectator in court sat three rows behind them. It was the same man Jake had seen at arraignment, the big guy with the high shirt collar and gray ponytail stuffed inside his corduroy sport coat.

"Don't look now, but take a look at the white guy over there," Jake said quietly to Kitty, "the one in the brown jacket. Has he talked to anyone in here today?"

"Not since I've been here. He was here when I walked in. Why?"

"We need to find out who he is."

Jake turned on his phone to check his messages and e-mail. There was a long e-mail from Billy Gillmon with several attachments. Jake decided to open it later on his laptop. With the service he had in the court room, it would have taken forever on his phone.

A few minutes later, Judge Williams ascended the bench, right on time. Jake made sure he turned off his phone. No need to be held in contempt.

"Gentlemen," she said, "what's your pleasure with the questions?"

Walton stood. "We have no objection to the court submitting the questionnaire to the prospective jurors when they arrive on the seventh, Your Honor."

"Do you wish to add any questions?"

"No, Your Honor," Walton said.

Jake was surprised. Out of curiosity, he decided to ask Willie Mitchell and Walton later if he could look over the questionnaire.

"That brings us to the Motion to Recuse," she said. "Mr. Summit, Ms. Bernstein, I've read your motion and supporting memorandum. I don't see the need for a lot of testimony…."

"We only intend to call one witness, Your Honor," Jordan said.

"Very well. Call your first witness."

"The defense calls District Attorney Willie Mitchell Banks on cross-examination, Your Honor."

Walton stood. "We'd like to enter an objection for the record, Your Honor. Calling opposing counsel to testify is…."

Judge Williams interrupted.

"I know it's not to be done lightly, Mr. Donaldson, but it is a Motion to Recuse and I do not see how the Court can deny the defense the right to cross-examine Mr. Banks, since it is his bias they are alleging should disqualify him and his entire office from handling the prosecution of this case."

"Yes, Your Honor," Walton said after bending down to confer with Willie Mitchell.

"If Mr. Summit delves into areas where he shouldn't, I'm sure you will be prepared to object."

Willie Mitchell walked around the prosecution table and stood in front of the witness stand, raising his right hand. Eddie Bordelon administered the oath.

"...I do," Willie Mitchell said and sat down.

Jake knew testifying was routine for Willie Mitchell because of *Batson vs. Kentucky* and subsequent U.S. Supreme Court decisions requiring prosecutors to testify under oath to establish racially neutral reasons for exercising peremptory challenges to excuse potential African-American jurors. Willie Mitchell had picked more than a hundred juries since *Batson,* and told Jake he had to testify to justify his challenges in many of the trials. Jake remembered telling his Criminal Procedure professor in law school it didn't seem fair that the D.A. had to testify in most jury trials to justify challenging minorities but the defense attorneys were rarely required to provide race neutral reasons for excusing non-minority prospective jurors. The professor's response did not surprise Jake. Most professors were anti-prosecutor.

"I'm sorry you feel that way, Mr. Banks, but that's the law. You'll just have to get over it."

"State your name for the record, please," Jordan Summit said, bringing Jake back into focus on the hearing.

"Your Honor," Eddie Bordelon said, raising a finger. His head tilted to the side and he listened intently to the headphone he held to his ear. Eddie nodded to the Judge and whispered "thank you," indicating he was ready to proceed.

Willie Mitchell testified about coaching Trevor in Little League, about his spending the night at the Banks' home a couple of times.

"Let's move on, Mr. Summit," Judge Williams said. "The State admitted all this in its response to your motion. Do you have anything else to support your allegation of bias?"

"Getting there, Your Honor," Jordan said and paused.

"Now, Mr. Banks, on how many occasions since the death of Abdul Azeem have you spoken to Trevor Brewer?"

Willie Mitchell thought a moment.

"I spoke to Trevor and his father Tom the day he was arraigned, helped with the bonding process. I spoke to Trevor one other time at his house in Dundee County."

"Was his attorney present?" Jordan asked.

"His father was there. Trevor doesn't have an attorney yet as far as I know."

"Did you discuss the charges against him?"

"I did."

"Did you tell him…?"

Eleanor Bernstein touched her co-counsel's arm and whispered something to him. Jake couldn't make out what was going on. Jordan addressed the Court.

"That's all the questions I have for this witness, Your Honor. I would re-urge the factual and legal grounds supporting the Motion to Recuse in the brief we filed previously with the Court."

"Anything for this witness?" Judge Williams asked Walton.

"No, Your Honor."

"Submitted?" she asked both counsel. They said yes.

"This Court is ready to rule. I've read the Motion to Recuse, the cases cited in the brief and defense counsel's arguments in support. I am well aware of the case law on this issue, and find no legal justification for recusal. I hereby deny the motion."

Jordan Summit stood with a document in his hand. He nodded to Eleanor, who delivered copies of the document to Walton and the Judge.

"Thank you, Your Honor. I have one last thing that I neglected to mention earlier. I apologize for the omission. This is a Motion and Order for the issuance of an out of state subpoena for a witness in Oklahoma City. His name is Gary Needham. He is an agent with the Alcohol, Tobacco, and Firearms division of the Justice Department."

"For trial?"

"No, Your Honor, for the hearing on the Motion to Produce Trevor Brewer's weapon set for the 21st. We've also subpoenaed Trevor Brewer."

"Any objection?"

"We would re-urge our general objection to the hearing and advise the Court that our offer to stipulate that the bullet from the Smith & Wesson struck Mr. Azeem close to the heart and that Dr. Nathan Clement established that wound as the fatal one."

"I cannot force the defense to stipulate, though it would certainly seem to be in order. They are entitled to their hearing. Let the subpoenas issue to Mr. Needham and Mr. Brewer."

Everyone stood while Judge Williams left the bench and the courtroom. Jake whispered to Kitty and walked toward the prosecution table. He stood at the rail for a moment, turned so he could observe the pony-tailed man. When the man walked out of the courtroom, Jake waited a moment, and followed him.

Jake kept his distance. He watched the man remove his corduroy coat and get into an older model pickup truck. As the man drove past, Jake saw him talking to a much smaller man with almost no hair in the passenger seat. Freddy was gesturing and grinning. Jake memorized the license plate number.

Got to find out who that is.

Chapter Thirty-Four

When Jake walked into his father's office, Walton and Kitty were sitting across the desk from Willie Mitchell. Sheriff Jones leaned against the wall next to the desk, slowly pushing off with his upper back to an upright position, then fading back into the wall and starting the process all over again. It was a nervous habit Jake had seen Lee perform dozens of times in Willie Mitchell's office.

"I need a license plate run," Jake said.

"Let me have it," Lee said. "Won't take a second."

Jake gave a small piece of paper to the Sheriff, who stepped out of the D.A.'s private office.

"How did Summit know about Gary Needham?" Kitty asked.

"Courthouse grapevine, probably," Walton said.

"Needham had to wait a while to see me," Willie Mitchell said. "He had never been here before, probably stopped at one of the offices downstairs and talked to a Deputy Sheriff or a clerk or office worker."

"Eleanor's got sources all over this courthouse," Walton said. "She's got friends in every office. You'd be amazed at how quickly information like that gets around inside this building."

"So he told someone he was here on a federal gun charge?" Kitty asked. "And they got word to Eleanor?"

"Maybe not the same day," Willie Mitchell said. "Everyone in this building knows Eleanor is co-counsel for Mule. They also know it was Trevor Brewer's gun that actually killed Azeem."

"Do you think Eleanor called Oklahoma City and found out about the double homicide?" Kitty asked.

"She might not have," Willie Mitchell said, "but I guarantee you Jordan Summit or one of his investigators did."

"But you're not contesting...," Kitty started.

"Doesn't matter," Jake said to Kitty. "If the defense can make the jury aware that Trevor's gun was used in a racially motivated homicide, it's going to make it that much harder to get the jury to convict Mule."

"Especially," Walton said, "when the jury finds out Trevor Brewer hasn't been charged with a homicide."

"Can't you keep that out?" Jake asked.

"Probably," Willie Mitchell said, "but someone on the jury venire or even the jury we select will know. Somehow the jurors always find out the things you don't want them to know. And the things you want them to know, sometimes you don't get that testimony in."

"What a system," Kitty said.

"Yeah," Willie Mitchell said. "It's crazy the way it works, but it's still better than all the other systems around the world. Not that it couldn't be improved greatly with a little common sense."

Lee Jones walked in.

"The truck is registered to Tracy Brewer of Dundee County."

"The woman behind the counter in Tom's shop," Jake said. "She didn't like me one bit when she found out who I was."

"She doesn't like you now," Kitty leaned over and whispered to Jake, "but you said she liked you when you were younger."

"She doesn't like any of us," Willie Mitchell said. "If the guy's using her truck, he's a Brewer."

"I didn't see any ponytails up on that hill," Jake said, "and that guy's got a serious ponytail he hides under his coat."

"How about if I drive over and talk to Tracy Brewer," Kitty said. "Maybe she'll tell me who's driving her truck."

"Good idea," Willie Mitchell said and looked up at Lee. "That all right with you?"

"She's much more likely to get information without me being in the picture," the Sheriff said. "They might not care for you guys over there at Brewer Hill, but they *really* don't like me."

"I'll go with her," Jake said, "if she doesn't mind my tagging along."

"I'm driving," Kitty said.

"How'd your Freedmen's Creek trip go?" Willie Mitchell asked Jake.

Jake described what he saw in his eighteen hours in the tree. Everyone in the room was spellbound.

"What the hell are they doing with AKs out there?" Lee said.

"Learning how to shoot them," Jake said, "and learning how to go hand-to-hand with a knife. There's several instructors that know what they're doing, men that move around like they've had military training. They're teaching teenagers and young adult men. I couldn't tell their exact ages."

"We've got to find out more information on Freedmen's Creek," Willie Mitchell said. "Why do the head honchos show up for every hearing and why are they so insistent we prosecute Trevor?"

"It's not because of Mule," Lee said.

"No," Willie Mitchell said. "I've watched them. They don't care what happens to Mule." He focused on Jake. "You've got to use your connections to get to the bottom of Freedmen's Creek, why they're so upset about Abdul Azeem's death. Can you do that for us?"

"I had plenty of time to think up in that pine tree," Jake said. "I believe we're going at their motivation the wrong way. The first thing I'm going to find out is exactly who Abdul Azeem *nee* Joseph Randall was. If we can figure out what he was up to, that might explain his connection to Mohammed X and Freedmen's Creek."

"Then maybe we can ferret out why they've gone into battle mode out there," Willie Mitchell said and turned to Walton. "I want you to get busy preparing for trial. I'll help you all I can."

"Lee," Willie Mitchell said, "you have enough in your budget to fly Kitty up to Oklahoma City? We need to know as much as we can about the double homicide that's got the feds all over this case."

"I'll come up with the money somehow," Lee said.

"The initial details you got from the FBI agent up there were good," Willie Mitchell said to Kitty, "but we need you to dig deeper. Find out everything you can about the double homicide and the investigation that might connect it to our case here. See what you can wrangle out of Gary Needham, too. Convince ATF we're on their side."

"I don't need to fly," Kitty said. "I've already mapped it out. It's only about five hundred miles. I can drive there in my car in about seven hours if the Sheriff will let me use his portable dash lights and siren in case I get stopped."

"No problem," Lee said.

"Jake and I can go talk to Tracy Brewer right now," Kitty said. "I'll head for Oklahoma City early Sunday morning, if that's okay with Lee."

"Absolutely," he said.

"All right," Willie Mitchell said. "Let's get busy. Walton and I start picking the jury thirty-one days from now. We don't have any time to spare."

Chapter Thirty-Five

Early Sunday morning Jake heard his phone beep. He looked out his window and saw Kitty pull into the circular drive in front of the Banks home, right on time. He walked down the stairs and out the front door into the darkness. Jake bent over into the low-riding BMW and kissed Kitty goodbye. He waved to her as she pulled out of the Banks driveway bound for Oklahoma City.

Standing barefoot in the pea gravel, he looked up. In spite of the slight hint of daylight in the east, there were plenty of stars still visible against a black sky. It was humid, like the night before at the duck camp. He checked his phone. *74 degrees. 5:30 a.m. October 9.*

Jimmy Gray would be picking him up in thirty minutes. Willie Mitchell had mentioned to Jimmy while walking Saturday morning that Jake would be talking to his people in Washington to help find out something about Azeem and the Freedmen's Creek operations. Jimmy said he was flying in his Learjet 60 to D.C. Sunday morning for a two-day American Bankers Association meeting and Jake was welcome to fly up and return with him Tuesday. When Willie Mitchell mentioned it, Jake jumped at the chance, calling Billy Gillmon immediately. Gillmon told Jake to come on up, they could get more done in the office together than communicating by phone.

Back inside the Banks home after seeing Kitty off, Jake stood under the shower long after he was clean. Their Friday afternoon trip to interview Tracy Brewer was a waste of time. She knew Jake and Kitty couldn't make her answer questions, and without a subpoena, Tracy knew she didn't have to go anywhere. It was clear to Jake that their attempted interrogation of Tracy was not, as Jimmy Gray would say, her first rodeo with law enforcement. She said nothing.

Jake smiled thinking about how intense Kitty was pushing Tracy to answer. One tough woman against another. As the warm water hit his head and shoulders, he daydreamed about the evening before at the duck camp. When they discussed the case in the swing on the porch, Kitty was all fired up about what she might uncover in Oklahoma City, asking Jake's opinion from time to time. Jake didn't give Kitty much detail about his plans, but he was looking forward to sitting next to Billy Gillmon helping him search cyberspace. The man was a marvel with his computer and the program he built, REMORA.

Jake was motivated to help prosecute Mule because of his relationship to Willie Mitchell, Walton, Lee, and Trevor. He had also inherited from Willie Mitchell a deep-seated desire to see justice done.

Kitty's passion was derivative. Jake's family and friends were now her family and friends. She also possessed an incredible desire to win. It was beyond ambition, part of her competitive nature. Jake figured it was her innate need to excel that enabled her to claw her way out of her dead end home life in Tacoma, away from her needy single mother's succession of abusive boyfriends.

In the porch swing, the La Crema Pinot Noir they shared talking shop began to blunt their discussion of the investigation. At the same time, it heightened their interest in each other. The night ended early, but not before several sessions of fevered lovemaking. In the shower, Jake felt waves of arousal thinking about the two of them in bed the night before. He turned off the hot water but remained for a while, the torrent of cold water cooling him down, bringing him back to the present. It was time to redirect his thoughts to the flight with Jimmy Gray and the cyber research with Billy Gillmon.

~ * ~

Jake took Gillmon up on his offer to meet the Learjet 60 at Dulles General Aviation. By nine-thirty Jake and Billy were in the DOGs' small suite of offices in the basement of the Homeland Security Building on 7th Street S.W. The flight from the Mid-Delta Regional in Greenville was ninety-five minutes and smooth as silk. Jimmy Gray said it was due to the time of day and the tail wind out of the southwest. Jake knew Jimmy owned the jet with three other Delta businessmen who shared the cost of employing a professional pilot and co-pilot full-time.

Billy set up a new computer with a twenty-seven inch monitor for Jake so the two of them could work side by side. On his own before Jake's arrival, Billy had already discovered a great deal about Abdul Azeem *nee* Joseph Randall. The name change documents from the Prince William County Clerk's office had been his starting point, so he brought up on his screen the court records, including fingerprints. With the prints and the rest of the data Randall was required to provide in order to become Azeem, Billy said gathering the early background information was a piece of cake. Jake looked at the trail of documents and records that Billy had pieced together and read Billy's narrative. The history was fascinating.

Joseph Randall was born in Baltimore in 1970 in a working class neighborhood in the Park Heights area west of downtown. His family life was stable. Both parents worked, and he did well in high school. With financial aid from the Baltimore Rotary club he earned a degree in accounting from Baltimore City College and went to work as a bookkeeper for a successful black attorney who was active in local politics. The lawyer saw Randall's potential and encouraged the young man to run for city council. Apparently Randall's personality was ill-suited for politics because he lost in a landslide. Angry at the entrenched Baltimore African-American political scene whom he thought were controlled by rich white businessmen, Randall became active in community organizing. He was making quite a name for himself until he slugged a white Baltimore policeman who was chasing a young black man in Randall's neighborhood. Broke the cop's jaw. The black city councilman who had defeated Randall so handily saw an opportunity to eliminate a possible future opponent. With the help of several leading Baltimore white businessmen and a few black Baptist preachers with political stroke, the incumbent councilman pressed the local prosecutor to throw the book at Randall. In unison, they claimed to the prosecutor they were showing strong support for local law enforcement.

The odds were stacked against Randall. The black lawyer who employed him urged him to take the deal. Outgunned and isolated, Randall pleaded guilty to a felony in exchange for a suspended sentence and a year's probation. Unable to get an accounting job with his felony record, Randall began studying the history and writings of Marcus Garvey and Malcolm X. As soon as his probation ended, Randall moved in with distant relatives in Brookline, Massachusetts, where he took the first steps on the path that would eventually have him working and recruiting all over the United States.

Jake coughed. He looked away from his computer.

"How'd you put all this together?" he asked Billy.

"Most of the background information about Baltimore up to the move to Massachusetts is in his probation file. Then I tracked Azeem wherever REMORA took me after he completed his probation and moved to Brookline."

Billy Gillmon designed and built the DOGs REMORA program from scratch in the basement of Homeland Security. REMORA traveled silently underneath the behemoth HSA computer network that accessed virtually every database in the United States and critical sources outside the U.S. Gillmon designed REMORA to move undetected through the universe of data, hidden in the shadow of the aggressive HSA system that was constantly invading, probing everything that moved in cyberspace.

"Starting in 2002," Gillmon said, "Azeem began to do a lot of driving. I followed credit card purchases through just about every state."

"Why was he traveling?"

"We'll get to that. The credit card had a Brookline address for billing from 1999 until early 2002, when everything started going to a post office box in Virginia. Everything after 2001 points to Virginia as Azeem's state of residence."

"Do we know why he moved there?"

"I think so. His name change petition filed in 2002 claimed Prince William County, Virginia as his legal domicile. From what I've uncovered, Virginia remained his domicile until he joined his seventy-two virgins recently, courtesy of Mule Gardner and Trevor Brewer."

Jake started to ask a question but Gillmon interrupted him.

"Before we talk about Virginia, why don't you ask me if his original Brookline address caused me to sit up and take notice?"

"Okay."

"All of Azeem's mail went to Frank's Pawn Shop in Brookline."

"The same place where Dunne and Bull took down...?"

"A Saudi named Farid al Dosari a.k.a. Frank," Gillmon said. "May he rest in peace. Frank's Pawn shop was a conduit for money to some of the 9/11 hijackers and their ground support."

"And al Dosari worked for Kassab," Jake said.

"That's right. Akmal Kassab, a.k.a Al Dubb, "The Bear." The man that shot David Dunne in Rock Creek Park last year. The man we've been trying to find ever since."

"Man-oh-man," Jake said.

~ * ~

Jake spent the rest of the day with Billy Gillmon in their basement office. That night, Jake had dinner with his brother Scott and his girl friend Donna Piersall. They both worked on the hill, Scott for Mississippi Senator Skeeter Sumrall, and Donna for the senator from her home state of South Carolina. Back in his small apartment not far from the DOJ main office building on Constitution Avenue, Jake lay on his bed thinking, his head resting on his interlaced fingers. He had spoken to Kitty earlier. She made it to Oklahoma City safely and was scheduled to meet with ATF agent Gary Needham the next morning. Kitty asked him what he had found out. Jake told her he'd fill her in when he got home, that he didn't want to talk about it over the telephone. Scott and Donna asked him to join them at Scott's apartment after dinner but Jake declined. He was still trying to sort out everything he learned from Billy Gillmon about Abdul Azeem.

Gillmon told him that after Azeem moved to Brookline from Baltimore, he apparently began to attend a mosque and became active in the Muslim community. Gillmon cited several newspaper articles in the local Brookline paper where Azeem appeared in photographs with other Muslims at the mosque. Gillmon found an ad for Frank's Pawn Shop announcing a new tax filing and tax refund loan business in the pawn shop, touting Joseph Randall as the store's accounting and tax expert.

Gillmon said after al Dosari was taken down in Frank's Pawn Shop by Dunne and Bull shortly after 9/11, the DOGs didn't pursue Joseph Randall because they found no evidence of his involvement in the WTC and Pentagon attacks. Randall surfaced the next year in Prince William County when he changed his name to Abdul Azeem. From 2002 until his death at the Gas & Go Fast, Azeem was a road warrior, driving all over the country. Gillmon said Azeem focused on California, Colorado and New Mexico in the West, Pennsylvania and upstate New York in the East, Virginia and North Carolina in the mid-Atlantic states, and rural counties in every southern state, including Yaloquena.

Late in the afternoon, when Billy Gillmon told Jake his theory on why Azeem was traveling, Jake took a deep breath. It had to be true. It explained why he was in Sunshine at the Gas & Go Fast. In her statement to Lee Jones' investigator, the clerk at the store said Azeem had been in the store on many occasions, passing through Yaloquena. She said he was always nice, but never told her why he was traveling through Sunshine.

In bed in his apartment, Jake turned on the television. He needed something to make him relax, take his mind off why he was in D.C. When they stopped working in the late afternoon, Gillmon told Jake that the next day they would spend studying the thirty to forty sites in different states that Gillmon believed Azeem visited in his travels. Gillmon said if he was right, and he was sure he was, it would explain why the young Muslims at Freedmen's Creek were training with AK-47s.

Chapter Thirty-Six

Wednesday morning at 8:30 Kitty and Jake sat in Willie Mitchell's office. Lee Jones leaned against the wall. Walton pulled a chair to the side of the D.A.'s desk.

"So, I found out nothing," Kitty said. "It was a wasted trip."

"Sure is coincidental that ATF Agent Needham got called away suddenly on a top-secret investigation Monday morning," Walton said.

"When I talked to him late Friday he said he would go over their file with me," she said. "When I got there the secretary said he was gone and she wasn't authorized to give me access."

"That's the feds," Lee said. "Cooperation is a one-way street."

"I met with OKCPD investigators and looked at everything they had on the homicide," Kitty said. "It didn't take long. They don't have much on the pistol because ATF was the primary investigative agency for that."

"Your FBI contacts up there?" Willie Mitchell asked.

"They were irritated at Needham, but nothing they could do." She paused a minute. "I'm going to keep calling Needham until I get him. I'm not sure if they have anything that would help us down here, but I'm going to look at that file at some point. I promise you that."

"The defense subpoenaed Needham for next Friday for their Motion to Produce Trevor's Smith & Wesson," Willie Mitchell said. "If he shows up for the hearing, we'll hot box him, show him a little home cooking. See if we can't convince him to share his files with us."

"If he's subpoenaed he has to show up, doesn't he?" Kitty asked.

"Feds play by different rules," Willie Mitchell said. "They can get a federal judge to sign a protective order like that." He snapped his fingers and turned to Walton, then Lee.

"I want Jake to brief you two on what he found out about Abdul Azeem in D.C. He spent a couple of hours with Kitty and me last night. Turns out Freedmen's Creek is not flying solo. It's linked to a bunch of compounds all over the U.S."

"At least thirty," Jake said, passing out a highlighted map of the United States to the others. "Maybe more. You guys ever hear of a fellow named Sheik Mabarik Ali Shah Gilani?"

Walton and Lee said no. Jake told them what he learned about Sheik Gilani in Gillmon's basement office.

"Sheik Gilani is a Pakistani. He founded Muslims of America on a trip to New York in 1980. It's a 501(c)(3) organization...."

"Tax-exempt?" Walton asked.

"That's right. And get this. It's linked to Jamaat al-Fuqra, a jihadist group with the avowed purpose of bringing down the United States from within."

"Jesus Christ," Lee Jones said. "How can our government give tax-exempt status to an organization like Gilani's?"

"Wait," Jake said, "it gets better. Muslims of America have an educational division that gets grants from states and private foundations in the U.S. to fund what they refer to as 'schools' all over the country.

"My guy in D.C. thinks Freedmen's Creek is one of them."

"This is unbelievable," Walton said.

"Listen to this. In mid-2002, California law enforcement shut down a Muslim charter school near Fresno that couldn't account for $1.3 million dollars of public money they had been given by California for education purposes. Fresno was one of the towns Azeem traveled to several times in 2002. From newspaper accounts I saw, these people lived communally on a thousand acre tract in the foothills of the Sierra Mountain. When the state shut them down, most of the members headed east to Virginia, which has become the command center for these compounds in the last seven or eight years. Virginia was Azeem's legal residence from 2002 until his death last month. We think it's why Azeem moved to Virginia, to be near their headquarters."

"Was this Fresno commune the only one in the U.S. to get in this kind of trouble?" Walton asked. "Seems like we would have read about this before now."

"No. The first Muslim compound busted in the United States was in Colorado in 1993. The members supported themselves by filing fraudulent state tax refund claims and lawsuits against the state. When the state police raided the encampment, they found automatic weapons, ammunition dumps, bombs, and maps of potential targets." Jake paused. "They had a shooting range, too."

Walton and Sheriff Jones stared at Jake.

"So," Willie Mitchell said, "looks like Freedmen's Creek is the same thing. Jake didn't see any bombs or maps, but he saw everything else."

"What evidence links Azeem to these thirty communes all over the country?" Walton asked. "How do you know he was involved?"

"I can't tell you everything, but my associate did a comparison of Azeem's travel over the last nine years, and everywhere he went...," Jake looked at Walton, "our information is there was a Muslim commune in the area. The computer analyzed the data and there's no doubt he was linked to each one of these places. Before he started coming down here to Freedmen's Creek, his credit card receipts show he spent a good bit of time in Memphis."

Lee Jones pointed to his map. "Freedmen's Creek is the only commune in Mississippi. The closest one outside the state is in Memphis, but there's a mark through it on the map."

Jake looked at his father.

"That was the Al Rashad mosque in Memphis," Willie Mitchell said. "It wasn't a commune, but it had a big outreach program. As you all know it shut down over two years ago."

There was a silence in the room. Every one of them knew the Memphis mosque was the source of the attempt on Willie Mitchell's life during the trial of El Moro, the drug smuggling Muslim convert. Willie Mitchell barely survived the attempt. He still had the scars, aches, and seizures to prove it.

"It makes all this real personal now," Willie Mitchell said.

"And it explains why Mohammed X is so irate about Azeem's death," Jake said. "If we're reading this right, Azeem was their link to funding. He was the connection with Sheik Gilani and the Muslims of America. With their money man gone to Allah and with the bright light this case is going to focus on their commune, the national leaders are going to cut all ties with Freedmen's Creek. No more money."

"And without money from their people in Virginia," Willie Mitchell said, "Mohammed X's utopia at Freedmen's Creek is history."

"And we're sure these people are violent?" Lee Jones asked. "They're not just intent on defending themselves?"

"They get their funding from U.S. organizations linked to Sheik Gilani in Pakistan," Jake said. "He's dedicated to the overthrow of the United States."

"You remember Daniel Pearl," Willie Mitchell said, "the Wall Street Journal reporter whose beheading you can still watch on the internet?"

"I sure do," Sheriff Jones said.

"Well," Willie Mitchell said, "when Daniel Pearl was captured, he was on his way to interview Sheik Gilani."

Chapter Thirty-Seven

Freddy showed up for the hearing early wearing his court outfit, the brown corduroy sport coat with his long gray ponytail tucked in. He knew he drew enough attention from the locals without the ponytail making it worse. It was the same reason he borrowed Tracy Brewer's truck to drive to the Sunshine courthouse. An older model truck was much less conspicuous than a customized Harley Blockhead in Sunshine. Even though Freddy made sure the motorcycle's engine was muffled enough to be within the legal decibel limits in every state, it was still loud. Just resting on its kickstand in the courthouse parking lot, the classic Harley attracted a lot of gawkers.

Tracy had turned out to be a lot of help to Freddy. She let him use her old truck anytime he asked, and she had a good friend working in the Yaloquena courthouse whom she did not mind calling to check on the status of the hearing and trial dates in the case. She was a powerful flirt, too, and sexy as hell, with her long black hair, high cheekbones, and those tits trying to bust out of her shirt with "Tracy" sewn on it. Freddy knew he was kin to her somehow, but like his old great Uncle Norbert used to say, *"Son, if it ain't good enough for family...."*

Tracy sticking her tits in his face reminded him of his ex, Brandi Trichel. Damn, that was one hot woman. Too bad she was crazy as a road lizard, but what the hell, Freddy figured they were all crazy because every woman he ever spent time with seemed nuts to him. Her parents were assholes, too. They didn't like Freddy worth a shit. He didn't mind it when Brandi told him to hit the road. He thought Oklahoma City was a dip shit town anyway.

For right now, Freddy fought off his lustful thoughts about Tracy. He figured keeping her at arms' length while he had this business to take care of was the best way to handle Tracy. There would be plenty of time later, on the next trip to Mississippi. Holding off would make it that much sweeter when he came back. Seeing Tracy in all her naked glory was one more reason to make sure he got the gun back from the authorities. If he didn't this might be his last trip to Mississippi, or anywhere else in the U.S. for that matter. He had what he thought was a pretty good plan, with a reasonable chance of success. He hoped it did, because he sure as hell did not want to spend the rest of his life in Mexico or Venezuela.

Freddy sat by himself in the fourth row behind the defense table. He watched the same bunch of dressed up, pissed off niggers walk into court and file into the first row. He couldn't figure out where the hell they came from. To Freddy, three of them did not look or act like Mississippi niggers; they talked like Yankees. There was the giant, who was black as the ace of spades, and the little shrimp with the big glasses. They bowed and scraped, walking on tiptoes around their boss man, the one in the green bow tie and light brown suit, with the rimless glasses and wet-looking hair plastered down on his head. Then there was the local guy with the Catholic priest collar. Freddy knew he was local by the way he talked, and he knew for damned sure the pencil-necked prick wasn't any Catholic priest. All things being equal, Freddy thought he would enjoy kicking all four of their black asses if he had the chance. Man, how he would love to turn Breed and Wrench loose on'em. And Wizler. Freddy chuckled at the thought of Wizler goose stepping and channeling Hitler, yelling all that white supremacy shit at the Muslims. What a trip that would be. All three of his men hated niggers worse than Freddy did, and they'd be tickled pink to harrass'em and rough'em up, but first things first. Business before pleasure.

Freddy watched the little bald-headed clerk walk in and sit behind his equipment. The clerk had the same routine as the first two times Freddy had watched him. He fiddled with his computer and his recording system, making sure it was working before the woman judge came in. When the little clerk had problems with his systems, which apparently was quite often based on Freddy's two prior trips to the Sunshine courtroom, Freddy could tell the clerk got nervous, worried the woman judge would get upset.

While the clerk worked on his systems this morning, all the lawyers showed up at once, walking into court together through the side door. Freddy thought they might have had some kind of pre-trial conference before court started. In his experience with the legal systems in Colorado and Texas, his lawyers had done that on a few occasions. Freddy wished he could have heard what his own lawyers said about him to the judges and the other lawyers involved in his own cases years ago.

Freddy watched the black woman lawyer wheel the little crippled nigger inside the rail to the defense table. Now there was a waste of humanity. "Mule" was what they called him in court sometime, and Freddy figured "Mule" was not worth the rigmarole his shooting had brought about, the court proceedings and all. If the little black son-of-a-bitch hadn't pulled his Saturday night special and started shooting at the Muslim, Freddy wouldn't be in the jam he was in. Mule's main lawyer, the stocky Summit guy, was good. Freddy knew a good lawyer when he saw one. The guy was sharp and forceful. The woman lawyer seemed smart, too, but she was quiet, mild-mannered. Freddy guessed that was why he was the number one lawyer and she was number two. He had no idea how Mule could afford such good lawyers working for him, because there was no way he had any money. Summit was no public defender. He was high-priced legal talent. The woman lawyer didn't seem like any slouch either.

Both the D.A.'s were good, from what Freddy saw in the first two court proceedings. The young one was smart, quick on his feet. The older one, the actual District Attorney named Willie Mitchell, Freddy could tell he was a powerful force. Even though the younger D.A. was doing all the talking, Willie Mitchell had a presence, a calm strength. He was in charge, just sitting there. The man was smart and experienced. Freddy didn't ever want to have to go up against District Attorney Willie Mitchell Banks, that's for sure.

Freddy was trying to get a look at the good-looking woman deputy sitting in the second row behind the D.A.'s table. She was in court the last time with the twenty-something-year-old man whom Freddy thought might be an FBI agent. The guy was in good shape, strong-looking and rangy. Freddy noticed he looked like the D.A., so maybe he was Willie Mitchell's son from out of town. That might explain why he wasn't in court today, gone back to wherever he came from. Good riddance.

The black woman judge walked in. Freddy stood up with everyone else. The judge nodded and everyone sat down. She looked over at the little bald-headed clerk, who checked all his equipment and gave the judge a reassuring nod. He was ready.

Freddy knew this hearing was about Trevor's gun, the fuckin' gun that had Freddy in such deep shit. The defense lawyer Summit wanted the D.A. to have to turn it over to the defense for them to inspect and test it. Freddy thought the judge was right when she said it didn't make any difference to Mule's case because both sides said it was Trevor's gun, not the twenty-two, that ended up killing the Muslim nigger. So, Freddy thought, why they fuck do they need to test it?

Should have destroyed that gun after Oklahoma City. Never should have given it to Trevor. But man, I hated to waste a good gun like that. Who would have thought it would end up killing the Muslim? Who would have ever thought the gun would have left the hill? Trevor never did.

Freddy figured the D.A.'s had the best side of the argument on the gun, and the judge ought to rule in their favor. No need to let the defense get the gun and send it to who knows where in the federal government to test it. Freddy knew if his gun got into federal custody, his chances of getting it back and saving his own ass were almost zero. If the gun ever left this little hick courthouse for the FBI lab in D.C., Freddy knew he was up shit creek. Forever. That's why he had a good plan to get it, and why it was important that the judge rule in the D.A.'s favor. Freddy was confident she would. She seemed to be a good judge, tough and smart, even though she was a nigger.

Chapter Thirty-Eight

Sitting at the prosecution table after Judge Williams took the bench, Willie Mitchell was glad the hearing this morning on Summit's Motion to Produce the Smith & Wesson had turned out to be such a goat rope. Both witnesses Summit subpoenaed failed to show. That's what took up most of the discussion in the pre-hearing conference. As Willie Mitchell had predicted last week, Judge Williams received a fax this morning before the hearing from the Oklahoma City ATF office. The fax was accompanied by a grainy copy of a federal judge's order quashing the Yaloquena County subpoena. The federal judge was vague in the protective order about how Needham's testimony would jeopardize "an important ongoing federal investigation." The federal judge said it would, and apparently that's all he felt like Yaloquena County officials needed to know. It all sounded like boilerplate to Willie Mitchell. In his experience with DOJ, explanations in jurisdictional conflicts only went one way. The feds never felt like they had to justify the exercise of their preemptive authority over federal agents testifying in state court. Willie Mitchell did not think there was some deep, dark secret agenda in ATF or DOJ regarding Trevor's gun. They liked to throw their weight around, sometimes just to show they could. From experience, he knew the feds did not like their agents testifying in situations the DOJ did not control. That was probably all that was going on here.

Since ATF Agent Gary Needham was a no-show for Summit's dog-and-pony show on his Motion to Produce the weapon, Willie Mitchell and Kitty's plan to interrogate Needham privately withered on the vine. Kitty told Willie Mitchell after the pre-hearing conference in Judge Williams' chambers she would stay on Needham by phone to get what information she could, even if she had to grovel. Willie Mitchell told her that's just what it would take—a submissive attitude to the fed's authority, and perhaps another road trip to OKC.

Needham's no-show wasn't a big deal to the D.A., but Trevor Brewer's was. Willie Mitchell asked Jake after the pre-trial to leave immediately for Brewer Hill to find out what happened to Trevor. Trevor was out on bail on his weapons charges. Failure to appear, failure to obey a court order, which is what the subpoena was, was a breach of the bail undertaking. It would be interesting to see what Judge Williams would do. Willie Mitchell knew it would depend on how hard Summit pushed it. The D.A. leaned over to whisper to Walton.

"Take up for Trevor as much as you can. Try to get Judge Williams to give him some time to come in. Maybe it was beyond his control."

"Mr. Summit," the judge said, "what is your pleasure on Agent Needham?"

"I don't see how this court can do anything, Your Honor," Summit said. "Therefore, I would just ask that the ATF fax and court order attached be filed into the record. I do plan to call Agent Needham as a witness at the trial of this matter in two weeks, so I will undertake to talk to his supervisors in hopes that I can get him here then."

"Good luck," she said. "Though my authority over a federal agent is limited, this Court stands ready to issue whatever orders are within my power to have Agent Needham here for the trial. Now, what about Mr. Brewer, your other witness?"

"The record reflects that proper service on Trevor Brewer was made by Dundee County deputies," Summit said.

"Yes, it does," Judge Williams said.

Walton stood. "Your Honor, may I be heard?"

"Go ahead," she said.

"This Court knows how unreliable service is in other counties when it's not the deputy sheriff's county judge issuing the subpoena. We would like to assist the Court in locating the witness, but we would ask Your Honor to hold off on revoking or forfeiting Mr. Brewer's bail until we get to the bottom of this. We certainly don't condone his ignoring the Court order, if that's what Mr. Brewer did. Our office would just ask that we make certain what happened to cause the non-appearance before Your Honor issues any new order."

"Mr. Summit?"

"That's fine, Your Honor. However, if it becomes clear that Trevor Brewer was properly served, I would ask the Court to forfeit his bond and keep him upstairs in Yaloquena County jail until the trial. That way it's certain he will appear for the jury trial."

"I think that's a reasonable request," she said. "Is that resolution acceptable to the State?"

Walton looked down at Willie Mitchell, who said "yes" quietly.

"Do you have anything else to offer in support of your Motion to Produce the weapon, Mr. Summit," Judge Williams asked, "other than the testimony of these two witnesses who failed to appear and the arguments and law set forth in your memorandum in support of your motion?"

"No, Your Honor. I would ask the Court to postpone ruling until we have a resolution of Mr. Brewer's non-appearance."

Walton stood but sat back down when Judge Williams answered.

"Jury selection begins two weeks from this Monday, Mr. Summit, and I'm not willing to delay the trial because of your Motion to Produce, which I must say, Mr. Summit, borders on the frivolous in my opinion. I'm ready to rule."

Summit sat down.

"I find no legal or factual justification for compelling the State to produce the Smith & Wesson for defense testing for the following reason: both sides agree that Dr. Nathan's conclusion in his written report is correct, that the Smith & Wesson fired by Mr. Brewer caused Abdul Azeem's death. There is no justiciable controversy involving this gun and the cause of death. The defense Motion to Produce is hereby denied."

"To which ruling the defense objects," Summit said.

"From discussions in chambers this morning, the District Attorney's office will offer the Smith & Wesson used by Mr. Brewer into evidence at the trial. Mr. Donaldson indicated it will be one of the first exhibits, along with Mr. Gardner's .22 automatic and the digital recording of the shooting. After the jury renders its verdict, Mr. Summit, I will entertain a motion from you to withdraw the weapon from evidence for whatever purposes you deem fit, as long as it is returned to the custody of the Clerk of Court to remain until further orders."

"Your Honor," Walton said, "as we indicated in chambers, the gun will still be needed by the State in our prosecution of Trevor Brewer on the stolen weapons charge. Also, DOJ through ATF has put us on notice that they might want to take possession of the gun after we are through with our cases down here. As the court is aware, it has evidentiary value in a homicide prosecution in Oklahoma City, according to DOJ."

"You may have to wait your turn, Mr. Summit," she said. "I suggest let's all wait to see what happens in this trial before we make any future plans related to the gun." She paused a moment. "What else can we dispose of this morning. Is all discovery complete? Any other preliminary matters?"

Jordan Summit stood. Willie Mitchell glanced over at Summit's client. Mule was sound asleep in his oversized white shirt and big wheelchair. Willie Mitchell had noticed Mule sleeping before Judge Williams took the bench this morning, and watched him doze through the arguments of both sides.

Well, a man needs his rest.

"There was only one outstanding discovery request that had not been satisfied through the close of business yesterday, Your Honor," Jordan Summit said, "but this morning Ms. Bernstein and I received all of the telephone records of Gas & Go Fast pertaining to the location in question. Counsel for the company delivered to us this morning the phone records for the twelve months prior to the shooting. We have yet to review them in detail, but on first glance, it appears that the subpoena *duces tecum* for the phone records is satisfied."

"Very well," the judge said. "Anything else?"

Jordan Summit and Walton Donaldson said no.

"I directed the clerk to deliver jury subpoenas to the Sheriff's office Monday morning to serve on one hundred prospective jurors. This is not a capital case. If history is any indicator, approximately sixty-five to seventy of the subpoenaed venire will appear for jury selection on November 7, which should be an adequate number from which we can select the jury. Some of those named will have moved or died or committed a felony since the voter rolls were last purged. Do either of you think we need more?"

Walton conferred briefly with Willie Mitchell.

"No, Your Honor," Walton said.

"That number should be adequate, Judge," Jordan Summit said.

"If there's nothing further, this Court is adjourned."

~ * ~

Mohammed X waited in the courtroom after the woman judge exited. It was an abomination seeing a woman in such a position, but he had no choice but to put up with it. He noticed the big white man in the brown coat leave the courtroom quickly. He had seen him in court before. Mohammed X assumed he was related to the murderer who was getting away with Azeem's murder.

He watched the young woman deputy walk through the rail to talk to the District Attorney and his aide. The hapless fool Bobby Sanders stood at the rail talking to Bernstein, the woman defense attorney. It was unbelievable how many women were involved in the case in official capacities. When the destiny of jihad was fulfilled in North America, things would be different.

Mohammed watched the District Attorney gather his papers. It was unusual how their lives seemed intertwined. In a perfect world, Willie Mitchell Banks would have had nothing to do with prosecution of Abdul Azeem's killer. It seemed to Mohammed that fate had a warped sense of humor. Then again, his own destiny had taken him a long way from Inglewood, California to this Godforsaken backwater. He prayed to Allah to reveal the nature of his next mission, now that this one seemed to be drawing to a close. He prayed the revelation would come soon.

Mohammed gestured to Abud and Samson. It was time to go. Leave the stupid infidel Bobby Sanders with the woman.

~ * ~

Freddy waited in Tracy's truck with the motor running for the dressed-up niggers to leave the courthouse. He had overheard bits and pieces of conversation in the courtroom and courthouse hallways to know they had it in for Trevor. He was fed up with their attitude. He didn't know how or when he was going to pay them a visit, but he was at least going to find out more about who they were. If he ever was in a position to get up close and personal with them, they wouldn't forget it.

From his parking spot he could see everyone come and go from the courthouse. After a few minutes, he saw the three Yankee-talking niggers walk down the courthouse steps and get into a Dodge Ram pickup with dark-tinted windows. He didn't know what happened to the local skinny nigger with the priest collar but he wasn't hanging around to find out. The Dodge took off, and Freddy followed. He knew a good bit about how to tail someone without being seen. It was a lot easier in a truck than on a Harley Blockhead.

Freddy followed them out of town on the highway to Kilbride, staying well behind them. The Dodge Ram was easy to keep an eye on. The Dodge passed the turnoff to Rivercrest and the Lonely Road Bar & Grill, the Dregs home away from home in Yaloquena.

A few miles west of Dundee County, the Dodge turned left. As soon as it did, Freddy stomped Tracy's truck and sped toward the turn. As he drew close, he could see the Dodge had driven north from the highway on the road intersecting the main highway at the Dregs' motel. He double-checked the motel parking lot to make sure the truck wasn't there.

In a few minutes Freddy spotted the back of the Dodge. He hung back until he saw the red brake lights flash and the Dodge turn left and stop. Freddy drove slowly past the fortress-like entrance set back about a hundred feet from the highway. He kept his left arm on the window blocking any view of his face. He saw the armed guard lift the bar at the gate and motion the Dodge Ram through.

Freddy drove on past the place at a steady pace. A mile up the road, he turned the truck around and drove south to pass the Freedmen's Creek entrance again. This time, he noticed the flag waving from the silver pole and the guardhouse at the closed gate.

Freddy wasn't sure what the place was, but he was going to find out. Breed might not acknowledge his heritage, but Freddy knew from experience that Breed was good at scouting. He could move silently and patiently, observing people without being detected. Even if Breed claimed he wasn't a real Indian or half-Indian, Freddy knew he sure could track and scout like one.

Freddy returned to the motel, rousting Breed and Wrench from a late morning "date" with the girls old greasy Buster Cloud found for them. He told Breed what he needed him to do, that he would drive him past the place the next morning. Freddy told Breed and Wrench to bring their women and meet Wizler and him at the Lonely Road. Freddy's plan had come together, and he wanted to celebrate, even if it was only eleven a.m.

Chapter Thirty-Nine

Jake stood by Willie Mitchell's farm truck in the parking lot of Tom's Automotive talking to Tom. It was ten in the morning.

"I know it's some serious shit and I got money on the line but I don't know where Trevor is."

"He didn't tell you anything about getting served with a subpoena by Dundee deputies?"

"He sure as hell didn't. I ain't saying for sure it didn't happen, but if Trevor had been served some papers seems like I'd have known about it. Not much happens on that hill that gets by me."

Jake noticed Tracy Brewer staring a hole through him from inside the office. Jake sensed that she was upset with him and probably everyone from Sunshine for continuing to interfere with the Brewer clan. He turned away so he didn't have to look at her.

"Daddy sent me to find Trevor before the law gets involved. He's got to come in and explain to Judge Williams why he didn't show up this morning in court in Sunshine."

"I ain't seen him today. Fact of business I ain't seen him all yesterday, neither."

"How can I find him?"

Tom thought a moment, wiping his hands, which looked clean already to Jake, on his dark red rag. Tom pushed his red cap with the STP logo back on his head.

"Tell you what. I'm going to make a call up there and get'em to spread the word you're coming up. You drive on up there, go through the *cummins* onto the trail that leads back to our cabins. You remember the way?"

"Yes, sir," Jake said.

"You park in front of Trevor's cabin. Start walking into the woods behind the cabin."

"How do I know which way to walk when I get in those woods?"

"You just keep walking. It won't matter what direction you're going in. You couldn't find him in a million years. Trevor'll find you. He'll know you're in them woods. Take my word for it. Only reason I'm calling up there is I don't want anyone else giving you any trouble. You carrying a gun?"

"Yes, sir."

"Good. I ain't sayin' you'll need it, I'm just sayin' there's Brewers up there, not none of my close kin, that'd just as soon shoot you as not."

Jake watched Tom enter the office and say something to Tracy. Jake couldn't make out what Tracy answered, but the two of them started arguing. Through the window, Jake saw Tom walk toward Tracy and shake his finger at her. Jake waited, continuing to watch as Tom picked up the phone and made a brief call. Tom cracked open the office door and waved Jake toward Brewer Hill.

"Go on ahead up there. They'll be expecting you. Do what I told you and you'll be all right."

Jake cranked the farm truck and drove a few hundred yards on the paved highway, then turned right onto the dirt and gravel road leading up Brewer Hill. Before he started up the incline, Jake stopped his truck at the end of the flat part of the road. Standing outside on the gravel, Jake strapped on his Colt XSE .45 caliber in its leather holster. His Glock 36 forty-five was already in its waist holster in the middle of his back. He checked both pistols to make sure there was a chambered round in each and they were ready to fire.

Jake had debated on the drive over whether to go up on Brewer Hill armed. On the one hand, the sight of an unescorted stranger with a sidearm strapped to his leg might prove to be provocative to the Brewers. An unarmed intruder might generate less concern. On the other, the last time he was on the hill the Brewers seemed to be itching for trouble. Trevor had to run off two of them who showed up with rifles in the clearing in front of Trevor's cabin. When Tom asked him if he had a gun on him, Jake took it as a friendly signal from Tom that carrying his weapons up there might be a good idea. Just in case.

He built up speed before hitting the incline to help the old Ford truck make it to the top. Jake glanced quickly to his left and right, checking the trees for Brewers. His main focus was keeping the truck in the center of the road.

The truck finally cleared the summit. Jake slowed to a stop in the common area. He saw several people in trucks on the edge of the clearing that seemed to be watching him. He moved ahead slowly toward the abandoned buildings. When no one intercepted him, he continued on the trail through the buildings and into the woods to Tom and Trevor's cabins.

There was nothing in the truck of consequence, so Jake left the truck unlocked and walked past the burn pit into the trees behind Trevor's cabin. He followed a well-worn trail. From the hoof tracks and droppings the trail seemed to be a major thoroughfare for cattle. Jake watched his step and took the lesser traveled path when the trail forked. Since he didn't know where he was going, he figured he'd choose the route that allowed him to avoid most of the cow patties.

After ten minutes of walking, he encountered a dirt road. Jake could tell it was a major truck artery because of the tire tracks. He walked north on the road until he saw a half-dozen cabins in the distance. Jake turned around. He did not want to disturb any Brewers, and from what Tom said, Trevor was in the woods, not in a cabin.

By one p.m. Jake was ready for a break. He hadn't come well-prepared for a hike. He was adequately armed, but had no water, no food. He sat a few minutes on a rotted log overlooking a picturesque valley north of Brewer Hill. Using woodsmanship he learned as a kid hunting deer and squirrels, Jake started out again, heading down hill where he could, hoping to find a creek with clear running water. After an hour, he found a slow-moving shallow stream. He knelt beside it and scooped up water in his palm. As he brought it to his mouth, an aluminum canteen hit his leg and fell on the ground next to him.

"That creek water's clean enough to drink," Trevor said, "b-but if you ain't from up here it might give you the r-runs."

Jake emptied his palm and drank from the dented canteen.

"Drink it all. I g-got plenty."

Jake finished and screwed on the canteen top. He tossed it to Trevor.

"Glad you found me," Jake said.

"I heard you were coming up here." He paused. "You know I never was served with any subpoena."

"Good. Then you didn't violate any court order. Why'd the Dundee deputy certify that he served you personally?"

"C-can't answer that. He came up here on the hill with the p-paper, asking for me. Every p-person he saw in the *cummins* anywhere near my age he asked'em, 'You Trevor Brewer?' They said he was real nervous-like. The first person that didn't say 'no, I ain't' right away, he g-gave the subpoena to. Said he was d-done. It was my c-cousin Burl took it. He and I k-kind of look alike."

"So you knew about the hearing this morning?"

"Yep. But n-nobody told me I had to be there."

Jake nodded. "You don't have to wear that sling any more?"

"I don't know how l-long I was supposed to w-wear it. I took it off yesterday and my arm didn't f-feel too bad so I left it off. Arm's sore and weak, but it'll h-heal all right without that sling."

"You spent the night in these woods?"

"Yep. No big deal. I've been doing it all my life. I got places to go that give me some shelter. Long as it don't rain I'm fine. It ain't cold yet. Come wintertime I'd have to prepare a little better."

"So, if you weren't served why'd you take off into the woods?"

Trevor kicked at some leaves.

"You can't hide from this stuff, Trevor," Jake said. "Tom's going to have to come up with a lot more money if your bail is revoked."

"I don't want to go back in that courtroom."

"You have to. And if Judge Williams doesn't believe you about not being served she can hold you in jail until the trial in a couple of weeks."

"I didn't do anything wrong."

"We know that. But your bullet's the one that killed the guy. No way you can get around that. Daddy's going to help you all he can. You believe that, don't you?"

"Y-yeah. I trust you and Coach."

Trevor grimaced like he was in pain.

"You don't want to have to talk in front of all those people."

"Y-you weren't there in court," Trevor said. "I c-couldn't get out a s-single word. I just froze."

"Let's walk back to your cabin," Jake said.

~ * ~

That afternoon, Walton, Trevor, and Tom gathered in Judge Williams' chambers around the telephone she moved from her credenza to the center of her desk. Jordan Summit was in his Jackson office, participating via the phone's speaker.

"As long as he appears for trial," Summit said, "I'm all right with that, Your Honor."

"Mr. Brewer, Trevor's father, has assured me that Trevor will be present in court for the duration of the trial."

"What about jury selection?" Walton asked. "Can Trevor wait until the first day of testimony?"

"Mr. Summit?" she asked.

"That's fine, Your Honor. No need for him to be there to watch the jury being selected."

"All right. Thank you, Mr. Summit."

Judge Williams hung up. She looked up at Trevor and Tom.

"You're very lucky Mr. Summit is not pressing the matter, young man," she said. "Don't push your luck again."

"No, Judge," Trevor said, "I'll be h-here."

Tom nodded, deadly serious, staring at the Judge's carpet.

"Okay," she said. "See you all in two weeks."

Walking in the courthouse hallway, Walton, Trevor, and Tom joined Jake outside the District Attorney's office.

"Trevor dodged a bullet in the judge's office," Walton said.

"I wish that M-Muslim at the store had dodged mine," Trevor said.

"It's going to work out," Walton said and walked into the D.A.'s office, leaving Jake and the two Brewers in the hall.

"Let me ask you both something," Jake said. "There's been a big white guy up here watching every hearing. He was there again this morning. He drove to court last time in an older model truck registered to Tracy Brewer. He's got a ponytail he tucks inside his coat."

Trevor glanced at Tom, who looked at the floor. Neither of them said anything.

"Do you want m-me to...."

"Go ahead," Tom said.

"That's my uncle."

"Half-uncle," Tom said.

"Freddy Brewer," Trevor said. "He's just here visiting."

"Why is he at every hearing?" Jake asked.

Trevor glanced at his father, who kept his eyes on his shoes.

"He w-wants to make sure I'm okay."

"What's he do for a living?" Jake asked.

"Used to own night c-clubs," Trevor said.

Tom patted Trevor's arm.

"We've got to go," Tom said. "I've got two jobs to get out tonight." He turned to Jake. "I'll have him here when the testifyin' starts."

Tom hustled Trevor down the hallway. Trevor looked over his shoulder at Jake and waved. Jake couldn't help but feel sorry for his friend Trevor. He had a good heart, but he grew up on Brewer Hill, his father in Parchman for much of his early life. Trevor wasn't hard and unforgiving, like the Brewers Jake had seen and Willie Mitchell had told him about. No doubt the other Brewers thought Trevor was weak because of his stutter. Jake could only imagine how much Trevor dreaded testifying.

Chapter Forty

Mohammed X sat on the large pillow with his legs crossed. He picked up his prayer beads from the low table and fingered them, moving from one bead to the next as he watched Abud pace. It was almost midnight.

"Your Eminence, I don't know what else to do," Abud said, pushing his giant glasses up on his tiny nose. "We are out of money. We've been cut off from everyone in Virginia. I've called other encampments as well. No one will talk to me."

"Calm down, Abud. Allah will see us through this."

Mohammed X knew he had to project confidence and serenity in the face of the crisis. The death of Abdul Azeem in September was a blow to the entire network of Muslim compounds throughout the United States. He was the conduit for money and advice from central command in Virginia. The last time the two of them communicated, Mohammed X told Azeem he was the "Johnny Appleseed" of Muslim training communes in America. From the time he escaped blame-free for 9/11 from Frank's Pawn Shop in Brookline and moved to Virginia to the home office, Azeem had personally recruited over one thousand U.S. Muslims to the cause. From 2002 forward, Azeem had a hand in the founding of two dozen of the thirty-five communes operating in the U.S.

Azeem's death was a double-whammy for Freedmen's Creek. Not only was Azeem the bag man providing their cash funding from Virginia HQ, his murder in Sunshine also resulted in their being totally cut off from central command and from any other compounds. Mohammed X guessed that word went out from Virginia immediately after learning of Azeem's death that Freedmen's Creek was to be quarantined. No one in the movement was to have contact or communication with the Mississippi brothers.

Abud was Mohammed X's operations officer, but he had never dealt with the home office except through Azeem. Mohammed X was sure it was the organization's method of insulating top management from any civil or criminal screw ups at the communes.

"Get some rest, Brother Abud," Mohammed X said. "Tomorrow is another day. We will find a way to work through this setback."

Abud left Muhammad X's quarters. His Eminence hadn't shown weakness to Abud, but Mohammed X knew Freedmen's Creek was doomed. Without the periodic cash assistance package from Virginia via Azeem, Freedmen's Creek would not survive. Their efforts to grow and store crops had been a total failure, and their animal husbandry was a joke. The only people in the commune with practical knowledge to share were his military instructors, but they were no help in other disciplines. The soil in the compound had too much clay content to grow crops efficiently and produce hay for animals. It was good for growing pine trees, but they weren't edible and were too few to harvest for sale. In their two years of existence, in addition to trying unsuccessfully to grow their own food, they had tried to earn money at different times by operating an automotive repair shop, a sewing facility to produce clothing for sale, and a contract painting crew to do jobs in the nearby communities. Everything they tried was an abject failure.

Exacerbating the dilemma was Mohammed X's failure to control his population. Their mission outreach was so effective their numbers had grown to an unmanageable number. With too many mouths to feed, no money, and enough food only for a few weeks, the commune was limping into winter, when things would only get worse.

Mohammed would make the announcement to his people after the trial of Lester Gardner. He felt they had enough to make it through the trial if it started on November 7 on schedule and didn't last too long. The woman lawyer Bernstein told the fool Bobby Sanders that Jordan Summit felt they could try it in one week. Mohammed X was certain they didn't have enough money and food to last until justice was done to the Brewer boy. So be it. White men had been dealing misery to black men for centuries, and Mohammed X knew he would have to get over this miscarriage of justice. He would just have to move on to whatever task the central command in Virginia wanted him to pursue.

Mohammed X made sure all the doors to his residence were locked and he was alone. He walked into his kitchen and reached for the Baker's Bittersweet Baking Chocolate package on the top shelf of the cabinet above the refrigerator. He removed the rubber band holding the package together and removed a dark brown plug of what looked like a misshapen square of baking chocolate. Mohammed X walked into his bedroom and retrieved a lighter and a clear plastic pipe from his dop kit, along with a glass bowl that fitted snugly on top of the closed end of the perforated pipe. He placed the plug in the bowl, turned off the lights, and reclined on his bed.

Mohammed X held the lighter flame to the dark plug and inhaled. He did it several more times in rapid succession, then placed the pipe and lighter on his night table and reclined. From past experience he knew it was important that he lie down before he felt the full effect.

He lay on his bed in darkness. He was grateful for the "chocolate" Azeem left him on an earlier visit. The bedroom was pitch black. In all his years Mohammed X had never experienced darkness like he had at Freedmen's Creek. In the early days before they had their outside lighting installed, when there was no moon, the darkness in the encampment was impenetrable. In California and Tennessee, Mohammed X merely thought he had seen darkness.

Mohammed X felt the opium pinning him to the bed. Unable to move, he revisited his early life with his slave name Calvin Ketchums. Born in Inglewood near LAX, his parents were devout Baptists. They dragged him to church with them, but Calvin was never comfortable there. From an early age, he thought the preachers were showmen, full of crap and on the take. As soon as he finished high school he moved to Oakland and got a job in a hotel. In an incredible stroke of bad luck, Calvin was caught going through a guest's suitcase. When he ran from the room with the man chasing him, he bumped into a Mexican maid and knocked her down some stairs. The stupid bitch hit her head and died. Calvin didn't mean to hurt her. Even though it was an accident, he had an appointed lawyer who told him to plead guilty to some kind of manslaughter. A year out of high school, and Calvin was on his way to San Quentin.

He studied under Ronald Johnson, who started the African Identity Movement, AIM, at SQ. Calvin learned a lot about slavery and the black man's two centuries of suffering at the hands of white America, how the wealth of the country was built on the backs on African labor. Johnson taught him Marxist philosophy as well. After his internship with AIM, Calvin fell in with a crew of other brothers at San Quinten and learned about Islam. His last two years inside, he immersed himself in the Quran and the words of the prophet. With the help of a Muslim jailhouse lawyer, he changed his name to Hakim Abdullah Al Rashad.

As Al Rashad, he started California Afro-Americans for Allah and raised enough money to build three mosques. His religious fervor merged with his militant tendencies and CAAA began buying and selling guns to raise money for the movement. The local cops accused CAAA of trying to blow up Candlestick Park, and they tried to pin the murders they linked to the gun smuggling to Al Rashad. When the FBI and ATF began investigating CAAA's involvement in bomb plots to take out Candlestick Park and San Francisco's Opera House, he saw the writing on the wall. Al Rashad left California for Memphis to let the heat die down. He began to worship at a small, peaceful Memphis mosque where in 2003, he met and was recruited by Abdul Azeem to start another mosque, one with much more aggressive goals. With Azeem's funding and organizational help, Al Rashad soon had his own mosque in Memphis with its own agenda. The mosque's ultimate mission was the violent overthrow of the United States government. To that end, Al Rashad accumulated guns and trained his followers in military tactics. He recruited and carried out missions within a two-hundred mile radius of Memphis. That's what brought his group into contact with the Yaloquena District Attorney two years before, and ultimately caused him to shut down the mosque and flee Memphis with the only two members he trusted, Abud and Samson.

He surfaced as Mohammed X and with Azeem's help, established Freedmen's Creek, not realizing the remote location was within District Attorney Willie Mitchell Banks' jurisdiction. Until Azeem's death, Mohammed X had never been to Sunshine, leaving external and outreach functions to Abud and Samson.

The opium was making it more difficult to concentrate. Phantasmagoric images clouded his sensorium, making it impossible to continue the walk through his past. He gave up and let the opium take him where it would. He moaned quietly as he entered a state between consciousness and sleep, unaware of where or even who he was. Later, he fell into a sound sleep, oblivious to the outside world for ten hours.

Chapter Forty-One

At three a.m. Willie Mitchell's phone rang. He heard it but didn't move because Susan always grabbed it, certain something bad had happened to Jake or Scott.

"Hold on," Susan said and gave Willie Mitchell the hand set. She put the pillow over her head.

"Unh-huh," he mumbled.

It took a few seconds to realize it was Walton. Willie Mitchell had been sound asleep, tired from the previous week's intense preparation for trial with Walton. With Walton being first chair, Willie Mitchell felt compelled to make sure Walton was prepared. The D.A. ended up working harder and more thoroughly than he would have to ready himself to sit first chair. It was a waste of manpower and he knew it. Walton was more than capable of preparing for Mule's trial by himself. It was not a complicated case, and they both knew the result would be a crap shoot. The evidence was easy to put on. The critical testimony with the greatest impact on the verdict would be the cross-examinations of Trevor and Mule. Everything else was a question of interpretation for the jurors. It would have been a much easier case if the digital record of the shootout had audio. Three issues could sink the prosecution case regardless of the facts proven at trial. The first was Abdul Azeem's religion. The second was the undisputed fact that Trevor's gun killed Azeem. The third was the history of Trevor's gun, to-wit: it ended the lives of an interracial couple in Oklahoma City under circumstances that were vague at best.

In the early stages of trial preparation, Willie Mitchell tried to keep his distance, to give Walton advice only when asked. What a dismal failure that strategy was. He had to admire Walton for his patience in dealing with his hovering boss. Walton was no shrinking violet. He was tough as a boot and aggressive as he needed to be in litigation without crossing the line and becoming obnoxious. It was an invisible line in the courtroom—overstep it and the jury thinks you're being an ass. Too timid and the jury thinks the other lawyer is pushing you around. *Be prepared for everything; be assertive and confident in the courtroom, but make the jury like you.* That's what he told Walton and Jake all the time. All young lawyers needed to keep that in mind. Privately, Willie Mitchell sometimes believed that the ability to pull it off was in one's DNA. You either had it or you didn't. It was one of those things you couldn't learn. No matter, he would keep harping on it as long as Walton or Jake or any lawyer-in-training would listen.

"Bring Heckel and Jeckel by here on your way," Willie Mitchell said into the phone. "You get on down there and don't worry about the trial. Gayle's situation is way more important."

He rested the phone on Susan's stomach. She pulled the pillow off her head and sat up.

"What's wrong?" she asked.

"Gayle's appendix ruptured. Nathan met them at the hospital and medevaced her to St. Christopher's. Nathan is worried about sepsis being already involved. Walton's bringing the twins over."

Susan threw the covers back and jumped out of bed into the bathroom. She brushed her teeth quickly and pulled on a workout outfit she had draped on a chair the night before.

"I'll put the coffee on," she said as she slid into her slippers and hustled downstairs.

Willie Mitchell was wide awake, too. He put on a pair of walking shorts, a tee shirt and sandals and walked down the steps and out on the porch. He knew Walton would be pulling into the driveway in minutes and need help unloading the twins' stuff. The door opened behind him. Susan gave him a mug of coffee.

"They should be here any minute," Willie Mitchell said.

"I'll go get their room ready," Susan said.

The twins had spent many weekends at the Banks home. Susan loved having them. Willie Mitchell looked forward to their visits, too. Walton's mother had died in Clarksdale and his father moved to Texas. Gayle's parents were divorced. Her father traveled much of the time with his young second wife. He wasn't interested in being a grandfather. Her mother wanted to be a good grandmother, but was still fragile from her breakup with the only man she ever loved. She lived in West Point, where Gayle grew up, on the eastern edge of Mississippi near the Alabama border. Even if her mother weren't distracted or depressed much of the time, West Point was too far away to be much help.

The twins were born in Sunshine in January 2006, delivered by Dr. Nathan Clement. Willie Mitchell and Susan were in Gayle's hospital room when they brought the boys in for her to hold for the first time. For the first few years of the twins' lives, whenever Walton and Gayle needed a break, or a long weekend, or wanted to stay out late for some event, Susan pleaded with them to let the boys stay with Willie Mitchell and her. Gayle and Walton were reluctant to impose at first, but as they came to realize how much the twins enjoyed staying with Willie Mitchell and Susan, they began to let the boys stay as often as Susan wanted.

Susan and Gayle grew very close, and Gayle was distraught when Susan told her she was going away for a while, a separation from Willie

Mitchell that lasted almost three years. When they reconciled and Susan returned home, she picked up where she left off with the twins.

When Kitty moved to Yaloquena to work for Sheriff Jones, Susan invited Gayle to walk with Kitty and her, and the two young women hit it off. Their lives were as different as night and day, but both Kitty and Gayle were outsiders in Sunshine, smart and good-looking. The three attractive women with first-rate figures walking for exercise together on the streets of Sunshine drew a lot of tongue-in-cheek wolf whistles from the old white men who walked or drove the streets of Sunshine. The men were harmless, but they still liked to flirt with pretty girls.

Walton and Gayle's six-year-old twins were fraternal with distinct personalities. Nicholas was the oldest by fifteen minutes. Payne was the tallest. Contrary to type, Payne was the biggest and most confident. Nicholas was smarter but more withdrawn.

During Susan's extended absence, Willie Mitchell had Sunday lunch at Walton and Gayle's home and referred to Nicholas and Payne as Heckle and Jeckle. They both started crying at the dinner table. He never understood why his whimsical reference to the talking magpies who starred in television cartoons in the fifties would upset them. In time, they began to like being called Heckle and Jeckle. Jimmy Gray was the only adult Willie Mitchell knew who was familiar with Heckle and Jeckle. When they were kids Jimmy and Willie Mitchell watched hours and hours of the talking magpies' cartoons on rainy Saturday mornings.

As soon as Walton's extended cab Ford Truck hit the pea gravel in the circular drive Susan popped through the front door to join Willie Mitchell on the porch. They walked down the steps and opened the back doors. Nicholas was asleep, pinned in by his seatbelt. Payne was awake and unlatched his seat belt when he realized where he was.

Willie Mitchell picked up the sleeping twin. Susan led Payne by the hand. They put them in bed in their room. Walton whispered to Payne that he was going to the hospital in Jackson to be with Mama and would call back to let everyone know the outcome of the surgery. Walton kissed Payne and told him to behave, to mind Susan and Willie Mitchell.

Susan switched on the nightlight plugged into a wall socket and closed the door. Outside on the porch, Walton hugged Susan.

"Thank you for keeping them," Walton said.

"They can stay here as long as needed," Susan said. "You know we love having them here."

He shook Willie Mitchell's hand.

"Sorry to leave you in the lurch like this."

"Don't give it another thought," Willie Mitchell said. "That's the upside of being a bad delegator. I can try this case standing on my head. All the hard work's done. You stay with Gayle as long as it takes."

"Call us as soon as you know something," Susan called to Walton as he hustled down the steps and jumped back into the truck, "and don't worry about the boys."

They watched him drive away. Willie Mitchell looked at Susan in the dim light leaking onto the front porch from the Victorian hallway fixture inside. No makeup, just a quick brush through her hair, and still she was beautiful standing there. He knew she was worried about Gayle.

"She'll be all right," Willie Mitchell said, giving Susan a hug and a brief but tender kiss on the cheek.

"I'll go check on the twins," she said. "Are you going back to bed?"

"No way. I'll go ahead and run. Maybe you could put some grits on and a couple of biscuits in the oven? Might as well get to the office."

Susan nodded. Willie Mitchell walked quietly upstairs to put on his jogging stuff.

Ten minutes later, Willie Mitchell set his watch and his iPod and disappeared into the darkness, the pea gravel crunching under his Sauconys.

Chapter Forty-Two

Willie Mitchell sat behind his desk at five-thirty and picked up the jury list. It was deathly quiet in his office. He was the only person on the second floor. The custodial staff would not arrive for another hour.

He and Walton had gone over the venire with the Sheriff several times in the previous two weeks, trying to learn as much about each prospective juror as possible. The venire was seventy-five per cent black, roughly reflecting Yaloquena's demographics. When Lee was unsure about a prospective juror, he called in a deputy who worked the relevant part of the county. The deputies knew the prospect or their family most of the time. If they didn't know anything about the person, Lee sent the deputy out to find out discreetly if the person might be a good juror for the State or one to avoid.

Willie Mitchell appreciated Lee's help because it helped him avoid antagonistic jurors. Jurors rarely admitted to having animosity unless the D.A. knew in advance the basis for it and asked them directly. Willie Mitchell knew a lot of people, but Lee knew more. The detailed information Lee provided also helped Willie Mitchell articulate race-neutral reasons for striking a prospect if called upon to testify about the use of his challenges. If Willie Mitchell had sent a prospect's relative to Parchman, it was a good thing to factor in the decision to accept or strike, and an important thing to add if the D.A. had to testify at a *Batson* hearing.

Willie Mitchell studied the remaining names on the list, whittled down from a hundred to eighty by the facts he had gathered with Walton and Lee's help. Selecting the best jury he could was probably more important than how he presented the evidence or argued the case. If he let Jordan Summit load the jury with people who weren't friendly to the prosecution, it really didn't matter what kind of case Willie Mitchell put on. Over the last week, working the fine details to get ready, Walton and Willie Mitchell agreed that convicting Mule in Yaloquena County was possible, but so was an acquittal. They also expected Summit to put Mule on the witness stand to testify in his own defense.

At 8:45, Willie Mitchell gathered his files and walked into the courtroom. Walton had called an hour earlier. He said Gayle would be in surgery for another hour and apologized again to Willie Mitchell. Willie Mitchell told him to forget about it. Down deep, Willie Mitchell was looking forward to trying the case. He had done his best to resign himself to second chair, but the excitement he felt now walking into the packed courtroom convinced him he would have been miserable listening to the action instead of being in the middle of it.

One of the world's worst delegators.

Willie Mitchell walked through the side door and stopped just inside the courtroom for a moment. Files under his arm, he smiled and nodded at the jury prospects and onlookers who filled almost every seat. There was no feeling like it. An occasional butterfly flitted under Willie Mitchell's sternum inside his chest, but quickly disappeared as he thought about the many cases he had tried in this courtroom.

There was no higher drama than waiting for the jury to announce its verdict after completing its deliberations. Many times collective gasps from a crowded courtroom followed the reading of the verdict. Willie Mitchell remembered many of those. The reactions that bothered him, though, the ones he heard at night when he was alone, were the cries of the mothers of the dead victims or the haunting wails from the mothers of the convicted defendants being taken away to Parchman for the rest of their natural lives or to death row. Willie Mitchell lived through many piercing calls in this courtroom for help from God above. His work produced them. That was the nature of his calling. If he did his job well, defendants went to prison for a long time. It was no cause for him to celebrate, but it was justice. Without someone like Willie Mitchell demanding that a jury make a defendant pay with his freedom for taking a life or maiming, there was no justice.

For Willie Mitchell, civil litigation, with its multi-million dollar verdicts and decisions leading to bankrupt companies, jobs lost, marriages broken, wages garnished, and paternity established, none of it held a candle to the drama of a criminal verdict. In murder trials, Willie Mitchell dealt in life or death. For the victims' families, he was their avenger of blood, delivering retribution for the death of a loved one. For the criminals and their families, he was their day of judgment, the wrath of God, the endgame they had been dreading. The families usually knew their loved one on trial was guilty. In Willie Mitchell's experience the families would never admit it, but they generally had little doubt that their baby boy or brother or husband did it. They just hoped somehow he wouldn't have to answer for it. Willie Mitchell was there to see he did.

Standing just inside the courtroom, he focused and recognized many of the prospective jurors. He wanted to be pleasant in acknowledging them, but careful not to go overboard and be accused by Jordan Summit of trying to curry their favor. Willie Mitchell took a deep breath and walked the few steps to the prosecution table. He put down his files and walked over to shake hands with Jordan Summit and Eleanor Bernstein, already seated at the defense table flanking their client in his large wheelchair. Without being unpleasant, he ignored Mule Gardner. Willie Mitchell never shook the hand of a defendant.

He sat at the prosecution table alone. That's the way he liked it. Willie Mitchell against everyone else. He pulled the jury list from an accordion file and looked at the first three names. He stopped there. He had gone over them so many times there was nothing more to gain from studying their names and his handwritten notes around them.

Willie Mitchell turned in his seat. Behind him on the first row were Jake, Kitty, and Lee. He shared with them earlier Gayle's medical situation. The three looked grim. He smiled and winked. As usual, Susan was not there. When Willie Mitchell was a young lawyer, Susan attended several of his jury trials. Realizing how the testimony Willie Mitchell took in stride must have seemed so brutal and inhuman to Susan's sensitive nature, he asked her to stop attending. She gladly agreed. After their two sons were in elementary school, Susan brought them to see Willie Mitchell try a few cases, all relatively non-violent offenses. For the serious trials in his early years as elected District Attorney, he wanted his young family as far away from the courtroom as possible.

He glanced at the Freedmen's Creek entourage in the first row: Mohammed X in his green bow tie, Samson the giant, and Tweety Bird Abud, together with their favorite infidel, Reverend Bobby Sanders. The four of them sat stone-faced. They were there to see justice rendered in the death of their associate Azeem. Willie Mitchell already knew they would be disappointed, regardless of the outcome of Mule's trial. The revenge they sought for Azeem's death was not going to be available with the set of facts that the D.A. was going to establish in the trial. It was Trevor's bullet that killed Azeem, but Mule started the violence. Trevor acted in self-defense, though Mohammed X would never believe it. It would not be the first time an interested spectator would be unhappy, leaving the courtroom after trial claiming Willie Mitchell was crooked, or incompetent. His favorite complaint was that the D.A. had been "bought off."

Two rows behind them, in the middle of a bench otherwise filled with prospective jurors, Willie Mitchell saw Freddy Brewer, who stared straight ahead, never making eye contact with the D.A. Willie Mitchell asked Kitty that morning if her federal associates had gotten back to her with details about some of the entries on Freddy's criminal record. Not yet, she said. She was also supposed to talk to ATF Gary Needham sometime today or tomorrow about Trevor's gun. Needham's "special assignment" for which he stood her up two weeks earlier in Oklahoma City had apparently ended.

After jury selection, with only a handful of spectators in the courtroom watching the opening arguments and the first witnesses, the tension in the chamber would subside. This morning you could cut it with a knife.

Chapter Forty-Three

Judge Zelda Williams walked into the courtroom behind Circuit Clerk Winston Moore. He was dressed to kill as usual with a matching bright red tie and pocket kerchief setting off his navy blue pinstripe Austin Reed suit. Willie Mitchell glanced at Eddie Bordelon and winked. Eddie's boss only came to court when it was packed with voters. After calling the venire roll, preening and harrumphing for an hour or so, he usually conferred quietly with Judge Williams and departed. Walking from the judge's bench to the side door, Winston's demeanor was earnest, all-business, intended to give his voters the impression he had to be about the people's business.

Willie Mitchell liked Winston, but along with Judge Williams and Eddie Bordelon, the D.A. was relieved when the Circuit Clerk left the courtroom. To them, his behavior was transparent and distracting. Willie Mitchell and Judge Williams were doing their best to conduct a serious trial, and were not interested in the political impact of their appearance.

Eddie tested his equipment and asked the judge for a moment to make sure it was working. He signaled to her and she started.

"Good morning, ladies and gentlemen," she said.

Judge Williams explained why they were there, the type of case, and explained their duties as jurors if chosen to serve. She went over the statutory qualifications, asking the jury prospects as a group to indicate if they did not meet a particular requirement. When some in the audience raised their hands, she had them approach the bench and tell her quietly why they might not qualify.

Clerk Winston Moore called the roll and the prospective jurors answered "here" or "present," like students. The judge introduced the D.A. and the defense attorneys, and named Lester Gardner as the defendant, reading the Grand Jury charges against him. As expected, Clerk Winston Moore huddled with the judge, and departed. Eddie Bordelon shook an old cigar box and pulled out twelve slips of paper. As he called each name, the prospective juror took a seat in the jury box.

"Now," Judge Williams said to the twelve prospects seated in the jury box, "the District Attorney will ask you any general questions he may have, then the defense attorney Mr. Summit will do the same. The attorneys will then ask you their specific questions, including any questions your answer to their general inquiries might have raised. Both sides have copies of the answers each of you provided in the questionnaire you filled out this morning. If they don't ask you something, it may be because it is covered adequately in the questionnaire.

"Mr. Willie Mitchell Banks," she said, "you may proceed."

Willie Mitchell walked to the small podium centered on the jury box. He glanced quickly at both rows of prospective jurors, six in front, six in back. He greeted them and introduced himself again, and described his role in the trial as District Attorney.

"Now," he said, "I have a few general questions I'd like to ask all of you as a group. I'll phrase the question so that you can raise your hand if you answer yes to the general question. I'll make a mark by your name on my list, and when I come back up here to ask each of you specific questions, I'll explore your response to my general questions. Everyone with me?"

All twelve nodded.

"Here's my first general question. You will learn that the victim in this case was born Joseph Randall but converted to Islam and legally changed his name to Abdul Azeem. Now, do any of you have any doubt that you can be fair and impartial in this case even though the victim is a Muslim?"

Willie Mitchell watched as two of the men raised a hand, then a third raised hers but took it down.

"Thank you," Willie Mitchell said looking at his jury seating chart, "Mr. Dupree and Mr. Conlay. Mrs. Wilkinson, did you mean to answer yes? I saw you raise your hand momentarily."

"I'm not sure," she said.

"Your Honor," Willie Mitchell said, "may I explore this general question with Mrs. Wilkinson at this point? It may save some time."

"Go ahead, Mr. Banks."

He quickly looked at the woman's questionnaire.

"I see you are a member of the United Pentecostal Church here in town," Willie Mitchell said to the fiftyish black mother of three grown children. "What do you think about the Muslim religion?"

Mrs. Wilkinson fidgeted. He noticed several other jurors move slightly in their seats.

"I don't like it," she said. "They claim Jesus Christ was not God but just another prophet. I see on television stories about them wanting to convert all of us Christians to their church. Our preacher told us about it two Sundays ago."

There it is.

Willie Mitchell wanted to turn around and see how the Freedmen's Creek men were reacting to the testimony, but he couldn't do it without being obvious. He would wait to ask Jake or Kitty or Lee at a break.

"I've seen those stories, Mrs. Wilkinson. But do you understand that Mr. Azeem's religion should not be an issue for this jury whose job it is to decide if this defendant Lester "Mule" Gardner is guilty of murder in the death of Mr. Azeem?"

"That's why I pulled down my hand. Even if I don't like the Muslim religion it doesn't make any difference in this case, right?"

"That's correct. Do you think you can render a fair verdict based on the evidence you hear in this courtroom and put aside the fact that the victim belonged to a religion that you disagree with or don't like?"

"I think I can."

"We have to be sure, Mrs. Wilkinson. Can you?"

She thought a moment. "I can."

Willie Mitchell looked at the two men who raised their hands. Mr. Dupree was older, white; Mr. Conlay a black man in an Orkin shirt.

"What about you gentlemen?" Willie Mitchell asked.

"Hold on, Mr. Banks," Judge Williams said. "Let's wait until you start asking specific questions for each juror to explore that with Mr. Dupree and Mr. Conlay. Do you have any other general questions?"

"I do, Your Honor." He paused a moment. "One of the witnesses in this case is Trevor Brewer, a young man from Dundee County. Do any of you know Trevor Brewer or any member of the Brewer family personally? If you do, raise your hand."

Not one of the twelve did.

"Have any one of you ever heard of the Brewer family of Dundee County?"

All eight of the black prospective jurors raised their hands. Two of the whites did. Willie Mitchell heard rustling and murmuring from the audience. Judge Williams tapped her gavel to quiet the courtroom.

"Regardless of what you might have heard about the Brewer family, would each of you be willing to put that aside and judge this case solely on the facts you hear from the witness stand," Willie Mitchell said, pointing at the witness stand, "and not from what you may have heard in the past about the Brewers?"

Everyone nodded. He looked at his notes and paused a moment.

"All of you will hear testimony in this trial describing what happened at the Gas & Go Fast this past September, and you will view a video disk of the events. Without suggesting that you commit to anything right now, do each of you believe in everyone's right to self-defense?" Everyone nodded. He thought a moment.

Need to get this out before Summit does.

"Ladies and Gentlemen, it will be established that the defendant on trial for murder in this case did not fire the bullet that killed the victim. I will offer into evidence the Smith & Wesson nine-millimeter semi-automatic handgun that actually fired the fatal bullet. The evidence will show Trevor Brewer to be the man that fired that weapon at the Gas & Go Fast that day."

Willie Mitchell expected Summit to object or intervene but he didn't. By their raised eyebrows and quizzical facial expressions, Willie Mitchell knew he had the prospective jurors' attention. He had made the decision to stop there and not mention that the gun was used in the murder of the interracial couple in Oklahoma City. In chambers, Willie Mitchell had put Judge Williams and Jordan Summit on notice that he objected strenuously to the gun's history being brought up in this trial. He stressed its irrelevancy to the guilt or innocence of Mule Gardner. Willie Mitchell did not file a Motion In Limine to get a ruling in advance because he wasn't sure how Judge Williams would decide the issue. If Summit started down that road, Willie Mitchell would interrupt and object, hopefully before the jury understood where Summit was going. He would ask the Judge to remove the jury from the courtroom and argue that the gun's history was highly prejudicial to the D.A.'s case. He would argue the damage the gun's history would inflict on his case far outweighed its relevance. He would urge the court to caution the defense not to bring it up. He would then cross his fingers.

"Without getting into the specifics at this point, can each of you listen to the testimony and render your verdict based on all the facts and circumstances surrounding the shooting at the Gas & Go Fast that are established in this trial, and not on some other information you may have heard about the shooting before today?"

Willie Mitchell was glad this part was over. It was awkward asking the "general" questions and difficult to avoid going into too much detail. It was a time-saving feature of Judge Williams' trial procedure that he generally liked, but one that defense lawyers usually abused. He sat down and watched Jordan Summit take the podium.

"Good morning, ladies and gentlemen," Summit said.

He introduced himself, his co-counsel Eleanor Bernstein, and his client, then surprised Willie Mitchell.

"I don't have any additional general questions for you folks right now. I believe the prosecutor covered the topics very well, and have nothing further to ask. Your time is important, and I do not want to waste it by being repetitive. The Judge will have us begin the individual questioning in a few minutes, and I will ask each of you a few things at that time. I've studied your questionnaires, and thank you for taking the time to fill them out. Because of your answers, it will streamline this part of the trial and hopefully limit the inconvenience that serving on this jury is for each and every one of you. Thank you."

It was unusual for a defense lawyer to forego face time in front of the jury prospects, but Willie Mitchell thought Jordan Summit had scored some points with his low-key courtesy and stated concern for the interruption of the jurors' lives. It also crossed the D.A.'s mind that Summit might be so confident of the outcome that he was ready to get to the testimony and verdict as soon as possible, and get on with his civil case against Gas & Go Fast.

Summit might be right. Could my case be that weak?

As always happened in Willie Mitchell's experience in jury selection, there were some light moments. The tension each jury prospect felt generated nervous laughter. Like in church, everything seemed funnier in the courtroom.

Late Tuesday, picking alternates, Jordan Summit asked a young black woman in white rubber boots and a plastic bonnet over her hair what she did in her job at the catfish plant. The way she almost yelled "de-bone fish" made everyone in the courtroom laugh. An older black man got a few chuckles the first day from the dozen-or-so people in the courtroom familiar with sciatica when he said he could not sit too long in one position because of pain running down his legs due to his "psychotic nerves" in his backside. In the afternoon of the second day of jury selection, a thirty-something white teacher's aide said serving on the jury would create a hardship because she took care of her grandfather who had "old-timer's" disease. No one laughed, but Summit cut his eyes to meet Willie Mitchell's.

Willie Mitchell's favorite jury prospect was the Orkin man on the first panel of twelve prospects, Mr. Conlay, whose initial response to each of Willie Mitchell and Summit's questions was to repeat the question with different inflection. Not just sometimes. Every time. Willie Mitchell jotted on his notes "Conlay Communication Concept," and thought the CCC methodology might be useful at cocktail parties or anywhere else where the content of conversation is irrelevant.

~ * ~

By day's end Tuesday, twelve jurors and two alternates had been chosen to serve. There were five black women seated, mostly older; four black men, trending younger; two fifty-something white women and one gruff white man in his sixties. The alternates were seated in chairs in front of the jury box. One was the young black woman who "de-boned" catfish; the other a middle-aged white woman, a retired teacher.

Judge Williams adjourned court for the day after admonishing the jurors not to discuss the case with anyone nor watch the television news or read the papers until the trial was over. They were led single-file out of the side door of the courtroom by the bailiff, through for the day.

"We'll start opening arguments at nine sharp," Judge Williams told the lawyers and walked out.

While Eddie Bordelon secured his desk and computer for the night, Willie Mitchell studied the jury seating chart. Overall, he was pleased with the selection. He thought the young men would be receptive to the idea that Trevor Brewer was justified in returning fire at Mule. Beyond that, it was a crap shoot. Every person on the jury panel knew who Mule was or had seen him pushing his cart along the highway at some point in the last five years. That's the way it was trying cases in a small town. Mule had stayed awake in his oversized white shirt and wheelchair most of the first day, but on Tuesday, Willie Mitchell noticed Mule napping during much of the questioning.

Jake, Kitty, and Lee walked through the rail gate and gathered around Willie Mitchell at his table. They talked quietly about the jury, Lee saying he thought it was a real good panel for them. Willie Mitchell glanced over at the Freedmen's Creek crowd. As usual, Bobby Sanders was huddled with his candidate for next year's election, Eleanor Bernstein. When Willie Mitchell made eye contact, he realized Mohammed X had been watching him. Willie Mitchell understood the man being upset at losing Azeem, but there was something personal in his hateful stare. Willie Mitchell knew he was on Mohammed X's shit list, but it didn't bother him. In almost twenty-four years prosecuting, the list of people who held a grudge against Willie Mitchell was long.

~ * ~

Jake stood slightly apart from the others at the table. He had watched Freddy Brewer leave the courtroom. In spite of what Jake now knew about Freddy's criminal record, sitting in the midst of the prospective jurors, Jake thought Freddy looked and acted like the concerned uncle Trevor said he was. He was the only Brewer representative in the courtroom. Maybe he was there to keep the clan informed and let Tom and Trevor know when Trevor had to appear.

Jake listened to Lee and Kitty's comments to Willie Mitchell, but kept his eyes on Mohammed X and his men. Abud and Samson didn't bother him, but there was something about Mohammed X that put Jake on notice. He hadn't been able to shake the feeling he had seen the man before. Now that Gillmon's research had linked Freedmen's Creek with the other militant Muslim communes in the country, Jake was concerned for Willie Mitchell. Azeem had supplied the Memphis mosque with funding and support before it was shut down after the attempt on Willie

Mitchell's life. Sitting on the first row in their suits and ties, the Freedmen's Creek group might not seem sinister to anyone else in the courtroom. Given what Jake had seen up in the pine tree, Jake knew otherwise. The deep-seated anger Jake sensed in Mohammed X toward Willie Mitchell wasn't justified by the prosecution of Mule. There was something else. Jake could not put his finger on it, but his subconscious was working on it. In the meantime, Jake would continue to be on high alert status. He could not shake the nagging feeling that Mohammed X was dangerous.

Chapter Forty-Four

At 8:40 Wednesday morning Freddy Brewer, Breed, and Wrench strode into the courtroom like they owned the place. Clad in full-blown Dregs getups, they strutted in and plopped down behind the prosecution table before Lee, Kitty, and Jake could claim their usual front row seats.

There was no brown corduroy coat for Freddy this day. He wore his tattered jeans and heavy boots, his black leather vest with DREGS on his back arcing over the demonic, forked-tongued red-eyed woman. His ponytail was out for everyone to see. So were the lightning bolt tattoos on his neck that had been hidden by the high shirt collar he wore at previous court hearings. Freddy wore nothing under his vest, but buttoned the front to meet the court's dress code. The top part of the German war eagle on his chest was visible above the vest, as were the woodpeckers on his forearms, the 1% inside a diamond on the back of each arm, and his jagged prison tats.

Breed and Wrench were dressed in their Dregs vests like Freddy, but they were more muscular and threatening. Freddy smiled a lot; Breed and Wrench never did. Breed wore his black hair pulled back into a braided ponytail. His beaded headband and scowl made him look like a fierce Comanche warrior. Wrench's long brown hair flowed freely down his back. His shark-like eyes were black and piercing, cold.

The three of them captured the front row. From time to time before court convened they stood up with arms crossed and turned their menacing faces to the rest of the courtroom observers. After thirty seconds or so of staring, the three heavily muscled and tattooed bikers would sit back down. The three Dregs were in standing mode when the Freedmen's Creek group walked in. Freddy and the others burned a hole through the Muslims, glaring at them as they walked down the center aisle to take their front row seats behind the defense table.

The Dregs were still standing and facing down Mohammed X and his men when Willie Mitchell, Jordan Summit, and Eleanor Bernstein entered the courtroom. Willie Mitchell put down his file and walked back out the side door, returning in less than a minute with Lee Jones, Jake, Kitty and four more deputy sheriffs Lee placed around the room. Lee walked through the rail and stood next to Freddy.

"Why don't y'all take your seats, please," Lee said quietly.

Freddy nodded to Breed and Wrench.

"We don't want any trouble in here today," Lee told Freddy after the Dregs sat down.

"Yes, sir," Freddy said. "We're cool with that. We're only here to see justice done."

Lee Jones walked across the aisle to the Freedmen's Creek group. He bent down to speak quietly to Bobby Sanders.

"I told them no trouble," Lee said. "They said all right. Let's keep everything under control on this side."

Bobby Sanders nodded and passed the word to Samson and Abud. Abud whispered something to Mohammed X. Lee Jones walked through the rail and sat next to Willie Mitchell.

"Everything all right?" Willie Mitchell said.

"I warned both sides. I don't guess we can keep the bikers out."

"No. Open to the public includes them."

Willie Mitchell turned to watch Tom and Trevor Brewer walk through the back door followed by Tracy Brewer and twenty other men and women Brewers of all ages and sizes. The Brewers took up rows two through five behind the prosecution table. Willie Mitchell glanced at the four Freedmen Creek men on the other side of the aisle in the first row. They were the only observers on the defense side.

"Why don't you, Jake, and Kitty sit a couple of rows behind Mohammed and his boys," Willie Mitchell told Lee. "Be ready for anything. The Brewers have them outnumbered."

"They all had to come through the scanner," Lee said. "We should be okay."

Willie Mitchell watched Eddie Bordelon walk in through the side door. As usual, Eddie kept his head down, frowning in concentration, worried about everything running just right in Judge William's courtroom. He took his seat at the Clerk's table and started fiddling with his computer and recording equipment. Not once did Eddie look up to notice the audience. Willie Mitchell whispered to Sheriff Jones.

"Would you let Judge Williams know what's going on out here so she won't be caught off guard when she walks in?"

Lee nodded and took off through the side door. Willie Mitchell motioned for Jake and Kitty to join him.

"Has Needham showed up yet?" Willie Mitchell asked Kitty.

"Not yet, but I spoke to him earlier and he's on his way."

"Make one more effort to get a look at his file on Trevor's gun when he gets here. See if there's anything in there we need to be ready for. I've got a feeling Jordan Summit and Eleanor have probably already seen everything in it. I don't want any surprises."

Jake and Kitty took their seats two rows behind Mohammed X and his men. Lee walked back into court. He gestured to Willie Mitchell that everything was fine and took his seat with Jake and Kitty.

The side door opened and the bailiff walked through, telling everyone to stand, calling for order and quiet, and announcing that court was now in session. Judge Williams walked in confidently and sat behind her elevated bench. She looked out over the courtroom.

"Before we bring in the jury this morning," she said, "I want everyone in this courtroom to understand that if there is the slightest disturbance or noise from any one of you, you will be immediately removed and banned from returning. Is that clear?"

Everyone in court was quiet.

"Anything from either the State or the defense before we start?"

Willie Mitchell and Jordan Summit shook their heads.

"Very well. Mr. Banks, we'll start with your opening statement."

Willie Mitchell turned to Lee Jones. He had asked the Sheriff to be ready to gather all the evidence from the evidence locker in his office and bring it into the courtroom after opening statements. Willie Mitchell would not have a long opening, twenty minutes or so, and Summit had indicated he would be brief as well. Willie Mitchell gestured to Lee, who walked out of court to retrieve the physical evidence, including what Lee's deputies had picked up from the crime lab on Friday and placed under lock and key in the Sheriff's office.

Willie Mitchell stood at the podium and told the jurors what he expected to prove. He reminded them of their commitment to be fair to the dead victim regardless of his faith. He told them the evidence would show that Trevor Brewer acted in self-defense and in defense of Azeem, that Mule started the violent episode and would have killed Azeem if Trevor had not intervened. As expected, Jordan Summit told the jurors the evidence would show beyond a reasonable doubt that Mule acted in self-defense, and that Azeem would be alive today and Summit's client Lester Gardner not paralyzed if only Trevor Brewer had left his weapon in his truck. The themes Willie Mitchell and Summit stressed in opening were no surprise to the jurors. They had heard the lawyers cover them extensively in the two previous days of *voir dire.*

After Summit returned to his table, Willie Mitchell turned to see Lee walk in the main door with a cardboard box holding the physical evidence from the crime lab, including Mule's .22 and Trevor's S & W nine millimeter, the dvd of the shooting, and the casings collected at the scene. Lee delivered the box to Eddie Bordelon who sat it on the small table next to his equipment. Eddie made another equipment check and nodded to the judge, who turned to Willie Mitchell.

"Call your first witness, Mr. Banks."

Chapter Forty-Five

Sheriff Lee Jones walked through the rail. As Willie Mitchell watched him, a sense of pride and loyalty came out of nowhere, flooding Willie Mitchell with emotion.

It was out of character, but since his brush with death two years earlier and his daily battles with the effects of that ambush, Willie Mitchell found himself treasuring the relationships that were important to him. He had enormous respect for Lee Jones. Because he was big and athletic, and blessed with character and a strong sense of right and wrong from his hard-working parents, Lee endured the hapless Yaloquena County public school system unscathed, and prospered through college, the military, and the state police. He could have gone anywhere, but chose to return home in an attempt to make a difference, to protect those that needed help, and steer in the right direction the thousands of youngsters in the city and county raising themselves.

"Would you state your name for the record, please sir," Willie Mitchell asked the Sheriff after he was sworn.

The D.A. asked Lee to tell the jury where he was that day in September when he got the call about the Gas & Go Fast Shooting, what he found when he arrived at the scene, and give a summary of how his office investigated the crime. Willie Mitchell moved Lee quickly through his testimony, including everything he did to secure the two weapons and casings found on the concrete.

Willie Mitchell walked to Eddie Bordelon's desk and asked Eddie for the two guns. He marked the twenty-two as State's Exhibit 2 and the nine millimeter Smith & Wesson State's Exhibit 3. He gave each gun to the Sheriff to identify, asking him to make sure each had no live rounds chambered or in their magazines. He waited while Lee examined each gun, then asked Lee to describe how he took custody of each gun that day at the Gas & Go Fast and delivered them to the crime lab. The D.A. offered the two guns into evidence. Summit had no objection. Willie Mitchell picked up the twenty-two and nine-millimeter off the narrow counter in front of the witness stand and returned them to Eddie's table. Eddie returned them to the cardboard evidence box on his desk.

Lee identified photographs marked as State's Exhibits 4 through 20 as having been taken that day in his presence. He described how he took custody of the digital recorder in the store and dispatched a deputy immediately to deliver it to the crime lab in Jackson with a request that they preserve the original at the lab and make a number of copies. With

Lee on the stand, Willie Mitchell was ready to show the jury the disk Robbie Cedars made at the crime lab from the digital recorder.

Walton had worked with Eddie Bordelon and the county electrician the previous week setting up the three big screen monitors in the courtroom, placing them so that the jury, Judge Williams, and the attorneys had an unobstructed view. Walton said they made an attempt to accommodate the audience as well, but those in the back rows would have to strain to see the images on the screen. An hour before court convened this morning, Willie Mitchell and Eddie Bordelon locked the courtroom and did a trial run with the D.A.'s copy of the disk to make sure the system worked and the screens were visible from all angles in the jury box.

Willie Mitchell and Jordan Summit had agreed in advance that there was no need for the D.A. to call the crime lab technician who had converted the digital images to the DVD format. Willie Mitchell had prepared a written stipulation for both of them to sign agreeing to the authenticity and accuracy of the DVD and confirming that the DVD would be offered into evidence jointly and marked for identification as State Exhibit One and Defense Exhibit One. Willie Mitchell would argue the action on the DVD supported the State's theory of the case, and Summit would argue it supported his. It would be up to the jury to decide which of the lawyers was right.

"Turn off the lights, Mr. Delrie," Judge Williams said to the bailiff as Eddie Bordelon placed the DVD in the player at the D.A.'s request. She looked into the audience. "There will be no reaction to the DVD, nor will there be any whispering in the courtroom during the playing of the disk. Anyone who does so will be removed. You may proceed, Mr. Bordelon. Play the disk."

Willie Mitchell turned his chair slightly so he could watch the monitor and also observe the jurors' reactions. The image was black and white and a bit unsteady at times, but it showed all the action: Azeem filling his tank, holding the nozzle trigger; Mule entering the screen from the right side of the monitor, walking herky-jerky up-and-down toward Azeem; a couple of minutes of uneventful conversation; an older model Ford pickup entering the lower left hand part of the screen image, parking at an angle close to the front door; Trevor walking in the store; Azeem putting a bill on the Taurus trunk then snatching it back before Mule could get to it; Mule and Azeem lowering their heads as if praying; Mule suddenly pointing his finger at Azeem, getting angrier, gesturing wildly and walking in a circle, up and down and around; Mule moving closer, appearing to threaten Azeem; Mule throwing his tennis shoe; Azeem turning the gas nozzle on Mule and spraying him with a thick stream of gasoline; Mule jerking to his cart and pulling a pistol; Mule shooting at Azeem twice; Trevor moving from near the front door toward his truck; Mule turning the gun toward Trevor and firing twice more; Mule and Azeem struggling; Azeem falling back against the gas pump; Mule turning quickly, his gun extended in the direction of Trevor's truck; Trevor squatting by his truck and firing twice as Azeem lurched from the gas pump to engage Mule again; both of them falling onto the concrete between the gas pump and the front door; and in the final scene, Trevor picking up Mule's .22 pistol and entering the store with both guns.

Willie Mitchell signaled to the bailiff to turn on the lights. The D.A. thought he heard the onlookers behind him exhale together. He definitely heard low rumbling and whispering, which Judge Williams silenced with a couple of light taps of her gavel. She had control of the courtroom, for which Willie Mitchell was thankful.

Willie Mitchell retrieved the remote for the player and took Lee back through the disk, freezing certain images and asking Lee questions, careful not to ask Lee's opinion or conclusions, just ask him what he saw. By eleven o'clock, the D.A. was finished with his direct examination. It was Jordan Summit's turn. Willie Mitchell handed him the small remote.

Summit's cross was relatively brief. There were no surprises. Willie Mitchell knew which parts of the action on the disk Summit would freeze and question the Sheriff about, and the defense attorney did not disappoint. Willie Mitchell was impressed with Summit's demeanor. He was very business-like, well-prepared and precise in his questions, no grandstanding or overreaching. He didn't re-plow ground that was already covered. He focused on the portions of the disk critical to his defense: Azeem turning the gasoline on Mule; the ambiguity of Mule's aim when shooting twice at or near Trevor; Trevor shooting twice and the two men falling hard onto the concrete. Summit did not try to commit Lee to an interpretation of the disk that was not warranted by the images. An excellent job of cross, Willie Mitchell had to admit.

Summit's mighty good.

When both attorneys were through with Lee Jones, Judge Williams looked at her watch.

"Gentlemen, it's 11:45. I see no reason to start the next witness's testimony then break for lunch. Let's adjourn and return at one-thirty with the State's next witness. Mr. Delrie, would you escort the jury? Everyone remain seated until the jury has been removed."

Willie Mitchell watched the jurors leave, making eye contact only if each juror offered it. When the side door closed behind the last alternate, Judge Williams tapped her gavel and adjourned court, walking briskly down the three short steps from her elevated bench to floor level and out the side door.

Willie Mitchell closed his trial book and turned around. Jake and Kitty walked through the rail gate and joined Lee at the prosecution table to compare notes with the D.A. about how Lee's testimony went and what the jurors seemed to focus on while watching the disk. While they conferred, a short, wiry man in a navy blue coverall uniform with *Big River Electronics* in red block letters on his chest and back, wearing a matching *Big River Electronics* cap and carrying a dark blue tool box walked between the prosecution and defense tables and stopped at Eddie Bordelon's desk. Eddie was busy, making notes on a yellow legal pad. He looked up and spoke briefly with the electronics repair man, smiled and nodded with enthusiasm. Eddie moved away from the desk to his table to finish his notes. The repairman kneeled behind Eddie's desk and connected his diagnostic computer to Eddie's machines, then adjusted knobs on his own device. He put on Eddie's earphones, started and stopped Eddie's computer and recording system several times, listening intently. He was talking quietly to Eddie about the courtroom's computerized recorder when a commotion started in the center aisle outside the rail.

Chapter Forty-Six

Freddy stood up after the Judge left the courtroom. He stretched and yawned, then walked a few steps to the center aisle, put his hands in his pockets and rocked back and forth, heel to toe, heel to toe. He broke into a broad grin.

SHOWTIME.

"Hey, fellows," Freddy said to Breed and Wrench. "Come over here a second. I want to ask you something."

Breed and Wrench joined him in the aisle.

"Y'all smell that?"

"Yeah," Breed said. "I've been smellin' it all Goddamned day."

Freddy turned toward Mohammed X, Abud, and Samson, still sitting in the first row. Bobby Sanders, who had been talking to Eleanor Bernstein inside the rail, heard Breed. He left Eleanor and joined his Freedmen's Creek pals.

"It smells like Jheri Curl," Freddy said. "Remember that crap? Brothers put it on their hair. Real greasy stuff."

Wrench chimed in. "I remember that shit. Dude I knew used to cake it on. His hair would drip. That shit went out in the eighties, didn't it? I thought Michael Jackson was the last one to use it."

"Apparently some people still put it on their hair," Freddy said.

"No, brother Freddy," Breed said. "Nobody's that stupid."

"Then how come I smell it so strong right here?" Freddy said, leaning toward Mohammed X and taking an exaggerated deep breath. "Oh, I see. It looks like the boss man in charge over here plasters his hair with it."

Samson stood up next to Freddy. Freddy made a point of moving his eyes slowly from Samson's chest to the top of his head.

"Whoo—eee," Freddy said laughing. "This boy here must be six-six. I didn't know they stacked shit that high."

Samson grabbed Freddy's vest with one hand and his ponytail with the other. Freddy laughed like a maniac as Samson pulled his head back by his hair.

Breed and Wrench tried to pry the man's huge arms away from Freddy. Samson was too strong. He switched to a headlock, then a chokehold. Freddy's laugh became a theatrical scream.

"Help. He's killing me."

Tom Brewer left his seat and stationed himself between the scuffle in the center aisle and the twenty or so Brewer spectators, telling Trevor and the rest of them to stay out of it. Lee Jones and his four deputies arrived at the Samson and Freddy set-to at the same time. Mohammad X and Abud continued to sit in their first row seats. Willie Mitchell, Jake, and Kitty stood at the rail watching the struggle. Eddie Bordelon joined them.

Lee and his deputies could not break Samson's headlock. With the five of them surrounding Samson and Freddy, it looked like a rugby scrum in the center aisle.

"Samson," Mohammed X said.

The giant released Freddy, who dropped to the floor, red-faced and sputtering. Freddy stood up rubbing his neck. He saw the Big River Electronics repairman walk up the side aisle and out the back door.

Lee Jones started in on Freddy, who held up his hands, palms toward the Sheriff.

"Sheriff," Freddy said, "I know it's my right, but I do not want to press charges. I was out of line, just trying to have some fun kidding around and went too far." Freddy extended his hand to Samson.

"No hard feelings, big guy."

Samson acted as if he didn't hear Freddy. He turned and sat back down in the first row next to Mohammed X.

"Come on boys," Freddy said loudly to Breed and Wrench. "Let's go get some lunch. We'll see you this afternoon, fellows."

Freddy strutted out the main door rubbing his neck, followed by Wrench and Breed.

~ * ~

Judge Williams banged her gavel at 1:30 sharp. She looked over the courtroom audience, the Brewers and the Freedmen's Creek bunch, and warned them that any further disorder would not be tolerated. She instructed the four deputies stationed around the courtroom to let her know immediately if they sensed any trouble and it would be dealt with right away. Willie Mitchell watched the expressions of the Brewers as they listened to the Judge. The three bikers were late for the afternoon session, so he felt the likelihood of a recurrence was slim until they returned.

"Call your next witness, Mr. Banks," the Judge said.

"State calls Trevor Brewer."

Trevor walked through the rail looking down at the carpet. He continued to keep his eyes downcast until he sat on the witness stand. For a moment he looked around the courtroom, then lowered his eyes to the narrow ledge in front of the witness chair, where they stayed for most his testimony.

Willie Mitchell was pleasantly surprised at Trevor. He stuttered some at first, but seemed to settle down and was stuttering hardly at all when Willie Mitchell asked him if he intended to kill Azeem.

"No, sir," Trevor said. "I yelled at the l-little guy to stop when I s-saw he was about to shoot the b-bigger man again. When he t-turned the g-gun on me that's when I shot. T-two times. I thought it w-was either him or me."

Willie Mitchell stood and approached Eddie's desk.

"S-3 please, Mr. Bordelon," Willie Mitchell said.

Eddie stood and reached into the cardboard evidence box. Willie Mitchell watched Eddie move things around inside the box. Then Eddie became agitated. He looked around his desk and table. He picked up the cardboard evidence box and turned it upside down. Mule's .22 and the seventeen photographs spilled onto the carpet, together with two Ziploc plastic bags of brass casings.

Eddie looked at the District Attorney. Willie Mitchell had never seen such a look of terror. Eddie's face was white as talc.

"It's not here," Eddie said, choking on his words.

Chapter Forty-Seven

Jake was looking out the window at the end of the hall outside the courtroom. He was on his cell phone, finding out Gayle's situation in the hospital from Walton and letting him know how the trial was going. Jake heard the door and turned in time to see Kitty rushing out of the courtroom. She was walking fast. Something was up.

"I'll keep you posted," Jake said and ended the call.

"You've got to get in here," Kitty said. "Trevor's gun is gone."

When Jake walked into the courtroom, he saw Eddie frantically searching under his desk. Willie Mitchell, Jordan Summit, and Eleanor Bernstein were helping, turning over books and pads.

"It's not here," Eddie told the Judge.

The courtroom began to buzz with movement and whispers. Judge Williams banged her gavel and demanded quiet.

"This court is still in session," she said and motioned to the lawyers. "Approach," Judge Williams said. "You, too, Mr. Bordelon." She turned to Trevor still in the witness chair. "Mr. Brewer, take your seat in the audience, please."

Trevor joined Tom and the rest of the Brewers. Jake and Kitty sat down next to the Sheriff. Lee leaned over to Jake. "I'm calling the crime scene guys from the State Crime Lab to fly up here right now in their chopper. Tell Willie Mitchell when you get the chance."

The Sheriff walked out. Jake watched the three lawyers and the Judge's clerk huddle in front of the bench, talking quietly to the Judge. She opened her palm toward Jordan Summit to calm him down.

"All right," she said, "take your seats and let's put all this on the record after Mr. Delrie removes the jury." She turned to the jurors. "Ladies and gentlemen, I apologize for this delay. As you have seen, an exhibit introduced into evidence this morning is missing. We're going to try to get to the bottom of this." She looked at her watch. "I'm not going to dismiss you for the day until we decide how we're going to proceed. Mr. Delrie will take you back to the jury room down the hall. I hope to be able to let you know something shortly."

Jake watched the bailiff remove the jury. Some of the jurors were wide-eyed; some appeared confused. Jake couldn't blame them. When the side door shut behind the last one, Judge Williams directed Eddie Bordelon to put on the record every bit of the discussion they were about to have. She said she wanted it for the Court of Appeal when they reviewed how she handled this matter.

Jake was two rows behind Bobby Sanders and the Freedmen's Creek men. From their whispering and body language he could tell they were upset, especially Mohammed X.

"Your Honor," Willie Mitchell said. "I don't think Mr. Bordelon should touch anything else around his desk and table. I believe we should treat it as a potential crime scene."

"I agree with the District Attorney," Summit said.

While the Judge considered the suggestion, Jake walked to the rail and got Willie Mitchell's attention.

"Lee's gone to call the crime lab," Jake told him. "They can get here within forty-five minutes in their new helicopter. It won't take thirty minutes to process the area around Eddie's desk and table."

Willie Mitchell left the rail.

"Your Honor," he said and conveyed what Jake told him.

"Mr. Bordelon," she said, "do you have your portable system available so that we can discuss this on the record without your having to disturb your desk or table?"

"Yes, ma'am," Eddie said.

"Let's get it set up right now."

Ten minutes later, Eddie was ready to go at a card table and chair in front of the witness box, an orange extension cord plugged into the wall behind the Judge's bench. Jake admired Eddie's ability to perform his job in spite of being a nervous wreck. Because of Eddie's personality, Jake knew the missing gun was about to cause the little bald clerk to have a heart attack.

"Are we ready?" the Judge asked Eddie.

He nodded and turned on his portable recorder and began to write on a fresh legal pad.

"For the record," Judge Williams said, "State's Exhibit 3, a Smith & Wesson nine millimeter pistol which was introduced into evidence this morning, has disappeared from Deputy Clerk Bordelon's desk. Mr. Bordelon, would you...?"

"Shouldn't he be sworn?" Jordan Summit said.

"He probably should, Your Honor," Willie Mitchell agreed.

Judge Williams administered the oath to Eddie and had him describe everything he remembered about S-3, the exact time it was filed into evidence, where he put it, when he last saw it, and when he realized it was missing. She asked him who had access to his work area.

"Just me and the attorneys, Your Honor. The bailiff...,"

"What about the Big River Electronics man?" Willie Mitchell asked.

"He just did a quick systems check," Eddie said.

"Had you ever seen him before?" Willie Mitchell asked.

"No. I asked him where Harry was. Harry's the Big River representative who takes care of all our computer and electronic systems, the microphones, everything. He said Harry was down in his back and he was taking Harry's calls."

"When did you call Big River to check your equipment?" the D.A. asked. "I know you had been having trouble for some time."

"I didn't," Eddie said. "The repairman told me Judge Williams called and requested the systems check because of this trial."

"I didn't call them," Judge Williams said.

"Do you have their number?" Willie Mitchell asked Eddie.

Eddie tore off a business card taped to his portable machine.

"Here's their contact information."

Willie Mitchell took the card from Eddie and turned to gesture to Kitty who met him at the rail. He gave her the card.

"Deputy Kitty Douglas will call their office right now and report back to us, Your Honor."

"I move for a mistrial," Jordan Summit said.

"The State opposes the defense motion," Willie Mitchell said.

"I've been expecting you to move in that direction, Mr. Summit," Judge Williams said. "I've been giving it some thought."

Jake had a sinking feeling.

"Before I rule on your motion, I'd like you to tell this Court, for the record, the relevance of the gun S-3 in this trial against your client."

"It's the murder weapon, Your Honor."

Willie Mitchell stood. "That's not a correct characterization, Your Honor. It's the weapon that fired the bullet that caused the death of Mr. Azeem."

"Wait a minute, gentlemen," she said. "Mr. Summit. Do you agree with what Mr. Banks said? His statement describing S-3, is it factually correct?"

"Yes, Your Honor."

"The District Attorney already established through the Sheriff's testimony this morning that S-3 fired the round that caused the death of Mr. Azeem. The jury has seen the weapon. Sheriff Jones handled it, held it up for the jurors to see, and checked it for live rounds. The jury watched him do that." She turned to Willie Mitchell. "Does the State offer at this point to stipulate as a matter of fact that S-3 was fired by Trevor Brewer and the bullet from S-3 caused the death of the victim, Abdul Azeem?"

"Yes, Your Honor," Willie Mitchell said. "We made that offer in pre-trial proceedings and it still stands."

"Now Mr. Summit, in light of what the District Attorney has just offered, tell me why this Court should order a mistrial? Seems to me if you will enter into the stipulation as offered it proves everything the defense needs for the theories set forth in your opening and in *voir dire*."

"A moment, Your Honor," Summit said.

He sat down and conferred with Eleanor for several minutes. When Summit stood up, Eleanor turned to look at Bobby Sanders and Mohammed X on the first row behind her. She shrugged and gestured to indicate they had little choice.

"On behalf of Lester Gardner, the defense accepts the stipulation and asks that the Court advise the jury of the stipulation."

"As soon as we reconvene," she said.

"And I would ask the Court to formally rule on my mistrial motion."

"In light of the stipulation entered into on the record in this matter by and between the State and the defense with respect to S-3, the defense motion for mistrial is hereby denied."

Jake sighed with relief. The trial crisis had been averted, but it left the more troubling question about who took the gun and why. He heard the back door open and saw Sheriff Jones and Kitty walk to the rail. She whispered to Willie Mitchell. He listened a moment.

"Big River Electronics," Willie Mitchell turned and announced to the Court, "did not send anyone to work on the courtroom system today. Harry, the repairman who services this equipment, is not ill and has been working all morning at the local radio station installing new equipment. He brought his lunch from home in a brown bag and ate it at the radio station. He has not left there since nine a.m. and is continuing to install their equipment right now. They have no other repairman working in Sunshine today, and are unaware if any of their uniforms have been stolen. They use a uniform service out of Jackson and are calling them now. They will report back to Deputy Douglas."

"Well," the Judge said, "I guess the mystery is solved. Sheriff Jones, I hope you can find and arrest the repairman, whoever he was."

"We're already on it, Judge Williams. And I've been in radio contact with the crime lab team on their way. The helicopter should be landing in our parking lot in twenty minutes."

"All right," she said. "This court is adjourned until four o'clock today, at which time Mr. Trevor Brewer will be back on the witness stand. Anything further?"

Judge Williams left the courtroom. Jake, Kitty, and Lee walked through the rail to join Willie Mitchell at his table. Jake watched Eleanor talk to Bobby Sanders and Mohammed X standing at the rail. Mohammed X began to tremble. He took a deep breath and motioned to Abud and Samson. He walked toward the exit, pausing in the aisle next to Tom, Trevor, and Tracy. He stared at them briefly, and left.

Atmosphere of Violence

Tracy jumped up and tried to climb over Tom to get to Mohammed X as he walked out. Tom grabbed Tracy and held her until they were gone.

Chapter Forty-Eight

Freddy left Wrench and Wizler for a moment and walked to the rolling side door they had forced open earlier at Tom's Automotive. He could see Breed squatting in a grove of trees on a hill a hundred feet from the shop. An occasional puff of smoke floated out of the metal barrel next to Breed. Following Freddy's instructions, Breed burned the Big River Electronics coveralls and hat with diesel, poking the ashes until every trace of fabric was gone. Freddy also had Breed watching the road to let Freddy know if anyone pulled into Tom's parking lot. Freddy waved until he got Breed's attention. Breed had never worn a wristwatch to the best of Freddy's knowledge, but Breed acknowledged Freddy by pointing to his wrist where he would have worn a watch if he had ever been a normal person. Freddy held up his right hand with his index finger and thumb a half-inch apart.

Freddy knew brother Tom would be in court all day with Trevor, accompanied probably by Tracy and at least a couple of his mechanics. Tom's Automotive would be closed for business. Freddy thought Tom would have everything they needed to destroy the Smith & Wesson right there in the repair shop. He was right.

Freddy studied the damage they had done to Tom's rolling door garage entrance. The door opening was plenty large enough for a tractor-trailer rig to drive into the garage. Tom could probably fix it. Unlike Freddy, Tom could fix just about anything. Freddy was only good at breaking and tearing up things. He walked back to Wrench and Wizler, careful to avoid looking directly at the flame. The men were both in welding helmets, with Wrench holding the industrial sized acetylene torch, concentrating the white and orange tipped blue flame searing what was left of the nine millimeter S & W clamped in a table vise. Wrench stopped his work and raised the visor.

"Almost done, boss man," Wrench said.

"Keep at it," Freddy growled.

Wizler pointed to the small, mangled and melted metal pieces on the floor cooling. He jumped and spun around, looking like an alien to Freddy with the helmet on. Freddy could hear him yelling but couldn't understand him through the helmet and over the noise of the torch. Freddy held his palms out. Wizler lifted his helmet.

"Melting that bitch," Wizler yelled and let the helmet visor fall back down to cover his face.

Freddy studied the gnarled and molten fragments on the floor. Two more pieces dropped from the vise onto the floor next to the others.

Wrench turned a knob on the torch and its flame disappeared with a pop. He gestured to Wizler to turn off the acetylene valve at the top of its cylindrical tank. Both men took off their helmets and flung them away. They skittered and slid across the concrete floor. Wizler unwound the clamp and the tiny remains of the S & W fell from the vise. Wizler knocked his heels together and thrust his hand out in a rigid Nazi salute.

"Ready for inspection, Mein Fuhrer."

Wrench picked up the metal pieces with tongs and dropped them into a bucket of water. Most of them were cool already, but a couple of the last fragments hissed hitting the water. Wizler took the bucket to the open door and poured off the water. He spread one of Tom's greasy red rags on the floor. He poured the lumps of metal onto the rag, tied the corners in a central knot and gave the bundle to Freddy.

"Let them run ballistics on this, Herr Brewermeister," Wizler giggled and rubbed his upper lip where his Hitler moustache used to be.

Wrench waved Breed in.

"Let's get the fuck outta here," Wizler said when they gathered in the garage. "I've got me a powerful thirst."

The Dregs cranked up their Harleys and revved the engines. The noise inside Tom's metal building was deafening. Freddy looked around at the mess his men had made. He laughed thinking about how pissed Tom would be when he saw the place. Still laughing, Freddy held up the red rag holding the misshapen gun fragments and roared out of the garage. Wizler shrieked like a banshee and followed. Wrench and Breed laid as much rubber as they could on Tom's formerly clean concrete floor, and took off to catch their boss man and his deranged sidekick.

~ * ~

Cruising southwest through Dundee county, Freddy wore his Nazi helmet and stayed right at the speed limit. Every half-mile or so, he reached into the red rag bundle stuffed inside his vest, grabbed a small metal fragment of the gun and tossed it into the ditch on the side of the highway. By the time they entered Yaloquena County, all the molten lumps were gone, spread over fifteen miles of the seldom traveled road from Kilbride to Sunshine.

He slowed to make sure his men saw him, then turned left on Rivercrest Road and into the Lonely Road Bar and Grill parking lot. When he dismounted, he took his lighter and torched the red rag, holding a small piece of the corner until the flames licked his fingers.

"Boys," Freddy said, "you are looking at a free man. Let's go in and celebrate with the honorable Buster Cloud, head chef of this fine establishment. All drinks and food you consume are on me. I don't know about you, but I've had about all of this law-abiding Freddy I can stand. Let's go in and see if we can't set the old Freddy free."

The four of them walked into the Lonely Road. It was three-thirty in the afternoon.

~ * ~

Judge Williams reconvened the trial at 3:50, ten minutes ahead of schedule. The crime lab techs had come and gone, dusting everything around Eddie's desk, table, and machines, then cleaning the area thoroughly to remove the fine black powder. They took comparison prints from Eddie, Judge Williams, and the three lawyers to eliminate their fingerprints if any were found.

Willie Mitchell was proud of how Trevor handled himself with Jordan Summit. At the outset when the trial resumed, Judge Williams told the jurors the terms of the stipulation the parties agreed to, assuring the jurors that the disappearance of the gun S-3 was irrelevant in light of the stipulation and facts already in evidence. She said the investigators would find the gun eventually, and to put the afternoon drama about S-3 out of their minds. She asked Trevor to return to the witness stand. In concluding his direct examination, Willie Mitchell had asked Trevor a few mop-up questions, and ended by asking him if he was sorry for Azeem's death. Trevor expressed his remorse honestly. Willie Mitchell asked him to answer any questions Mr. Summit might have.

Consistent with his prior strategy, Summit was direct and to the point. Even answering Summit, Trevor's stuttering was mild. He came across as truthful and sincere in Willie Mitchell's opinion. When Summit paused at the end of his questions, Willie Mitchell was ready to jump up and object if Summit tried to ask anything about Trevor's gun being the murder weapon in the Oklahoma City double homicide. To his credit, Summit didn't bring it up.

Judge Williams adjourned court for the day, reminding the jurors to avoid watching television or reading any newspaper. She told them to be back in the jury room no later than 8:45 the next day, because testimony would start at nine sharp.

After the jurors and Judge Williams left, Willie Mitchell turned to watch the Brewers walk out. Trevor waved briefly but Tom kept his head down. Tracy looked at Willie Mitchell for a second, but didn't acknowledge him in any way. Willie Mitchell had told Trevor earlier that after his testimony he didn't have to stay for the rest of the trial. Trevor assured the D.A. he would not be back unless the D.A. sent word to Brewer Hill that he was needed again.

Willie Mitchell closed his trial book and walked through the rail to join Lee, Kitty, and Jake. He asked Lee for an update on the search for the phony Big River Electronics repairman.

"I've got everybody I can spare on it," Lee said.

The D.A. pointed to the back door as the last Brewer left.

"They're the likely suspects," Willie Mitchell said. "With the gun no longer around, Trevor's prosecution goes up in smoke. Can't convict him without the gun."

"I didn't even notice the repairman," Lee said. "You think he was one of the Brewers?"

"Who knows," Willie Mitchell said. "They all kind of look alike."

"It sure wasn't Freddy or those two bikers in court," Lee said.

"I don't know," Jake said, "but when I drove to Freedmen's Creek to climb that pine tree and watch the compound, I got behind four motorcycles on the Kilbride highway. They pulled off the road into the old motel on the highway. I didn't think much of it, but I know there were four bikers. There were only three bikers in court this morning, Freddy and the two mean-looking guys. After a hearing a couple of weeks ago I followed Freddy to his truck to get his tag number to try to figure out who he was," Jake said. "That was before I knew he was a Brewer. In Tracy's truck that day, Freddy had a little guy with almost no hair riding with him. I don't know if he was Brewer, but maybe he was the fourth biker I saw on the highway. Maybe he was the River City repairman who took the gun this morning."

"Well, let's find Freddy and ask him," Willie Mitchell said.

"We're trying," Lee said.

Inside the rail, Eddie walked toward the side door carrying the cardboard evidence box.

"Sorry that happened with the gun," Willie Mitchell said to him.

"This is the worst day of my life," Eddie said and walked out.

Willie Mitchell knew he wasn't exaggerating.

Chapter Forty-Nine

From three-thirty to five, the Dregs drank one beer after another, replaying Wizler's magnificent theft of the Smith & Wesson right under the nose of everyone in the courtroom. From force of habit Wizler stroked his upper lip as if the Hitler moustache were still there.

"It'll grow back," Freddy said laughing.

"It just feels funny," Wizler said. "Wish you hadn't made me shave it. You know the hardest thing about the whole caper?"

"Trying to keep the little bald guy from figuring out what you were doing up there, I imagine," Wrench said.

"Naw, man. The hardest thing was keeping from busting out laughing when I was walking out the courtroom it was so fuckin' easy."

"That would have blown the whole thing," Wrench said.

"Yeah," Freddy said. "Can you imagine the look on that black bitch judge's face if she had caught sight of Wiz's gold swastikas in his front teeth?" He paused while they all roared. "And what if she saw that two-inch gap between Wiz's front teeth?"

"I bet she'd have wanted a swastika of her own," Wizler said giggling and slapping his knee. "Mud people like gold inlays."

By six-thirty, the Dregs had consumed two-and-a-half cases of beer and were hungry. Freddy had stayed ahead of Buster, putting down more cash as the grizzled bartender demanded they pay in advance for their beer. When Freddy ordered four of "Lonely Road's finest cheeseburgers," Buster stood by the table waiting. Freddy looked up. He had about all of Buster he could stand.

"What are you waiting for old man?" Freddy asked, an edge to it.

"Be twenty dollars," Buster said, wiping his right hand on the front of his greasy apron.

"We been eatin' here well over six weeks now," Freddy said. "Probably spent over three or four thousand dollars cash with you. And you're going to stand there and wait until I put up twenty fuckin' dollars to cover four of your greasy fuckin' burgers that you ought to be paying us to eat?"

Buster didn't move or change his expression. Freddy took a deep breath, reached in his pocket and threw some bills at Buster. The bartender picked them up off the dirty floor and walked behind the bar to make the burgers.

"If we weren't having such a good time," Freddy said, "I'd kick that son-of-a-bitch's ass. But I don't want to spoil our party, at least not right now." He looked at his men around the table, raising his beer bottle to clink with theirs in a toast. "Here's to Wizler and his Academy Award winning performance today."

They laughed and clapped Wizler on the back. Freddy took a pull on his beer, smiling at his men, keeping an eye on Buster moving slowly behind the bar, placing his precious fuckin' patties on the grill.

But for the four Dregs this Wednesday afternoon, Buster Cloud's struggling Lonely Road Bar & Grill would have had been empty. The Dregs had it to themselves until about seven, when three scruffy commercial fishermen who lived on Rivercrest road stopped in to guzzle a beer. They ordered another for the road and left.

About seven-thirty, the two girls Breed and Wrench had been "dating" in Yaloquena County showed up. They finished their first beer sitting on Breed and Wrench's laps. For their second, third, and fourth, the Dregs pulled up chairs for the women. After an hour, Freddy watched Wrench's woman, the one with brown and rotting upper incisors flanked by black stumps of canines and molars, whisper to Wrench. Wrench raised his eyebrows and followed her into the ladies room where they stayed for a couple of minutes. Freddy watched them walk out of the bathroom and back to the table. Wrench smiled and winked at Wizler. Wrench's girl grabbed Breed's woman by the wrist and left the Lonely Road arm in arm, laughing and talking. Wrench sat down.

"That didn't take long," Freddy said.

Wrench stuck his closed fist in the middle of the table, turned it palm up and opened his fingers. Inside a glassine packet were at least two dozen slightly yellow methamphetamine crystals. Freddy snatched the packet from Wrench's palm.

"Who's in charge here?" Freddy bellowed.

"You are," Wrench said. "I just thought since Wizler loves crank more than life itself, and he did such a good job today, that...."

"What have I told you about thinking?" Freddy said, glaring at Wrench a moment, then breaking into a big grin. "But in this case you thought right."

The four of them laughed and hooted. Freddy tossed the packet to Wizler, who pushed his chair out of the way and from a standing squat, did a flip and landed on his feet. Wizler reached into his pocket and pulled out a small glass pipe. Freddy clapped and yelled at Buster.

"Buster," Freddy said, "bring me some tin foil."

"Take it outside," Buster grumbled when he brought the foil.

Between the time the two women left until midnight, the Dregs had the place to themselves. They alternated between drinking one beer after another and fifteen minute trips to the parking lot to smoke the crystal meth. By midnight, their blood alcohol levels were off the charts and they were revved up on crank, still the only patrons of the Lonely Road.

"Closing time," Buster said at 12:05, rubbing his week's growth of white stubble and taking off his grimy apron.

"Give us some time here, Buster," Freddy said. "You're making money and we're having a party."

"Nope. Get moving."

To celebrate with his men, Freddy had put aside what an asshole Buster had been to him for six weeks, talking back to Freddy, making demands, smarting off. With the gun destroyed, he no longer had to be law-abiding Freddy. He could now treat Buster in the manner he thought he deserved. A good ass-whippin' would be a nice way to say goodbye; a going away present for the Lonely Road proprietor.

~ * ~

At the Banks home after dinner, Willie Mitchell, Susan, Jake, and Kitty sat around the old pine table in the kitchen. Susan had added sautéed sliced sausage to Zatarain's red beans and rice mix and served it with a green salad and Gambino's French bread Martha Gray brought her from New Orleans. Martha had flown down with Jimmy for an ABA regional meeting in the French Quarter at the Royal Orleans.

The mood around the table was somber. With Trevor's testimony behind them, Willie Mitchell's only remaining witnesses were the clerk at the convenience store, Tyretta Neely, and a few deputies to establish chain of custody. Summit had surprised Willie Mitchell by agreeing to allow Dr. Nathan Clement's written report to be placed into evidence rather than require the doctor's testimony. Summit finally acknowledged that the stipulation had rendered everything else surrounding the cause of death to be irrelevant.

Willie Mitchell noticed Jake deep in thought, his mind far away.

"What's up," he asked Jake.

"Mohammed X," Jake said. "That guy bothers me. He's got a weird affect about him. Maybe I've seen him on television before."

"I doubt it," Kitty said.

The wall phone rang and Susan answered it. She listened for a while, and gave the phone to Willie Mitchell.

"Who is it?" he asked, not wanting to talk.

"It's Walton. Gayle's back in ICU. He says she's taken a turn for the worse. I'm going down there. You stay with the twins."

"I'm going with you," Kitty said, following Susan out of the kitchen.

Chapter Fifty

"It's twenty after midnight and you got to leave," Buster said to the Dregs on his third attempt to roust them.

"I been meaning to ask you, Buster," Freddy said, "how did you come up with the name of this place?"

"Didn't," Buster said. "I guess the man I bought the place from did. Never asked him. Been called that for years."

"It's a good name."

"Whatever you say, just get moving."

Freddy pushed back from the table, grabbed an empty longneck and threw it hard against the cinder block wall behind the bar.

"Hey," Buster said.

Freddy grabbed another bottle and smashed it on the concrete at Buster's feet. Buster hardly moved. He looked down at the shattered glass around him.

"You better straighten up," Buster said. "You're paying for any damages you do to my place. I'll see to that."

Freddy burst out laughing.

"Did you hear that, men? We're going to have to pay for tearing up old Buster's lovely establishment."

Wizler jumped up, grabbed a bottle by the neck with each hand, twirled them in front of him like Zorro, then lunged forward and threw them hard as he could against the bar. Glass flew everywhere. Breed and Wrench pushed back their chairs, grabbed empty longnecks and began flinging them in every direction.

From the look on his face, Freddy could tell Buster was no longer angry—now he was frightened. It was about time.

"Look here at Buster, boys," Freddy said laughing. "He don't know whether to shit or go blind."

Freddy grabbed two handfuls of Buster's dirty shirt, pushing him against the bar. Freddy's stuck his face a half-inch from Buster's.

"We're fixin' to tear you a new one, Buster, and we're going to smash and crash this shit hole place of yours just 'cause we can."

Buster's eyes were wide. Freddy wasn't through. He jerked the old man around, pushing his head toward the floor.

"And you see these big heavy boots of mine? If you call the cops tonight, tomorrow, or next week, over even next month, I'll come back here and personally break your fuckin' ankles with my boots. You understand?"

Freddy pushed him away. Wizler shrieked like a maniac and turned the table over into Buster, knocking him back against the bar again. Freddy grabbed Buster to steady him, brushing imaginary dirt off the front of his nasty tee shirt.

"You all right, Buster?" Freddy asked, then sucker-punched the bartender, a hard blow right on the nose.

Buster fell backward into the bar then slid down onto the concrete.

"Pick old Buster up out of that broken glass before he gets cut or something worse, boys."

Breed and Wrench pulled the old man to his feet and held him against the bar while Freddy punched him, alternating rights and lefts. Freddy hit him with a right that shattered the old man's left eye socket. Breed and Wrench let Buster go. He fell over, hitting hard on the concrete. Wizler kicked him in the gut, then broke a longneck half-filled with Coors Light over Buster's head.

Freddy and his boys stared at Buster on the floor, bleeding from his nose and eyes, a gash on his head, and from cuts on his bare arms and neck where he fell on the broken glass.

"Pick that table up," Freddy barked, "and gather round. We've got some more unfinished business to take care of before we haul ass out of Mississippi."

~ * ~

The planning session took an hour, but that included a fifteen minute crystal meth break. With Buster knocked out, there was no further need to be discreet. They smoked it right at the table. Tiny embers floated down, burning small holes in the crude map of Freedmen's Creek drawn by Breed on paper Wizler retrieved from Freddy's saddlebags.

Buster groaned a time or two but appeared to still be unconscious on his concrete bed littered with beer bottle shards. It looked to Freddy like the old man had stopped bleeding.

"I know you boys got sick of watching those spooks in their suits and ties all duded up in the courtroom this morning," Freddy said, "but how do you think I felt putting up with their arrogant black asses sitting there like big shots every time there was some kind of hearing? Talk about chap my ass? And the head nigger in charge has a hard on for Trevor, wanting the D.A. to charge him with murder, and him having nothing to do with the shootout at the store on the highway except a white man defending himself." Freddy paused a moment and turned to Wrench. "You and Breed go get The Bomb. Let's put it together right here on this table before we leave. We're going take it out there to the Muslims and tear some of their shit up." They stood and lurched out the door. "Wizler, my man, get us four more Coors Lights."

"Are we staying to see what happens to the charges against Trevor?" Wizler asked as he passed out the beer.

"Shit, no. I did what I came to do."

"Can they prosecute him on that gun charge with the gun gone?"

"Don't know. Don't care."

Breed and Wrench sat down to assemble The Bomb. Freddy and Wizler guzzled beer and watched them work. The Bomb was kind of a homemade medieval battle flail. It consisted of three parts: a solid steel ball the size of a baseball with an eye bolt on one side; a stout wooden handle with a swivel eye bolt welded to a metal cap on one end of the wood; and a heavy steel chain tethering the steel ball to the wooden handle. After a couple of minutes Breed grabbed the wooden handle and stood, swinging the ball slowly at first, gathering momentum, then holding The Bomb above his head, the deadly steel ball traveling in a circle above. The muscles in Breed's right arm bulged and strained as he increased the speed of the ball and walked toward the Budweiser clock hanging from the ceiling over the bar. Breed was the only Dreg strong enough to wield The Bomb. When the steel ball connected with its target, the Budweiser clock exploded. A thousand pieces of blue and red neon tubing and wood and plastic clock housing rained down everywhere in the Lonely Road.

"Looks like it's working okay, boss," Wizler said.

Breed lowered his arm gradually, slowing the ball and chain until the ball moved in an arc like a pendulum. Breed brought the ball to rest on the floor. He glared at Wizler, showing his teeth.

"Like to put The Bomb against your head," Breed said.

Freddy laughed. "Don't hurt my little huckleberry, Breed. His little pin head's got too much brains in it. Soon as we get back to Texas the money's going to start rolling in thanks to Wizler's magic electronic readers." He gestured to Breed. "Sit back down here now and let's go over this map you drew us again, make sure we're all on the same page."

Breed described everything he learned about Freedmen's Creek in the four scouting trips he had made in the last week, pointing to the map. Freddy took over and went over the plan step by step starting the Dregs at the front gate and moving them around the compound. He asked if there were any questions and his men said no.

"Let's get it on," Wrench said.

"Hold on," Freddy said and turned to Wizler. "You watch old Buster enough to know where he kept his Lonely Road stash? We need to get back the money we've spent in this place the last six weeks."

Wizler stood at attention, clicked his heels and straight-armed the Nazi salute. "*Javol, mein Fuhrer,*" Wizler said. "As you ordered."

Wizler walked behind the bar and disappeared from view. In a few minutes, he popped up with a wad of cash in one hand and a long-barreled revolver in the other.

"Bring the cash," Freddy said, "leave the pistol."

Freddy chuckled when Wizler gave him the money. Wizler's pupils were so dilated his eyes looked black; so stoked with crystal he could not sit still. Wizler jerked and jumped, giggled and blew air threw the gap in his front teeth.

"Calm down, Wiz, before you blow up." Freddy did a quick count of the money. "Almost ten grand here." He looked down at Buster out on the floor. "With this much bread you'd think the nasty son of a bitch could buy him a new tee shirt and apron or two."

He counted out over two thousand dollars for each of his men and stuffed the rest in his pocket.

"Two final things," Freddy said. "As soon as our playtime is over with these colored folks, each one of you lights out for Texas alone. Breed, you head west until you hit Mississippi One and take it north to cross the river into Arkansas at Helena. I'm crossing at Greenville. And Wizler, you and Wrench head south on U.S. 61. Wizler crosses at Vicksburg, Wrench at Natchez. No stopping until you cross into Texas and no riding together. You should be out of Mississippi by 4:30 or 5:00 a.m. at the latest. Lay low by yourself for a while at a whore house motel of your choice and keep your bike stashed somewhere. Don't wear your vest. We'll meet up back in San Antonio one week from today."

"And the second thing is," Freddy said, opening his palm to reveal the last four crank crystals, "let's light these babies up."

They smoked the meth and stood up to leave. Freddy walked to the bar, reached over and picked up a bucket half-filled with ice cubes and water. He poured it on Buster's face. Buster sputtered as he came to.

"Pick him up," Freddy said to Breed and Wrench.

They stood Buster against the bar again. He was going in and out of consciousness, so Freddy felt it important to get Buster's attention to make his point. He slapped the old man, gently at first, then with more force. The old man opened his eyes and tried to talk.

"Hey," he said, "don't...."

"Shut up," Freddy said, moving within an inch of Buster. "Look at me. Are you awake enough to understand me?"

Buster nodded his head. His eyes stayed open.

"We're leaving and taking our money with us."

Freddy grinned. His nose touched Buster's.

"You call the law on us, old man, and I'll come back and break your ankles, like I said. And after that, I'll kill you. Comprendez?"

Buster said "yes, sir" through his broken nose and split lips.

"Good," Freddy said, "but just in case."

He wound up and launched an uppercut that caught Buster under his jaw and almost ripped off his head. Freddy gestured to Breed and Wrench to let the old man down easy onto the concrete this time.

"Let's ride," Freddy said.

Wizler grabbed four more bottles of beer from behind the bar and the Dregs left the Lonely Road Bar & Grill. The last one out, Freddy made sure to turn over the sign on the door to read CLOSED.

Chapter Fifty-One

They walked their bikes in silence the last quarter of a mile to the Freedmen's Creek gate. Like Breed predicted, the single guard was asleep in the small guardhouse. Freddy and Breed parked their Harleys on their kickstands. Freddy gestured for Wizler and Wrench to stay on their bikes while Breed and he took care of the guard.

Inside the small guard house, Freddy tapped the guard on the head. When the guard opened his eyes and jumped up, Breed cold cocked him, knocking him out with his deadly right fist. They took off the guards' pants and shirt, ripped them into strips and hog-tied him. Freddy picked up his AK-47 while Breed engaged the gate motor. They walked outside to their bikes as the gate rolled open.

"Where's Wizler?" Freddy whispered to Wrench.

Wrench pointed to the flag pole. Wizler had shinnied up the pole and was on his way down with the green, black, and red flag draped over his shoulder. Back at his Harley, Wizler tied one end of the flag around his neck like a cape, the black crescent down around his knees.

Freddy gave a signal and the four of them pushed their Harleys through the gate on the main road downhill to the community center. At the center, Freddy and Wizler turned their bikes to the left, Breed and Wrench to the right.

"We ready?" Freddy asked and almost started laughing at the delight on the faces of his three men. The meth was making Freddy's head buzz.

"Hey, Freddy," Wizler said, "I feel like a Viking. You know, a fuckin' Viking, before a raid. Vikings were some raiding mother-fuckers. You know?"

Freddy chuckled. "Yeah, man. Vikings, that's what we are. Raiders of the night. All right, my Viking brothers, start your engines on the count of three, turn on your lights, and let's do some damage."

The bikes roared to life, like only Harleys can do. Headlights flashed on and the Dregs took off, Freddy and Wizler on the road going past the living quarters, Wrench and Breed in the opposite direction, on the narrow road between the community center and kitchen leading to the mosque and Mohammed X's residence.

Wizler turned on his sound system, blasting his homemade brew of pounding industrial metal dubbed with voiceovers of Adolf Hitler's speeches, *der Führer* at his maniacal best. Wizler cut doughnuts in the grassy area in front of the FEMA trailer housing units. When several of the trailer doors opened, Wizler whistled through the gap in his teeth and shrieked, roaring closer to the trailers, the black crescent flag waving behind him.

Freddy knocked down the door and tore through the gymnasium, peeling out and ripping the mats. Wrench did the same thing in the mosque, tearing down everything he could, leaving black skid marks and circles all around the prayer floor. When Wrench rode out of the mosque, Wizler sped by in front of him on the road to the amphitheatre, holding the edge of the burning flag flapping behind him. Wrench smiled, something he almost never did.

On his way back from his first run past the mosque, Breed tore through the Freedmen's Creek vegetable gardens. He opened the wooden gate and rousted the cattle, driving in circles in the pen until all the cows were out roaming the roads and paths of the compound. Riding out of the cow pen, Breed began swinging The Bomb at every structure he rode by, crunching metal and splintering wood.

~ * ~

Samson woke up in the FEMA trailer he shared with Abud when Wizler and Freddy made their first pass. He quickly put on his pants, grabbed his automatic rifle and stuck his head out the door. Wizler was cutting doughnuts in the grass fifty feet away to the grating sound of atonal heavy metal and excerpts from a speech in some foreign language.

Samson didn't recognize German. Even regular English was a second language to the big man. He grew up Ambrose Bryant in the Sea Islands near Beaufort, South Carolina speaking Gullah, later known as Sea Island Creole English. Raised by his grandmother, Ambrose was always self-conscious about his size. He went as far in school as he could on the island and had to transfer to the high school on the mainland after eighth grade. The kids made fun of the way he talked, careful not to do it while standing too close to Ambrose. He adjusted, learning regular English as quickly as he could.

Ambrose was by far the strongest young man in his high school, winning the South Carolina All-Class high school power lifting title at the state tournament in Columbia his junior and senior years. His grandmother talked him into accepting a full scholarship to Louisiana Tech in Ruston. He competed on Tech's well-respected intercollegiate power lifting team, but struggled with classroom work because of his language deficiency. Louisiana was like a foreign country to him, and after two years of being called "Pump" and "Gullah Gorilla" by his teammates, Ambrose had enough. At age twenty he was recruited by a talent scout for professional wrestling and trained at the World Championship Wrestling center in Atlanta. His agent and handlers settled on "Gomba the Lion Killer" as his ring name. They dressed him in leopard print and told him to grunt and act mean. Even in interviews to promote the next scripted battle royal, his bosses told him to grunt and roar and gesture wildly, but never talk.

Ambrose was arrested for possession of steroids but turned it into a felony battery when he beat up the two arresting officers. In prison, his size and weightlifting ability gained him notoriety, but with it came more teasing and abuse. When an Imam in prison asked him why he let white and black Christians exploit and degrade him, Ambrose began to listen. After a year of prayer, he converted and took the Muslim name Samson al Kadeesh. His prison Imam arranged for him to continue his Islamic education in Memphis when he left the penitentiary. The Memphis Imam, Mohammed X, immediately recognized Samson's potential value as a bodyguard. Samson became friends with Abud Rahman in the Memphis mosque. The three of them fled Memphis under cover of darkness to escape assassination, eventually relocating at Freedmen's Creek.

"Who's making all that noise?" Abud asked, putting on his oversized glasses. "Are those motorcycles?"

"You stay here," Samson told his friend.

Samson walked out of his trailer with his AK-47. He walked in the darkness toward the community center, stopping at the gate of a chain link fence. He opened the gate and threw a large metal switch on a pole, illuminating the outside lighting throughout the compound. His eyes had not quite adjusted to the bright light when he exited the small chain link enclosure and stepped onto the path.

By the time he saw Breed speeding past him on the Harley it was too late to move. The Bomb caught him in his left temple, bursting through his skull, the solid steel ball obliterating his brain. The giant man was dead before he hit the ground.

~ * ~

With the lights on in the compound, Freddy knew it was time to clear out. He passed by Mohammed X's building one last time, flipping him off as he rode by, throwing his head back laughing. He made eye contact with the head man and was happy to see the look of recognition in Mohammed X's eyes. Freddy wanted the black son of a bitch to know who was fucking with him. The Dregs had only been in the compound a couple of minutes, but with their bikes and The Bomb they had done some major damage.

Freddy blew past the community center, took a sharp left at what was left of the gym, and approached his three men stopped on the road in front of the residential trailers. When Freddy pulled up next to them, he saw Samson. Lying on the path was the giant bodyguard, the top of his head ripped off and his brains strewn in a straight pink line across the road.

"We need to jet, bro," Wizler said to Freddy.

"No kidding," Freddy said. "Let's boogie."

The Dregs roared out of Freedmen's Creek and onto the highway. They didn't stop until the Freedmen's Creek road made a tee intersection with the Sunshine to Kilbride highway.

"Dude had an AK," Wizler said. "He was going to kill one of us for sure. Breed saved our asses."

"Good work," Freddy said to Breed. "Chunk The Bomb into the river when you cross at Helena."

Freddy watched them take off, tightened his helmet and headed toward Sunshine at the speed limit. He started whistling and thinking about his favorite East Texas titty bar on a piney woods peninsula at Lake Sam Rayburn east of Lufkin. There was this little blonde there. She was no Brandi Trichel, but she'd do in a pinch.

Chapter Fifty-Two

Willie Mitchell finished his direct examination of the Gas & Go Fast clerk Tyretta Neely at 10:30 Thursday morning. She was his last witness. Willie Mitchell almost didn't call her to the stand because she added little to what the jury had already seen on the video. The only element it lacked was audio, which Trevor provided as best he could. He heard only the last few words of the argument leading up to the shooting. Trevor had done better than the D.A. expected in testifying about what he heard and what happened that day.

Though Tyretta added nothing to what happened outside, Willie Mitchell decided to call her to the stand because she did corroborate Trevor's testimony about his coming in the store after the shooting. Her description of Trevor's actions inside added to the State's theory of the case that Trevor acted only in self-defense and in defense of Abdul Azeem. His behavior inside the store was that of an innocent passerby caught up in a bad situation. He had no reason to run. Trevor had done nothing wrong. In legal arcana, no *mens rea.*

While waiting for Summit to begin his cross, Willie Mitchell turned around. What a difference a day made. The courtroom was virtually empty—no Brewers, no Muslims, no Dregs. Jake and Lee sat together. Kitty had not returned from the hospital in Jackson. The Reverend Bobby Sanders was alone in the front row behind Mule. Willie Mitchell noticed Bobby checking the door every few minutes, no doubt looking for his friends from Freedmen's Creek.

Willie Mitchell did not expect Summit to do much with Tyretta on cross because her testimony on direct didn't contradict the defense version of what happened at the gas pump. Out of habit, the D.A. picked up his pen to make notes of the questions and answers. After Summit lobbed a few perfunctory questions about ground covered by Willie Mitchell on direct, Summit took off in another direction.

"Now, Ms. Neely, I want to ask you about previous problems with customers or conflicts between customers at your store."

"All right."

"Have you had disturbances in the past?"

"Sometimes."

"On how many occasions?"

"Not too often."

Summit held up a binder containing what looked to Willie Mitchell to be about two hundred pages.

"I have here, Ms. Neely," Summit said, "phone records for your store for the last year. These were provided to me by your employer Gas & Go Fast Company pursuant to a subpoena issued to them."

Tyretta nodded. "Okay."

Summit opened the binder and flipped through the pages. Willie Mitchell noticed that some of the documents were marked with tabs and highlighted with yellow and green markers.

"I don't want to bore you, the jury, or Judge Williams with questions about every 9-1-1 call emanating from the store over the last year, but it appears that there was a call for the police from the store's phone about once a month, on average, Ms. Neely. Is that consistent with your recollection or experience?"

"That's probably about right. Sometimes the calls don't be for fights or arguing. Sometimes a customer needs help with something, some emergency, you know, and we make the call."

"There was one call where a car caught on fire."

"Yeah. Something like that."

"But sometimes these calls are because of trouble, fights, or what have you, is that right?"

"Sometimes. It ain't too bad."

"Your Honor," Willie Mitchell said, "I don't want to object to this line of questioning if it's shown to be relevant to this matter. I think an inquiry into the 9-1-1 records themselves would be a more productive source for the exact nature of the calls. They're kept on file at the 9-1-1 office in the basement of the courthouse and are public records."

"Mr. Banks is correct, Your Honor," Summit said. "I only have a couple of additional questions and I'll be through with this witness."

"Go ahead," the Judge said.

"I noticed in reviewing these records, Ms. Neely, that there are several calls around seven a.m. every day to various local numbers. Do you know the nature of these calls?"

"That's not me calling. The manager usually be making those calls. When I work the morning shift sometimes I see the manager make calls around that time, but I'm busy and don't pay it much attention."

"So you don't know about the calls?"

She shook her head no.

"You'll have to respond orally," Judge Williams said.

Tyretta looked at the judge.

"So the microphone can pick up your answer for the record."

"Oh. No, sir. I don't know."

"That's all I have for Ms. Neely," Summit said.

Willie Mitchell didn't mind Summit using his cross to develop his civil case as long as he kept it brief, which he had. In Mule's civil suit for damages against Gas & Go Fast, Summit had to prove that the previous fights or shootings at the store created, in the words of the Mississippi Supreme Court, an "atmosphere of violence" so that the owner, Gas & Go Fast, owed a greater duty to its business invitees to protect them from harm. Willie Mitchell knew the premises liability case law. A property owner could fulfill the duty by hiring private security or restricting hours of operation so that its customers would be safer. The D.A. also knew that this particular Gas & Go Fast location was not a regular source of trouble for local law enforcement. He couldn't remember a single violent incident at the store in the last few years. But Willie Mitchell also knew that with the right jury and a defendant company with deep pockets, any verdict was possible, regardless of the evidence.

"Mr. Banks?" the Judge said.

"May I have a moment?"

Judge Williams nodded. Willie Mitchell went quickly through his trial book, double-checking, making sure all his trial exhibits were filed into evidence and all the testimony that he intended to offer was in. He thought for a moment.

"I have no further witnesses, Your Honor. The State rests."

"Mr. Summit?"

"If we could take a short recess, Judge Williams, I'll be ready to call my first witness shortly."

"Very well. Remove the jurors, Mr. Delrie."

After the jury left, she tapped her gavel and recessed court. Willie Mitchell stood for her to leave, and turned to his gallery. Bobby Sanders walked briskly out of the courtroom, leaving Jake and the Sheriff. Willie Mitchell stepped outside the rail to join them in the center aisle.

"What do you think?"

"If they follow the law," Lee said, "they'll convict him. Trevor was minding his own business. The video shows Mule started it all."

"What about you, Jake?" Willie Mitchell asked.

"It depends on what kind of case Summit puts on."

"What was that about the phone calls?" Lee asked.

"That's all related to the civil suit," Jake said to Lee. "He's doing some unofficial discovery. The lawsuit for damages he and Eleanor filed is the only reason Summit is handling this criminal trial." Jake paused. "Is that store location dangerous?" Jake asked Lee. "Lots of fights or robberies, things like that?"

Lee shook his head. "Nah," he said.

~ * ~

Willie Mitchell wasn't surprised when Summit put Mule on the witness stand as his first witness. The parties had already stipulated and the jury had been instructed that Mule's gun did not kill Azeem. Summit's strategy boiled down to establishing that Mule was in fear for his own safety and acted in self-defense. Summit had already gotten on cross from Trevor, Lee, and the clerk Tyretta everything he could to help make his case. Proving justification now depended solely on Mule's testimony. Because Mule's prior criminal record consisted only of petty crimes, nothing violent, Summit had nothing to lose by putting Mule on the stand. Willie Mitchell knew from talking to Lee and the deputies who dealt with Mule that he was something of a con artist, quick with an answer for everything. Mule had a lot riding on his testimony, his freedom for sure, and possibly money in the civil suit. As prepared as Summit had been in every aspect of pre-trial and trial, Willie Mitchell suspected Summit had spent a good bit of time woodshedding Mule, going over and over what Summit wanted Mule to say. After thirty minutes of Mule telling the jury about his life and his background, Summit moved to the crux of the defense.

"Now, Mule, the jury has seen the video of what happened between you and Abdul Azeem that day, so there's no need for me to cover everything it shows. I do want to draw your attention to the point at which Abdul Azeem grabs the money off the trunk of the Taurus and talks to you. What exactly did he say?"

Mule mumbled. Willie Mitchell had to hand it to Summit. He had Mule acting sufficiently humble in recounting his past, contrite for the misdemeanors he had committed, and apologetic for his drinking. Summit led Mule down the path and Mule did a good job following. Mule was ashamed of his past conduct. Summit suggested and Mule agreed reluctantly that his drinking and inability to work resulted from his disability and the abuse he had taken as a child and adult because of the way he walked.

Summit made it clear to the jury it was not Mule's fault he was born poor on a plantation without medical care, resulting in his leg deformity. Willie Mitchell remained stoic during Mule's testimony. He refrained from objecting because he didn't want the jury to get the impression he was heartless or that he was trying to keep them from learning the facts about Mule. Most of the testimony was irrelevant to the homicide, so the D.A. let it go. Summit continued to impress Willie Mitchell. Whenever possible, Summit referred to the victim by his full Muslim name, Abdul Azeem. Summit also placed Mule in his wheelchair on the riser in front of the Judge's bench facing the jury. Mule was at eye level with the jurors.

"You'll have to speak up and speak clearly," Summit told his client. "I know this is difficult, but the jury must be able to hear and understand what you are saying about what Abdul Azeem said."

Mule sat up in his wheel chair as straight as he could. His oversized white long-sleeved shirt was buttoned at the collar, still leaving a full inch of clearance around Mule's skinny neck. He looked the jurors in the eye for a minute.

"He told me if I wanted the five dollar bill I had to pray to Allah," Mule said, starting out too loud, then modulating his voice.

"Did that make you angry?"

"Yes, sir, Mr. Summit, it surely did."

Summit paused a few seconds, adding to the drama. Willie Mitchell glanced at the jurors. They were hanging on Mule's every word.

"What did you tell Abdul Azeem?"

"I said I wasn't praying to no Allah. I said he weren't my God."

"What did Abdul Azeem say then?"

"I don't want to say."

Summit stood up, pushed his chair under the table and stood behind it gripping its back.

"You must, Mr. Gardner. Tell the jury exactly what Azeem said at that point."

"He said Jesus wasn't no God. Said he was a lesser prophet. Lesser than his prophet Mohammed."

"Did he say anything else?"

"Yes, sir. Then he said...." Mule paused, swallowed. "He said Jesus weren't nothing but a man, and not much man at that."

Willie Mitchell thought he heard a couple of audible gasps from the jury panel. He dared not look over to see. He'd ask Lee and Jake later.

"And that," Mule said, "that made me mad. So mad I couldn't control myself. That's when I threw my shoe and went after him, like it shows on the video. I weren't letting him get away with talking 'bout Jesus Christ like that."

"What happened then?"

"He turnt that gas hose on me, soaking me down. I thought I was done for."

"Why did you think that?"

"I just knew the man, the Muslim Azeem or whatever, I knew he was fixin' to light me up."

"What do you mean?"

"Why else would you spray gas on somebody? I figured he had a lighter or matches and was going to set me on fire like they do those monks in China. Kill me."

"Your Honor," Willie Mitchell said, "may we approach?"

Willie Mitchell enjoyed the feigned look of surprise on Summit's face. When they stood before Judge Williams, the D.A. whispered.

"Judge, I haven't objected, but there's no foundation for any of this. There's no evidence the victim had a lighter or matches on him, and it's apparent from the video that the victim made no attempt to set the defendant on fire."

"State of mind, Your Honor," Summit said quietly. "My client's state of mind at that point is most relevant. Self-defense justification is based on what my client perceives the threat to be, and as long as his perception is reasonable under the circumstances, it is up to the jury to determine if Mr. Gardner acted reasonably in defending himself."

Judge Williams looked at Willie Mitchell.

"He's right, Mr. Banks. But I imagine you already knew that. Take your seats and let's continue."

Of course he's right. I had to do something to interrupt Mule's tour de force. Much more of this and there's no way the jury will convict.

"Did he do that, Mr. Gardner?"

"Do what?"

"Did he light you on fire?" Summit asked.

"I thought he was about to but I didn't give him the chance. That's when I got my gun out of my buggy. I wasn't going to get burned up by that Muslim without puttin' up a fight."

Willie Mitchell thought he heard a juror say "un-huh" in quiet agreement with Mule. Absent some miracle, Mule's performance had just won him an acquittal. Like the savvy lawyer he was, Summit wrapped up in a hurry. Willie Mitchell was sure Summit had gotten more out of Mule's performance than he ever expected. Mule had been a hell of a witness. Willie Mitchell was positive everything Mule said about Jesus and Azeem torching him was made up out of whole cloth, the result of suggestions by Summit. But Summit would never have told Mule to lie. He was too smart for that. Willie Mitchell knew all Summit had to do was ask Mule leading questions when the two of them were preparing for trial. And Willie Mitchell knew there was nothing he could do about it. Bear down on Mule in his wheelchair on cross-examination and the jury would hold any slip-up against the D.A., not Mule. They would feel sorry for the paralyzed defendant, think Willie Mitchell was a cold, mean bastard, and acquit Mule as fast as they could.

Summit turned Mule over to Willie Mitchell. Willie Mitchell cleared his throat and looked at notes he made of Mule's testimony. He said "Mr. Gardner," then felt himself falling into the black hole that engulfed him when he went into an *absent* seizure. Willie Mitchell sat motionless at the prosecution table, but he was no longer there.

~ * ~

Judge Williams had seen it before. As soon as she recognized Willie Mitchell descending into his *petit mal* trance, she interrupted him.

"Just a minute, Mr. Banks."

She knew Willie Mitchell could not hear her. She made eye contact with Jake. Zelda could tell Jake knew what was going on. She watched Jake walk through the gate and pull up a chair to position himself between his Daddy and the jury. Jake whispered to Willie Mitchell as if he could hear.

"I've got something I have to tend to," the Judge said to the jury. "We'll take a short recess and reconvene in fifteen minutes. Mr. Bailiff, take the jurors back to the jury room for a coffee break."

The bailiff led the jury out. Zelda noticed a few of the jurors cast puzzled glances at the D.A. and Jake. After the jurors were gone, Judge Williams adjourned court and walked down to Willie Mitchell's side. The little bald clerk Eddie Bordelon joined them.

"He'll be all right in a few minutes, Judge," Jake said. "Thanks for catching it when you did."

"Take all the time you need, Jake," she said and walked out. Eddie nodded support for Jake and left with Judge Williams.

Willie Mitchell sat looking down at his notes, as still as a mannequin. Jake put his arm around his Daddy's shoulders. Lee walked through the gate.

"How long?" the Sheriff asked.

"Ten minutes. Maybe fifteen."

Jake looked over at Summit and Eleanor Bernstein. They stared at Willie Mitchell. Eleanor leaned over to Summit and whispered in his ear. Summit turned to Eleanor and began asking questions quietly.

Eleanor stepped on the riser and bent over to say something to Mule, who was studying the D.A. in silence. Mule nodded in response to whatever Eleanor said.

Jake continued to hold his father, waiting for the seizure to pass.

~ * ~

Twenty minutes later, Willie Mitchell asked Mule if he had any evidence to support his belief that the victim had a lighter or matches. The quality of Mule's response convinced Willie Mitchell that he would do nothing but dig the hole deeper if he tried to discredit Mule. After twenty minutes of cross, the D.A. turned the witness back. Summit wisely had no re-direct. Willie Mitchell had scored a few points on cross with Mule, but not enough to resurrect the strong possibility of a conviction. At best Willie Mitchell thought a lesser-included-offense might still be in play. He would cover that in closing, arguing that the death of Azeem warranted a conviction of some lower grade of homicide, if not the felony murder Mule was charged with.

After the bailiff rolled Mule carefully down from the riser and back to the defense table, Judge Williams asked Summit to call his next witness. Summit asked for a minute and huddled with Eleanor.

He ought to rest. Nothing could make his case better after Mule's performance.

"The defense rests, Your Honor," Summit said.

"Very well," the Judge said and turned to the jury. "Ladies and gentlemen, the part of the trial where the parties present evidence and testimony is over. We will adjourn for lunch and reconvene at two p.m. when Mr. Banks and Mr. Summit will present their closing arguments. It will then be my duty to instruct you on the law." She looked at her watch. "With any luck, you should be retiring to the jury room to begin deliberations by four o'clock."

Most of the jurors smiled as the bailiff led them out. Willie Mitchell guessed it was the possibility of wrapping up their duty tonight. With the jury, judge, and court personnel gone, Willie Mitchell closed his trial book and joined Lee and Jake in the aisle next to their bench. There wasn't much to say, no need to ask Willie Mitchell what Lee and Jake thought. He could tell from their demeanor their assessment of the probability of conviction was the same as his.

Jordan Summit pushed Mule out the center aisle, pausing as he reached Willie Mitchell.

"I'm going to be brief in closing," Summit said.

"Don't blame you. I won't take long."

Willie Mitchell made eye contact with Eleanor. She quickly averted her eyes and walked toward the back door ahead of Mule. Eleanor stopped when the door opened and Kitty burst in.

"Has Needham testified?" Kitty asked.

"With Trevor's gun missing I decided not to call Needham to testify," Summit said. "He arrived in town late last night. I met him for coffee this morning and released him from his subpoena. He's on his way back to Oklahoma City."

Kitty's shoulders slumped.

"I drove really fast from Jackson to get here. I was supposed to get a look at his file from the Oklahoma City case," she said.

"He asked me to give you this," Summit said and pulled a large envelope from his briefcase. Kitty's name was written boldly on the envelope with a black Sharpie. "It's a copy for you to keep. He said he told you on the phone a few days ago he would let you see the file when he was here."

"Thank you very much," she said, breathing a sigh of relief.

Summit rolled Mule out the door and Eleanor followed. The courtroom was cleared except for Lee, Jake, Kitty, and Willie Mitchell.

"I wonder what Eleanor thinks of her political opponent after what she saw in here today?" Willie Mitchell said.

"It means nothing, Willie Mitchell," Lee said. "Nothing at all."

"What?" Kitty asked.

Jake took her by the arm and led her out.

"I'll tell you," he said.

The door closed behind them. Willie Mitchell looked at Lee.

"Bad timing," Willie Mitchell said.

"No big deal, partner. Just like this case. Nothing we can do about Mule making all that stuff up. He was pretty effective up there."

"Yep," Willie Mitchell said. "Mule sure told a good story."

Chapter Fifty-Three

The sun was peeking through the pine trees east of Freedmen's Creek by the time the men Abud supervised completed bathing and enshrouding Samson's body in a white cotton sheet. All that was left was Mohammed X's recitation of the *Janazah* ritual prayer over the body and burial in the deep hole Mohammed had his men digging since three a.m. The leader had chosen a spot in the dense woods in the most remote portion of the property.

Abud tried to organize the men to carry Samson's body on a wooden plank. The body was so heavy and the plank so unwieldy that Abud settled on placing Samson's remains in a low-riding metal trailer and towing it behind one of the commune's four-wheelers. The procession began at six-thirty. Mohammed X limited the mourners to the warrior class of men, the ones trained to shoot and fight. He wanted them to be emotionally wrought at the death of their beloved Samson at the hands of the Brewers. The more his death incited the men, the more receptive they would be to what he had planned for them.

The service in the woods was brief. Mohammed X ordered Abud to make sure the body was deep and to spread pine straw and limbs over the disturbed soil to hide the grave. Mohammed X did not want Samson's body unearthed by whoever ended up owning the thirty acres. It was sorry land and had dealt Mohammed X plenty of misery in the two years the commune existed. He understood now why the freed slaves who started Freedmen's Creek as a utopian village after the Civil War eventually abandoned it.

Mohammed X had known this day was inevitable since Azeem's death. The hierarchy in Virginia had treated Freedmen's Creek the way he would have, cutting off all funding and all communication. They were out of money and food, but still had plenty of weapons and ammunition. Freedmen's Creek would cease to exist after today. Mohammed X wanted it to go out with a bang.

Abud walked into Mohammed X's office. He stood until Mohammed X gestured. Abud sat on the big pillow across the low table from his master.

"It is done," Abud said.

"Is it well-concealed?"

"Yes. You could walk right past it and not discover that the ground had been opened for Brother Samson's burial."

"Good."

"Some of the men are angry. They want to call the Sheriff."

Mohammed X laughed. "What for? The authorities will not help us. It is never a good idea to draw attention to ourselves."

Abud appeared disconsolate.

"Don't worry, my little comrade. We will avenge Samson's death."

"How?"

"Gather every man woman and child into the mosque. In thirty minutes I will address them." He paused. "Everyone. No one is to miss what I have to say. Go now. Send Obeh to me immediately."

Abud nodded and left.

~ * ~

After their thirty minute private meeting, Mohammed X was convinced that Obeh was incapable of leading a successful assault on anything. Unfortunately, Obeh was the best candidate he had. Obeh was intent on avenging his friend Samson, hated white people, and was not afraid to die—all prerequisites for the mission. Mohammed X did not know if Obeh's willingness to give his life in the cause was due to religious fervor and friendship, or due to Obeh's life being miserable and pointless by Mohammed X's standards. No matter, Obeh would have to do.

"After our convocation begin preparation for the attack. You have the rest of this day and tonight to teach your men what they will need to know before dawn tomorrow. Any questions?"

"Just one, Your Eminence. Who is our target on that hill?"

"Target? Kill them all."

Mohammed X dismissed Obeh. It was now time to address the great unwashed. He took several minutes to adjust his suit and tie and part his hair just so. He put on his beige brocade Sherwani suit jacket with metallic embroidery and his white silk *shorah* with its black leather binding to keep it snug on his head. Mohammed X took one last look in the mirror. He liked what he saw.

~ * ~

Mohammed X strode purposefully toward the raised platform at one end of the expansive prayer room in the mosque. He gestured for Abud to join him, directing him to stand far enough to the side to make it clear to the people that Abud was being honored, but his status was certainly well below that of Mohammed X.

Mohammed X looked out on the crowd. The brothers and sisters were riveted. They knew something big was up. The commune had lost a well-loved member. No meeting like this had ever occurred. Mohammed X made a quick estimate of the crowd. It seemed everyone was there. He noted how ragged and tired his people appeared. No wonder. Being on half-rations the last several weeks was barely enough to keep them alive.

He buried his chin into his chest for a moment, eyes closed as if deep in contemplation. When he extended his arms for several seconds, a hush descended. He raised his head. He looked out on his flock. He was smiling, peaceful. He began his address.

Brothers and Sisters, thank you for joining me in our holy place of worship. I join you today in mourning the loss of Brother Samson. He was a wonderful and powerful man, full of faith and love for each of you. He was a faithful servant, cut down in the prime of his life. His sin? Trying to defend all of us from the infidels who invaded our home this morning.

Samson was not the first to die for us. Abdul Azeem was also assassinated by the murderous white devils who live like animals on the hill not far from here. Who will the crusaders kill next? I ask you to consider what I believe is true: They will not stop until we are all dead.

The law is against us. The government is against us. We will not call the local Sheriff to arrest those responsible because the local Sheriff is on the side of the infidels. I have seen him with the Brewers in court. The Sheriff and the Brewers are united as Christians in their hatred for us. I assure you the Sheriff celebrates Brother Samson's death.

Infidels killed Azeem in their town. Now they break into our sanctuary and kill us. Should we flee? Should we stay and fight? Each of you must answer that question in your own heart.

The white devils killed Abdul Azeem to starve us and destroy our sources of revenue. I know you are hungry. I know the hunger has caused you to become restless. I have made a choice. I know how I will respond to these murderers. I will stay and fight. I will do my best to kill these men. I hope you will join with me, but if you choose not to defend our way of life, you are free to go. After today, Allah's Temple at Freedmen's Creek will no longer exist.

Mohammed X smiled like a kindly father as the rumble of whispers grew loud. One angry man stood and raised his voice.

"My family and I left our home and jobs to join Freedmen's Creek. You told us you would take care of us, that our lives would be blessed by Allah. Now you say it's over. What are we to do? Where are we to go?"

"Kill the infidels," another man shouted.

Some men stood to support him, but others booed.

Brothers. Sisters. There's nothing more we can do. I feel the pain and loss. I put everything I had in this holy land. I am losing more than any of you. It hurts my heart to tell you these truths. Those of you who will join me in avenging the deaths of Azeem and Samson, come forward and gather with Brother Obeh over here.

He pointed to the corner of the prayer room to his left.

Those of you who choose to leave, I wish you the best. You may meet with Brother Abud after I leave to discuss the schedule of bus departures. May Allah be with you.

Mohammed X walked deliberately from the prayer room. When the door closed behind him, he heard shouts and screams. He walked into his residence and locked the door behind him. He fixed himself a cup of tea and sat on the pillow behind his desk thumbing through his most recent road atlas of the United States. Virginia would be his first stop. The leaders of the movement would reassign him somewhere, especially when they learned of the slaughter of the white Christians on Brewer Hill carried out by Obeh and his warriors.

Chapter Fifty-Four

Bobby Sanders had to find out why they hadn't shown up for the trial this morning. He parked his black Escalade in the parking lot just inside the gate. He thought it strange that the gate was open and the guardhouse empty. The crescent flag was missing, too. He locked his SUV and walked down the slight incline toward the community center.

He stopped where the path split. To his left, he saw thirty or forty people milling around in front of the FEMA trailers. A malnourished cow walked past the people toward Bobby. He turned to continue to the center and saw several cattle grazing in the vegetable garden. No wonder. The fence was down.

Bobby knew something bad was happening. He walked between the center and the cafeteria to the mosque. Outside the building he saw a dozen men in uniform with automatic rifles listening to one man in a maroon beret. The men and their leader turned and glared at Bobby. He walked quickly into the mosque, hoping he didn't get shot on the way.

Bobby breathed easier when was inside the mosque. It was bedlam, but at least no one had guns. Abud was in the front of the prayer room. At least fifty men and women were gathered in front of him, yelling questions and pumping their fists. He watched Abud try to quiet the people. Abud looked Bobby's way and gestured to the people he'd be right back.

"What's going on?" Bobby asked him.

"I'd rather the master explain. Go to him."

Bobby left the mosque and walked the short distance to Mohammed X's residence. He knocked several times and waited.

"Come in," Mohammed X said when he opened the door.

Bobby sat on the large pillow in front of the low table.

"What is going on out here?" Bobby asked.

"We are disbanding the facility," Mohammed X said. "I've been called on another mission for our faith."

"I knew when you weren't in court this morning it was something important. I saw Abud in the mosque. Where is Samson?"

"He's already departed for the new location."

"Well. It's a shame you're leaving."

"This property, this county is too inhospitable. We've had nothing but trouble. The murder of Abdul Azeem was the last straw. Nothing is going to be done to the Brewer who killed him."

"I'm not giving up...."

"Listen to me. Stop playing by their rules. You people here in Mississippi are just as oppressed as our forefathers in the slave ships. The sad thing is you don't even realize it. You protest and play at their politics. You take money from their government. They give you just enough to keep you alive. But that's not living. It makes you dependent on white people. Break your chains of servitude. Be a man. Fight the white devils. Hurt them. That's the only thing they understand. Make them fear you."

Bobby didn't know how to respond. Mohammed X stood and looked down at Bobby on his pillow. He wasn't smiling. Bobby got the hint and walked to the door.

"I'll go see if I can help Abud," Bobby said.

Walking away with his back to Mohammed X, Bobby felt the same as he had earlier when he hustled into the mosque to avoid the gang of men armed with AK-47s—threatened.

~ * ~

Mohammed X locked the door after Bobby left. He took a deep breath. The significance of the day was sinking in. Now that he had time to think about it, he was actually happy to be leaving Freedmen's Creek. He was a city boy. He was tired of the piney woods, fed up with the Deep South, and bored with his uneducated followers.

"Dumb as dirt," he muttered to himself.

He did regret they were disbanding before carrying out at least one terrorist attack on a soft target in Sunshine or Jackson. He would explain it all in Virginia. The followers at Freedmen's Creek were devout but hapless. Mohammed X didn't think they were capable of pulling off a successful attack, no matter how much training or time spent on the shooting range. The ex-military men training the others were adequate technique-wise, but they weren't leaders. Obeh was the best commander in the bunch, but that wasn't saying much.

"Time to pack a few things," Mohammed X mumbled as he removed his Sherwani suit jacket. He began to gather the clothes and things he thought he would need, including the $50,000 he had skimmed off Azeem's deliveries and saved for a rainy day. That day was now upon him. After he sent Obeh and his men to attack Brewer Hill, Mohammed planned on loading up the Dodge Ram in the garage of his personal headquarters and hitting the road.

~ * ~

Bobby spent the rest of the day helping Abud organize the frenzied exodus from Freedmen's Creek. Abud assured him the armed men would not harm him as long as he was with Abud. Still, Bobby was nervous and kept looking over his shoulder. His instincts told him to get out of there, but Abud needed his help. The people fleeing the compound were pathetic.

After the sun went down and the two silver busses left on their final run with the last of the families, Bobby was tired. Abud had arranged with Red Cross shelters in Yazoo City, Greenwood, and Jackson to take the members in on a temporary basis. Bobby was impressed with Abud's organizational skills. He had pulled off a logistical nightmare on very short notice.

They walked together from the parking area toward the gym. It was an eerie experience for Bobby. The place was like a ghost town. Hungry cattle munched grass, meandering past clothing and belongings strewn around the commune. Gusts of wind blew papers around. As they walked past the gym and turned toward the mosque, Bobby was startled by an extended burst of gunfire from a slew of automatic weapons. He looked at Abud.

"What's that about?"

"Not everyone chose to leave."

"What do you mean?"

Abud shrugged. They walked further.

"Mohammed X told me Samson left this morning."

Abud stopped in his tracks. He spoke quietly.

"You have been of great assistance to me today. I could not have completed this without your help." Abud paused. "His Eminence would not want me to tell you this. You must keep it secret."

"Sure."

"Samson is dead."

"Dead? How?"

"At around two o'clock this morning we were attacked by the bikers from the courtroom. The ones with the vests. The Brewers."

"They killed Samson?"

"With some kind of primitive weapon. Destroyed his skull."

"You're sure it was them?"

"I saw them with my own eyes. So did Mohammed X. We knew them from the courtroom, sitting there in front with the rest of the Brewer family behind them."

"Damn," Bobby said. "You should call the Sheriff."

"He's in with them."

Bobby looked at Abud as if he were insane.

"Sheriff Lee Jones? No way. I've known him most of my life. He's a bully and too friendly with the D.A., but he ain't no friend of the Brewers, believe you me."

"That's how it appears to Mohammed X. I trust his judgment."

"Listen to me, Abud. That's just plain wrong."

"It doesn't matter. Samson's death will not be reported."

"You've got to do something."

"We are."

"What?"

"We are avenging his death ourselves. There's no justice to be had in your court system here."

"You're going to do something to the bikers?"

"We're going to kill them. We attack in the morning. As soon as there's enough light. It is Allah's will."

"Wait just a minute," Bobby said. "You can't just go over there to Dundee County and shoot up those people. That ain't right. Besides, those Brewers are not easy to kill."

"We'll see."

"I can tell you for a fact. I don't care how many men y'all got trained and armed to go up on that hill and take revenge for Samson's death, those Brewers see a bunch of niggers in uniforms with guns coming up on their hill they're going to shoot first and ask questions later. And they say the Brewers can shoot like nobody's business."

"Mohammed X has already given the order."

Another protracted volley of automatic weapon fire rang out. Bobby turned toward the gym and saw a number of men armed with automatic weapons approaching.

"You better leave while you can," Abud said. "Cut through the path between the community center and the cafeteria. And run, don't walk. Get out of here before something happens to you. You see those men. Their blood is up. They want *jihad*."

Bobby grabbed Abud's hand and shook it, then took off like a shot into the darkness between the two buildings. He began to duck and weave as he got closer to his SUV. He grabbed his keys from his pocket on the run and punched the open button on his remote. The Escalade interior lights came on. The brake and parking lights flashed. Bobby jumped in, cranked it up and sped out of the parking lot through the open gate. He picked up speed when he hit the road and didn't breathe easily until he slowed down to turn on the highway to Sunshine.

"I got to call somebody," Reverend Bobby Sanders muttered and picked up his phone. "Those fuckers are crazy."

Chapter Fifty-Five

Willie Mitchell sat behind his desk, Jordan Summit across from him. It was a little past eight. The two men were alone, waiting for the jury to report. When the jury began its deliberations, Mule had been picked up by his friends, a big man named Red and a smaller man Albert. Albert had given Summit his cell number and said they would have Mule back in the courtroom five minutes after Summit called. Eleanor Bernstein told Summit she would wait at her office for his call.

"I never thought it would take them this long," Willie Mitchell said. "I figured an hour, tops, to get your acquittal."

"You did a good job in closing emphasizing the lesser included offenses. Always good to give a jury choices."

"Mule put on quite a display," Willie Mitchell said.

"No kidding. He was nothing like that in trial prep. I worked and worked with him, but I never expected him to be so effective."

"You know what they say, when the curtain opens and the klieg lights come on...."

Summit took a sip from his bottle of water.

"Sorry about my seizure."

"You've got nothing to apologize for. It was handled very well by Judge Williams and your son. I'm not sure the jury even noticed."

"I don't know when it's going to happen. It just...."

"I'm telling you, it was no big deal. Fifteen minutes out of four days of jury selection and trial."

They sat in silence a moment.

"You really did a good job with your case," Willie Mitchell said. "It's so much easier prosecuting when the defense counsel is professional and organized. I've seen Judge Williams virtually have to take over a case to help some of the defense lawyers get through trial."

"Works both ways, Willie Mitchell. Not all prosecutors are like you. Some like to hide the ball like it's all a big game. A lot of them are just not very smart."

"You want another water?"

"Please."

Willie Mitchell walked through the reception area to the refrigerator in the back of his suite of offices. The afternoon had been uneventful. They started closing arguments right at two. He took thirty minutes, Summit about forty-five, then Willie Mitchell took less than ten minutes for rebuttal. Court was recessed and Summit, Eleanor, and Willie Mitchell had a half-hour conference with Judge Williams to hammer out the final jury instructions. It took another half-hour for the Judge to read the instructions to the jurors in open court. The jurors began deliberations a little before five. The only surprise to Willie Mitchell had been the jury ordering supper to be brought in to the jury room at seven o'clock. He thought he would have been home by then, having chalked up a loss. Not unheard of in his career, but not his typical outcome.

He gave Summit the bottle of water and sat down.

"Sorry about this political stuff coming up," Summit said. "I had no idea until I overheard the little preacher with the priest collar and Eleanor talking at a break. I guess she's serious about running against you."

"Apparently. Maybe it's time for me to move on."

"I hope you don't, Willie Mitchell. I mean that." He paused. "Anyway, I want you to know it was a big surprise to me. Even if I had known in advance, I'm not sure I could have done anything differently. She brought me into the case after she got Mule committed. At that point she was in charge."

"No problem."

Willie Mitchell appreciated the comment. He and Summit were miles apart philosophically and in how they used their respective law practices, but Summit was smart and efficient. He was like an engineer, straight-forward and unabashed in his pursuit of his goal, which in this case was the personal injury claim for Mule against Gas & Go Fast. Winning the criminal case was only the first step. It was an important step, but Summit still had a long way to go to proving Gas & Go Fast liable for Mule's paralysis. Willie Mitchell knew for a fact the location on the highway was nowhere near the kind of place where an "atmosphere of violence" existed, putting customers at risk.

"Let me ask you something," Willie Mitchell said. "Have you ever seen a bigger waste of time than going over jury instructions with the judge on a case, nit-picking every word and phrase, arguing like crazy to get a particular sentence included? That same sentence is buried in the middle of twenty pages of stuff the judge is going to read to the jury."

"Only thing it's good for is to give me grounds for appeal if the judge doesn't include something I want," Summit said. "You want to know what I think? I think the jurors stop listening after five minutes. You can see their eyes glaze over. Besides, half of the jurors these days can't understand much of what they read in a newspaper. How are they going to listen to these complicated statements of law, splitting hairs over this and that and make any sense of it? I can tell you. They don't."

"Amen," Willie Mitchell said.

He watched the stocky Summit walk to the window and look out, patting his jet black hair that never moved. Kitty walked in the door.

"I need to talk to you," she blurted to Willie Mitchell.

Chapter Fifty-Six

Jake sat at the primitive antique pine table in the kitchen eating a sandwich he made from his mother's chicken salad, the best chicken salad in the world. He left Willie Mitchell and Summit in the D.A.'s office. Kitty was holed up in the Sheriff's office going over the Oklahoma City file Needham left for her. Susan was still in Jackson with Walton and Gayle. No one needed him for anything at this moment, and he had to get something to eat. He was starving.

Jake knew Willie Mitchell was going to lose, but what did it matter? Abdul Azeem was a stranger to Yaloquena. No one was in court rooting for Mule to be convicted, and no one was going to be upset when he was acquitted, even the Muslims. The Freedmen's Creek people didn't care what happened to Mule, they were there just to put pressure on Willie Mitchell to do something about Trevor. Jake knew they weren't stupid, just blinded by their racial and religious animus. The Brewers were from Dundee County, so even if they got royally pissed at Willie Mitchell they couldn't vote in Yaloquena.

Damn Eleanor Bernstein.

Jake wasn't sure Willie Mitchell ought to run for re-election anyway, but he wanted his Daddy to leave on his terms, not be pushed out by someone else. Jake knew Eleanor was a decent lawyer, not as good as Walton, but still more effective than most public defenders. She had plenty of trial experience, too. Mostly losing, but that was the nature of her practice. You represent guilty people all the time, you're going to lose the vast majority of your cases.

"Crap," Jake said when the phone rang.

He didn't recognize the number, but with everything going on, he had to answer.

"Hello."

"Mr. Banks."

"No. This is Jake."

Jake recognized Bobby Sanders' voice. He was either upset or excited, Jake couldn't tell which.

"I need to speak to your father."

"He's at the courthouse waiting for the jury to come back with a verdict."

"What's that number?"

"He's not going to answer the phone," Jake said. "He'll just let it ring. I'm going back up there in a minute. What do you need?"

"I need to talk to him."

Jake sensed the preacher's intensity.

"Look, Bobby, I know everything that's going on with the case. You can tell me." Jake stretched the truth a bit. "If your information is important, you've got to tell me and I'll get word to him right away. There's no other way to reach him."

There was silence on the line a few seconds.

"Something bad's fixin' to happen."

"What?"

"I just came from Freedmen's Creek. It's scary out there. All the regular folks left that place today like they got the plague out there. Except for Mohammed and Abud, and the platoon of soldiers they got with automatic rifles, everybody else is gone."

"What are they planning?"

"They fixin' to attack the Brewers at their place in Dundee County sometime before daylight tomorrow."

"You sure they're serious? Maybe they're just talking."

"This ain't no joke. You tell your Daddy I'm sure about this. I just left from out there. They mad as hell. I was afraid their soldiers were going to shoot at me."

"Why are they so mad at the Brewers?"

"Because they say those biker Brewers, the ones in court, attacked the camp at two or three this morning and tore the place up. Abud said he saw them with his own eyes. Mohammed X did, too."

"Anybody hurt?"

"You know the big man, Samson?" Bobby said after a moment. "They killed him."

"Who killed Samson?"

"They're not sure. One of the bikers."

"They call the Sheriff or State Police?"

"No. And they ain't going to."

Jake thought for a moment.

"All right, Bobby. I'll leave right now and get this information to Willie Mitchell and the Sheriff. You did the right thing calling."

"Yeah," Bobby said, "I ain't in favor of no violence. What the Muslims planning on doing with their little army and all their assault rifles ain't called for. I'm for doing things the right way, the legal way, not this."

"I'll take it from here, Bobby. I've got your cell number on my phone. You go on home and calm down. I'll keep you posted."

Jake hung up, grabbed the last of his sandwich and wolfed it while taking the stairs two at a time. He stood on the stool in his closet and tossed his black bag and the three plastic gun cases on his bed. He slipped under the bed and pulled out his Ithaca pistol-gripped shotgun, got his KA-BAR knife from under his desk, and pulled every gun from his drawers. He studied all his weapons and equipment on the bedspread while he put on his tactical gear. In a couple of minutes he was dressed in black: combat pants and a long-sleeved knit shirt, military boots, baseball-style cap. He strapped on his Colt XSE 1911 .45 caliber in its black holster. Jake emptied the long black bag onto the bed. Now to fill it with what he was taking with him. The first thing he put back in the bag was his black Kevlar body armor vest and helmet.

He put in both rifles, the Colt M4 Carbine and the H&K 416. Jake took the Mossberg 590 out of its case. He smiled as he glanced at the mantra David Dunne had engraved on the barrel: *You never know.* He decided to take it rather than the Ithaca 37. Jake threw in his Glock 30 .45 caliber pistol, frag grenades, two SOG knives and the night vision goggles. He tossed in plenty of ammunition.

A few minutes later, Jake was in Willie Mitchell's farm truck, his arsenal in the bed of the pickup. He answered his cell.

"You coming back to the courthouse?" Sheriff Jones asked.

"No. Something's come up."

"What could be more important than this? Something happen with Gayle in the hospital?"

"No."

Jake's mind was racing. He needed to tell someone what was going on in case something happened to him. Kitty would be upset if she knew. Willie Mitchell would demand that he turn around and go back home. Lee was probably the best person to know.

"You by yourself?"

"In my office," Lee said. "Nobody's here."

"Close your door and I'll tell you."

Jake waited a few seconds. Lee said it was closed.

"I'm driving out to Brewer Hill."

"What the hell for?"

"Bobby Sanders called looking for Willie Mitchell. Said it was important. I talked him into telling me. Mohammed X has disbanded the commune. All the followers abandoned Freedmen's Creek today except for Mohammed X, Abud, and their militia. Samson's dead. Abud said Freddy Brewer's biker gang attacked the compound at around two this morning. Tore the place up and killed Samson."

The Sheriff was silent on the other end.

"Abud told Bobby they're going to attack Brewer Hill."

"And just what do you plan on doing about it?"

"I'm not sure, but the Brewers need to be warned. That's where I'm heading now."

"Just hold on," Lee said. "This is a law enforcement matter. I can call over to Dundee County...."

"There's no time for that," Jake said. "Besides, you don't have the firepower to go up against a platoon of trained men with AK-47s out at Freedmen's Creek. I spent a whole day in the top of a pine tree watching them training and shooting. They're not Green Berets, but from what I saw, a lot of your deputies would be killed."

"State police...."

"Not enough time to mobilize their assault units, Lee. And Sheriff Cheatwood in Dundee County's not going up on that hill. You heard what he said."

"Yes. Besides, he's only got a half-dozen deputies working for him. Most of them are just good-old-boys from what I hear."

Jake checked the truck's speedometer. He didn't want to be pulled over by a deputy or trooper with his arsenal in the back and dressed like a SWAT team member. Jake let Lee work out the situation for himself. He'd figure it out. Jake's going out there was the only option.

"Okay," Lee said. "But you're not going up Brewer Hill by yourself. Where are you now?"

"I'm still in Yaloquena on the road to Kilbride."

"You wait for me at Tom's Automotive. I'm coming with you. I'll be there in twenty minutes, soon as I tell Willie Mitchell what's going on."

"No," Jake said, louder than he should have. "You cannot tell him any of this. He can't leave the courthouse right now, and there's no way he'd go along with what I'm doing. You'd probably make him have another seizure if he knew."

Lee Jones was silent.

"Come on, Lee. You've got to keep all this to yourself."

"All right, dammit," Lee said. "But you sit right there in that parking lot at Tom's and wait for me. Don't go up on that hill."

"Deal, Lee. Just get to Tom's fast as you can."

Chapter Fifty-Seven

Summit excused himself from Willie Mitchell's office when Kitty interrupted them. The defense lawyer said he had calls he had to make and would be out in the hall. Kitty sat down across from Willie Mitchell.

"Freddy Brewer took the gun," she said.

"How? He was in court, but he was never inside the rail."

"I don't mean he personally stole the gun off Mr. Eddie's desk, but he set it up, had one of the Brewers or somebody impersonate the Big River repairman."

"No leads on the repairman?"

"No. He disappeared. We'll never find him. Don't even have a decent description. All people remember is the uniform."

"How do you know Freddy was behind it all?"

"Look at this," she said, placing a report on the desk. "It's from the file Agent Needham left with Mr. Summit to give to me. The person reporting the nine millimeter missing was named Brandi Trichel. She bought the gun in her name from a gun shop in Oklahoma City about eight months before she told the police it was stolen."

"Okay."

She put another report on Willie Mitchell's desk and pointed to a highlighted portion.

"This is a follow up report. This time, the complainant is referred to as Brandi Brewer."

"Brewer?"

"It's no coincidence," Kitty said. "As soon as I saw it I called Agent Needham. He's already back in Oklahoma City. He called Brandi Brewer for me. Get this. She was married to Freddy Brewer. She bought the gun in Oklahoma City, where she's from, a couple of months before she married Freddy. Her pistol went missing when she filed for divorce and kicked him out. She didn't accuse Freddy Brewer in the complaint of being the thief. Needham said she told him just now on the phone that she thought Freddy took it, but she never had proof and didn't want to get tangled up with Freddy again. Brandi told Needham she filed the theft complaint with OKC police just so she could make a claim for reimbursement on her homeowner's policy. She didn't want to have to testify against Freddy over this gun. She wanted to stay as far away from him as she could. At the time she made the complaint she had gone back to using her maiden name, Brandi Trichel."

"Freddy stole the gun from her and used it to kill the couple in Oklahoma City," Willie Mitchell said. "He gave it to Trevor on his next trip home."

"How could he be that stupid?" Kitty asked. "Why didn't he just dump the gun after he killed that couple?"

"Criminals don't like to throw their guns away. I can't tell you how many cases I've tried where the defendant hid the murder weapon rather than get rid of it. And Freddy probably figured giving it to Trevor was as good as burying it. He knew Trevor would never leave the hill."

"I told Needham all this," Kitty said. "They're putting Freddy on their AFAP list. He said they'll eventually pick him up."

Willie Mitchell shook his head.

"This time Freddy probably threw the gun in the deepest lake he could find. Without the gun, the case against him for the OKC murder is all circumstantial. The federal prosecutors will have to convince a jury that Freddy stole it from his wife, even though she admits she has no proof Freddy took it."

"I think they can."

"There's something else?"

Kitty placed another document on Willie Mitchell's desk. She pointed to the portion highlighted in bright yellow. Willie Mitchell read it on the desk, then picked up the report and leaned back in his chair. He continued to read and after a moment, tossed it back on the desk.

"The Dregs were at the Grand Southern Plains Road Rally in Oklahoma City the weekend the couple was murdered," he said.

Kitty stared at her hands a moment.

"Right after Azeem was killed and the crime lab in Jackson had gotten a hit on Trevor's gun being used in the double homicide in OKC, you had me call the FBI office in OKC. The agent I talked to told me the names of the gangs at the rally the weekend of the murder. I wrote down Bandidos, Outlaws, Hell's Angels, but I didn't write down the names of the small biker gangs he mentioned that I had never heard of. There were several of them. If I had done my job right, I would have recognized the Dregs name on their leather vests in the courtroom yesterday morning. It would have been in my notes. We would have figured out they were there to retrieve the gun and put a stop to it. It's all my fault."

"That was two months ago you talked to the FBI agent," Willie Mitchell said. "We had a lot going on at the time. Don't beat yourself up over this. This is the way things happen in the real world. At the beginning of a complex investigation, you never know what's going to turn out to be critical. Stuff falls through the cracks all the time and we find out later it was important. It's all part of it, Kitty. If you're going to be an investigator, you've got to accept it. Next time, you'll be more thorough. You'll pay closer attention to things in the early stages of a case you may think are irrelevant."

The bailiff stepped into Willie Mitchell's office.

"They're ready," he said and left.

"Come on," Willie Mitchell said to Kitty. "Let's go take our medicine. Get Lee and Jake and meet me in the courtroom."

~ * ~

Ten minutes later, Judge Williams was on the bench. Jordan Summit and Eleanor Bernstein sat at the defense table. Mule Gardner slumped in his wheel chair between them, nodding off. Willie Mitchell overheard the three of them talking earlier before the Judge took the bench. He could tell Mule was drunk by the way he was talking. Summit and Eleanor shushed Mule, trying to get him to lower his voice. Summit looked over at Willie Mitchell and rolled his eyes.

While the jurors filed into the box, Willie Mitchell heard Kitty whispering behind him. He joined her at the rail.

"I can't find them," she said. "No one in Lee's office knows where he is. Neither Jake nor Lee are answering my calls. I left a message for both of them."

"Okay," Willie Mitchell said and took his seat.

"Has the jury reached a verdict?" Judge Williams asked the panel.

An older black woman, a retired school teacher, stood.

"Are you the foreperson?" Judge Williams asked her.

"I am," the lady said, holding up the written verdict form.

Eddie Bordelon hustled over and retrieved the verdict. He took it quickly to Judge Williams. She studied it a moment and gave it back to Eddie to return to the woman to read.

"Madame foreperson, what does the jury find?" the Judge asked.

"We find the defendant, Lester Gardner, not guilty."

Willie Mitchell took a deep breath. It was what he was expecting. He looked over at the defense. Summit and Eleanor shook hands, smiling. Mule slept through it all.

Judge Williams thanked the jurors for their service and released them. When the side door closed behind the last alternate, Judge Williams addressed the defense.

"After your client sleeps it off, you can tell him he is released from his bail obligation and free to go about his business. This court is adjourned."

Judge Williams tapped her gavel and left the courtroom.

Willie Mitchell shook hands with Eleanor and Summit and walked out with Kitty.

"On to better things," he told Kitty as he held the door for her.

Chapter Fifty-Eight

Lee Jones slowed his wife's Toyota Venza when he saw the flashing blue lights at the Rivercrest Road turnoff. He pulled into the small parking area in front of the Lonely Road Bar & Grill behind two of his patrol units. Lee had been out of radio contact for twenty minutes. When he hung up after talking to Jake he made the decision to use his wife's car rather than his Sheriff's vehicle, the black Tahoe with the Yaloquena emblem on the doors. If Lee were questioned later by the press or the State Police about what happened in Dundee County, he wanted to be able to say he was not on official business, that he received a call for help and was on a personal mission to help a friend. He knew it would make little difference legally because he was Yaloquena Sheriff twenty-four hours a day, no matter where he was in the United States. Everything he did was "official," but taking Yancey's Venza to Dundee County would support his claim that it was personal. When dealing with public perception, Lee knew using the Venza would support the appearance of the private nature of the acts, which sometimes was more important than the actual facts.

Deputy Sammy Roberts greeted his boss. Lee hired Sammy out of the Marines. He was a no-nonsense, flat-bellied black man with a military bearing, a native of Tunica, the northernmost county in the Mississippi Delta.

"What's up, Sammy?"

"Buster Cloud, 60, owner of this place, beaten up pretty bad."

"Who called it in?"

"One of the commercial fishermen lives south of here on Rivercrest. He's a regular, got suspicious when the bar wasn't open for business. Walked in and saw the owner out cold on the floor."

"We know how it happened?"

"Late last night, or rather after midnight this morning, some bikers who had been hanging out here a month or so beat up the old guy and robbed him."

"You talk to him?"

"Deputy Jimenez did. He was here first. By the time I arrived the old man had passed out again. He's got some really bad head trauma."

"What else did he tell Jimenez?"

"He said the bikers were planning something else. He wasn't sure what. Said he was in and out of consciousness. He did hear them planning on splitting up and getting out of the state as soon as they did their other job. He didn't know their real names except for the leader, who went by

Freddy. Dregs was written across the back of their vests. It's the same guys that were in the courtroom for Mule's trial."

Lee knew what the Dregs' other job was. Freedmen's Creek. After killing Samson they were now going into hiding, no telling where. Lee turned around when the ambulance pulled into the parking area. Two EMTs jumped out and hustled into the Lonely Road.

"As soon as you can, Sammy, get the owner's statement recorded. Follow them to the hospital. Get this place roped off and call the crime scene crew at the State crime lab. They're going to get tired of hearing from us. They just worked up the scene in the courtroom yesterday."

Lee looked at his watch.

"You're in charge out here, Sammy. I've got to take care of something else. Put out an APB for Freddy Brewer and a description of the other Dregs. Charges are aggravated battery and attempted murder. Notify the State Police. Contact Kitty Douglas and let her know what happened. Ask her to notify the FBI and let Willie Mitchell know."

"No problem, Sheriff."

"And Sammy. Don't tell them you talked to me. I know this is weird, but under no circumstances are you to tell them where you saw me or what direction I was headed. They ask about me you tell them you haven't seen me. Trust me on this."

"That an order?"

"That's an order, Marine. You with me?"

"Yes, sir," Sammy said.

Lee started Yancey's Venza and began backing out. He stopped when he saw the EMTs walking out of the bar to talk to Sammy. Lee pulled back in and rolled down his window.

"Bartender didn't make it," Sammy said to Lee.

"The charge is now first degree murder," Lee said. He raised his window and took off on the dark highway towards Kilbride.

~ * ~

Jake saw the eastbound vehicle flash its brights and slow down on the Kilbride highway. When the small SUV turned into Tom's parking lot he recognized it. Yancey Jones' Venza.

"So, I see you're on unofficial business," Jake told Lee.

"Every little bit helps when dealing with reporters."

"I don't blame you."

"I'm in Dundee County, outside my jurisdiction, heading into something I ought to stay out of if I had good sense."

"If you want to head back it's okay with me," Jake said. "In fact I think it would be the smart play."

"No way. I'd rather get my ass shot off than tell Willie Mitchell I let you go up on that hill by yourself."

Jake laughed. "You armed?"

"Just my service weapon." Lee patted his holstered pistol. "Glock nine. It'll have to do."

"We can do better than that."

Jake shined his small LED flashlight in the bed of his pickup. He held open the black bag for Lee.

"I've got a Colt M4 and an H&K 416," Jake said. "Pick one and I'll take the other. Got an extra Glock .45 caliber pistol you can carry. And take a frag grenade and plenty of ammo."

Lee leaned against the farm truck.

"About time you leveled with me, Jake. You're not just an Assistant U.S. Attorney in D.C."

"Yes, I am," Jake said, "but I'm also part of another group."

"David Dunne's. Whatever that is."

"And we have to leave it at that. I'm on the side of the good guys, Lee, and that's about all I can tell you."

"I'll take the M4. Reminds me of my service days. And the baby Glock. Are those night vision goggles?"

"Yes. We may not need them. Bobby Sanders said the attack will be at first light before dawn."

"You ought to take'em anyway. You can't always rely on what Bobby says to be true. And before Mohammed's warriors get here, we've got to survive driving up on Brewer Hill at night. Those goggles might come in handy."

"The Brewers know I'm coming up. I called Trevor."

"They know I'm with you?"

"No. I'll call Trevor back and let him know."

"I'd appreciate that. And what about all the other Brewers? There's a bunch of them up there and they all might not get the message."

Jake patted Lee on the back. "We'll be okay."

"If Bobby wasn't bull shitting you, a bunch of people are going to die on this hill in a few hours."

"They will. But if you took your deputies and went to Freedmen's Creek to try to stop them, you'd have a lot of dead deputies. They've got AK-47s, new ones. I saw with my own eyes they know how to use them."

"There's not enough time to get the State Police mobilized."

"No," Jake said. "Not nearly enough."

"Like you said on the phone, Sheriff Cheatwood's not going to send his men. Since we've got a little time maybe could get some of my deputies to join us up on the hill."

"Then it would definitely become an official act of your office, in a county where you don't have jurisdiction. From what I've seen of the Brewers, we don't need any more men. We just need to make sure all the Brewers know the Freedmen's Creek militia is coming. Maybe help them defend themselves."

"If I kill someone up on that hill, I could get in a lot of trouble, Jake. Lose my job for sure, maybe get prosecuted."

"Very possible," Jake said. "That's why I told you on the phone there was no need for you to be here. You ought to leave. After it's over, I'll tell you how it went down."

Lee's phone buzzed. He looked at the number.

"It's Kitty," Lee said, closing his phone.

"Aren't you going to answer?"

"Hell, no," Lee said. "We've got to get up on that hill."

They checked their weapons, made sure they were loaded and ready, and got in the farm truck. The Sheriff told Jake about the Dregs beating Buster Cloud to death in the Lonely Road. Lee said the State Police and FBI were being notified.

Jake started up the hill. The Ford's headlights were old sealed beams, throwing a yellowish light a hundred feet up the steep incline but not illuminating much on the periphery except oak tree trunks. He glanced out the driver's window. Beyond his headlights it was as dark a place as Jake had ever seen.

"You know," Lee said, "gunshots are probably an everyday occurrence up here. No one's going to pay much attention."

"I don't know, Lee," Jake said, squinting into the distance up the hill, "I doubt they've heard automatic weapons."

"But who's going to hear it? Except for Tom's repair shop, there's not a building or house within miles of this place."

The truck's headlights reflected in the eyes of two Catahoula curs on the side of the road. After the dogs watched the truck pass, Jake saw the two of them take off up the hill into the darkness.

The farm truck strained against the incline for another few minutes before it sailed over the ridge onto the flat ground of the commons. Jake slowed to a stop. When the dust settled in front of the truck, five men with rifles and shotguns stepped into the headlights. Two cur dogs trotted behind them and sat on their haunches.

One of the men in worn out denim overalls carried a double-barreled shotgun. He walked to the driver's side. He spit a stream of tobacco juice on the ground and peered into the cab.

"You Jake Banks?" the man said.

"Yes, sir," Jake said.

"I figured you was," the Brewer said, eyeballing Lee Jones.

"Tom said it'd be you and one other. Didn't say nothin' about...."

The Brewer stopped and spit again.

"You know the way to Trevor's place?"

"Yes, sir."

"You go on through the *cummins* here on the path between them old buildings yonder and follow the trail through the trees to the next clearing."

"Yes, sir," Jake said and drove off slowly as the other Brewers parted to let the truck pass. Every one of them stared at Lee Jones.

"I don't think he believed you when you said you knew the way," Lee said. "Some rough-looking white people."

"Yeah," Jake said. "Let's go see a couple of more."

Chapter Fifty-Nine

Jake saw Trevor in the truck's headlights on his front porch. Jake parked in front of the cabin, stepped on to the porch and shook Trevor's hand. Lee stood behind Jake.

"Sheriff," Trevor said to Lee, extending his hand. "Thank y-you for coming up here with Jake. I know you d-didn't have to."

"Where's Tom?" Jake asked.

"Over at his place. He'll be here in a minute."

Jake heard a sound in the distance. It was an old horn of some kind. There were three short notes followed by one long one.

"What's that?" Jake asked.

"R-Redneck intercom," Trevor said and led them inside.

Jake recognized the Brewer Hill Skins CD on Trevor's player, but the volume was turned way down. Still, Jake could hear Trevor's clear, strong voice.

"That your fight song?" Jake asked.

"Nah," Trevor said. "I just like listening to it."

Tom walked in the cabin. He kept his eyes on the floor as he approached Jake and Lee. When he stood next to them, he looked up.

"We thank you for calling Trevor," he said and looked back down. "You know, we ain't done nothin' to those people at Freedmen's Creek."

"I know," Jake said. "Freddy and his Dregs did. But you're getting credit for it."

"Trevor said you told him the bikers killed that big'un."

"They did."

"And they killed a bar owner named Buster Cloud," Lee said, "at his place just inside Yaloquena County. Word is they've left the state."

"They tore up my shop, too," Tom said. He looked up briefly at Lee. "Appreciate your comin' up here, Sheriff. This ain't your fight."

"I'm with Jake," Lee said.

"All right, then. I'm sorry for all my half-brother's done. He give that pistol to Trevor and got him in all this trouble. Now he's gone and killed people and look who's having to answer for it. This is just how Freddy did growing up. Stir somethin' up and skedaddle, leaving me or somebody else to clean up his mess. All that fighting he used to do down in Kilbride. He never got in no trouble, but other Brewers did. It was lots more peaceful up here when Freddy run away at sixteen. Whenever he comes back, there's trouble."

Through the window, Jake noticed a flame in the center of the clearing in front of Tom and Trevor's cabins. Tom walked to the window then outside on the porch. Trevor gestured for Jake and Lee to join Tom and him on the porch.

When Jake and Lee stepped out the door, Jake couldn't believe it. In the short time they were inside, at least two hundred men, women, and children had assembled in silence in the clearing around a bonfire dragged into the center on an A-shaped frame of long wooden poles behind a sturdy work horse. One of the Brewers unhitched the horse and led him through the crowd as the flames engulfed the pile of limbs, sticks, and the A-frame poles. Jake studied the Brewers.

It was the oddest collection of human beings Jake had ever seen. All the men held rifles or shotguns. Some boys and young teens were shirtless, with painted faces, carrying Indian war clubs decorated with paint stripes and feathers. Some of the clubs had wooden balls on the end; some had sharp, jagged ends. Some of the women were armed with rifles and long knives. The men were in all shapes and sizes, in all manner of dress. The women were more attractive than the men, most with high cheekbones and dark hair like Tracy Brewer. The younger women had youthful faces, but their bodies were fully mature. Some wore jeans and tee shirts; some full-length plain cotton dresses.

What was even more incredible to Jake was the discipline. They gathered in the clearing outside Trevor's cabin without making noise. They stood around the bonfire, unsmiling and absolutely silent. Jake looked at Tom in a new light. He was clearly their leader, and their allegiance was absolute.

Tom stepped off the porch and walked to Jake's truck. He lowered the tailgate and stood on it. To Jake's amazement, the crowd continued to be quiet, the only noise the hissing, popping, and cracking of the limbs and sticks in the fire. Jake, Lee, and Trevor remained on the porch, watching Tom's back as he spoke.

"You all know," Tom told the crowd, "we ain't never hurt nobody up here that ain't deserved it. We ain't never took nuthin' from nobody that wasn't rightfully ours. We've been the same for years. We tend to ourselves and expect others to do the same."

Tom was calm, his voice steady and matter-of-fact. He made no effort to incite the Brewers.

"These two outsiders behind me on the porch, the young one who's Trevor's friend, he's the one called to warn us about these colored Muslim soldiers coming up here to kill us for something my half-brother Freddy done. They say Freddy and his biker friends killed one of the head Muslims over there in Yaloquena where they live. The other man on the porch, the law man from Yaloquena, he just told me Freddy and his men done killed another man this morning, the old man runs that honky-tonk Lonely Road down in the flatlands."

The crowd was hushed, no reaction to what Tom said.

"Now, we didn't do nothin' to these men coming here in the darkness to kill us, but we sure as hell are going to defend ourselves. These two outsiders say there's nothing can be done to stop these people from coming up the hill. They are a'comin' with automatic machine guns and they supposed to be well-trained. They supposed to attack at first light, but we're going to take up positions right now and wait, just in case they decide to come early. You all know what each of you's supposed to do in a situation like this. These two outsiders up here on Trevor's porch, they're honorary Brewers for this fight."

Jake caught himself nodding to faces in the crowd, reinforcing what Tom was saying.

"All right," Tom said, pointing to a much older man holding what looked to Jake like an old Sharp's rifle. "Caleb, you take your sharpshooters and take up positions south of the *cummins*, some up in the trees, some hidden below the ridge."

"Wilbert," Tom said, "you get the cur dogs patrolling the southwest slope soon as you leave here. You and Jerome keep'em on patrol."

Jake and Lee listened while Tom gave out orders. Each group trotted away from the bonfire to take up their assigned positions. Listening to Tom's description of where he was placing each group and what they were to do, Jake figured out Tom's strategy was to allow the attackers to clear the ridge and head into the commons. Trevor had told Jake the northeast side of Brewer Hill was too steep for an assault, that throughout Brewer history, attackers including the Chickasaws and renegade Confederate troops always came up the southwest slope.

"You women take the young children to bed. The older ones can watch long as they're in a safe place. Don't want to see any war clubs from you young'uns until after the shootin's done. The rest of you men take up your positions. These people will come up the hill and we'll let'em into the *cummins*, but they won't be goin' back down."

Jake checked his watch. It was after midnight. He wasn't tired.

Four hours, maybe five, and the shooting begins.

Chapter Sixty

Abud drove the flatbed truck with side rails past the abandoned guardhouse at Freedmen's Creek. He was not happy about it. Abud's abilities were administrative and organizational. He wasn't a holy warrior; he was a bureaucrat. Since the Virginia office cut off funding and contact after Azeem's murder, Mohammed X had Abud doing things outside his comfort zone.

Like driving this truck to Brewer Hill.

Abud had turned fifty this year. Born Andre Nelson in Minneapolis and baptized into the neighborhood African Methodist Episcopal Church, he was the oldest of six children. Andre was always the responsible one, helping his mother take care of the others. When all his siblings were out of the house, he moved to Detroit and at twenty-six began working on a Ford assembly line. He married a Detroit girl and joined her church, Ebenezer Baptist. They had two daughters. He thought they were a happy family. His wife and daughters were active in the church. When his girls were twelve and ten, Andre learned that his wife's activities at the Baptist church included servicing the preacher regularly in the Sunday School room. Andre said he forgave her when she promised to mend her ways, but it was difficult for Andre to maintain his previous level of devotion at Ebenezer. He became interested in Islam, studying the doctrine and communicating online with Muslim recruiters. One Sunday in 2005, Andre got up from his pew during the hypocritical preacher's sermon about faith and family. He walked outside, got into the family car, and drove to California to join a Black Muslim group run by a man he considered holy, a man he came to know later as Mohammed X. Andre changed his name to Abud Rahman and never saw his wife and daughters again.

After the holy man's difficulties with federal and state authorities in California, Abud moved with him to Memphis, where the holy man started a mosque with financial assistance from Islamic brothers in Virginia. Abud was his right hand man, joined by the giant Samson al Kadeesh. The three of them were later forced to abandon the Memphis mosque to avoid an attempt on the holy man's life. With help from the Virginia office and Abdul Azeem, they founded the Islamic commune at Freedmen's Creek, where the holy man was reborn as Mohammed X.

Abud was upset with Mohammed X. After two excellent years of teaching, converting, and training converts to fight and shoot, they were once again fleeing in the dead of night to start over somewhere else. Mohammed X's ritual blessing of the warriors before they left for battle was a nice touch, but Abud was disturbed to hear Mohammed X tell Obeh after the blessing there was no need for reconnaissance on Brewer Hill. Mohammed X huddled with Obeh studying Brewer Hill on Google Earth. Abud didn't know much about military tactics, but he was fairly certain that an hour studying a two-year-old satellite photo was a poor substitute for actual intelligence.

Abud glanced in the rear view mirror. A dozen warriors stood hanging on to the side rails occasionally raising their AKs above their heads and yelling. Abud knew if they were stopped by a state trooper there would be a gunfight, but at three in the morning, he doubted law enforcement was anywhere around the lightly traveled road.

There was no conversation with Obeh. Mohammed X had elevated Obeh to leader of the militia only a couple of days before. In Abud's opinion, there was scant evidence Obeh was capable. His chief attribute seemed to be unbridled blood lust and hatred of white people. He promised Mohammed X he and his men would kill all the Brewers and return at daybreak to Freedmen's Creek in triumph. Abud glanced at Obeh as they drove. Obeh was sweating, his eyes wide. He mumbled, sometimes squeezing the handle of the machete in his right hand. Obeh kept a tight grip on his AK-47 with his left hand. The extra AK Obeh brought with him lay on the bench seat between them. Abud made sure the rifle's short barrel was pointed away from him. When Obeh tossed it there, he didn't seem to care which way the dangerous end pointed.

From what little Obeh told him, Abud gathered that Obeh's strategy was to hide in the trees halfway up the hill until first light, then six teams of two warriors would spread out and stealthily climb the hill. When they reached the top, they were to open fire on anything that moved. They would then spread throughout the hill, killing the sleepy Brewers as they found them. Obeh assured Mohammed X that without automatic weapons, the Brewers were no match for his men. The battle would be one-sided and brief.

After dropping off the soldiers at the mid-point of the incline, Abud's only task was to drive the flatbed on top of the hill after the firefight was over, load the men and drive them back to Freedmen's Creek to rejoin Mohammed X and receive further instructions.

It didn't seem like much of a plan to Abud, but Mohammed X approved it when Obeh sketched out the details with a stick in the dirt outside the mosque. Abud just wanted it over with so he could rejoin Mohammed X in the morning and drive off to their next assignment.

Abud turned onto the Brewer Hill road. He drove up the hill on the dirt and gravel until Obeh pointed into the woods and grunted. Abud left the road and parked in the trees. The warriors jumped down from the truck and sat on the ground to wait. Abud looked at his watch. He estimated they had about an hour until daybreak. Abud rested his back against an oak tree. He would be glad when the fighting was over.

~ * ~

"It's almost four a.m.," Kitty said to Willie Mitchell in the kitchen of the Banks home.

"I know," he said, filling a carafe with water to make more coffee.

"We have to do something, call somebody."

"No, we don't."

Kitty had been calling Lee Jones and Jake since the jury returned its verdict the night before. At first, Willie Mitchell thought it might be bad cell service, but by eleven, he knew Jake and Lee were up to something they did not want to share with Willie Mitchell and Kitty. He had a hard time convincing Kitty to accept it. Finally, she realized that driving somewhere was not an option when they didn't know where to go. Not even the Sheriff's office knew where Lee was. That was another tip off to Willie Mitchell.

"You trust Jake, don't you?" he asked Kitty.

"You know I do. He might be in trouble, not able to call."

"Jake's a tough cookie, pretty smart. It's not likely he's gotten involved in something he can't handle. Lee Jones is the same way. We have to just sit tight and wait. Jake and Lee will call us when they can."

Kitty plopped down in the chair at the old pine table. Willie Mitchell knew she was frustrated. Good time to change the subject.

"Susan talk to you about going to see your mother?"

Kitty stiffened. "No."

"She said she was going to. When's the last time you saw her?"

Kitty looked away. She rubbed the back of her hand under her nose and blinked. He knew she was holding back tears.

"Susan wants to take you to Tacoma. She thinks she can come up with a better place for your mother than that state hospital."

"Mother doesn't know she's in the world," Kitty said.

Willie Mitchell was quiet for a minute.

"It won't hurt to go see her now, will it? When's the last time you were up there? It was before you got hurt in New Orleans, wasn't it?"

Big tears streamed down Kitty's cheeks. Willie Mitchell grabbed Kleenexes from the flowery square box on the kitchen counter.

"Don't get upset," he said. "You need to go see your mother and Susan wants to go with you. We'll pay for the trip."

"It's not that," Kitty said, sniffing irregularly, trying to stop sobbing. "I just hate to see her in that place."

Atmosphere of Violence

"I know," Willie Mitchell said, "but you have to."

Chapter Sixty-One

"They're waiting in the trees on the west slope," Tom said when he walked back to Trevor's porch. "About a dozen of them. Probably waitin' for daylight to attack. I reckon we've got no more'n an hour before they come up the hill."

Tom left Jake, Lee, and Trevor on the porch and walked toward the commons, passing the smoldering embers of the bonfire.

"How's he know that?" Jake asked Trevor.

"Once you t-tipped us off, Tom sent scouts all around the h-hill, some of em down where the incline b-begins. They're like squirrels, some of these B-Brewers he sends up in the trees. Ain't no way to see them if they d-don't want you to. Even in the daylight."

"How do they get word to Tom?"

"Different w-ways. Only Brewers can know. Let's j-just say it's kind of something like bird c-calls. Maybe I'll teach you one day."

Trevor popped his fist lightly on Jake's bicep and chuckled.

"I want to get a better vantage," Jake said. "Let's go up around the commons to wait. Maybe in those old buildings. Can you check with Tom and let him know?"

"No need t-to. They'll all see us moving. Brewers can see good in the dark, lots better than flatlanders. Bred into us. But we can't get inside those old buildings. Those spots are already taken."

Jake carried his H&K 416 and Lee the Colt M4. Jake filled a small black backpack with ammunition, his night vision goggles and one SOG knife. He gave the other to Lee. He threw in two frag grenades.

Trevor said "f-follow me" and led them on a slow walk through the big oak trees to the edge of the commons. Trevor pointed to something south of the last of the abandoned log buildings. Jake couldn't see anything until he put on his goggles. There was a depression, kind of a natural foxhole that Trevor was walking toward. In a few minutes, the three men were prone in the hole, their weapons pointed toward the southwestern edge of the commons where Tom said the Freedmen's Creek assault force would gather under the ridge before their attack. The sky behind them showed the first sign of light. Not long now.

In the greenish glow of his goggles, Jake saw a blur in the distance coming over the hill into the commons. In a few seconds, Jake made sense of what he saw.

"There's four dogs coming this way. They are hauling ass."

"That'd be the Catahoula c-curs. They're trained to r-run through the commons when strangers come up the hill. T-taught to be quiet, no barking. Homemade s-silent alarms."

"The fighters are headed this way," Jake said, still looking through the goggles. "Can you see them?"

"Yep," Trevor said. "There they are."

"I don't see anything," Lee said. "Still too dark for me to see."

"They're getting closer," Jake said. "Wait, I can see something moving up in the trees behind them. There's activity on the ground behind them, too."

"Them's sharpshooters up in the t-trees. Like Tom said. Let'em in. Don't let'em out."

"There's enough light now for me to make out the sharpshooters," Lee said. "I'd have never have noticed them if I hadn't been looking for them."

In his night vision goggles, Jake watched six two-man militia teams advancing, a hundred feet apart. In front of them he saw one man, signaling.

"Stay d-down," Trevor said. "It's f-fixin' to start."

Jake heard a strange whistle. Rifle shots exploded from the holes where windows used to be in the abandoned log building closest to them.

Jake saw four of the attackers fall, the others hit the dirt on their bellies. The leader screamed "fire" to his remaining men and the Muslim soldiers unleashed a barrage of automatic weapons fire on the building.

At the same time, Jake saw the next building light up with rifle and shotgun blasts at the militia. He watched the soldiers shift positions and fire their AKs into the second building, just in time for the Brewers in the first building to fire another burst at the militia.

Jake saw the leader wave and heard him scream. His men that were still able began crawling backward away from the buildings. They retreated halfway back to the ridge when the leader signaled and shouted again. The militia stood up and ran for the cover of the ridge, bent over and zig-zagging.

Gunfire rained down on the soldiers from the ridge and from the top of seven or eight oak trees. In less than fifteen seconds from the time they began to run for the ridge, all seven of the remaining attackers had been shot multiple times.

"Let's w-wait a while," Trevor said in the hole. "Tom'll s-say when."

Jake stared at the two coveys of corpses, one close to them, the other nearer the ridge. Through his night vision goggles he saw the bodies on the ground. No movement.

"Damn," Lee said to Jake. "Glad we could contribute."

"Tom told us up front they didn't need us," Jake said. "Apparently he was just being hospitable when he said we could stay."

Jake took off his goggles and stuck them in his backpack. He waited for his eyes to adjust. There was enough light in the sky now to see most of the commons. He heard the strange sound again, kind of a whistle.

"All r-right," Trevor said. "Let's go see."

The three of them left the depression. Jake watched Brewers walk out of each of the four abandoned buildings on the northeast side of the commons. Jake elbowed the Sheriff.

"Two of the buildings didn't even have to fire a shot."

"Yep," Trevor said, "Tom's big on backups in any skirmish."

~ * ~

Sitting in the flatbed, Abud checked his watch. It had been ten minutes since the last shots were fired. Perhaps, he thought, he had underestimated Obeh. Maybe Obeh was right saying the Brewers were no match for the AKs. Abud looked through the oak canopy above him. The sky was much lighter.

Abud started the truck and let it idle a minute. He drove slowly through the woods to the gravel incline. He had never been in a shootout and wasn't sure how long one might take.

He grabbed Obeh's extra AK off the seat, placed the butt of the gun on his lap and let the end of the barrel stick out of his window. It would show Obeh that Abud was ready to support the cause, even though Abud had never fired a rifle in his life and certainly had no idea how to shoot the AK-47.

~ * ~

Jake and Lee watched the young boys begin checking the bodies in the commons. Jake thought the boys ranged in age from six to ten. Tom had given the order minutes earlier for them to "check for breathers" and to finish them off. So far, Jake was relieved that everyone they checked was dead.

Jake, Lee, and Trevor followed the young boys into the commons. Tom walked with them carrying a shotgun in a firing position.

They were no more than twenty feet from the group of bodies nearest the ridge when a militia member on the ground raised up on his elbow and began spraying the ground with AK fire, struggling to get the barrel high enough to kill. The boys scattered and hit the ground. Tom moved in front of Jake and raised his shotgun.

Out of the corner of his eye, Jake saw Lee Jones dive like a linebacker into Trevor, taking him to the ground. When Tom unleashed both barrels of his shotgun at the one surviving soldier, everything became quiet again.

The young boys returned. One of them smashed his war club into the skull of the soldier who had just tried to kill them. Jake knew Tom's shotgun had already taken him out, but he guessed it didn't hurt to be thorough.

Jake looked up when he heard a piercing whistle from the top of an oak tree on the ridge.

A flatbed truck topped the hill and barreled into the commons toward them, but not for long. A barrage of rifle fire from the treetops and the ridge tore into the tires, the body, and cab of the truck.

The truck's momentum carried it towards them, but it slowed as it approached, stopping ten feet from the dead soldiers on the ground. Tom walked to the truck and grabbed the barrel sticking out of the driver's window, tossing the AK into the pile with the other AKs the boys had gathered from both sets of bodies.

Jake was close enough to the truck to recognize "Tweety Bird," the Freedmen's Creek Muslim who was in the courtroom with Samson and Mohammed X for the hearings and the first three days of trial.

Jake heard the man groan. He walked to the truck and opened the door. "Tweety Bird" lay back against the seat, eyes closed, his big glasses shattered in his lap. Jake looked at the wounds in the man's torso. He was alive, but wouldn't be for long. He mumbled something.

Jake made sure both the man's hands were empty and no weapons were within reach. He moved closer and listened.

"Al Rashad," the man muttered. "Tell Al Rashad."

It hit Jake like a ton of bricks. He grabbed Lee.

"I've got to go."

Jake ran southwest toward Trevor's cabin.

~ * ~

When Jake took off, Trevor stepped toward his father, holding his side. Halfway to Tom, Trevor faltered. Lee was there to catch him. Lee laid him gently on the ground and removed Trevor's hand. There was a hole in the front of Trevor's shirt and a growing bloodstain around it. Tom knelt beside Trevor and pulled up his shirt to reveal an entry wound above Trevor's left pelvis. Tom turned Trevor over. A much-larger exit wound was in Trevor's lower back.

"Get Nadine and her girls," Tom called out.

In less than a minute, an older woman with wild gray hair ran through the crowd followed by three women Lee estimated to be in their early twenties. Nadine knelt next to Trevor and examined his wound. The

Sheriff watched her check out the exit hole in Trevor's lower back. She whispered something to Tom kneeling beside her. One of the young women gave Nadine a bottle filled with tea-colored liquid. She poured it over Trevor's wounds. He stiffened but didn't cry out. Nadine and the younger women wrapped Trevor's waist in white cotton bandages interspersed with dark green herbs of some kind. Tom squatted next to Trevor and watched Nadine work. He tapped Trevor on the arm.

"Damn, son. This is the second time you been shot in less than three months. Getting' to be a habit. You need to be more careful."

Trevor smiled weakly. Nadine nodded to Tom, who gestured to some Brewers who had driven their pickup to the commons. The men picked up Trevor and placed him in the back of the truck on an old mattress. Nadine and the women climbed in the back of the truck. The driver waved to Tom and drove away from the scene.

"Taking him to the hospital?" Lee asked.

Tom and the other Brewers around him laughed.

"We don't know much of what's in books," Tom said, "but up here on this hill we know how to take care of a bullet wound. He'll be fine. Nadine said it just went through the fat on his side, missed his kidney and anything else important."

"Good," Lee said as Jake blew past the battle scene in the old red farm truck. Lee Jones and Tom watched the truck's wheels leave the ground as it flew over the ridge onto the gravel road and out of sight.

"I'll get a man to take you into Sunshine, Sheriff," Tom said to Lee. "Looks like your partner's in a hurry to put out a fire somewhere."

"Thanks," Lee said. "What's the plan now?"

"We got a routine for this," Tom said. "Not sure you ought to be here to witness it."

"Tom," Lee said, "I didn't see anything go on up on this hill this morning of any consequence. I don't figure I'll see anything up here from now on that I'd care to remember or share with anyone."

Tom almost smiled, looking up from the ground at Lee.

"Well. I guess it won't hurt." Tom turned to the scores of Brewers gathered in the commons around the bodies and the bullet-riddled flatbed truck.

"Where's Leon?" Tom called out to the crowd.

A wiry man with a short-billed welding cap stepped forward.

"First thing, check on the little man in the truck."

Leon hustled to Abud's flatbed and checked Abud.

"He's a goner, Tom."

"Good. Get your welders together. And I mean everybody." Tom looked around. "Where's Justin?"

A tall man with a long neck and protruding adam's apple came forward.

"Is the D-6 runnin' all right?"

"Shore is," Justin said.

"Crank it up and run it over here. Bring enough heavy chains to drag this flatbed over to the welding shed."

Justin walked off at a brisk pace.

"Damn," Lee said to Tom. "You got a D-6 bulldozer?"

"Sure do. With an oversized U-blade on it. You ain't dealing with no amateurs up here."

Tom pronounced it *arma-toors*. It took a second, but Lee got it.

"We got a first rate motor grader and two heavy duty backhoes, too. We got roads to tend to, ponds to dig out and levees to maintain."

"Oh," Lee said.

"Leon," Tom said, "when Justin drags this truck over to the welding shed, I want you and all your boys to get on it with your torches. I mean every hand you got. I want this truck cut up into little pieces. See what looks worth saving on the engine and get rid of the rest. I want you and your boys to finish today."

"Okay," Leon said, running off with ten men and boys behind him.

"Willie Brewer," Tom called out.

A grizzled old man stepped forward. Lee thought he looked like the local that gave Ned Beatty a hard time in *Deliverance*.

"Get Luther to get a team of dray horses together and y'all get'em out here and drag what's left of these soldiers off. Take'em to your hog pens. Burn the clothes and throw the bodies to the feral pigs."

"Waste disposal's about the only thing those wild hogs are good for," Trevor said to Lee.

"Okay you youngsters," Tom said to the boys, "I want all these automatic weapons picked up and put in a pile. Then I want you to spend the rest of the day picking up brass out of the *cummins*. I don't want to find a single hull up here when you're through."

The boys scattered to pick up the AKs and the spent shells.

"Roy Gene," Tom said.

A man Lee guessed was in his twenties stepped up.

"Melt all these AK-47s down," Tom said.

"Pretty good weapons to go to waste," Roy Gene said.

"We ain't got no need for'em," Tom said. "They didn't do these fellers any good."

Tom stared at a clod of dirt and kicked it. He spit a dark stream at the clod and looked up at Lee, right into Lee's eyes. For the Sheriff, it was a first.

"I want to thank you for saving my boy," Tom said. "You hadn't taken him down like that those bullets would have tore right through him. You saved his life."

Lee Jones extended his hand and Tom took it.

"Trevor's a good young fellow," Lee said.

Tom continued to grip Lee's hand.

"I want to tell you something," Tom said. "And I want you to tell the D.A. Mr. Banks. I didn't rape that woman in Kilbride. What I done time for? I wasn't guilty. I wanted you and the D.A. to know."

Chapter Sixty-Two

Jake glanced at the scene of the massacre in the commons as he sped past in Willie Mitchell's red farm truck. He sailed off the ridge onto the gravel road and put pressure on the brake. He was in a hurry, but wouldn't do any good if he wrecked on the way. Driving up or down the hill took full concentration.

When he reached the bottom of the incline he sped up. Careful not to fishtail out of control, he turned on the paved highway and raced toward Sunshine.

Al Rashad. Tell Al Rashad.

Al Rashad had probably already fled Freedman's Creek, but Jake had to be sure. Maybe he would get lucky. If Jake missed him, he'd turn up somewhere else under a new name. It might be years or decades before Jake could get another lead on him, even with David Dunne and Billy Gillmon's help.

The first time he saw Mohammed X in the courtroom, Jake was certain he had seen him before. Now he knew, thanks to the dying declaration of Al Rashad's right hand man. Several years before, David Dunne had shown Jake photographs of Al Rashad in Jake's silver 4Runner as they drove to his mosque in Memphis, trying to get to the bottom of his involvement in the deaths of the prospective jurors in the trial of El Moro in Sunshine. In the photos Al Rashad wore heavy dreadlocks and a dense, black beard. No matter. Mohammed X was Al Rashad.

Jake gripped the steering wheel and turned north past the motel onto the Freedmen's Creek road. He prayed he would come face to face with the man who ordered Willie Mitchell killed. Had it not been for David Dunne, both Willie Mitchell and Jake would be dead at the hands of the two hit men Al Rashad sent to kill them at the Jackson Reservoir.

Jake turned into Freedmen's Creek and slowed down to get his bearings. He had never seen the place at ground level, and he took a moment to get oriented. He was looking for Mohammed X's building, the one that seemed to be his office or residence.

Freedman's Creek was a ghost town. Litter everywhere, starving cattle roaming, everything in disarray. It looked nothing like the place he watched closely for a day from the top of a pine tree.

Jake turned right on the narrow road between the community center and the cafeteria. The mosque was dead ahead. When he cleared the cafeteria building, he looked to his right and saw Mohammed's residence. He killed the engine.

Jake pulled his Colt XSE out of his drop down rig. He made sure his Glock 30 was secure in the holster at his waist in the small of his back. He checked his pocket for the SOG knife.

Jake walked past the mosque to Mohammed X's building. He checked the front door quietly. It was locked. He walked down the side of Mohammed X's building. As he neared the back, a man cursed.

"Mother fucker," the man said loudly.

Jake took a deep breath. With both hands on his Colt in an upright position, he stopped at the corner of the building and took a quick look.

There was a two car garage in the back of the building. The door was rolled up, the garage wide open. Inside was a Dodge Ram truck.

Next to the truck was a four-wheeler. There was a man bent over the engine compartment of the four-wheeler, turning a wrench. Jake moved closer, his gun ready. On the hood of the Dodge, Jake saw a revolver. It looked like a Chief's Special, a thirty-eight.

"Son of a bitchin' bastard mother fucker," the man said.

"That's some foul language for a holy man," Jake said.

The man whipped around.

"That four-wheeler battery's not gonna cut it, Al Rashad," Jake said. "It's too little to start this truck."

"Who the fuck are you?" Mohammad X said.

"You don't remember me from court? I was sitting on the other side of the aisle from you and your men. Remember?"

"No. I've never seen you before."

"Maybe this will jog your memory. Do you remember trying to kill my father, Willie Mitchell Banks, couple of years back? You nearly succeeded, and almost killed me in the process, too."

"I'm sure you have me confused with someone else."

"No. You sent two of your followers. They ended up dead. Just like all those militia men you sent to Brewer Hill. They're dead, too. Fourteen by my count, including Abud. That's your m.o. You send people out to get killed. And you don't care."

Jake followed Mohammad X's eyes. The Imam was looking at the Chief's Special.

"You got a car?" the holy man said. "I'll give you ten grand for it."

"You're a liar and a killer, and don't care anything about Allah."

"Look, boy. If you're going to take me in, let's go. I'm tired of fuckin' around here with you. You ain't got nothing on me. And even if you did, your worthless old man couldn't make it stick."

"I'm not taking you in."

"Then get the fuck outta my way."

"One last question," Jake said, "what should I call you? Al Rashad or Mohammed X? Or should I go all the way back to Calvin Ketchums? You choose."

"You can't shoot me. You're some kind of law officer. Take me in or leave."

Mohammed X turned back to the four-wheeler. He spun around and threw a wrench at Jake. Jake ducked and Mohammed X went for his revolver.

Jake had plenty of time. He shot Mohammed X twice in the torso, the bullets entering through his right rib cage, shattering two ribs on the way to his heart and lungs.

Mohammed X fell back against the truck and on to the concrete floor. He rolled on his back, struggling to inhale. He grabbed at the front of his shirt, trying to rip it open to check his wounds.

Jake walked over. Mohammed X looked surprised.

Jake placed his Colt two inches from Mohammed X's forehead and fired another round right between his eyes.

Mohammad X of Freedmen's Creek, *a.k.a.* Al Rashad of Memphis, *a.k.a.* Calvin Ketchums was dead.

Back in the farm truck, Jake pulled slowly out of the Freedmen's Creek gate. The sun peeked above the eastern horizon. It was going to be a pretty day.

Jake thought about the five dollar bill Abdul Azeem jerked away from Mule's grasp at the Gas & Go Fast a couple of months ago. If Azeem had just let Mule have the five, things would have worked out better for him. Probably for Al Rashad, too.

Chapter Sixty-Three

Two days after Christmas, Willie Mitchell was in his office going over his year-end checklist. He was ready to get out of Sunshine. He and Susan were welcoming the New Year in a private *cabana* on a small, white sand beach in Cozumel, their favorite hideaway. He looked forward to the little Mexican sparrows picking the crumbs off his plate as he ate breakfast with them on the porch, just two feet from the hammock.

Ethel Morris stood at his door. Her hair was short and gray, but it looked much better than her wig. She said the doctors were encouraging. Ethel looked much stronger. He hoped she was telling him the truth about the prognosis.

"Jordan Summit is here," she said. "He wants to know if he can see you for just a minute."

"Absolutely," Willie Mitchell said.

He walked around his desk and greeted Summit.

"This is a nice surprise," Willie Mitchell said. "What brings you back to our humble courthouse?"

"Business. I couldn't leave without stopping in."

"What are you doing working this week? I thought you big city lawyers shut down for Christmas and didn't come back to work until after the New Year. Haven't you made enough Benjamins this year?"

Summit laughed.

"I can always use a few more. You know how insurance companies are. They like to clear their decks at the end of the fiscal year."

"Whatever happened to Mule's civil suit you and Eleanor filed? The premises liability claim against Gas & Go Fast."

"That's why I'm here. We settled."

"You're kidding," Willie Mitchell said. "I did some checking after Mule's acquittal. Mule's shooting was the only crime at that location involving bodily harm in the last five years. Not exactly an atmosphere of violence."

"I know," Summit said.

"The law says Gas & Go Fast has to use reasonable efforts to provide a safe place for its invitees to buy things. It doesn't say they have to provide a safe place for its customers to have a shootout."

Summit chuckled. "That's pretty good. I'll have to remember that the next time I turn down one of these premises liability cases."

"You must have settled for nuisance value."

"Not exactly," Summit said. "Policy limits."

"Bull," Willie Mitchell said. "You're pulling my leg. The liability limit was a million."

Summit nodded. "That's what they paid."

Willie Mitchell leaned back. "No way."

"Judge Williams just approved the settlement agreement. It's filed into the record. The insurance company insisted it be part of the suit record. You can go into the Clerk's office and check it out. Or call Eddie Bordelon. He clocked it in."

"Tell me how you did it."

"I found out that Mainland Insurance," Summit said, "the company that provided the million dollars of coverage at the Gas & Go Fast is merging with Northern Trust Insurance on December 31. Mule's lawsuit is the only pending claim Mainland has on this type of liability policy. They quit writing new policies in Mississippi years ago because of all the premises liability claims. Mainland made an exception for Gas & Go Fast because they insured the Sunshine location for two decades and never had a claim filed. They let Gas & Go Fast continue the existing liability coverage, and Mainland kept collecting the premium every year."

"So as a condition to the merger...."

"You got it. When Mainland called me and made a low ball offer to settle, an alarm went off up here." He pointed his index finger at the dark mat of curly black hair covering his temple. "I started checking around. I raised a lot of campaign cash for the Commissioner of Insurance his last election, so I called him about Mainland to see if he knew anything."

"And he knew everything," Willie Mitchell said. "The companies had to get his office to approve the merger agreement. The Commissioner had the whole document, including, I bet, a requirement that Mule's case be settled."

"It was on the list of conditions in the merger document."

"Chicken doo-doo turned into chicken salad."

Summit started laughing. "It was nothing but luck. And it didn't hurt the settlement when I told Mainland about the antitrust suit I would be filing in federal court in Oxford."

"Antitrust?"

"Remember those phone calls the store clerk Tyretta Neely said the manager made around seven every morning?"

"Sure. I was going to object if you took it any further."

"It had no relevance to the criminal case against Mule or to the premises liability claim. But something about the calls bothered me, so I had my investigators and paralegal check them out. Turns out the manager at the store called the managers he knew at other convenience stores on the strip at the same time every morning. Calls averaged about thirty seconds, but they were made every day."

"The dumb ass managers were talking about the price of gasoline."

"You are one hundred per cent correct. My investigator followed the Gas & Go Fast manager around a little. In the course of investigating he sat down on a bar stool next to the manager at this local juke joint. We had the investigator wired. After a few drinks he started asking the manager about gas prices, how they seemed to go up and down at the same time. The manager just opened up. My investigator said he didn't think the manager knew what he was doing was illegal. He said his boss man had said one day if everyone on the highway would kind of cooperate on prices, that everyone could make a lot more money and he could pay his people more."

"You saying the owners of the stores knew it was going on?"

"No. The owners didn't know. My investigator said the store managers were talking about gas prices on their own, thinking they were showing some initiative."

"What was the name of this bar?"

"Club Ivory," Summit said.

"Did you know that's Mule's favorite place?"

"I do now. My investigator said Mule was in there that night, buying everybody drinks."

"Have you done a gas price survey on the stores?"

Summit shrugged. "Yeah. It didn't turn out like I thought it would."

"No collusion on prices?"

"No. The actual prices don't show any pattern of acting in concert. In fact, the price data shows just the opposite."

"If you can't prove that the prices moved in tandem then you can't prove causation or damages," Willie Mitchell said.

"Probably not, but since I can prove the calls were made I can hire a couple of economists I've used in the past as expert witnesses. They'll put some lipstick on the price data and make it look better to a jury. Juries don't know beans about economics."

Willie Mitchell nodded. Listening to Jordan Summit talk off the record about his personal injury tactics was putting a damper on Willie Mitchell's holiday cheer. The sad thing was Summit was only doing what every p.i. lawyer in the state would do under the same circumstances.

"I've already gotten a call from two of the majors. They're pretty sensitive about their public image these days, especially after the BP spill in the Gulf. The two companies I talked to are willing to pay a little money to make it go away. A little money to these big oil companies is still a lot of Benjamins."

"So you haven't filed your antitrust suit yet?"

"I've drafted it and it's ready to file. I hired a public relations firm and they were the ones to advise me to send a copy of the proposed complaint to the two oil companies I'm now talking to. After the two companies read the proposed complaint they asked me to hold off until they get back to me. I expect to hear from the other five companies this week. My p.r. people say the two companies I've talked to are contacting the others to pool together a fund they're willing to pay me to make it all go away and avoid the bad publicity."

And there it was. For all the camaraderie and shared litigation experiences, Jordan Summit was using the legal system in a way Willie Mitchell believed was dishonest. Willie Mitchell viewed Summit's claim as extortion, threatening unfounded legal action unless the prospective defendants paid him money—a lot of money. Summit's investigation showed no price-fixing and no effect on pricing. Consumers were not overcharged. Summit was prepared to file the suit anyway. There would be no repercussions for him. No ethics violation, no criminal or civil penalty for filing a claim when he knew consumers were not harmed. It was the way the personal injury and tort systems worked all over the country. Bogus claims filed every day and nothing done to reprimand or punish the lawyers or claimants. Willie Mitchell blamed the legal profession, the judges, the legislatures, and the media. Hundreds of thousands of lawyers in the United States started out each day searching for a case against a defendant with deep pockets to drag before a jury made up of poorly educated citizens, citizens eager to punish companies that the media constantly vilified as greedy and heartless. The legal system no longer seemed fair to Willie Mitchell. In fact, he knew it wasn't.

"It's funny," Jordan Summit said, "how all this came out of a worthless lawsuit and a subpoena request that was nothing more than a fishing expedition," Summit said. "An old trial lawyer told me when I first started practicing that you have to 'cast your bread upon the waters.' He was right."

"You mind me asking the breakdown of Mule's settlement?" Willie Mitchell said. "If it's not being too nosy."

"Not at all. It's all in the agreement I just filed with Eddie. I also attached the contract Mule signed with Eleanor and me."

"He hired you for two trials."

"Right. The deal was no charge for the criminal defense. But if we got a settlement out of Gas & Go Fast on the premises liability claim, our fee was fifty per cent off the top, before expenses."

"So how much did Mule end up with?"

"He had to pay off his maintenance loan with the loan company to keep him alive while his case was going. That was fifteen thousand. State Medicaid office filed a lien for his surgery and hospitalization, and rehab and meds. Anyway, it was two hundred thousand. He also had about seven or eight small judgments against him the judge made me pay off. They came to a total of fifty thousand."

"So Mule ended up with about $235,000 in his pocket?" Willie Mitchell asked after doing some quick math.

"That's it, and some change. Of course, it's tax free. Housing Authority got wind of his settlement and they told him he has to leave public housing. Between his ongoing medical care, his housing expenses, his tab at Club Ivory, I don't figure Mule's money's going to last very long."

"He's not eligible for Medicaid with that money in the bank," Willie Mitchell said, "and he's too young for Medicare. He's uninsurable, so medical bills will make him indigent again in a year or so."

"I give it eight months, tops," Summit said. "That's enough about Mule. How's your boy Jake doing? And Kitty?"

"Jake went back to D.C. right after Mule's acquittal."

"He's with DOJ up there, right?"

"Right. Kitty's still working for Sheriff Jones."

"Lee seems like a nice guy. Eleanor told me the Freedmen's Creek people flew the coop."

"Yeah. Out of money, apparently. They just took off and abandoned the place. It happened the day Mule was acquitted."

"I guess you couldn't proceed against Trevor without the gun," Summit said. "Did y'all ever catch the repairman you thought stole it?"

"No. Trevor's getting married, by the way. Jake had to tell him he couldn't make the wedding. The girl's sixteen. Guess who was the only flatlander invited to the nuptials."

"You?"

"Nope. Lee Jones. Turns out they think Lee is a rock star up on that hill."

"Those Brewers are something else," Summit said. "I wonder who does their legal work?"

Willie Mitchell smiled. "An old firm by the name of Smith & Wesson, I think." He paused while Summit laughed. "You know what Trevor's dad told me when I talked to him about Trevor getting married?"

"This ought to be good," Summit said.

"Tom said on Brewer Hill, sixteen ain't too old to get married if the girl's taken good care of herself."

Summit laughed and slapped his knee. He stood up.